Praise for t

"Readers looking for ⌐
variety need look n⌐
covered."

Bitter Waters

"An engrossing, thrill-filled adventure, full of fascinating alien—and human—weirdness." —*Locus*

"The series is worth the price." —*VOYA*

"Wen Spencer's Ukiah Oregon stories owe more to the Detective genre than to Science Fiction, which is what makes them so compelling. Oh, sure Ukiah is half alien, a hundred or so years old, once lived as an Indian, ran with wolves and can't be killed short of incineration, but every PI has baggage. . . . The SF aspects of it are fun . . . But take away the alien parts and you've still got a great action/detective story, which is why you should pick up Wen Spencer's trail wherever her literary muse takes her next." —*SFRevu*

"The rocketing pace . . . had me glued to the pages."
—SF Site

"An exciting science fiction thriller that stars a vulnerable and powerful hero who is impossible not to cherish . . . a must read." —BookBrowser

"[Spencer] has blended in private investigation, science fiction, and fantasy into a rip-roaring tale. . . . More books like this would probably expand the Science Fiction and Fantasy genre's readership. . . . A book that keeps going from strength to strength, the action just won't stop, and it will appeal to fans of a wide spectrum of fiction." —The Alien Online

"The continual character development adds another dimension to the story. . . . The tension builds nicely . . . An exciting chapter to the continuing adventures of Ukiah Oregon." —Rambles

"Ms. Spencer has a mighty fine imagination."
—Science Fiction Romance

continued . . .

Tainted Trail

"Spencer continues to amaze, cranking up both suspense and wonder." —Julie E. Czerneda

"A fun read, definitely worth checking out." —*Locus*

"Spencer's skillful characterizations, vividly drawn settings, and comic exploitations of Ukiah's deceptively youthful, highly buff looks make the romp high light entertainment." —*Booklist*

"A unique and highly entertaining reading experience." —*Midwest Book Review*

Alien Taste

"Each and every character is fascinating, extraordinarily well-developed, and gets right under your skin. A terrific, memorable story." —Julie E. Czerneda

"Revelations ranging from surprising to funny to wonderfully inventive. A delightful new SF mystery with a fun protagonist." —*Locus*

"Spencer has written an intriguing contemporary science fiction tale. Her characters come alive on the page and their uniqueness will grab and hold you." —*Talebones*

"The characters are fully developed and understandable. This novel is keeper shelf material." —BookBrowser

"Spencer takes readers on a fast-paced journey into disbelief. [Her] timing is impeccable and the denouement stunning." —*Romantic Times* (4 star review)

"A fabulous mix of science fiction, suspense, romance, and the nature of wolves, in a story like none you've ever seen." —Science Fiction Romance

A
BROTHER'S
PRICE

WEN SPENCER

A ROC BOOK

ROC
Published by New American Library, a division of
Penguin Group (USA) Inc., 375 Hudson Street,
New York, New York 10014, USA
Penguin Group (Canada), 90 Eglinton Avenue East, Suite 700, Toronto,
Ontario M4P 2Y3, Canada (a division of Pearson Penguin Canada Inc.)
Penguin Books Ltd., 80 Strand, London WC2R 0RL, England
Penguin Ireland, 25 St. Stephen's Green, Dublin 2,
Ireland (a division of Penguin Books Ltd.)
Penguin Group (Australia), 250 Camberwell Road, Camberwell, Victoria 3124,
Australia (a division of Pearson Australia Group Pty. Ltd.)
Penguin Books India Pvt. Ltd., 11 Community Centre, Panchsheel Park,
New Delhi - 110 017, India
Penguin Group (NZ), cnr Airborne and Rosedale Roads, Albany,
Auckland 1310, New Zealand (a division of Pearson New Zealand Ltd.)
Penguin Books (South Africa) (Pty.) Ltd., 24 Sturdee Avenue,
Rosebank, Johannesburg 2196, South Africa

Penguin Books Ltd., Registered Offices:
80 Strand, London WC2R 0RL, England

First published by Roc, an imprint of New American Library,
a division of Penguin Group (USA) Inc.

First Printing, July 2005
10 9 8 7 6 5 4 3 2 1

PUBLISHER'S NOTE
This is a work of fiction. Names, characters, places, and incidents either are the
product of the author's imagination or are used fictitiously, and any resemblance
to actual persons, living or dead, business establishments, events, or locales is
entirely coincidental.

The publisher does not have any control over and does not assume any responsibility for author or third-party Web sites or their content.

To Ann Cecil and June Drexler Robertson

ACKNOWLEDGMENTS

Thanks to Ann Cecil, W. Randy Hoffman, John Schmid, and Linda Sprinkle for all their help.

Chapter 1

There were a few advantages to being a boy in a society dominated by women. One, Jerin Whistler thought, was that you could throttle your older sister, and everyone would say, "She was one of twenty-eight girls—a middle sister—and a troublemaker too, and he—he's a boy," and that would be the end of it.

Certainly if a sister deserved to be strangled, it was Corelle. She was idly flipping through a magazine showing the latest in men's fashions while he tried to stuff a thirty-pound goose, comfort a youngest sister with a boo-boo knee, and feed their baby brother. Since their mothers and elder sisters had left the middle sisters in charge of the farm, Corelle strutted about, with her six-guns tied low and the brim of her Stetson pulled down so far it was amazing she could see. Worse, she started to criticize everything he did, with an eye toward his coming of age—when he would be sold into a marriage of his sisters' choosing.

She had previously complained that he chapped his hands in hot wash water, that trying to read at night would give him a squint, and that he should add scents to his bathwater. This morning it was his clothes.

"Men's fashion magazines are a joke," Jerin growled, trying to keep the goose from scooting across the table as he shoved sage dressing into its cavity. If he hadn't spent years diapering his seventeen youngest sisters and three little brothers, the goose might have gotten away from him. The massive, fat-covered goose, however, was nothing compared with a determined Whistler baby. "No one but family ever sees their menfolk! How do these editors know what men are wearing?"

"Things are different with nobility," Corelle countered, and held out the magazine. "It's the whole point to a Season: to be seen! Here. This is the pair I want you to make for yourself."

Instead of good honest broadcloth trousers, the fashion plate showed kid-glove-tight pants with a groin-hugging patch of bright colored fabric. Labeled underneath was *Return of the codpiece: it allows the future wives to see what they are buying.*

Jerin wrestled the goose into their largest roasting pan. "Don't even think it, Corelle. I won't wear them."

"I'd like seeing you say that to Eldest."

"Eldest knows better than to waste money on clothes no one will see." Jerin worked the kitchen pump to wash the goose fat from his hands. Much as he hated to admit it, Corelle's aim was dead-on—he wouldn't be able to face Eldest and say no. Two could play that game, though. "Eldest is going to be pissed that you went to town and got that magazine. She told you to stay at the farm, close to the house."

"I didn't go to town, so there." Corelle, nonetheless, closed the magazine up, realizing it was evidence of a crime.

So where did she get it? Jerin swung the crying little girl holding on to his knees up onto the counter beside the goose. It was Pansy, when he had thought it was Violet all this time. "Hey, hey, big girls don't cry. Let me see the boo-boo. Corelle, at least feed Kai."

Corelle eyed the sloppy baby playing in his oatmeal. "Why don't you call Doric? It's boys' work. He should be learning all this from you before you get married. Your birthday is only a few months away—and then you'll be gone."

Luckily Pansy was crying too hard to notice that comment.

"Doric is churning butter and can't stop," Jerin lied. "If you want to spell him, I'm sure he'd rather be feeding Kai instead."

Corelle shot him a dirty look but picked up the spoon and redirected some of the oatmeal into Kai's mouth. "All I'm saying is that the—that certain families are making noises that they want to come courting and see you decked out in something other than a walking robe and hat. Hell, you might as well be stuffed in a gunnysack when you're out in public—at least as far as a woman knowing if you're worth looking at or not."

"That's the point, Corelle." Jerin had gotten the mud and crusted blood off of Pansy's knee and discovered a nasty cut. He washed it well with hot water and soap, put three small stitches in to hold the flesh together, and then, knowing his little sisters, bandaged it heavily to keep the dirt out. He ordered firmly, "Now, don't take it off," and unlatched the lower half of the back door to scoot Pansy outside.

In the protected play yard between the house and the barns, the other sixteen youngest sisters were playing reconnaissance. Apparently Leia was General Wellsbury; she was shouting, "Great Hera's teat, you Whistlers call this an intelligence report?" According to their grandmothers, this was the phrase uttered most often by the famous general after their spying missions. Accurate, it might be—but too foul to be repeated in front of the three- through ten-year-olds.

Jerin shouted, "Watch your mouth, Wellsbury!" and went back to the goose. At least the goose had nothing annoying to say.

The same, unfortunately, could not be said of Corelle. "You need some nice clothes so we can show you off and make a good match. People are saying you're not as fetching as rumored."

As if anyone cares what I look like, as long as I'm fertile. Jerin made a rude noise and seasoned the goose's skin. "Who said that?"

"People."

Then it all clicked together. The criticism, the magazine, the clothes, and a certain family annoyed that the Whistlers were landed gentry—despite their common line soldiers' roots—making them a step above their neighbors. "You're talking about the Brindles!"

"Am not!" she snapped, and then frowned, realizing that she had tipped her hand. "Besides, they have a right to see what they're getting before the papers are signed. None of them has ever laid eyes on you outside of a fair or a barn raising—which is hardly seeing you at all."

"You better not be thinking of bringing them here while Eldest is gone. She'll have your hide tacked to the barn! She doesn't want them past the east boundary fence unless the whole family is here."

"Nay neighborly of 'er," Corelle retorted with such an up-country drawl that it could have been straight out of a Brindle mouth.

"*Not* neighborly of *h*er." Jerin heaved the goose up into the oven and slammed shut the oven door. "You sound like a river rat, half drunk on moonshine."

"What does it matter, how we talk?" Corelle deemed herself finished with Kai, now that his bowl was empty. She drifted away from the high chair, leaving the mess for Jerin to clean up. "The Brindles think we're putting on airs, paying so much attention to speaking correct Queens' diction. All we're doing is annoying our neighbors."

Jerin worked the kitchen pump to wet a towel to wash up Kai. "Who cares if we annoy the Brindles? None of our other neighbors are bothered by how we talk. And you know why we speak this way, even if the Brindles don't. Our grandmothers paid with their lives to buy us a better lot in life—for their sake, we don't give up an inch of what they won us."

Corelle made a great show of rolling her eyes. "No one is going to marry you for your *dic-tion*. They're going to marry you for your dic—"

Jerin twirled the damp towel into a rattail and snapped it like a whip, catching her on the exposed skin of her wrist.

She yelped, more out of surprise than pain. Anger flashed across her face, and she started toward him, hands closing into fists.

He backed away from her, twirling up the towel again, heart pounding. When they were little, only Corelle would risk Eldest's wrath to hit him, and now their older sisters were far from home. There was the sudden, tiny, fearful knowledge that Corelle was wearing her pistols. "Don't make me get the spoon!"

She checked and they glared at one another across the cocked and ready towel.

"You be civil, Corelle," he finally managed. "You have no need or place to talk low to me. Eldest will decide what I wear, whom I see, and whom I marry, so there's no call for you to be fussing at me over it."

Corelle pursed her lips together as if to keep in bitter words, her blue eyes cold as winter sky.

In the high chair behind Corelle, Kai started indignant squawking.

"Take care of the baby," Corelle snapped, to give herself the last words of the fight, and stalked out of the kitchen.

Jerin had just put Kai down to sleep when he heard the first rifle shot. He froze beside the cradle, listening to the sharp crack echoing up the hollow.

Maybe it was just thunder, he rationalized, because he didn't want it to be gunfire. He replayed the sound in his mind. No, the sound definitely came from a rifle.

Who would be shooting in their woods? Damn her, had Corelle gone out hunting? Eldest had told all four of the middle sisters to keep at the house, to forgo even fence mending, while their mothers and elder sisters were gone.

Another shot rang out from the creek bottom, then a third, close after the second. The back door banged open. His younger siblings spilled into the house like a covey of quail, the littlest sister running in first, the older ones doing a slower rear guard, scanning over their shoulders for lost siblings or strangers.

Blush, second oldest of the youngest sisters, stationed herself at the door, tapping shoulders to keep count. "Drill teams! Prepare for attack! Shutter the windows, bar the doors, and get down the rifles. Fifteen! Sixteen!" Blush snapped, and tagged Jerin. "Three." Then pointed to the cradle. "Four?"

"Four boys," Jerin said automatically, although stunned. Sixteen? There should be seventeen youngest, and the four middle sisters.

Blush dropped the bars on the upper and lower halves of the back door. First downstairs, then upstairs, the shutters banged shut and their bars rattled into place. Little girls moved through the shutter slats of sunlight, working in teams of mixed ages to load two rifles and guard every window.

"What's going on?" Jerin asked. "Who's shooting? Where are Corelle and the others?"

Blush gave a look of disgust that only a twelve-year-old could manage. "Corelle, Summer, Eva, and Kira went over to the Brindles', courting Balin Brindle. Heria said she thought she heard riders in the woods. She took her rifle and went out to have a look-see."

"Heria!" The fourteen-year-old oldest of his youngest sisters had more courage than sense. "Holy Mothers above!"

"Eldest is going to skin Corelle alive," one of the youngest whispered.

There was a ripple of agreement.

"Watch the windows!" Blush barked.

Too precious to risk in a fight, the boys were left with

nothing to do but whisper. Liam complained about his blocks, left outside in the sudden retreat. Doric speculated that it was only Corelle in the woods, doing a bit of hunting while coming home from courting. Jerin would have liked to believe that—but Corelle knew perfectly well there was no need for fresh meat with the elder half of the family gone and a thirty-pound goose in the oven. Most of the youngest still ate like birds.

"What do we do?" a youngest asked Blush after several minutes of silence.

Blush clutched one of the family's carbine rifles. "We stand guard until Corelle comes back."

A thunderous pounding at the back door stopped them cold.

Blush scurried to Jerin's side, the soldier training that had been carrying her vanished, leaving only a frightened twelve-year-old. "Jerin?"

Jerin swallowed his fear and whispered, "Identify the enemy and establish numbers."

Blush nodded rapidly, her eyes wide and rounded with fear. Still, she managed to shout, "Identify yourself!"

The pounding stopped. "Let me in! Let me in! Let me in!"

A sigh of relief went through the room.

"It's Heria!" Doric cried and was immediately hushed.

"Everyone, get to posts." Blush struggled to return to their training. "What's the password, Heria?"

"I don't remember!" Heria wailed beyond the door. "Lemme in!"

Blush looked at Jerin, unsure what to do.

"Use the spyhole." Jerin gave Blush a slight push toward the kitchen door. "Make sure she's alone. Then let her in, but only open the bottom half of the door."

Blush had to fetch a stool to reach the spyhole. She covered the delay by calling out, "You know we can't let you in without a password, Heria!"

There came a minute of cursing that would have made their father blush and their grandmothers proud. Finally,

Heria remembered the week's password. "Teacup! It's 'teacup'!"

"Well, the whole county knows it now!" Blush complained. "She's alone! Let her in."

Heria pushed her rifle and ammunition pouch in first, then scrambled in on hands and knees. Once inside, she remained crouched on the flagstones, panting, as the door was bolted shut again. The red stain of blood on her shirt made Jerin forget to stay out of the way. He dropped down beside her.

"Are you hurt?" He tried to get her up so he could see where she bled. "Did someone shoot you?"

Heria shook her head, squeezing his shoulder comfortingly, and gasped. "Not my blood." She swallowed hard. "The—they didn't have guns, only clubs and sabers. There's a soldier—in the creek!"

"Did you shoot her?" Jealous admiration tinted Blush's question.

Heria shook her head. "No. Riders chased her down out of the woods by the bend. They knocked her off her horse, into the creek. I thought they were going to kill her, and we'd get blamed, so I shot at them. The first shot just startled them." Which meant she probably missed, and they hadn't realized how lucky they had been. "They didn't start to run until the second shot. I winged one of them."

This got a murmur of admiration from the others.

Jerin hushed them. His youngest sisters might not see the danger remaining with the riders gone. "But they didn't kill the soldier?"

"She's got a big bruise on her forehead and she's out cold in the creek."

"In it?" Jerin cried. "Oh, Heria, you didn't leave her to drown, did you?"

"No, of course not," Heria said, which earned her a few dark looks from her sisters. "I got her sat up, put some rocks behind her, then laid her back down. It was the best I could do because I couldn't move her other-

wise. She's Corelle's size and all dead weight." Which
meant the soldier was nearly as tall as Jerin. "I didn't
know what else to do. She's out of the water, and I've
got her pinned so if she only half wakes, she's not going
to roll in and drown."

"Good!" Jerin said. He was relieved that the entire
younger half of the family was all accounted for, sound
and secured. Now if only the older half were here, armed
and ready!

"What about the riders?" Blush pressed Heria. "How
many were there? Did they look like a raiding party?
Are they coming back?"

"I saw five women. They didn't look like sisters, didn't
act like sisters. They looked like river trash. Dirty. Ragged. Poor. I winged the biggest."

As she spoke, Jerin glanced about the kitchen at the
girls clustered around him. Most barely came to his chest
and only Heria weighed more than a hundred pounds.
Three or four of the older girls combined could get the
soldier out of the creek and to the house. But that would
leave girls under ten to guard the boys.

"I'm going down to the creek and getting the soldier,"
he announced, standing up.

"What?" all his little sisters shouted.

"If she's alive, we can't let her die on Whistler land,"
he said.

"Damn right we can!" Blush snapped. There was a
roar of agreement.

"We can't!" Heria shouted. "Jerin's right. It's the law.
We have to lend aid to travelers in distress."

"Who would know?" Leia, the third to oldest, argued.
"We just say that we never found her until after she
died."

"Her attackers would know," Jerin pointed out.
"They probably know that the soldier is alive, and that
at least one of us knows it, because a Whistler shot at
them."

"Who would they tell?" Blush asked. "It would be

stupid for them to tell anyone. They'll be admitting to beating the soldier up."

"Better than being blamed for murder," Heria snapped. "What do you think they'll say if the Queens Justice catches them? 'Yes, we killed her,' or 'Oh, no, she was still alive when we got chased off'?"

Silence fell as his sisters recognized the truth of Heria's argument.

"The quicker we go," Jerin finally broke the silence, "the quicker we get back."

"No!" Blush cried. "We just won't send for Queens Justice. We can bury her in the woods. No one need know."

"Won't wash." Heria stood up. "There's her horse, to start with. Do we kill it and bury it too?"

"We could drive it off," Blush said.

"I'm eldest here," Heria said. "Jerin and I are going down to the creek. You stand ready."

They didn't like it, but they had been raised as soldiers and the line of command was clear. Heria was eldest; she was to be obeyed.

"Come on," Jerin said to Heria. "Show me where the soldier is."

Despite everything, he was nearly too angry to be scared. "I can't believe Corelle went off chasing after Balin's pants. Eldest told her not to leave sight of the house while they were gone."

"Eldest is going to kill her." Heria trotted to keep up with his long strides. She held her carbine rifle ready, her wide-brimmed hat thumping on her back with each step.

"One can hope so." He scanned the rolling pasture nervously. This was their main cattle field and thus, thankfully, bare of anything between the height of the short grass and the tall hickory trees. In a single glance, he could see that the pasture was clear of strangers. They would, at least, not be taken by sneak attacks. He looked back at the sprawling stone farmhouse, looking toy-sized on the hilltop.

"I was thinking, Jerin, maybe we should just kill this soldier. Hold her under, let her drown, then take her up onto the bank. We'll tell the Queens Justice that we did all we could, but she died anyway."

"Heria!"

"We don't know anything about this woman. She might be a murderer or a husband raider. We can't just take her into the house, give her access to our men!"

"No! You know what Grandmothers always said; the best way not to get caught for a crime is simply not to commit it. Besides, she probably has sisters, maybe close by. What if they found out we didn't help her, that we hurt her? They could take us to the Queens Justice and strip the family of all possessions."

And legally, as a boy, he was a possession. "After we get her to the house," he said, "you should ride quick to fetch the Queens Justice. Then go on to Brindles' farm and tell Corelle what's happened."

"I should go for Corelle first."

"There are only four of our sisters at the Brindles' farm. You saw five riders. We don't know how many more might be in the woods yet. I'd rather have a troop of Queens Justice here instead of our sisters."

"Don't worry. If anyone tries for you, I'll shoot them." Heria put her rifle to her shoulder and pretended to shoot it. "Bang!"

Jerin shook his head, wishing their mothers were home, or at least their elder sisters were nearer at hand. Corelle, and the sisters that looked to her, were all going to be in big trouble for leaving the farm unguarded.

A woman in her early twenties lay faceup in the wide, shallow creek, red hair rippling in the water like flowing blood. A purple knot marked her forehead. The soldier wore a black leather vest over a green silk shirt and

black leather pants. Rings graced every finger of her left
hand, with the exception of the wedding finger, and a
diamond-studded bracelet looped her left wrist. Her
right hand remained soldier-clear of clutter.

Jerin glanced about the creek bottom. The marsh
grass, cattails, and ditch weed on the far bank had been
trampled as if a great number of horses had ridden down
into the creek, then back out again. A thick screen of
brush cloaked the woods beyond the pasture's stone
wall, and jackdaws and chickadees darted through the
branches, apparently undisturbed by humans too near
their nests.

Why had the riders tried to kill this woman? Were
their reasons desperate enough for them to return?

"Did the riders see you?" he whispered to Heria over
the gurgle of water. "Do they know you were alone?"

"I don't know. I hid myself like Grandmas taught me."

Their grandmothers had been spies for the Queens.
They had taught all their grandchildren, regardless of
sex, how to be clever in war. Jerin wished they were
alive and with him now; maybe they could decipher
the dangers.

Standing around guessing wasn't solving anything. He
pointed to the woman's horse, a fine roan mare, eating
grass along their side of the creek, saddle polished glossy
and decorated with bits of silver. "Can you catch her
horse, Heria?"

"Easy as mud: dirt and water." Heria moved off
toward the horse, talking softly to it.

Jerin scrambled down the steep bank into the water
beside the soldier. He disarmed her first, undoing her
sword belt buckle to tug free the belt and scabbard. He
tossed it to Heria's feet as she brought back the horse.
Jerin found the woman's fluttering pulse, then stooped
lower to examine her forehead. Marked clear on her
skin was evidence of what had struck her—a steel-shod
truncheon. On her wrists, forearms, and shoulders were
marks of other blows.

Faced with the clear proof of attempted murder, fear became a cold, sharp-clawed beast skittering frantic inside of him. Jerin looked up, eyes to the woods again, ears straining.

Chick-a-dee-dee-dee-dee, called the little birds, flirting in the brush. Deeper into the woods, something unseen crashed in the bracken and then went still. Jerin bit down on a yelp of fear and levered the soldier over his shoulder like a sack of potatoes. He scrambled quickly back up the bank.

Heria had tied the mare to a sapling, leaving her hands free to shoot. She crouched in the weeds, scanning the woods as Jerin juggled himself and the soldier up into the saddle.

"Get on behind me," he ordered Heria.

"I can walk." She untied the mare and handed him the reins. "It would be easier."

"Not quicker. Get on."

She scrambled up. "When we get to the house, I'll ride out for the Queens Justice," Heria said as he kicked the mare into a smooth canter for home. "I'll tell them that Blush and Leia are here alone with you and the boys. That will bring them quick. Then I'll go out to the Brindles' for Corelle."

A slight stirring made him look down at the woman in his arms. She opened her eyes and looked up at him in surprise, apparently confused by her wounds. Memory seeped in, tainting her look with fear, stiffening her in his hold.

"Hush, you're fine, you're safe," he crooned softly in his best fatherly-comfort voice.

Her eyes closed, a smile slipped onto her lips, and she relaxed against his chest.

At the house, he got his youngest sisters to unlock and open the kitchen door for him to carry in the woman.

"Blush, have someone go help Heria saddle up one of the horses. Have them stable the red mare, but don't take time to unsaddle it or anything. Kettie, lock the door behind them, and stay here to let them back in. We didn't see any raiders, but they might still be close by."

Out of spite, he carried the soldier up to the middle sisters' room, to put her in Corelle's bed. Chaperoned by a dozen curious children, he stripped off the woman's wet clothing.

"Emma and Celain," Jerin said to the ten-year-olds, oldest of the girls around him, "bring up tea and whatever sugar biscuits are left over from yesterday. You will have some when you get back, so please, don't eat any beforehand. Ask Kettie to help you while you're down there. Have Blush or Leia carry up the teapot when the water is hot."

So it became a tea party after he dried the soldier's hair, bandaged two of the wounds that bled still, and slipped one of Corelle's sleeping shirts on her. She opened her eyes from time to time, to watch him groggily, still apparently unable to move. When the tea arrived, he made hers heavy with honey and cream, coaxing the warm drink into her. His baby sisters gathered around the bed, wide-eyed, sipping tea and munching on sugar biscuits, watching every move the soldier made.

"Jerin! Jerin! Corelle and the others are home!"

Somehow his middle sisters had missed the soldier's horse in the barn. They didn't notice that the youngest weren't out to play. They hadn't seen that the windows were shuttered and the doors were locked. They couldn't have—because they strolled lazily across the barnyard toward the kitchen door, arguing again about Balin Brindle and whether to take him as a husband or not.

Neither family had the cash to buy a husband; both could afford a husband only by selling or swapping their brothers. Where the Whistler family had the wealth of four sons, Balin Brindle was an only boy. If Jerin's sisters took Balin as a husband, Jerin would most likely marry the Brindle sisters as payment. Thirty Brindles—with no hope of a second husband to lessen the number! True, many of them were younger than Heria, so it would be years before he needed to service them all, but still! Worse yet, they were all ugly to him—with horsey faces, horsey laughs, and heavy hands. At a barn raising, he'd seen two Brindle sisters brawl with one another, a furious fight in which he thought they would kill each other. The other Brindle women had stood around, shaking their heads, as if it were normal, as if it were common. A Brindle mother finally stopped the fight with kicks, punches, and curses more fearsome than the sisters'.

No, he didn't want to be wed to the Brindles. Just the thought of it usually made him sick. Today, though, his middle sisters' continued consideration of the union infuriated him. They knew how he felt—and the fact they left the farm unguarded to continue the courtship made him rage.

Arms crossed, he waited at the kitchen door, seething as they strolled toward him.

"He has beautiful eyes." Corelle was in favor of the match, of course, else she would not have allowed a trip to the Brindle farm.

"He has a temper with the babies," Summer snapped, never happy with her role of younger sister and follower; yet she could never stand up to Corelle. "You could almost see him cringe every time the littlest one cried, and he never once tended to her. His father, bless his feeble body, looked to her every time."

"His father wasn't too feeble to father the baby," Corelle quipped.

"I've heard that Balin did, not his father. He's tumbling with his own mothers."

"Summer!"

"Oh, come on, admit it—there's a twelve-year gap in

the babies and then they start back up. His father is so feeble he couldn't work from the top, and so brittle he couldn't endure the bottom."

"Well, then we know the boy's fertile."

"And throwing only girls."

"We can pick up other husbands. We have four brothers."

"I don't want him as a—" Summer noticed Jerin at the door, the angry look, and then the empty play yard, the barred shuttered windows, and his damp clothing. "Oh, sweet Mothers, Jerin, what happened?"

"Thank you, Summer, for noticing that something is wrong. I can't believe you, Corelle, going off and leaving the farm unguarded!"

"What happened?" Corelle asked, guilt flashing across her features, then passing, as it always did. Corelle never believed what she did was wrong—she was as good at lying to herself as she was to anyone else.

"Heria heard riders in the woods. Poachers or raiders. She went down to the creek—"

"Heria heard something," Corelle snickered. "She heard the wind, or a herd of deer, or nothing."

"Well, then you won't mind that 'nothing' is taking up your bed, Corelle. The Queens Justice should be here soon to deal with that 'nothing.' They might escort the 'nothing' back to the garrison, or perhaps, 'nothing' will stay in your bed, being that she hasn't spoken since I carried her home half dead from the creek where her attackers left her to drown."

They gaped at him. Then Corelle reached in the opening to unlatch the bottom half of the door, pulled it open, and pushed past him to rush upstairs. Kira and Eva followed her without a word to him, as rudely intent as Corelle.

"I'm sorry, Jerin," Summer said before hurrying after them, tagging along as usual, unable to find the will to break free to stand on her own. "I should have stayed."

But still she followed to leave him alone in the kitchen.

Jerin checked to make sure the goose wasn't burning, then went up to the man's wing of the house. He sat on his wedding chest to take off his damp boots, and stripped out of his wet, muddy clothes.

There! His middle sisters were home, and Queens Justice would arrive soon, settling everything for good. All that remained was the possibility of marriage to the Brindles.

Oh, he hated the thought of marrying the Brindles! He hated everything about them, even their farm. Poorly made with no future expansion in mind, their farmhouse was already crowded and in desperate need of repair and additions. The Brindles proudly pointed out new barns and outbuildings, but no thought had gone into their locations. None of the barns sat west of the house, to act as a windbreak to driving snow and freezing wind. None of the outbuildings abutted; thus there was no enclosed and sheltered play yard. The pigpens sat upwind and close to the house. Sturdy oaks that would have shaded off the summer sun had been cut down to make room for rickety chicken coops. Softwood maples and poplars now grew too close to the house, threatening to take out part of the roof with every storm.

And everything, everywhere, from the weed-choked garden to the sticky kitchen floor, showed signs that the Brindles had a tendency toward sloth. The problems with the farm could be solved—maybe. He might be able to push them into changing their farm to suit him.

But the fact would remain that the Brindles themselves were ugly, brutish, and three times more in number than he ever wanted to marry.

He didn't know where his seven elder sisters stood in the matter; they had stayed closemouthed on the subject, which he took as a sign of disapproval. Had he read them wrong? Did Corelle stand as a weathercock for their older sisters' minds? Certainly the swap of brothers would tie them close to their next-door neighbors, putting cousins on their doorstep instead of strangers.

Jerin shuddered and clung to the knowledge that at
least Summer opposed the marriage with good, solid
points. If Summer did, then perhaps also Eva, who usually echoed Summer's desire—but also her inability to
stand against Corelle's will. Likewise, though, Kira followed Corelle's lead almost blindly. Two for, two
against, if Summer and Eva had the courage to stand
against Corelle. Too bad Heria would not be old enough
for a say in the marriage; she disliked the Brindles.

If the seven elder sisters all opposed the swap, they
outweighed the middle sisters completely. If they too
were in disagreement, he didn't want to even consider
the way the vote might fall.

He didn't want to marry the Brindles! If such things
were strictly up to his mothers, then he knew his desire
would be considered first. In the matter of husbands,
though, their mothers bowed to the women who would
actually bed the man.

Jerin dressed and picked up his muddy clothes to rinse
them clean before the dirt could set. He would have to
keep hoping things would work out the way he wished.
To be disheartened—when his older sisters might all
agree with him—was silly.

Blush's voice suddenly rose from the front door in
shrill panic.

"Riders coming in!" Blush screamed. "Corelle! Summer! Eva! Riders are coming!"

Jerin ran to his dormer window and looked out. A
dozen of riders, maybe more, were coming across the
pasture from the creek bottom. The Queens Justice
would come from the other direction, from out across
the grain fields.

The riders stopped in the apple orchard, out of volley
range. Some of the riders split off from the main group
and circled the house, checking the barns and outbuildings.

Their horses were fine, showy specimens, well cared
for but ridden hard. Like that of the wounded soldier's,
their saddles and bridles gleamed with polish and bits of

silver. Blonde-, black-, brown-, and red-haired, the riders lacked the unity of sisters. Somewhat comforting was the fact that half of them wore uniforms of the Queens Army—but then again, Jerin's grandmas had been soldiers when they kidnapped his grandfather.

The riders converged under the apple trees again, discussed what they found and started for the house. When they reached optimal volley range, there was a clatter of rifles being slid through the slits in the shutters.

"That's far enough!" Corelle's voice shouted from the dining room window. "We've summoned Queens Justice and they will be arriving soon. We suggest you move on."

A black-haired woman on a huge black horse shouted back. "In the name of the Queens, we ask for a parley like civilized women, not this screaming at one another through walls."

There was a whispered discussion in the dining room as the middle sisters conferred. Corelle suddenly ran back into the kitchen, unlatched the bottom half of the back door, and ducked out, snapping, "Lock it behind me" to Kettie. A moment later Corelle trotted around the corner of the house, rifle in hand, looking tall, cool, and unafraid.

For the first time in months, Jerin loved her and almost wept at the sight of her outside, alone, in front of the armed soldiers.

"So we talk," Corelle stated.

"I'm Captain Raven Tern," said the black-haired woman.

"Corelle Whistler. This is the Whistlers' farm. You're trespassing. We will defend our property and the lives of our younger sisters."

"You have a roan mare in your stables that doesn't belong to you." Captain Tern motioned to the horse barn. Heria must have put the roan in the first stall, making the mare visible from the barnyard. "It belonged to a red-haired woman. Where is she?"

Corelle gave them a cold stare, then finally admitted,

"We found the woman down in the creek, beaten and nearly drowned. We brought her home, as the law states we should, and gave her comfort. We've sent for Queens Justice. They will deal with the matter."

There was a shift in the group—shoulders straightening, heads lifting, flashes of smiles—as if the news was good, as if they had expected the soldier to be dead and didn't want to hear that unpleasant report.

"She's alive?" Captain Tern asked, her voice less harsh.

Corelle considered for a moment, then nodded slowly. "She is alive and, from time to time, awake, but has taken a blow to the head that has left her disoriented. We don't know who attacked her. We don't want trouble. We have children here to protect."

Tern gave a slight laugh. "You're not much more than a child yourself. Where are your mothers? Don't you have any elder sisters?"

Corelle clenched her jaw, not wanting to answer, but the truth was too obvious to deny. If there were any older women in the house, they would be out talking to the strangers. "Our mothers and elder sisters are not here. They will be back shortly."

One of the riders in the back, wearing a broad-brimmed hat, pushed forward. The young woman stopped even with the captain, and swept off her hat. The setting sun glittered on her flame red hair, red as the soldier's hair.

"Do you know who you've saved today?" the woman asked.

Corelle shook her head. "The woman hasn't spoken yet, hasn't given her name."

"She is Princess Odelia, third oldest daughter of the Queens."

Corelle took a step back. "I suppose," she said faintly, "that makes you a princess?"

"Yes, it does. I'm Princess Rennsellaer."

Chapter 2

Princess Rennsellaer, current Eldest of the Queens' daughters, sat in the shade of the apple orchard, secretly glad for the chance to relax her nerves. She had been growing more and more sure that she'd find her sister Odelia dead, and that she would have to return home and tell her mothers that not only had the long-awaited cast-iron cannons been stolen, but another of their daughters had been killed.

The worst came when the peaceful-looking farmhouse suddenly bristled with rifle barrels, and it seemed that she and her guard had ridden into a trap. Their fears had quickly been allayed by the shouted challenge—the house held nothing more than frightened farmers defending their own—but the close call rattled her.

She was unnerved enough to wait, as the farmers asked, for Queens Justice to arrive and act as trusted go-betweens. In the course of a few hours, the stolen cannons had moved from all-important to trivial, losing priority to Odelia's safe return. Cannons could be replaced; her sister could not. What surprised Ren was that the captain of her guard, Raven Tern, had not fought the delay.

She said as much to her captain. "I'm amazed you agreed to this. We could be waiting on the Queens Justice for hours. I thought you would want to push your way in, get Odelia, and get on with finding the cannons."

Raven made a fist and tapped the sword tattoo on the

back of her hand. "Didn't you notice the Order of the Sword mark on the girl, Ren? Crib father initials under the pommel, and on either side of the hilt, makes three generations of career soldiers. A family of line soldiers earning stud services from the military cribs wouldn't be able to afford this farm; it probably was a land grant for valiant service. A reward for loyalty proved by fire. Short of the local garrison, this is probably the safest place for Odelia to hole up in."

"Why not bully them into turning Odelia over?"

"The girl we parleyed with was, what—seventeen?— and scared silly. If she's the oldest one in the house, then those twenty rifles are in the hands of frightened children. Frankly, I'd rather not have to execute an eight-year-old because she shot you by accident."

"The family might have been soldiers, Raven, but they're farmers now."

Raven shook her head. "We're talking third-generation soldiers. They're like a different species by that stage, and all they know is training their daughters to fight alongside of them. Every girl in that house probably got a toy gun as a teething present, and a real gun at the age of eight. Every window is shuttered and barred. The doors are reinforced and barred. The house probably has food enough to last a siege, and access to fresh water. You could throw a hundred soldiers against those twenty children and lose."

Ren eyed the house in question. Mostly stone, with a slate roof, it looked like a fortress. Flowers grew around the footing, softening the impression, but she noticed for the first time the lack of bushes near the house. The trees were in full summer foliage, yet the house remained unscreened, allowing a view for miles in three directions. West of the house were barns and outbuildings, checking winter winds. None of the buildings touched the house directly—they could be set fire to and not take the house with them. A cupola, she noticed now, on the highest peak of the house, looked over the barn roofs to the west. A dark line of a rifle barrel showed that even the cupola was guarded.

In this remarkable house, instead of lying dead in woods, her charmed younger sister found refuge.

It figured.

Ren laughed aloud as it occurred to her how typical the event was of Odelia's life. "Odelia always had the luck of a cat. A countryside full of sheep-witted farmers, and she finds a veritable fortress to land in."

"I see you've stopped worrying about her."

"Currently she seems safer than me. That is, if these farmers weren't part of stealing the cannons."

"Doubt it," Raven said after considering it for a while. "Locals might have run the barge aground—sandbars change overnight—but they wouldn't have left it there for us to find. The barge was left because it couldn't be moved. What with the draft horses in the barn and twenty little sisters, this family could have pulled the barge free. Whoever is riding herd on those cannons, they're scrambling right now."

"The attack on Odelia was a distraction."

"Most certainly," Raven said. "A handful split off to keep us busy so the rest could deal with the cannons and small arms."

Ren cursed softly; they had been so close to catching the thieves. "Damn Odelia. Why'd she have to go off alone?"

"She wouldn't be Odelia if she had a lick of common sense."

"Riders!" came a call from a sentry. They turned and watched the troop of Queens Justice ride up. The leader was a graying, trim woman with a crooked nose. She blinked in surprise at the royal presence, then flashed a snaggletoothed grin at the princess and her captain.

"Lieutenant Bounder, at your service, Highness. Heria Whistler came to fetch us, saying that a soldier had been left to drown in their creek. One of yours, I take it?"

"My sister Princess Odelia."

Bounder blanched. "Mothers above, is she all right?"

"She's in there." Ren waved toward the imposing farmhouse. "They wouldn't let us in until you arrived."

Bounder laughed. "Sounds like them, making royalty stew like a neighboring farmer. Glad to see you had sense to wait for us. You have to cat-foot around the Whistlers."

"They're trouble?" Raven asked.

"Oh, not trouble, just dangerous to corner," Bounder said. "At the local fairs, the Whistlers don't start the trouble, but they always end it. No nonsense, just pow, and lay the other girls out flat. You'd think the farmers around here would learn, but every year it seems one of them has to be taught what it's like to cross someone trained to fight."

"I didn't know farmers were so quarrelsome," Raven murmured.

"It's all on account of the men," Bounder said.

"Pardon?" Ren was sure she misheard. Men fighting?

"The Whistlers' menfolk." Bounder grinned and clucked her tongue suggestively. "The Whistlers trot them out at social events and women fall over themselves to get near them. But the Whistlers don't share them out, and sooner or later, someone won't take no as an answer."

Raven glanced uphill, eyes narrowed in speculation. "Their mothers are away and they've got men to protect."

Bounder nodded. "Like I said, I'm glad you waited."

With Queens Justice on hand, the rifles were put up, the windows unshuttered, the doors unlocked, and the visitors invited in to check on the sleeping princess.

Inside, the house had the same military stamp: clean, neat, uncluttered, and orderly. The smell of roasting goose filled the house. There were only four teenage sisters; the rest were tiny, giggling girls that ducked shyly out of rooms and behind cover whenever looked at di-

rectly. Over the mantel, though, was an impressive array
of medals. Death for Country. Queens Medal of Honor.
Queen Elder Cross of Victory. Queens Order of
Knights!

Raven had paused with Ren to look at the medals,
and aahed at the Order of Knights. "*Those* Whistlers."

"You know of them?"

"Aye. Famous, infamous Whistlers," Raven murmured quietly, then glanced at a doorway, sending a giggling host of girls into hiding. The sister called Corelle
reappeared to lead them upstairs. "I'll explain later."

Ren sat on the edge of the bed, suddenly frightened
for her sister over again. Odelia lay so still and pale on
the farmer's narrow bed, oblivious to Ren's presence.
When a hand on Odelia's shoulder failed to wake her,
fear and despair mounted in Ren's chest. "Odelia?"

Odelia sighed deeply. "Rats."

"Rats?" Ren blinked in surprise and relief.

"I've been playing sick for hours hoping they'll let
him come back." Odelia opened her eyes and sighed
again. "And now you're here."

"Him? I'm frightened for your life, and you're ogling
farmers' husbands?"

"Oh, he was too young to be a husband." Odelia sat
up in bed—then looked concerned. Clasping her hand
over her mouth, she fought a battle to keep from vomiting, then—carefully—lay back on the pillows Ren
propped up behind her. "Okay, I wasn't totally playing,"
Odelia admitted quietly. "But he was very, very
handsome."

"Lieutenant Bounder said the Whistlers had handsome menfolk, but I assumed that was compared to the
farming standard."

"Look at the sisters, Ren. Then think of a man along
those lines with hair all down his back instead of a military crop."

Ren recalled the oldest sister. The girl had been striking enough to remember despite the day's flood of stressful events: clear pale skin, black hair, large blue eyes, and a full mouth. Ren snorted at the woolgathering, dismayed that Odelia managed to lead her so astray from important issues. For the sake of the country, it was good that Odelia was not the oldest. Her charmed life left her seeing things slightly skewed.

"Odelia, I can't believe you were beaten half to death, left to drown, and all you're concerned about is the handsome son of poor landed gentry."

"I'm still alive. The bruises will heal. Why dwell on the past? The future holds the chance to steal a kiss or two from the prettiest man I've seen my whole life."

"Because whoever tried to kill you is still out there, you're weak as a kitten, it's an hour's ride to the garrison protected by the Queens Justice, and the cannons are still missing."

"So I stay here, while you look for the cannons." Odelia's face went soft with apparently dreamy thoughts. "Maybe he'll come check on the poor unconscious princess." She slipped back down in the bed, pushing away the pillows. "Don't tell them I woke up."

"You're hopeless." Ren had been stifling the urge to take up a pillow and hit her sister. In moving about, though, the sleeves of Odelia's nightshirt slipped up past her elbows. Ren found herself staring at the large black bruises marking Odelia's forearms where she had apparently fended off killing blows.

Odelia's attackers almost killed her, would have surely if they had not thought the water would finish their work. If they had stopped to administer a sounder beating, used a sword instead of a truncheon, used a pistol—

Ren shuddered at the thought. To owe her sister's life to the sloppiness of cruel strangers and the lucky clear thinking of the daughters of farmers! So instead of hitting Odelia with pillows, Ren tucked her sister into the borrowed bed.

*   *   *

Raven leaned against the wall in the hall. "I heard you two talking. She's awake? How is she?"

Ren shut the door quietly. "Scheming to steal kisses from the farmers' beautiful son."

Raven shook her head. "That sounds like Odelia."

"She won't be able to ride to the garrison. It would make her happy to stay here. It would allow her to continue her schemes."

"It would make me happy to stay here," Raven stated. "With the Queens Justice looking for the cannons and Odelia's attackers, this place is safer than the local garrison. Apparently the lieutenant's predecessor allowed the town to grow up to the walls of the garrison, replaced a stone wall with a wood one—to cut cost—and so forth. All in all, it would be like guarding lambs in a brush lot."

"And the famous, infamous Whistlers? Are they safe?"

"They seem to have smoothed around the edges from the last I'd heard of them."

"And what have you heard of them?"

Raven smiled at Ren's impatient tone. "The grandmother Elder, or maybe the great-grandmother Elder of this lot, did something that got herself executed, her sisters cashiered, and their daughters blacklisted. To keep the family alive, the Eldest bullied the Sisterhood of the Night to take her and her sisters in."

"The thieves' guild? Bullied?"

"Aye, had the family switched into training as thieves. They were better than most, being already trained to work together under fire and fight well enough to break free if caught. Well, the War of the False Eldest started, and things were going badly. The False Eldest knew our defenses and we knew nothing of Tastledae. We sent in scouts, but they were all caught and executed. Then, somehow, Wellsbury picked up the Whistler girls."

"Soldiers trained as thieves, or thieves trained as soldiers."

Raven nodded. "They were a motley crew, all born

to the Order of the Sword, so each had a different father, and different grandfather more often than not.
They fought like wildcats with everyone and everything.
They lied, they stole, they ignored orders, and they won
the war. Wellsbury started them with spying, but expanded that to wreaking general mayhem behind enemy
lines. There had been thirty of them to start, only about
ten survived the war, and they cashed out after being
knighted."

Ren looked at the well-ordered home. "Their grandfather and father must have had strong character to turn
a motley crew of spies into this well-run army."

Raven nodded in agreement. "I've heard so many
women go on about wanting a biddable husband, but
I'd rather have a strong-willed man who can keep your
children in line. Weak husbands make spoiled children."

Ren leaned against the wall, rubbing at the bridge of
her nose, weighing the few options available. "Okay,
Odelia stays. I want to send a report downriver to let
our mothers know she's safe and that we might miss the
opening of Summer Court. Trini will have to preside as
Elder Judge. See what the Whistlers have in the way of
riding horses. After I'm done with my report, I want to
head out."

Raven shook her head. "It's dusk, Ren, we're dead
tired, in a strange land, and they've had one go at a
royal princess today already. Let Bounder search for the
cannons. Or do you really want Odelia to be Eldest?"

The last made Ren laugh, but she conceded the point.
"Okay. Okay. Halley, though, is two months older
than Odelia."

"No one has seen Halley for four months," Raven
said quietly.

Ren sighed, closing her eyes against the pain that truth
triggered. "There is that."

Jerin and the boys moved to his bedroom to ride out
the royal storming of the house. Heria brought him prog-

ress reports, as well as complaints of hunger growing among their younger sisters.

The Princess Ren was pleased at finding her sister alive and well. When Princess Odelia had gone missing, she had feared the worst. Seeing that the younger princess was not fit to ride, it was decided that the royal party would spend the night. Knowing their mothers would have a fit if Princess Ren was housed in the barn, Corelle offered up both the youngest and the older sisters' bedrooms. They were graciously accepted.

Nothing had been said, Heria complained, about dinner, and all the baby sisters were starting to whine and cry. Knowing full well that his sisters couldn't organize dinner to save their lives, Jerin came down from his bedroom to take control of the kitchen.

Heria had only one pot on the stove, just breaking into a boil. It contained peeled and sliced potatoes. The youngest were divided between raiding the pantry and peering in at the goose, trying to decide if it was done.

"Is that enough potatoes?" Heria asked, chasing girls out of the pantry.

Jerin dodged the little girls to consider what they had on hand for dinner. "How many are in Princess Rennsellaer's party?"

"Fifteen. Ten privates, two lieutenants, a captain, and the two princesses," Heria reported. "All of the guard are fathered out of the military cribs—Order of the Sword tattoos range from second generation to sixth. One of the privates is sister to the younger lieutenant; otherwise, there are no other sibling pairs. All but Princess Odelia are currently armed with a pistol, a brace of knives, and a saber. They also have standard-issue rifles and bayonets, but those are geared with their personal items upstairs."

"They each have a hundred rounds of rifle ammunition, and only fifty rounds of pistol ammo." Blush's tone indicated she thought it was a paltry supply. "They have

no food supplies nor grain. Each woman has a personal
purse, totaling sixty-seven crowns, eighty-six gils, and
fifteen quince between them, but they're not carrying
a cashbox."

"Blush!" Jerin hissed in surprise. "You didn't search
their gear?"

Blush looked at him with surprise and hurt. "They
won't be able to tell."

Leia, who was younger than Blush by an hour, and
twin-close as a result, added in, "Princess Rennsellaer
has a royal seal in her traveling desk, and Captain Tern
has hers secured against spies."

It was difficult to tell which desk created the most
interest. Immediately plans were laid for a series of reconnaissance missions to see said desks by the rest of
the youngest siblings, Doric included.

"No!" Jerin stated firmly. "You will not invade the
princesses' privacy or that of their guards any further.
They're guests in this house, and they will be treated
with respect."

"Oh, pooh," Heria risked grumbling, but the rest held
their tongues in the face of his glower.

"And that's plenty of potatoes," Jerin told Heria.

Fifteen hungry women. There would be no leftover
goose for lunch tomorrow. The potatoes would make
things stretch, but one could eat only so many before
getting bored. "Get a bushel of sweet yams scrubbed up,
and we'll put them in the oven after the goose comes
out." He handed out gathering baskets. "The rest of
you, out to the garden. Pick a full basket of peas, and
cut a quarter row of asparagus—make the stems long
as possible."

Summer hurried into the kitchen just as he set the
goose out. Her eyes went wide at the sight of him.
"What are you doing?" she whispered fiercely, throwing
a look toward the front of the house, where the royal
party gathered in the parlor.

"I am cooking dinner." Jerin picked up the tray of

now scrubbed and pierced sweet yams and slid them into
the empty oven. "Roasted goose, sage dressing, mashed
potatoes, gravy, blanched asparagus, boiled peas, sliced
winter apples, cheese, fresh bread, butter, and yams."

"They're going to see you and the boys!" Summer
cried.

"Not if they don't come into the kitchen," Jerin said.
"And you middle sisters handle the serving in the dining room."

If Summer's hair had been longer than the military
crop, it seemed she would be pulling it out by now.
"How are we going to keep the royal guard out of the
kitchen? They're probably going to check the food for
poison."

Jerin got out their largest platter and dual meat forks.
"Like we keep poison on hand to kill off visiting
princesses."

"Jerin!" Summer wailed.

He closed his eyes and counted to ten. "Summer, the
goose was going to burn if I didn't get it out, and the
youngest are hungry, and we have guests—royal guests.
If Corelle did the cooking, truly we would be poisoning
the princesses."

"What if they see you?" Summer frowned at the door
as if she expected the royal guard to burst through it
any moment.

"Then they see me!" He lifted the goose out of the
roasting pan and onto the platter. "She's the crown princess. She's not going to ride off with me."

"One of her guards might grab you and desert," Summer said.

"I'm sure the army knows where their families are
located," Jerin said.

Summer glared at him. "Jerin, will you take this
seriously!"

"I am!" He drained the drippings into a cook pot and
set it to boil. "Only the crème of military are picked for
royal guard. If they see me, the worst that will happen

is that they'll offer for me—and frankly, I think that's a better fate than the Brindles."

"Don't be naïve, Jerin." Summer crossed her arms and gave him a level look. "There are things to be done with a boy that have nothing to do with marriage."

He stared at her, and then blushed hot. "I wouldn't do anything like that."

Summer glanced at the little girls around them, listening intently, and whispered, "You wouldn't have much of a choice. It's why they call it rape."

He rolled his eyes at that. "Trust me, if any of them were carrying crib drugs, our little sisters would know."

As a distraction, it worked. Summer turned on the youngest in a full rage. "You little brats! You stay out of their rooms!"

Jerin moved on to the potatoes, which needed to be drained by now, and mashed. "Dinner will be ready in twenty minutes or so, though the sweet potatoes will be coming out later. The boys and I will eat in the keeping room, and then go upstairs right afterward. Heria can make sure the little ones eat, and Corelle can clean up with the girls."

"I will make sure you have a clean kitchen for morning," Summer said.

"Thank you, Summer. I'll make sure our mothers know who acted the idiot and who didn't today."

Summer suddenly caught him into a hug. "Oh, Jerin, I was an idiot! I knew we were leaving you and the babies alone! I let Corelle bully me into going. What if they had been raiders? We could have lost everything."

"I know. I know. Now, let me finish dinner."

Jerin had picked at his dinner and then left the kitchen without thinking of taking a snack. Later, he found himself so hungry that he couldn't sleep. Finally, he couldn't take it any longer. The house was silent. No one was up. He could slip downstairs, he told himself, grab something to eat from the pantry, and return with no one being the wiser.

He crawled out of bed, and stood a moment in darkness. Normally he'd pull on his trousers in addition to his nightshirt before going downstairs. Tonight, though, his three younger brothers were in his room, restless in their strange beds. He would have to light the lamp to find his trousers. He could imagine a cascade of events, starting with the lamp waking the boys and ending with the rest of the house awake.

It would only take a minute to run downstairs and raid the kitchen. I don't need trousers. My nightshirt reaches my knees—it's nearly a walking robe.

The kitchen seemed huge in the darkness. Flames still danced in the hearth; Summer must not have properly banked the cook fires. He frowned, crossing to the hearth, not sure if he should take the time to settle the fire.

"So my sister isn't imagining things," a female voice drawled in the darkness.

Jerin startled backward, almost into the flames of the open fire pit. There was motion, and arms pulled him away from the fire with a low croon of "Careful, careful."

"Your Highness!" His heart hammered in his throat as he recognized a gleam of red hair and delicate features before his body eclipsed the firelight.

"I didn't mean to frighten you," the princess murmured, a dark form with strong arms about him. "My sister claimed a beautiful man carried her up from the stream, but I thought she imagined it. Who would let a man risk his reputation so?"

"A sister who will soon be in deep trouble with her mothers and older sisters."

"Sister?" One arm lifted from his hip to run fingers through his waist-long hair. "You're not a husband?"

He bit his lip. Husbands were more dearly protected

by the law than brothers. He shouldn't have spoken—
each word he said was a danger to him.

"Come, come," Princess Rennsellaer coaxed gently,
"I'm not going to carry you off like some husband
raider."

"I'm a brother. I'll be of age in two months."

The princess turned him slightly so the fire was to her
back, the light a gleaming halo about the nimbus of her
shadowed hair. Her fingers touched his cheek, trailed
down to cup his chin. "Your family runs to good looks."

"Our grandfather was an exceedingly handsome man,"
Jerin admitted, aware suddenly that he wore only one
sheer layer of cotton, that she wore nearly the same, and
then her left hand cupped his buttocks, pressing his body
to hers. "I came down for a bite of something."

"I have something here you can nibble on," she murmured, catching his hand, guiding it under her sleeping
shirt. Her skin was soft, warm, and firm. His body re-
acted to the touch while his mind floundered in panic.
How much force could you use denying the crown princess without bringing trouble down on your head?

"Your Highness, please." He tried to sidestep, but she
moved with him.

"You desire me," she noted, running her hand over
his body.

"I desire to marry well," he murmured hoarsely. "For
fifteen years I have stayed chaste and pure. I would not
like to fail two months shy of the goal."

She chuckled. "I'm amazed that you've seen any
women besides your sisters."

"They take me to social events." He was babbling
now, unable to stop. "How else would families know we
seek a marriage alliance? We go to fairs, festivals, and
such. The girls compete in races and wrestling, and the
boys talk about how their sisters make them crazy and
how lonely it is, being the only man among so many
women." He moaned softly now, as her hand had not

stayed idle. "That is nice," he admitted, "but I wish—"
Truthfully he didn't really want it to stop. "I wish—"

She stepped him back, pressing him against the stones
of the hearth, and kissed him tenderly. Her mouth was
sweet, and warm, and electric on his. He couldn't find
anyplace safe to put his hands; they tended to flutter
like birds looking for a roosting place. He whimpered
partially in delight of the many sensations bombarding
him, partially in the helplessness of his situation.

"Highness—um—I don't think—we shouldn't be—oh,
gods—I—" While his mind raced to form some sentence,
any sentence, he stumbled on an awful thought. *If not
for this once, the only intimacy in my life will be with the
horsey-faced, heavy-handed Brindle women. Who would
know what we've done? Who would guess? Who would
tell? Certainly not my sisters.* With those thoughts, he
allowed his hands to alight on her hips, then explore
upward, under her nightshirt.

In the last year of his life, Jerin's father had told him
how one man could keep ten women happy. It had been
a frank, embarrassing, sometimes mystifying set of dis-
cussions. There hadn't been an opportunity for Jerin to
try any of the techniques outside of his increasingly
erotic dreams. It was somewhat satisfying, judging by the
princess's reaction, to discover he remembered a goodly
portion of his father's lessons.

They could have taken the last step. They lay on the
warm flagstones before the cooking fire, glistening with
sweat. She reached for him, his body responded as before, but this time, the edge taken off his desire, he was
able to stop her.

"No." He kissed her to soften the refusal. "To go this
far was foolish. To go on would be stupid."

She gazed at him, her hair reflecting back the flame-
red firelight. "It was wonderful."

That pulled a wry smile out of him. He caught her

hand before it could cause more mischief, and kissed her palm, nuzzling the sensitive spot on her wrist. "We can't do more. It would ruin me."

She looked away, watching instead the dance of firelight on the whitewashed ceiling. She was silent for many minutes, to the point that he was afraid he had angered her. "You are right. You are not yet old enough to marry, and I seduced you in your mothers' kitchen. It would be best that I don't take your virginity on your mothers' Hearth."

She gave it the old name. Jerin vaguely remembered that there were ancient rules of hospitality tied to the Hearth, remnants of days when starting a fire didn't mean just using a match, and homes consisted of just one large room.

"Please"—Jerin reached for his abandoned nightshirt—"let me go back to my room and you go back to yours?"

"I could come tuck you in," she murmured.

"We'd wake my brothers."

She startled. "There are more?"

He told her his brothers' names and ages. "Please don't tell my sisters that I've told you. They're afraid that you'll carry me off."

"Or seduce you in the kitchen."

He blushed. "Well, yes."

She giggled and then sobered. "Run up to bed, love, and be careful not to wake your brothers."

He slipped reluctantly out of her arms. "It's my sisters that I worry about."

Chapter 3

The black, bitter cold snow tasted of soot, mud, and blood. Ren slowly levered herself up, spitting out the tainted snow, puzzled by the odd flickering shadows, the endless, shapeless roar that beat on her ears, the heat across her back. Why was she facedown in the slush-covered street? A loud crack made her turn, and she gaped at flames towering up into the night sky, consuming the broken timbers of a building. The theater! What had happened? She had been standing on the theater stairs a moment before—had it been just a moment? But surely it must have been longer—the whole building was engulfed. Then realization struck her. The others were still inside. She opened her mouth to scream when the shape of a crumpled human finally found meaning in her mind. Her sister Halley lay at the top of the steps, half in the doorway. Ren tried to stand, but something was wrong with her legs. She struggled on anyhow in a haze of pain, crawling, frantic. She had to get to Halley. Had to get Halley away from the fire. No matter how hard she tried, though, she could not get closer. The doorway itself was on fire now, about to collapse in burning timbers onto her sister. Oh, merciful Mothers, let her save Halley!

Ren snapped awake, whimpering in fear, the smell of smoke thick under her nose. She sat up in alarm, instantly disoriented by the placement of the window, the low rough-timbered ceiling, and the plain lines of the furniture.

Oh, yes, the Whistler farm!

The events of the last few days must have triggered her old nightmare about the explosion at the theater. On impulse, she had decided to visit the armory upriver at North Branch. It had been a leisurely six-day trip from Mayfair on the royal stern-wheeler, but they had arrived to find the armory plundered and set afire. As they were still docking, the flames reached the gunpowder room. Great flowering blooms of flame rose in the night with a sound that could be felt, a heat that seared the skin even at a hundred feet away.

The scorching heat, the thick black smoke, and the charred bodies curled into the fetal position. Old impressions of the theater explosion that had killed her elder sisters and Keifer joined with new. No wonder her old nightmares were resurfacing.

Her cold rage at her helplessness reawakened too. Without thought to Odelia's and her own safety, Ren had led a pursuit of the escaping thieves from the armory back downriver. When the royal party found the thieves' barge run aground, she ordered a landing against Raven's advice. Stupidity at its highest order: going into unknown territory after an unknown force. Only Odelia's amazing luck had kept her safe.

At least there wouldn't be new nightmares to join the old one.

Dawn gleamed in the window, small noises indicated a house awakening to a normal day, and the smell of smoke vanished. Maybe, Ren rationalized, the stench had been the tail end of her nightmare.

She stretched, stiff after a night in a strange bed, and caught another whiff of smoke. She pulled the shoulder of her nightshirt to her nose and sniffed. Woodsmoke. No wonder she was dreaming about the fire. With a curse, she yanked the nightshirt over her head, wadded it into a ball, and was about to throw it across the room when she caught the smell of him. Ren buried her nose into it. Jerin. Beautiful, talented, sexy Jerin. She let the memories of him crowd out the nightmare. His sweet kisses. His warm skin. His long, silky hair. The delight he triggered in her body. The last made her giggle, hugging the shirt to her. Oh, she must be insane—as insane as Odelia! Making love to a farmers' son on the kitchen floor. Her mothers would die! His mothers would kill her!

Raven's tap came at the door.

"Enter," she called, trying to control her grin and failing.

"We are in a good mood." Raven used the royal plural. The captain carried a steaming pail of water.

"We are." Ren unrolled the nightshirt and carefully folded it, vowing to herself never to wash it. A farmers' son, no matter how beautiful or talented, could never be prince consort. Last night, though, had been glorious, and stopping where they did made it all the more pure.

Raven lifted one eyebrow in question and poured the water into the washbasin bowl. "The Queens Justice rode in with the false dawn. They spent the last of yesterday sweeping the woods and the neighboring lands for five miles. A lot of tracks, many from us when we were searching for Odelia. No sign, though, of the guns or Odelia's attackers. They'll be combing them again today."

"I didn't expect any." Ren stashed the folded nightshirt into her travel bags. "The thieves had since the night before last to tuck the guns away. The Whistlers found Odelia hours before we arrived, and we waited about an hour for Queens Justice to arrive. Odelia's attackers would have been complete fools to wait around for a second chance."

"So you think they're gone?"

"Certainly it's a far more comforting thought than the idea of them lurking behind every bush, looking for an open shot." Ren splashed warm water onto her face.

"Bounder had a theory on why the attackers didn't use pistols. She says that the Whistlers are notoriously rough on poachers. A shot fired would have brought them out in force, and no one in their right mind would want to take the Whistlers on."

Water dripping from her chin, Ren looked at Raven. "Only locals would know about the Whistlers. She thinks one of the locals had a go at Odelia?"

"Heron Landing apparently has a good bit of river trash." Raven named the nearest town, home of Bounder's garrison, at least ten miles from the Whistlers' farm. "Seasonal workers, outcasts, drifters, all of whom have been in the area long enough to learn about the Whistlers, and wouldn't be above doing some dirty work for hire. It would fit the description of the riders Heria saw."

Disposal tools. Did they even know who Odelia was? Or had they been told just to kill the red-haired woman on the roan mare? Considering her family's reputation at meting out severe punishment for regicide, one could almost be sure that the hired thugs were kept ignorant.

Still, the ignorant disposal tools were human beings. They might have seen or heard something they weren't supposed to, information they'd gladly trade for their lives.

"Is there a sheriff for Heron Landing?" Ren asked.

"Aye."

"Have the sheriff round up all the trash. Check them for studded truncheons. Find out where they were yesterday. See if any of them heard of someone hiring for a killing. Have her use whatever means she needs to find us a lead."

"Yes, Your Highness." Raven gave a slight bow and left.

Ren dried her face, watching the door close behind the captain of her guard. Raven never called her "Your Highness" in private, never bowed. Why the sudden change? Was this some subtle hint that Raven thought Ren was finally acting like a firstborn?

Jerin woke shortly after dawn as normal. He bathed quickly in the washbasin, brushed out his hair, braided it into one long braid, and pulled on his best shirt, a blue chambray that matched his eyes. After waking Doric and helping the ten-year-old brush out his hair and braid it, Jerin sent him out to gather eggs in the henhouse. Liam and baby Kai, Jerin gathered up and carried downstairs into the kitchen.

Corelle, Eva, and Kira had gotten up earlier to tend the stock. Heria had the cook fire built up for breakfast. Summer had organized the youngest sisters and they were carrying in pails of fresh milk for breakfast.

Jerin now put the many hands to work setting tables, fetching jars of clotted cream from the springhouse, opening crocks of blackberry jam and apple butter, cutting slices of yesterday's leftover bread to toast, fetching a wheel of sharp white cheese and slicing it down, mashing cold potatoes to make potato pancakes, and boiling the fresh eggs. As there were guests for breakfast, Jerin had Heria fetch a leg of ham from the smoke shed. For the occasion of guests too, he brought out a crock of maple syrup. He had no more than opened it when every finger in the room seemed to gravitate toward it.

"No fingers!" He tapped Doric's outstretched hands with his long mixing spoon. "Wait for it."

There was a collective gasp of surprise. Jerin glanced up and noticed that every eye was focused on the door to the dining room. He turned and found Princess Ren leaning on the doorjamb, watching him with a slight smile on her lips. The memory of her kisses burned suddenly across his senses, and he looked down.

Heria, Blush, and Leia slid between him and the princess, the set of their shoulders pure defiance.

"Heria." He turned her toward the cook fire. "The egg sandglass has run out. Get the eggs from the fire. Blush, start the potato pancakes now, so they'll be hot with the eggs. Leia, run out to the barns and let your sisters know that breakfast will be in ten minutes."

"Jerin!" They protested in chorus, their eyes locked on the princess.

"Go!" he said kindly but firmly, giving each a small nudge.

They went to their appointed tasks, though it was clear where their attention remained.

"They don't trust me." Princess Ren came to the high cooking table that he worked at, and took a seat on the stool there. The black-haired captain took Ren's place at the doorway; she seemed to view the kitchen full of knives and children with a mixture of anxiety and bemusement.

"Family history makes us leery." Jerin scooped up baby Kai and slid him into a high chair battered by nearly three dozen babies. He tickled a pure baby giggle out of his brother and spoiled him with a spoon dipped in the maple syrup. Princess Ren watched him and he found himself watching back. Her eyes were deep green, deeper than her sister's. Her red hair, like a flame, was spun from threads of red, orange, and gold. Her skin was creamy white and unblemished.

He found himself wishing they had taken that final step the night before. He blushed at the thought and looked away.

"What happened to make you leery? Your family lose a husband or a son?" Princess Ren asked.

"Well, actually, it ran the other way," he admitted. "Our grandmothers kidnapped our grandfather during the War of the False Eldest. He had not come willingly."

The princess reached out for the maple syrup and he tapped her fingers out of habit. She looked up at him, startled, while he stared at his spoon, horrified.

"Ummm, no fingers." He dipped a spoon into the syrup and handed it to her.

She smiled at him and lapped the spoon with the tip of her tongue, making a show of licking it clean. It recalled her leaning over him, her tongue touching his bare skin. His body responded to the memory. His blush became a complete burn as she noticed his arousal in his trousers.

"It's sweet," she murmured, "but not as tasty as you."

He felt like flipping a towel over his head and hiding. He felt like running from the room in embarrassment. He felt like leading her upstairs and letting her use her tongue on him again. The last put shudders of desire through him.

He struggled to find a less intimate subject. "How is your sister?"

Amusement fled Princess Ren's eyes. "She tried to get out of bed and failed. She nearly fainted when she stood up."

"I'm sorry."

Ren frowned a moment, then shrugged. "I'm thankful she's alive."

Jerin finished slicing down the ham, his hands trembling so much he had trouble controlling the sharp knife. "So," he said, trying not to seem as anxious as he felt, "you're going to be staying another night."

The smile returned to Ren's face. "If not more."

He looked at her, wanting her, wondering how he was going to resist her.

"Riders!" came a call from one of the princess's women, and the kitchen went still.

"It's Eldest! It's Eldest and the others!" Leia's voice followed the call.

There was a general rush for the door to see their seven elder sisters return. Corelle, not surprisingly, ran to meet them, talking low and fast, making sure they heard her side of the story first. They had apparently already heard some version of the news. Their horses were lathered and blowing from a hard riding. Their rifles sat in saddle holsters, instead of being wrapped well and strapped to the back of their saddles. Eldest gave Corelle a scathing look as she dismounted. She unholstered her rifle, saying, "See to the horses. We'll talk later." She threw her reins to Corelle and came on to the house.

Eldest looked first to Jerin, then scanned the children

for the other boys. Seeing that the family's greatest
assets were safe, she locked gazes with Princess Ren.

"Your Highness," Eldest said quietly, handing her
rifle to Heria without a glance. "Welcome to the House
of Whistler."

"Thank you, Eldest Whistler."

Heria ducked away to return the rifle to the gun rack.
The other children stood, waiting for orders.

Eldest glanced about the kitchen at the food threatening to burn unattended. "Get breakfast on," she stated.
"We'll wash up and eat, then talk."

So this was what little Whistler girls grew up to look
like, Ren mused, studying the recently returned elder
sisters. If the Whistler family had been a motley crew
during the War of the False Eldest, they had weeded
out all the variants in the last two generations. Without
exception, the Whistler clan was black-haired, blue-eyed,
and good-looking. The military heritage that showed in
the children as broad strokes became unmistakable in
the women. Regulation short haircuts, clothes tailored
along the lines of an infantry uniform, rifles in hand, and
six-guns riding low in tied-down hip holsters. Beyond the
outward appearances, there was the military precision to
the way they rode in—handing exhausted horses, damp
greatcoats, and weapons to younger sisters—and they
settled wordlessly to the breakfast table smelling of
horses and lye soap. Food was eaten in tense silence,
broken occasionally by a younger sister trying to report
a wrong or misadventure. Eldest Whistler silenced the
girls with a look.

Unlike the night before, Jerin and the younger boys
sat with the family instead of hiding in the kitchen. Still,
Jerin sat at other end of the table, at Eldest's right hand,
with the other boys well barricaded behind their sisters.

Eldest broke the silence, naming a town a day's travel
downriver of Heron Landing. "We were in Greenhaven
last evening, when we heard that there had been an at-

tack on the farm. No one knew any details, just that one of our little ones had ridden in for Queens Justice."

"I went for Queens Justice," Heria said, "because Corelle and the others weren't here."

"Heria!" Corelle cried as if stabbed. "We were just next door."

"You were supposed to be here!" Heria snapped, to which the nine- and eight-year-olds added their backing.

"Hush." Eldest Whistler quieted that family dispute with one look and a single even command. "We will talk about that later."

Ren looked down at her plate to cover a bolt of jealousy. Command of a family came so easy for someone who held her position from her first breath, blessed with the name of Eldest. In their cradles, younger sisters were told, "Listen to Eldest—she'll be Mother Elder when she's grown," even when the sisters were younger only by months or days. Ren wished she had that luxury in her own family, then, chiding herself for being small-hearted, wished instead that her elder sisters hadn't been killed, making her Eldest over sisters well practiced at disagreeing with her. She had not, in fact, even been the natural leader of the middle sisters. Halley had commanded Odelia, Trini, Lylia, and herself from the time they had left their cradles until the night Ren had become the Eldest.

Halley was younger by only six months. Six months that had never mattered before.

"We don't air family problems in front of strangers," Eldest Whistler stated as one who is never argued with. She finished the last bite of her eggs and pushed away the empty plate. "So, Your Highness, what brings you upriver to Heron Landing?"

Her eyes asked, "What troubles do you bring to my home?"

Ren glanced about the table, at the family trained by the best spies that Queensland had ever had, and decided that perhaps it would be best to take them into her confidence. "While we didn't engage the Imomains in full war, it has been a costly effort to keep them off our shores. Our coffers are low, and we can ill afford the drain on tax revenue that smuggling represents. Worse, smuggling on the rivers has increased tenfold in the last decade. The Queens contracted with a family of gun-makers upriver at North Branch to produce guns to be the teeth in our efforts to bear down on the smugglers. Princess Odelia and I decided to do a surprise inspection." Actually, Ren had dragged Odelia into duty, determined the younger princess would act her age and rank. "We had interrupted a raid on the armory. While we managed to prevent the theft of six naval guns, all the small arms and a series of cast-iron cannons were taken. The cannons are our main concern now."

"Cast iron?" Corelle scoffed. "You can't cast iron barrels uniformly. Under pressure they burst, killing everyone within dozens of feet. No one's made cast-iron cannons since Deathstriker burst twenty years ago."

Eldest frowned at her sister's rudeness, but added, "Bronze is the best metal for cannons."

Even after two generations of farming, they remained well schooled in the art of war. Until a few months ago, what they said had been true.

"Unless you want to rifle them." Ren pointed out the true flaw of bronze. "Bronze is too soft of a metal. The friction wears down the rifling in a short amount of time."

Jerin had been listening with his amazingly blue eyes open wide. He leaned to his Eldest sister and whispered, "How do you make a cannon a rifle?"

Eldest answered, obviously aiming her answer more to the very youngest of her sisters than to Jerin. "Rifling is cutting spiral grooves down the bore of the weapon, any weapon. It makes the shot fly straighter, so your aim is truer. Smooth bores, weapons without the grooves, you might as well point in the general direction, pull the trigger, and hope."

Ren nodded at this patient explanation. "The Wainwrights at North Branch proved they could make a reliable, cast-iron, breech-loaded cannon."

"Completely reliable?" Eldest asked.

Ren shrugged. "Extremely reliable—I would call nothing 'completely.' Apparently the novelty of their method isn't in the reinforcement of the cast iron forward of the breech—others have tried that and failed—but in the method of attachment." While his sisters listened passively, Jerin nodded slightly to indicate he followed the explanation. Ren controlled the urge to smile encouragement to him. "A wrought iron band is allowed to cool in place while the gun is rotated, which allows the reinforcement to clamp on uniformly around the circumference of the breech. We ordered eight ten-pounders. The Wainwrights called them the Prophets: Joan, Bonnye, Anna, Judith, Gregor, Larisa, Nane, and Ami."

"At Greenhaven," Eldest reported, "they were saying that the Wainwright place blew up, that their ammo went up and took out the shop and the house."

Ren shook her head. "The thieves killed the family in their beds long before torching the place. They managed to carry out all the small arms, the pistols and rifles, and the Prophets before we arrived. They were trying to move the great naval guns when we rode up, and they set fire to the shop to cover their retreat."

She and Raven had been to the Wainwrights' home several times to see the new weapons tested and to order various guns. While not as prolific as the Whistlers, the Wainwrights had numbered around twenty women and girls with a handsome young husband that they proudly showed off. Not one survived the murderous attack.

Raven cleared her throat and covered Ren's silence. "It was easy to track the cannons. Each of the Prophets weighs nearly nine hundred pounds and they are roughly six and a half feet long. Multiply that by eight, and it's quite an operation to move them. The thieves used two coal wagons and made four trips from the gun shop down to a waiting coal barge. Half the town saw them, but thought it was the Wainwrights' normal weekly delivery of coal for the forges."

Ren took up the story again. "The coal barge with the Prophets and small arms left with its load. There were two more barges waiting for the naval guns. The thieves scuttled them to foul river traffic. It gave them several hours' start on us. We might have caught up with them if they stayed on the river, but the barge and its tug ran aground, so they started overland."

"They ran aground above Heron Landing?" Eldest Whistler guessed.

Ren nodded. "They made a makeshift raft and floated the cannons and other crates ashore one at a time. We found a safe landing and unloaded our horses. Odelia"— Holy Mothers knew what Odelia had been doing— "became separated from the rest of us, and was attacked. We think it was more of a distraction than a planned assassination."

"So these guns are still in the area?" Eldest Whistler asked.

"Is there a reward?" Corelle asked.

"Do you think the riders will come back?" Jerin asked.

"The riders were probably hired to delay pursuers." Ren sought to reassure Jerin. "They have no reason to come back. As for the cannons and small arms, the Queens Justice has found no sign of them."

Two of the younger sisters were rude enough to laugh.

Eldest Whistler stood up, motioning Ren and Raven to follow. "Lieutenant Bounder is a good soldier, but she and most of her command are new to the area. Nor does she have many good trackers under her." Eldest led them to the small, well-appointed parlor. There she opened the doors on a cherry cabinet, revealing a set of shallow drawers. She pulled out the top drawer and took out a map. She laid the map on a small side table. "How far upriver from Heron Landing did they hit the sandbar?"

"About five miles." Raven answered. "Bounder said it's timberland belonging to the Fiddler family."

Eldest Whistler grunted, tapping a section of the map. "I thought it might be there. Look, the river runs fairly straight north to south through all of Queensland, but here, it makes a twenty-mile U east to west, and back again. When you're on the river, it's not obvious. The lay of the land fools you; only this ridge lies between the northern and the southern point." Her finger with a torn fingernail traced a short line over the said ridge. "It's less than three miles, but unless you've walked this straight line, or seen the map, you would never guess you could skip so far downriver so quickly."

Ren cursed softly and tapped the downriver part of the U. "I don't suppose the river is shallow here?"

Eldest shook her head. "Fairly deep. If they brought the guns to here, it would be easy to load them onto another boat."

"Why move them at all?" Corelle asked. "Seems like a lot of work for nothing, when they could hire a boat to go upriver and unload the barge."

Eldest threw her a disgusted look. "It would have been stupid to leave them stranded with the princesses somewhere close behind them. Secondly, this confuses the trail. Think of the trail they would have left if they had hired a boat to go upriver to the stranded barge. Every ship captain they tried to hire, the crew of the ship they finally hired, any passengers already on the boat, any ship that passed while they were transferring the load, and Holy Mothers knows who else would have known what ship the guns are now on. The princesses could go downriver until they saw that ship and stop it. If the thieves had managed to already off-load the guns, there would be witnesses to where and when.

"By moving the guns, they're no longer linked to the

barge. Picking up cargo is so common it's invisible in comparison to a salvage job. And, unless you've seen a map of the river, it seems unlikely that anyone could move a dozen heavy crates so far downriver in a span of a few hours."

"We'll never find them again," Ren whispered.

"They've only had one day to secure a ship. The guns might still be here." Eldest reached over to the gun rack and took down a rifle. "If they are, we can stop them."

The other Whistlers took this as a signal and armed themselves, down to the little ones, excluding only the boys. For one panicked moment, Ren thought she might have the whole clan ride out with her. Eldest Whistler, however, motioned to the middle and youngest sets of Whistler sisters to put up their rifles, with a firm, "You stay here and guard the boys and Princess Odelia."

"You don't have to come." The Queens Justice's opinion aside, Ren wasn't sure the farmers were up to riding with her guard.

"I've spent my whole life learning how to fight," Eldest stated. "Once in my life, it would be good to actually ride out to battle. I don't think the chance to ride in the Princesses' Guard will come around twice."

Certainly, it would help to have someone who knew the lay of the land to guide them.

"Glad to have you, then," Ren said, and earned a wide grin from the woman.

They surged out of the house, carried along in a wave of excited, and thankfully now unarmed, children. While saddling their horses, Ren caught sight of Jerin helping his older sisters saddle up. He moved with assurance among the horses, handling the bridles and saddles with ease. As she watched, he kneed a black mare in the middle to make her suck in her stomach. He clinched the saddle girth tight, tied it, and then looked up to meet Ren's gaze.

He wanted her. She knew the look now, having seen the physical evidence of his desire paired before with his level blue gaze. Just knowing that he wanted her did magic to her body. She dropped her eyes before anyone noticed the exchange. The Whistlers would not be so happy to ride beside her if they knew what she had done with their little brother in the kitchen.

Suddenly the idea of them at her back with rifles did not seem so wise. She glanced at Eldest Whistler, wondering if this was an exercise in revenge.

You're crazy, Ren told herself as she swung up into her saddle. *Eldest just rode in. She wasn't here to witness anything. You've heard everything that everyone had to say to her.*

Then she remembered Corelle darting up to her oldest sister, earnestly pouring out some story. Eldest's flash of anger could have been toward a lax sister making excuses—or at the news their brother had been compromised.

Ren scanned the milling women and children for Corelle. The middle sister stood by the padlock's gate, holding it open as riders were already trotting through. As if sensing Ren's gaze, Corelle turned toward her as she rode up to the gate. Cool, calculating resentment filled the girl's face.

She knows.

Ren kept her face passive as she rode past, and tried to ignore the itch between her shoulder blades. Had Corelle told Eldest? Was she riding into a trap?

If the Whistlers fought the way they rode, it was no wonder they won the war.

Showing little evidence that they had ridden all night, the Whistlers led cross-country, over fences and creeks, with seemingly reckless abandon. When one watched, though, not one horse so much as stumbled. Ren wondered if they were attempting an extremely subtle form of assassination: ride out with the princess and let her break her own neck trying to keep up.

The last mile they cut through rows of shoulder-high

corn, the leaves cutting and grabbing at both sides, and
came out onto a dirt path. Fresh wagon tracks crushed
the grass growing on either side of the path. The path
ran along the cornfield and, a half mile farther down,
dipped into woods. The river was near enough to smell
over the bruised corn and the hot horses.

The Whistlers dismounted, tied off their horses, and
went silent as wolves into the woods. Ren wanted to
follow, but she knew her own value. Her life wasn't
worth the capture of the cannons. There too was the
niggling thought that the small woodlot would be a perfect ambush site by the Whistlers. She signaled to her
women to ready weapons, wishing she had told Raven
of her indiscretion. Now, on the cusp of battle, would
be a foolish time to make her women doubt their allies.
On the other hand, letting the captain of her guard ride
blindly into an ambush seemed particularly stupid.

She fought her conscience while silence came from the
woods and one lone cicada droned loudly.

A Whistler came trotting out of the woods and tugged
on her cap bill in salute. "There's signs that a riverboat
tied off and something heavy was loaded. No cannons,
but there are a couple of fresh graves."

"Show me." Ren dismounted.

A screen of brush in the woods proved to be false, a
deliberate attempt to hide the path down to the river.
On the high bank some forty feet from the river's edge,
the thieves' camp showed evidence of being used often.
River stone shielded a fire pit from the river. Evergreens
hid a corral of sapling stringers. A well-beaten path led
down to a spring-fed streamlet, a wooden bucket beside
it waiting for the next visit. A secretive camp, but one
long-standing, not erected overnight. The corral and fire
pit both had seen winter. Thinking of the cornfield she
left behind, Ren guessed at the origin of the camp.

Beyond the corral, five of the Whistler sisters worked
at digging up the graves. Ren signaled to Raven and her

women to help with the unearthing and continued on to where Eldest Whistler crouched beside the fire pit.

"Whiskey runners?" she asked Eldest, meaning the original creators of the campsite. Was it just irony that the thieves used a smuggling camp while stealing cannons meant to fight river smuggling, or had they known what the cannons were going to be used for, and stolen them as a preventive measure?

Eldest shrugged. "Anything taxed going up and down the river. From the number of horses, tents, and footprints, we figure there were about twenty women in all. There are six graves. Heria saw five riders, so that may be them plus one." She touched the ground and lifted her fingers up to show that they were now tinged red. "This is the killing ground."

Odelia could have been the plus one. Ren controlled a shiver.

"The killing started here at the fire." Eldest wiped clean her fingers. "The worst of the blood has been scraped up, probably buried with the victim. There were guns fired." She tapped a scar of white on a river stone that served as a fireside seat. She pointed out fresh gouges in trees at chest height. "The dead were dragged up there to be buried. Things were cleaned up. That was yesterday, or the night before that. The survivors loaded a riverboat this morning around dawn." Eldest held her hand out over the white ash in the white pit. "The coals are still warm."

Ren swore softly. "They had wagons. I can't imagine them loading them—too noticeable. Can we track those?"

Eldest shook her head, and waved toward the shimmer of water through the trees. "Pushed them in the river and let the current take them."

"All dead ends." Ren stalked about the clearing, cursing. They had missed the thieves by a few hours. It was, perhaps, just as well. With her guard and the seven Whistlers they numbered only twenty-one. True, they outnumbered the surviving thieves, but the campsite had

hidden defenses. A jumble of boulders, a fallen tree, and
another set of rocks came together to form a disguised
wall to shield defenders. Three approaches were uphill
with the river at the attackers' backs.

Ren skirted the disguised wall to consider the only
downhill attack. A blur of motion was her only
warning—Eldest Whistler came over the low wall in a
flying tackle. Eldest slammed into Ren's waist, and they
tumbled onto the ground, Ren on the bottom, a shoulder
smashing into her gut.

Shit! Ren rolled free, reaching for her pistol, thinking,
*Stupid! Stupid! Ruin their brother and then let them take
you out in the middle of nowhere and separate you from
your guard!* Her pistol had been knocked free during
the tumble, lost in the dead leaves. She jerked free her
knife, and scrambled into a fighting crouch in the dead
leaves.

Eldest crouched a dozen feet from her, unarmed. Eldest made a stiff motion with her hand, palm downward.
"Stay still." She flashed another hand signal, a quick stiff
chop that flicked off to the right. "Traps."

Ren froze in place. Traps? She was an idiot! Outside
the camp and beyond the defense wall, of course there
were traps! She glanced back at where she had been
walking. A pole tipped with a dozen sharpened stakes
pinned her hat to a tree. Eldest hadn't attacked her—
she had saved Ren's life.

Putting fingers to her mouth, Eldest gave two shrill
whistles. "'Ware! Traps!" Hearing her warning echoed
through the encampment, Eldest turned back to Ren.
"Are you all right, Your Highness?"

Ren nodded, sheathing her knife, feeling stupid. "You
startled me."

Eldest grinned. "Did I, now?"

"Yes, but thank you."

"Another one there, and behind you." Eldest pointed
out a trip wire to either side of her. "Best just hop the
wall."

Raven was coming down from the graves as they slid over the wall. "You might want to see this," she said, but her face belied her words. Whatever they found was horrible to see.

"What is it?" Ren did not want to go unprepared to the grave site.

"They've killed a man."

It was not enough warning. Ren gagged at what they showed her. Arms tied behind his back, his trousers down around his ankles to expose scrawny hairy legs, paunchy stomach—no dignity afforded him in death. Blood spotted his privates; his rapists had either been virgins or on their menses. Blood had clotted on his face and nose, had pooled in his eyes, and his ears. Drug vials littered the grave with him, paper labels proclaiming EVERLAST. A crib drug, meant to keep the men passive, willing, and able.

Her women had uncovered the grave, and they stood silent, staring at the body. The younger Whistlers hung back, their fierceness stripped by their shock, unable to even look at the man. Her eyes furious, Eldest knelt beside the corpse and covered his nakedness with her coat.

Ren didn't want to look at the body, even with it decently covered. She didn't want to think of a rich Wainwright home now reduced to ash, of the intelligent women who were now burned shells, nor of the handsome husband showed off to visiting royalty. She turned instead to Raven. "It's Wainwrights' husband, isn't it?"

"Yes," Raven said. "His name was Egan, if I remember right."

"They overdosed him?" Ren guessed. It was a common problem in cribs, and even in a few families where the number of wives was high.

Raven looked bleak and confused. "They cut out his tongue, I suppose to ensure his silence, but botched it completely. Either he choked to death on his own blood, or he bled to death."

"Holy Mothers!" Ren trembled. "What kind of animals could do this? Rape a man, then maim him so. What if he got you with child? What do you tell your daughter? 'I tore your father's tongue out after I raped him'?"

Raven shrugged. "When your family's been bred out of the cribs, you don't talk about how you got pregnant. You go into an unlit room, a man half incoherent with drugs ruts on top of you, breaks your hymen—hopefully plants a fertile seed—and you leave. What's there to say except it was dark, painful, and bloody?"

Ren glanced at the gathered women. The women of her guard—all fathered from cribs—were passive in the face of this horror. The Whistlers, two generations removed from the cribs, looked panic-stricken. Did you have to have a loving father to understand the horror?

"Your Highness." Eldest struggled to keep fear from her face. "There's nothing here for us. We need to go! We need to get back to our brothers!"

Jerin! Odelia! Ren nodded even as she glanced to Raven.

"The other five are river trash." Raven indicated the other five shallow graves holding women in dirty ragged clothing. "The largest is wearing a bandage on her arm."

"Odelia's attackers."

"They've been shot, searched, and buried. There's nothing to identify them with."

Ren looked out upon the river. The trail ended here, then, at least for her. Summer Court opened in less than a week, and she needed to return home to Mayfair to act as Elder Judge. "There's nothing here for us. Let's go."

With no twenty sisters and one wounded princess to feed, Jerin did not hold dinner. He sent a tray of food up to Odelia with Summer, and the family ate a quiet dinner. He put the leftovers in the warming ovens for the others. Cleanup would have to wait until the others had eaten.

His announcement that it was bath night was greeted

with much groaning and moaning. He supervised the water brigade to fill the tanks of the bathhouse boiler, and had the fire built up. As the water heated, he sent the little ones up to their rooms to strip down and to troop back for the cold-water scrub and hot-water communal soak.

He went up to his quarters, undressed, and realized there was a good chance Ren and her women would return before he finished bathing. He couldn't go out in just a towel as usual. He opened his wedding chest and found his grandfather's silk bathing gown. It slid on like a cool, soft hand. Just in case Ren saw him, he also put on his only piece of jewelry, a small golden deer encrusted with green stones strung on a gold chain.

Eldest had told Jerin once that most neighboring families found the Whistlers' bathhouse a source of mystery. Apparently most families bathed less frequently, in laundry tubs set up in the kitchen. It seemed an uncomfortable way of bathing. Mother Elder often told them what her mothers went through trying to build the bathhouse. Grandfather had wanted one, so Grandfather got one, despite the fact his wives were clueless on how to build one. Apparently it was just one more of the many traditions Jerin's grandmothers had bent themselves into pretzels over for his grandfather's sake. Grandpa wanted all the menfolk to read and write? They were educated. Grandpa wanted the boys to play alongside their sisters, learning to run, climb, ride, shoot, and defend themselves? They were taught.

Jerin was going to miss the bathhouse. He was going to miss his freedom even more. He continued to soak even as his sisters turned to prunes, got out, and trooped back to the house. How had his grandfather convinced his grandmothers to build the bathhouse? He could not imagine his grandmothers giving in to childish displays of temper. Nor could he imagine his grandfather throwing a fit—he had been a quiet-spoken, dignified man.

Perhaps wives were like sisters. You chose your battles instead of engaging in every skirmish, negotiated terms whenever possible, and fought as cleanly as possible in hopes that the other person would react in kind. He would know soon, whatever the case. Within the next few months, his sisters would choose a betrothal offer that suited them, and he would marry on or shortly after his birthday.

He climbed out of the lukewarm water, finding comfort in being clean and warmed to the core. If nothing else, he would have to insist his wives build him a bathhouse.

It was full night when he stepped out of the bathhouse. Stars studded the sky and the crickets were in full voice.

"I've caught you again." A woman's voice made him start. Princess Rennsellaer came out of the night.

Jerin pulled the silk wrap tight about him. "How is it, Princess, you keep catching me with next to nothing on?"

"Luck, I guess." Ren reached out to finger his wrap. "This is beautiful."

"It was my grandfather's." Feeling naked, he stepped back into the shadows of the bathhouse door.

"The kidnapped one during the war?" Ren followed him into the shadows.

"Yes." He blushed. "It was all he was wearing when my grandmother Tea snatched him."

Ren laughed, running hands over the silk gown. "I suppose he wasn't very happy."

"No, he wasn't. My grandmothers were common line soldiers, unspeakably low for a prince to marry. After his entire family was put to death for Queen Bea's murder, though, he became more philosophical about life."

Ren took a sharp gasp inward. "What? Your grandfather was part of the False Eldest's family?"

"Prince Alannon. General Wellsbury had slipped my grandmothers into Castle Tastledae to break the siege.

Grandmother Tea found Grandpa alone and unguarded, so of course she took him."

"Of course," Ren murmured, pulling him out of the shadows to eye the bathing gown closely. "This is the only thing he had?"

Jerin glanced nervously about for his sisters. They wouldn't be happy about his talking to Ren with next to nothing on. "A necklace. And some hair combs."

"Does your family still have them?"

Jerin fumbled the green deer out of his gown. "Grandpa gave the necklace to me before he died. Doric has the hair combs. Liam and Kai weren't born yet. He said we should never forget our blood is royal."

Ren looked aghast. "Commoners can't marry royals."

"My grandmothers didn't marry him until they were knighted."

Ren laughed, caught between amusement and shock. She cupped the deer in her hand and gazed at it. "Do you know how long my family searched for Prince Alannon?"

"My grandmothers were quite anxious to keep him."

Ren laughed, then fiddled on her fingers, counting generations. "We share great-great-grandmothers." She tapped on her index finger, then stepped down to her middle finger. "Your grandfather was cousin to my grandmothers." She wiggled her ring finger. "Our mothers are first cousins once removed, or second cousins?"

"I'm not sure." He leaned over to touch her pinkie. "This is us?"

"First cousins twice removed, or second cousins once removed, or third cousins."

"Are there such things as third cousins?"

"I'm not sure," she admitted.

"Perhaps it's a good thing we did nothing in my mothers' kitchen."

"Pshaw, sharing great-grandmothers means nothing."

"Are you sure?" Jerin tucked an errant lock of hair

behind his ear. "There seems to be a great deal we're not sure of."

She pulled him to her, her hands slipping into his gown to stroke his damp bare skin, her mouth warm and sweet on his. Her kiss left him breathless, trembling, and wanting more but not daring to go on, because this time he would not be able to stop. She held him, nuzzling into his hair. "I am sure," she whispered into his ear, her breath hot, "that you are a beautiful man, in a beautiful silk gown, and I want you."

"I—I—" He wavered, then steeled himself to pull out of her arms. "I can't. I want to, but I can't do it—I can't betray my family. We've come so far from being thieves, but only because twenty of my grandmothers died in war, because Grandmother Tea lucked into finding Grandfather, because my mothers worked until they dropped to make this farm bountiful. I hate being the coin of their future, but—but—"

And he knew, suddenly, that any look, or word, or gesture from her, and his will would go. He fled her, fled his own desire.

Chapter 4

Jerin was not sure if he was relieved or disappointed that Odelia came to breakfast the next morning. She looked pale, weak, and battered, but pronounced herself up to riding. She spent the meal watching Jerin's every move until Ren teased her for being a bird dog at point. Jerin had to admit there was an uncanny resemblance between the princess and a hunting dog locked on to a pigeon: the unwavering gaze, the orientation of the body toward the target, and the trembling desire kept carefully in check.

As he feared, Ren announced that with Odelia fit to ride, they would be leaving. By setting out immediately, they would have a good chance of making the four-day journey downriver to Mayfair in time for the opening of Summer Court, where the princesses would preside as judges. Eldest offered the use of the Whistler dogcart to Heron Landing, where the royal steamboat was tied off. Odelia agreed that the small buggy would be safer than trying to take the ten miles on horseback to town. Breakfast finished, the women went out to hitch up the dogcart and saddle the horses. It happened so quickly, it wasn't until Jerin set the last dirty plate next the kitchen sink that he realized the princesses were going, going for good, and that he'd never see Ren again. Suddenly it seemed something amazingly precious had slipped away, something he couldn't grasp, no more than he could hold air.

The paddock seethed with horses and women and children. Jerin stood at the edge, watching Ren give commands. Somehow she detached herself and came to him without seeming to seek him out. They stood in silence as Jerin tried to think of something he could say. Certainly not "Don't go," or "I think I love you," or even "Don't leave me here to marry the Brindles." With his sisters near at hand, even "I'll miss you" was dangerous. "Come back and visit" was impossible; he'd be married and gone within a few months.

Finally, he found something acceptable. "Keep yourself safe."

She looked away, a hint of tears in her eyes, but then looked quickly back, as if she didn't want to waste one moment of their time together. "I will. I would feel better if your mothers were here too, in case there was an attack."

"They'll be back in a week." Eldest joined them, Raven on her heels.

Jerin bit down on his disappointment, only nodding to Eldest's comment. "They're in Annaboro." Ironically, the princesses would pass Annaboro halfway downriver to Mayfair.

"What takes them down there?" Raven asked.

"They took our two-year-old fillies down for market," Eldest said.

"They go the extra distance to visit their sisters and brothers," Jerin added.

"Sisters and brothers?" Ren asked, clearly startled by their rare proliferation.

"Our grandmothers had twenty-four daughters and three sons," Eldest explained. "They split the family in half. The elder twelve sisters stayed here at the farm, and swapped the oldest brother for a husband. The youngest twelve swapped the middle brother, and got the brother's price from selling their youngest brother. They started a trading house in Annaboro with the money."

A call took Eldest away. Jerin continued since the subject seemed safe.

"Our mothers take our bloodstock down every summer to sell. Sometimes they take us along, so we stay close to our cousins. In the winter, when trading is slow, our aunts, uncles, and cousins come to visit us."

"I see," Ren murmured. "What do your sisters plan with their wealth of brothers?"

The question made his stomach drop. "We might split the family again: eleven older sisters, seventeen younger. With the four of us boys, my sisters could swap two brothers for husbands, and sell the other two. Eldest is already twenty-eight; she and the others want a husband soon. I'll—I'll probably be swapped for a husband." He closed his eyes to force himself to say in a neutral voice, "Maybe with the neighbors. Doric will be of age in six years, but none of the youngest sisters will be quite old enough then, so they might sell him. Liam and Kai—sell one, swap the other."

"It sounds so cold."

"Actually it isn't that bad. With four boys, there is no pressure to accept the first offer."

Ren reached out to clasp his hands. "Keep safe."

With the royal party departed, the farm seemed emptier than two days previous when Eldest and the others were still gone. This being a laundry day, Jerin washed out the trousers he'd rescued Odelia in, and the sheets soiled by dreams of Ren. Her perfume clung to his nightshirt and he stood smelling it, wishing now that they had finished the deed. Finally, he added it to the soapy water, saying to himself, "Silly, silly boy."

When Corelle appeared, wanting to make sure he wasn't ruining his hands with the hot wash water, he threw a bucket of dirty soap water at her. Corelle leaped at him, fist upraised, and vanished under a pile of screaming, flailing girls. The youngest dragged Corelle down by sheer volume as she punched and kicked. Jerin cursed and started snatching the littlest ones out of the fight before they could get seriously hurt.

"Stop it! Stop it!" he yelled, plucking Violet out of the fray. The four-year-old had a bloody nose already. "Damn it, Corelle, you're going to hurt someone!"

"Good!" she roared.

Heria appeared suddenly, summoned by the fighting. "Corelle, do you want to be thrown out of the family? Stop it now, or I'll see it done!"

It shocked all the girls into stillness.

"Who do you think you are?" Corelle growled, wiping blood from a split lip.

"Eldest is pissed enough for you going off and leaving the boys unguarded, Corelle. You shouldn't be fighting with the little ones, and if you hit Jerin, I'll tell. Eldest will throw you out for sure."

"I'll tell! I'll tell!" Corelle whined and shoved Heria hard, knocking her to the ground. "Oh, shut up!"

Corelle stormed away, leaving behind little girls too angry to cry. Worse, they still had to carry the heavy baskets of wet linens down to the clotheslines and hang up the sheets. In the end, they pinned up only forty of the sixty sheets, creating walls of white that rippled in the wind. Blood from dripping noses, cut hands, and bloody lips splattered the rest of the sheets and they needed to be rewashed.

At dinnertime Eldest announced Corelle's punishment for leaving the farm unguarded: her personal items, with the exception of weapons and work clothes, would be divided out to the youngest sisters and she would be given no more pocket money for the rest of the year. Hinting at a day spent inventorying Corelle's belongings, Eldest read the list to be parceled out: Corelle's flashy buckskin mare, her fine-tooled saddle bought at last year's fair, her gold money clip, her two silk shirts, her tooled leather belts with silver buckles, her silver curry-comb, and even her coveted keepsake box inlaid with mother-of-pearl. To give the youngest sisters credit, the greed in their eyes dimmed to pity as the list continued until only guns and knives were left to Corelle.

"That's not fair!" Corelle yelped.

"I could throw in a horsewhipping too, if you like," Eldest snapped.

"What about the others?" Corelle indicated Kira beside her, Eva and Summer across the table.

"*You* were left in charge." Eldest jabbed a finger at Corelle. "*You* decided to go to the Brindles'. *You* will pay for this."

"No!"

"Yes," Eldest calmly stated. "You left four brothers' prices, our entire future, the only hope we have to buy a husband and have children to care for us when we're old—*all of that*—unguarded when you had been specifically told not to leave the farm."

"Fine!" Corelle stood up. "There's nothing I want," she said, and then paused to run her tongue over her lips in a manner that made Jerin recall Ren delighting him, "that I can't get for free."

Eldest caught Corelle by the hair and muscled her down into her chair. "First, you have let your hair grow too long. I suspect Balin Brindle to be the cause, but you *will* cut it shorter. Secondly, you're acting a little too knowledgeable for someone your age. Again, I suspect Balin Brindle to be the cause, and that better not be the case. That's how syphilis enters a family—one sister dallying outside of wedlock."

"He's clean, he promised me!" Corelle protested, indignant.

Eldest slapped her hard. "You do not put your family's lives on the line with a promise from an outsider. Tomorrow we will take you to a doctor and see what she says about how clean you are. I warn you: if you've gotten yourself infected with something, you will not be wife to our husband. If we have to, we will throw you out of the house."

"No!" Corelle cried. "I haven't done anything wrong!"

"You'd have us be like the Treesdales? Ignore the situation so our husband gets infected? Have him pass it to all of us, and then all the youngest sisters as they come of age? Do you want the whole family to die a hard, slow death? Do you remember how the Treesdales suffered? The pain? The babies born dead, born twisted? They're gone, Corelle! The whole family gone, because Zera Treesdale got the itch to try out a crib."

Corelle hunched down, ducked her head, and pouted. "He's not in a crib, and we're going to marry him anyhow."

"No, we aren't!" Eldest stated, then forestalled an argument by explaining, "They approached us. We listened. That was all. That is not an agreement for marriage. Frankly, Corelle, we can do better than them. We have land, money, and breeding. We've got Queens' blood in us, and don't you forget that. You're acting like a cat in heat, presenting yourself to anything that might want to service you."

"At least I'm not servicing women on the kitchen floor in the middle of the night!" Corelle hissed.

Jerin clapped hands to his mouth to trap in a cry of protest. Corelle witnessed him and Ren? Eldest turned toward him, saw his face, and went white.

"Corelle, go to your room," Eldest said.

"I'm not a child!" Corelle whined. "I have a right to hear—"

"Now!"

Corelle flinched backward from Eldest, shot an angry glare at Jerin, and then bolted from the room. Her footsteps thundered up the stairs and her door slammed shut with a bang.

Jerin sat frozen, hands still over his mouth.

"The rest of you too." Eldest indicated the youngest sisters, and they filed out.

"Who was it?" Eldest asked quietly, emotionlessly, when he was alone with his middle and oldest sisters.

His voice would only come out as a whisper. "Princess

Rennsellaer." Unbearable silence followed. He had to break it. "She didn't mount me." The silence continued. "She was sitting in the dark when I came down for something to eat. I didn't see her until she had me in her arms, and—and—I tried to resist. I asked her please not to—and she pushed me against the hearth and kissed me. She didn't mount me—we didn't go that far. Father told me ways to make a woman happy, and that satisfied her."

"The bitch!" Eldest muttered finally. "Come to our home, eat our food, sleep in our beds, and then rape our little brother!"

Jerin wrung his hands, feeling guilty for not confessing that he had done nothing he hadn't wanted to, that it wasn't truly rape. He was afraid, though, of his sisters' fury, and the cold disapproval he would have to live with until he married well, proving he wasn't ruined by the incident. His life would be bearable only by claiming the part of wronged innocence.

Still, it galled to leave the dangerous word floating there, uncountered. "I'm still a virgin, technically. In the end, when I said that going farther would ruin me, she let me go off to bed alone."

The level of anger in the room lessened slightly. He rocked slightly in his chair, chiding himself for being a coward. Should he tell them how he surrendered to the seduction, enjoyed giving pleasure to the princess, and received ecstasy beyond description? Who was the true hussy in this family?

"Do you think," Summer said quietly into the stunned silence, "he did enough to catch any diseases she might have?"

"She's a princess!" Jerin cried.

"She's a rapist," Eldest snapped.

"She didn't rape me. She didn't try to use any crib drugs on me. I'm still a virgin."

"She took you. Maybe not completely, but still she took you against your will."

Was it rape? He didn't know. Certainly if she had let him go when he first asked, he would have fled back to his bed, remaining chaste in his lips, his hands, and his memories. Now only parts of him were virgin. He wavered in the belief of his virginity. Maybe being a virgin was like planting a garden—you could turn the earth and rake down the soil all you wanted, but until you pushed a seed into the dirt, you hadn't created a garden. Or was being a virgin like a frosted cake, where once someone stole a slice, you couldn't proudly serve it to visitors?

He realized that while he debated his virginity, his sisters were discussing the issue of diseases. It would be too soon, they had decided, to tell if he had caught something. They would take him to a doctor, but one far away, so his reputation would not suffer.

He remembered with sudden, sickening clarity how experienced Princess Ren had seemed, how sure her touch, how skilled her kisses. If she could have any man that she wanted, then what was to say that she hadn't already taken them all? What was to say she wasn't diseased? Had they been intimate enough for him to catch something from her? God, they could barely have been more intimate!

If he was diseased, who would take him as husband?

The answer was obvious. The Brindles would take him.

The thought made him cover his eyes and weep.

Eldest pulled him into a hug, murmuring, "Hush, honey, hush," as the rest of the family fled or were shooed away.

"I'm sorry. I'm so sorry," Jerin sobbed.

"We don't blame you, honey," Eldest murmured.

"I could have fought."

"She's a princess. All her life people have obeyed her commands. You're a boy. All your life you have listened to others. It was up to her to stop at any no you gave, even if it was whispered."

"Please don't hate me, but I didn't say no. I protested some, but I didn't say no, not until the very end, and she listened to it." He could not look at Eldest when he admitted, in a whisper, "I liked what we did, only I was afraid to do more."

When silence was the only answer, he peeped at her. Eldest gazed unseeing across the room. When she finally looked at him, her eyes were sad. "I don't hate you. Truly, it is easier to know you gave in to passion. It hurt to think you had been pinned and taken against your will in our very kitchen. I'm still angry with her. Making advances on you is akin to dangling candy before a child."

"I'm not a child. In a few months, I'm going to be a married man."

"That's not what I meant. Jerin, have you not noticed how we are with Doric compared to Heria? Boys are cuddled by everyone from the day they are born. Heria, we discipline sternly. We've taught her how to protect what belongs to us. Doric would think nothing of a stranger wanting to cuddle with him. Heria would look for knives."

Sell one, swap the other.

Jerin's last words rolled about in Ren's head during the ride to Heron Landing. Strange how two days could change one's perspective. She had presided over countless marriage cases—all those bitter battles over money and men as if one were interchangeable with the other. Every season for the last six years, she had attended the society functions designed to bring prospective wives and the sisters of unmarried brothers together—buyers and sellers. When she was sixteen, she had even married a man her older sisters had bought.

It seemed as if she had stood on the moon and watched the process from that emotional distance. Now, gods have mercy on her, she saw with her heart engaged.

Sell one, swap the other.

Gods, how cold, like they were horses or pieces of furniture. But the man in question wasn't either. The man was Jerin. Beautiful, sweet Jerin, who had asked for nothing but her own safekeeping.

Sold to strangers. Given to strangers.

She tried not to think of horror stories she had judged. True, humans could inflict terrible cruelty upon one another, regardless of sex. Men, though, had no legal protection or recourse. They were their wives' property. She could not even count the times she had heard of men committing suicide to escape impossible situations.

Surely Jerin had the right of it—with four brothers his sisters could refuse offers. Eldest Whistler impressed her as an intelligent, reasonable woman. Ren trusted that Eldest would choose good wives for her brother.

I'll probably be swapped for a husband . . . maybe with the neighbors.

Ren remembered with a start that Corelle and the younger sisters had been off courting the neighbor boy. She wondered what kind of women these neighbors were.

Queens Justice met the royal party at Heron Landing. Ren greeted Lieutenant Bounder with a nod. The officer had been out to the campsite to ensure that the river trash received proper burial and that the body of Egan Wainwright was sent north to be buried with his wives.

Raven took out her portable desk and scratched out orders onto a piece of stationery. "If you find anything else out, report to me."

"Keep an eye on the Whistlers," Ren commanded. "It's unlikely they'll be bothered for their part in this— but one can't be sure."

"The Whistlers can probably fend for themselves better than I can look out for them," Bounder said.

"Perhaps," Ren allowed, then pressed on. "I don't want a repeat of last time, the menfolk and the youngest alone, the older sisters out courting the neighbor, and death nearly at the doorstep." Ren tried to remain casual as she finally asked, "What do you know about these neighbors?"

Bounder snorted. "Not as much as I would like."

"Meaning?"

"The Brindle women are lazy brutes that like to pick fights. They're horrible farmers, but they still manage to build new barns and outbuildings. I suspect they might be one of the families that smuggle in my area, but so far I haven't caught them at anything. Just a matter of time."

Ren felt like she had been struck. If the Whistlers swapped brothers with their neighbors, and the Brindles were then arrested for smuggling, the weight of the law would fall on Jerin. Since men were considered property, they could be taken as part of the heavy fines against smuggling. Such men usually went to cribs belonging to the Order of the Sword, which serviced the army, or were sold to private cribs. *Her Jerin in a crib?*

Her Jerin, indeed! She scoffed at herself. As if she could marry mere landed gentry.

Yet—yet—was he not the grandson of royalty? And was she not to be the Queen Mother Elder?

She found herself smiling. Her Jerin, indeed.

The Bright River lazed through the rolling hills of upland country, down to the great falls at Hera's Step. Each bend was the same as the last—high banks scoured by the winter ice and spring flooding, a fringe of trees lacing the uncertain flood zone, and, beyond, fields and sprawling farmhouses. Women and children in the fields would unbend from their work to wave at the passing paddle wheel. The pilot followed river traditions and blasted the great, ear-deafening steam whistle to each group of wavers.

Rennsellaer paced the decks, watching fields, workers, and countless little towns appear before them and slip along their sides to vanish behind the ship. It grated that someone had killed her people, taken her weapons,

attacked her sister, and vanished without a trace. She
wanted to hound the thieves to their lair and see them
punished. *Leave the tilling of the fields to the farmer's
mule,* as her Mother Elder would say. As future Queen
Mother Elder, she should be dealing with the entire
army and not just eight missing cannons. Stopping at
every town to personally conduct the search would be
pointless. Raven had already sent orders to every garrison downriver, and the Queens Justice was scouring the
countryside for the cannons.

The plain truth would be easier to cope with if she
weren't stuck with nothing to do but watch changeless
scenery glide past.

Besides, she and Odelia needed to attend Summer
Court. If Halley did not reappear, only Trini and Lylia
remained at Mayfair. Ren had no fears that Trini could
act as Elder Judge; her sister was quietly stubborn—no
one would be able to bully Trini into a decision. Lylia?
Lylia had turned sixteen at the beginning of the year
and was eager to speak her mind. Unfortunately, her
mind was filled with odd notions and sweeping reforms,
some of them far from practical. It would be best if Ren
and Odelia were on hand to dilute Lylia's presence.

Denied the release of seeking out the cannons, Ren
struggled instead with the perfect set of arguments to
convince her mothers to allow a marriage with the Whistlers. She well remembered the declaration of undying
love her older sisters gave for their first husband, Keifer.
As disappointing as that marriage was, no passionate
pleas would work for her. Her only hope, it seemed, lay
with establishing that the Whistlers' grandmothers had,
beyond a doubt, kidnapped and married Prince Alannon
after they had been knighted. The date of their knighting
would be a simple matter of checking the Book of
Knights. Hopefully they had properly recorded the marriage, although she couldn't see how they had managed
to keep it quiet when the prince's disappearance had
been so widely publicized. Then again, if their claim was

valid, they had managed to spirit him out of a castle under siege by the entire royal army, through half of Tastledae, and then across the channel.

Their success at secrecy could be the undoing of her hopes.

Still, if she could show they had reasonable access to the castle on the date of the prince's disappearance, it would be a start. Wellsbury's memoir recorded the war in minute detail, so getting a copy of her book would be the place to begin.

At Hera's Step, a queue formed of boats waiting to pass through the lock, bypassing the massive waterfalls. The royal stern-wheeler docked to wait their turn through the locks and take on coal. Normally Ren would ride out to perform devotions at the temple wreathed by the omnipresent spray, overlooking the mile-wide curve of the falls. This time Odelia, with a contingent of their guard, would have to uphold the family obligations. Ren went with her own guard to a small bookstore located at the heart of town. If she found a copy of Wellsbury's memoir, she could use the rest of the trip scanning it for references to the Whistlers.

Raven accompanied neither princess, going instead with their pilot to the lock offices. She wanted to check the logbooks. Careful records were kept on the lockage fees; not even a rowboat could bypass the waterfalls unrecorded.

Raven later found Ren at the bookstore, gathering startled looks and curious stares from the regular patrons. Between the "royal red" of Ren's hair and the royal guards, everyone knew she was one of the five adult princesses. From their whispers, it was clear the patrons were mistaking her for Halley.

"I've got a list of ships that passed through the locks since the barge ran aground," Raven said, pulling out a small tablet that she carried, the sharpened nub of a teeth-worried pencil tucked between the pages. Ren noted the pencil with chagrin; recent events were cracking Raven's legendary poise. "There are approximately a dozen ships a day of the tonnage needed to haul the cannons."

Ren glanced over the list and shook her head. "The haystack is growing quickly."

"Did you see this?" "This" being a newspaper folded and tucked under Raven's arm. When Ren shook her head, Raven unfolded it to reveal the front page.

It was the Mayfair daily newspaper, the *Herald*. Dated only two days before, its headline exclaimed in huge dark print, PRINCESS ODELIA STRUCK DOWN!

"Oh, damn." Ren snatched the paper out of Raven's hand. FATE OF PRINCESS UNKNOWN, read the second headline in only slightly smaller print. The article took up the entire front page but contained very little real information. Rumors gleaned from crews of ships passing through Heron Landing made up the bones of the story. Snippets of reports from the Queens Justice fleshed it out. It accurately recorded that Odelia had been attacked, left for dead in a stream, and found by local, thankfully unnamed gentry. Odelia's condition, however, was speculated on wildly, putting her at death's door. Worse, the article raised concerns about Rennsellaer's safety, and went on to repeat rumors about Halley's dropping out of the public eye. The article finished with an unsubtle reminder that Trini, at age twenty, and Lylia, who recently turned sixteen, were the only other adult princesses; Ren's other five sisters were clustered around age eight.

Had her report via Queens Justice reached her mothers before this hysteria? The article noted that no information was forthcoming from the palace.

"Is there a more recent paper?" Ren asked.

"Not yet. They say it normally takes two days for it to travel up from Mayfair."

Ren swore, spotting at last a copy of Wellsbury's memoirs and plucking it up. "See if our ship can be moved to the head of the lock queue. I want to get to

Mayfair as quickly as possible. The noble houses are probably up in arms about this. We need to get home."

The paper was two days old, and it would be another two days, at safe speeds, before they reached Mayfair, meaning the nobles would have four days to panic. Hopefully her mothers would have received her report and released some kind of calming news. Still, she and Odelia would both have to make public appearances as soon as possible.

Chapter 5

Mayfair first appeared in the distance as a haze on what had been a perfect summer morning sky. Great billowing plumes coughed up from the smokestacks of a score of steamboats joined with hundreds of smaller smudges from the kitchen chimneys and businesses ranging from bakeries to wheelwrights. Later in the summer, when the heat would trap in what the winter winds scoured away, the smoke would hang like a permanent fog over the city.

Ren's ancestors built their summer palace on fairgrounds located at the confluence of rivers. For a hundred years or more, the area remained fairly bucolic, a royal park reserved for ambles through groves of live oaks and foxhunts over the downs. The sprawling city of Portsmouth was the capital at that time, and the royal family spent three seasons at the badly named winter palace. During the War of the False Eldest, though, Portsmouth proved vulnerable to enemy ships, and swamp fever outbreaks spread from the poor to the noble families. Ren's mothers were sent to the summer palace when they were young; when they became Queens, they moved the capital to them.

Unfortunately, much of the surrounding land had been sold to finance the war. The groves of live oaks were leveled for sprawling city blocks. Soon factories and mills hugged the riverbanks, gathered to Mayfair by the gravity of power. The irony being, of course, that the capital had been moved to a healthier clime, only to have squalor close in around it.

The royal stern-wheeler had stopped at Annaboro the night before to let off a messenger. Because the river made numerous lazy turns, a woman on a fast horse could reach Mayfair before the ship traveling at night speeds. As the ship docked at Mayfair, the princesses' court uniforms and royal carriage would be waiting.

The city bells were ringing seven when the royal stern-wheeler steamed up to the landing. As usual, ships jockeyed for the limited docking space. Raven got the princesses' uniforms onboard somehow, then went off to see to the boat's docking. Ren dressed quickly; Summer Court would open within the hour.

As she stepped out of her cabin, a large stern-wheeler crawling upriver toward them let out a series of quick, urgent-sounding blasts on its steam whistle.

"Hoy!" the pilot of the stern-wheeler shouted. "Sister!"

Ren tensed until she recognized it as her sisters-in-law's *Destiny*. Cotton bales stacked the *Destiny*'s decks, clear evidence it was returning to Mayfair from the south. The whistle tooted again, and Kij Porter waved from the pilothouse. Seeing that Ren spotted her, she turned the stern-wheeler over to a younger sister and hurried to the railing as the ship came along Ren's.

Like herself, Kij hadn't been born Eldest of her family. The blast that killed Ren's sisters and husband also killed several of Kij's oldest mothers, and her Eldest. That common point formed a bond of friendship between Ren and the older woman, much stronger than it could have been if their sisters had survived.

Shaggy and rumpled, Kij didn't look like the Duchess of Avonar. Apparently returning from a long difficult trip, Kij suddenly no longer seemed young, as if she had crossed over to middle age since Ren last saw her. Dark smudges underlined her vivid blue eyes, and her ash-blonde bangs hung down almost to the tip of her nose.

Still, the Porter beauty that had made her brother, Keifer, exquisite remained. Kij leaned her lanky frame over the railing to better show Ren the headlines of the newspaper she held out.

Well, that answered the question of whether the type size was as large as Ren had feared.

"I saw the *Herald* yesterday!" Kij shouted. "How is Odelia?"

"She's fine!" Ren shouted back. "She's with me, getting dressed, late as usual!"

Kij glanced ashore and saw the royal coaches waiting there. "You're not planning to make the opening of Summer Court after what you've been through?"

"Good gods, yes!" Ren said. "If we don't show, the rumors will have another day to run rampant. Will you be there?"

Ren asked out of courtesy. Any noble house could attend, but usually only those involved in the current case made an appearance.

Kij scrubbed wearily at her face and then shook her head, laughing. "No! No. We aren't interested in anything scheduled for today. Besides, I'm bone tired. You've got more fortitude than I do, sister!"

A flash of gold hair streaked along the rail of *Destiny*'s top deck, and a moment later little Eldest Porter scrambled up beside Kij. She squealed at the sight of Ren.

"Auntie Ren!"

"Hoy, Eldie," Ren called to her only niece. The girl was living testament to how badly Kij had taken the loss of her mothers, sister, and brother. In a grief-borne panic, Kij had visited a crib the day after the bombing. Luckily, all she came away with was a child.

Still, it had been enough to ruin an offering months in the planning, and it had been the stated reason for many rejections since then, despite Kij being able to produce medical records proving she was clean. Ren suspected that the truth was that many families were jockeying for a royal match of their own, and only used Kij's possible infection as a cruel, convenient snub.

When we marry Jerin, Ren thought, *those families will be regretting their heartless rebuffs.*

"Auntie Ren!" Eldie shouted again, bouncing up and down on the railing in excitement. "Look, I lost my top teeth!" She grinned, showing off the gap between her canine teeth.

"I see! You're bigger every time I see you! Look at you. How old are you now? Ten?"

"No, five!" her niece giggled. "I'll be six at summer's peak! Auntie Ren, can I come and see the youngest today?"

Kij's youngest sisters were in their teens, leaving Eldie without anyone to play with except her slightly older aunts. A sad way to grow up; Kij must have been crazy with grief.

"Summer Court opens today!" Ren called back. "Zelie and the others have to attend. Tomorrow?"

"Perhaps," Kij told them both. "We're scheduled to continue upriver to home tomorrow—if today goes smoothly."

Odelia came out of her cabin, wondering whom Ren was shouting at. There were greetings exchanged at full volume, the missing teeth were displayed, and then the two great ships parted. Ren's tucked in close to the landing, while Kij's—with Eldie blowing a farewell on the steam whistle—moved on upriver to find a berth.

"We could have missed the morning session and bathed like civilized women at the palace," Odelia complained as the carriage pulled away from the docks.

Ren glowered, picking up the case binder. "Focus, Odelia, focus."

Odelia ignored her binder, choosing instead to rest her head, eyes closed, against the padded wall of the carriage. "I'm focused on a hot bath and a meal prepared by Cook."

Ren shook her head, scanning the cases they were to judge. The first one made her curse, startling her sister. "Raven!" At her call, her captain pulled her horse alongside of the carriage window. "Someone has shuffled the caseload. I left instructions that the Wakecliff inheritance wasn't to be tried until we returned home. We weren't expected to make this morning, so it shouldn't be first case up."

"I'll look into it while you're in court." Raven's look turned dark.

Ren slumped back in the carriage, raging at this new miscarriage of justice. The opening day's schedule would have been posted in the *Herald* a week ago. By the laws protecting civil rights, once made public, a hearing time couldn't be changed, even by the royal judges. This guaranteed that a hearing couldn't be moved to a time unknown to the claimants.

The Baroness Wakecliff family had managed the impossible this winter: fifty-eight members, from great-grandmothers down to infant granddaughters, had all died within one season. Not all at once, which actually would have been more understandable, but here and there in escalating tragedy. The first ten or so had been drowned in a midwinter shipwreck. Then a fire ripped through the nursery wing late at night; twenty-three mothers and sisters, all under the age of ten, died in their beds. A half-dozen adults, one of them a beloved newly wedded husband, died of burns and smoke inhalation suffered while trying to reach the children. Rev Wakecliff had died trying to give birth to a dead baby boy. Kareem Wakecliff committed suicide when she learned of all four tragedies in a single day. Eldest Wakecliff took to drinking heavily, and died of alcohol poisoning after a carriage accident, claiming another six Wakecliffs, triggered a binge.

Ren wasn't sure how the other ten had died. It little mattered; by then all the women of childbearing years and younger had already been killed. The Wakecliff family was dead long before the last member took her final breath. Had any member survived, however, Ren would have been spared trying to determine who received the inheritance today.

While there were no clear heirs to the great Wakecliff fortunes, three powerful families had issued nebulous claims. Ren had planned to carefully study all claims prior to hearing the case. Someone, however, had juggled the docket.

The royal carriage pulled up to the front of the courthouse. They were last to arrive, the normal confusion of coaches already cleared. As usual, Raven entered the building at a stride that was nearly a run, four of Ren's traveling guard half a pace behind their captain. The rest of the guard stood anxious for a signal that the foyer was clear, and then opened the carriage door.

They swept into the courthouse, flanked all around by the guards, through the foyers. Raven was at the courtroom doors, waiting. Just as Ren and Odelia reached them, Raven swung open the double doors.

Normally the room seemed to be built on too ponderous a scale, as if the plan of the architect had been to crush the handful of participants by sheer height and breadth of marble. This was the first time Ren had seen a sea of humanity reduce the room to almost claustrophobic size. Almost every noble house—Mother Elder, Eldest, elder sisters—sat in attendance, completely screening the massive marble columns and walls.

Trini sat in Elder Judge position, her mouth moving, but her voice, which barely carried to the back of the room when it was empty, couldn't be heard. Lylia perched on the edge of her throne beside Trini's, eyes eager. In the royal box overlooking the judges' thrones and the speaker's floor, their youngest sisters, Zelie, Quin, Nora, Mira, and Selina, watched over what someday would be their duty to uphold.

Trini spoke again, whatever she was saying lost in the surflike roar of voices.

Lylia nearly quivered with the tension in her, and then shouted, "Silence! The court is now in session! Bailiff! Call the first case!"

"That's it, Lylia," Odelia murmured fondly as silence fell. "Give them hell."

The bailiff came from her alcove to the center of the speaker's floor. She cleared her throat, opened her mouth to call the first case, and then caught sight of Ren and Odelia.

"All rise for Their Royal Highnesses, Princess Rennsellaer and Princess Odelia!"

They started forward into stunned silence. Then with a renewed roar, the observers came to their feet, clapping.

Clap, Ren thought, *but some of you bitches are very unhappy to see us.*

Trini and Lylia stood too, not applauding, but their relief plain to read. Trini sidestepped to her normal position and Ren took the throne of the Elder Judge. She made no signal to silence the crowd, taking the opportunity to scan the gathered nobles, wondering which of them had changed the docket and why.

There were three noble families, all baronesses with massive estates of their own, who had semivalid claims: Dunwood, Lethridge, and Stonevale. The network of marriages, however, extended those three by five- or sixfold, evidenced by the number of women crammed into the courtroom. Whichever family snared the vast estate would need trusted adults to immediately take control of the far-flung shipping fleet, manage the extensive vineyards, oversee the tenant farms, and repair the half-burnt Wakecliff Manor. The heirs would turn to their sisters-in-law, who would in turn lean on their sisters-in-law.

Most likely, every woman present had a vested interest in the outcome. Any one of them could have moved the case forward.

Slowly the cheering of Ren and Odelia's appearance

lessened and then died to a soft murmur of whispered comments between family members.

Ren nodded to the bailiff.

"This court is now in session." In her clear, carrying alto, the bailiff announced the first case. "Now judging on the orphaned estate of family Wakecliff, all lands, furnishings, and moneys herein. All petitioned claimants, make yourself be known."

There was a brief, undignified scramble as claimants made unseemly haste to be first to make their case. Ren motioned the bailiff to her and set the petitions in alphabetical order. Judging by the smiles on the Dunwoods and the frowns on the Stonevales, "first" was being construed as "favored."

"The family of Dunwood claims the orphaned estate!" Eldest Dunwood spoke for her family, even though her mother was present, most likely because their claim was through her brother. "Our beloved brother, Cedric, had been married to Eldest Wakecliff and her sisters for five months. Perhaps a short period of time, but the law does not set a time limit. We're the only clear heirs here."

That triggered a howl of protest from the other two families and their various sisters-in-law. Ren scanned the room quickly, trying to get a feel of who supported whom. The Dunwood sisters were the youngest claimants, but came from a vigorous line. Their mothers and aunts numbered in the sixties, with two uncles, a husband, and a younger brother to bring the number of possible families directly involved to five. Indeed, the elder Pilot sisters sat sprinkled among their Dunwood sisters-in-law, heads together in conference. Ren tried to recall the name of the family that married the Dunwood boy, then remembered he was Lylia's age, and would be coming out this season.

Eldest Lethridge waved to be recognized, and reluctantly, Ren gave her the floor. "Your Highnesses, yes, the law states that the sisters-in-law are the favored heirs of an orphaned estate, but that favoritism is based on children. Cedric Dunwood Wakecliff fathered no living children! The child that killed Rev Wakecliff was the only throw that made it to term, and it was dead before her contractions started. The Dunwood claim is thus void."

Eldest Dunwood frowned. "It would be void if there was anyone with a better claim, but there isn't. It's well known that the Wakecliffs were strongly traditionalist. In the three hundred years of its recorded line, the Wakecliff family has never split. They have no cousins."
. "Not true!" Lethridge cried. "Our mothers' brother married Mother Elder Wakecliff and her sisters. Our uncle was producing children up to his death. We are Eldest Wakecliff and her sisters' first cousin."

"Our claim of sister-in-law overrides yours!" Dunwood shouted.

Eldest Stonevale waved to be recognized. Ren motioned to the bailiff to silence the others and give the floor to Stonevale. As the woman moved to the speaker floor with pointed looks at the others, Ren flipped through her case binder, studying the extensive properties listed. She wished she had been given time to research it at length. In the past hundred years, through a series of desperate measures and bad judgment, vast tracts of land originally owned by the crown had been sold, some of them belatedly proving to be vital to security. Unfortunately, the new owners were rarely interested in selling back the properties. Only orphaned estates such as this one provided a chance to recover them.

Stonevale announced her dubious claim. "The family of Stonevale claims the orphaned estate. Our grandfather was Grandmother Elder Wakecliff's brother. The blood of Wakecliff flows in our veins. We have the strongest claim here."

"Men are property," Dunwood snapped. "They can't inherit an estate any more than that chair can."

"We're not men. We're women!" Stonevale hissed.

Dunwood said, "The daughters of a brother cannot lay claim to aunts' property!"

"Don't be dense!" Stonevale snapped. "The law states that descendants through the female line inherit before sisters-in-law, but there are none in this case, and it doesn't state which sisters-in-law inherit first. Living blood is stronger than a dead brother, especially one who didn't father any children! We're comparing a living Wakecliff descendant versus a—a—a burned chair!"

"How dare you say that in our hour of grief?" Dunwood howled in rage, and leaped at the older woman. Court guards moved in, setting up a barrier between the scuffling women and the princesses first, and then breaking up the ensuing fistfight.

Ren winced, trying to ignore the scuffle and focus on the properties at stake. One of the names suddenly leaped out at her: Tuck Landing. She'd forgotten about the notorious anchorage point located within the Elpern Bank holding. In truth, Ren didn't care which family received the money. Tuck Landing, though, she would be loath to hand over to any of them. A hundred years before, in what was tantamount to outright theft, the ownership of Elpern Bank and its anchorage had changed from the crown to the Wakecliffs. Since that time, it had become a major weakness. Both invasion forces that landed on Queensland soil had originated at Tuck Landing. Collusion was suspected but never proved in both cases.

"We are the current sisters-in-law!" Dunwood was shouting. "Listen to the words! By law, we are Eldest Wakecliff's sisters."

Lethridge was not to be outdone. "My family is sisters-in-law to Mother Elder, which makes us your mother, and mothers inherit before daughters."

"We are the blood of Wakecliff!" Stonevale shouted, shedding some of that blood from a broken nose.

Even as Ren realized that this squabble over the estate provided the crown a chance to take back Elpern Bank, it dawned on her that she might have stumbled onto the true reason the docket had been changed. Lylia certainly wouldn't have the experience to spot the inclusion of vital real estate. Trini might have missed it. They would have judged the case, and the chance of regaining Tuck Landing would be lost.

Still, she couldn't act without her sisters' agreement, and she didn't want to discuss it in front of the assembled nobles. "Have we heard enough?"

Her sisters nodded.

"Well, I haven't had breakfast," Ren announced to the courtroom. "Bailiff, recess the court for an early lunch. We'll announce our decision after lunch."

"All rise!" the bailiff shouted.

The crowd came to their feet, respectfully silent. Ren led the way to the judges' chambers. As the door closed behind Lylia, she heard the bailiff shout, "This court is in recess! Court will adjourn in one hour!"

Out of the public eye, Trini and Lylia greeted their sisters with hugs along with cheeky remarks on Lylia's part. The far hallway door opened, and Raven entered the chambers, escorting the lunch servers. "I thought you might want to discuss this in private." The lunch table was wheeled in, and then the servers bowed out. "I hurried the kitchen for you."

"You're a true gem," Ren said, the smell of food making her suddenly ravenous. "Did you find out who tampered with the docket?"

Raven shook her head. "In a few more days, I might be able to question the clerk staff closely enough to crack it, but not in this short time. There are several families serving as clerks, and quite a bit of bickering between them. I've got a surplus of suspects."

"I want whoever took the bribe and made the changes found," Ren said. "I want them out. I will not have my court manipulated like this."

"Yes, Your Highness." Raven bowed and left them to deliberate.

"Wow, Ren, that was so queenly," Lylia breathed.

Odelia grunted, settling down to lunch. "Why is that when I talk like that, people call me bitchy?"

"Because you only talk about your supper and baths in that tone," Trini chided quietly. "Ren is demanding respect for higher causes."

Odelia stuck out her tongue, ate a bite of lunch, and then asked, "So, what made you go to point like a bird dog?"

Ren opened her binder and tapped at the property list. "Tuck Landing. It's part and parcel of Elpern Bank. Wakecliff tore down the watchtower and built their manor with the stone. This is the crown's chance to get the landing back. Once we recover it, we can build a garrison and a war harbor, and we protect the whole southeast as it was protected for a thousand years."

They nodded in understanding, and ate in silence, each to her own thoughts.

"How do we do it?" Lylia pushed her empty plate away and leaned against the table.

"The combined inheritance taxes of all the estates are quite sizable," Trini murmured, eyeing her binder. "The moneys in escrow will not cover it all. We can declare that the crown has chosen to handle the reckoning. We seize the entire estate, do an accounting of debts and taxes, and deduct Elpern Bank as payment, then release the rest of the estate to the heirs."

Ren winced. It seemed like a perfect plan, except the numbers would not balance. "I doubt if the taxes are that sizable."

Trini shrugged. "We can figure a reasonable price for the sale of Elpern to the crown. Deduct the taxes from the sale price, and add the difference to the estate."

"They're not going to like it," Odelia half sang. "Elpern's yearly income, in the long run, would outstrip any

price you set on it. They'd probably rather pay the tax
from their pocket than have it taken out beforehand in
the form of prime land."

"None of them have clear right to the land," Ren
growled. "Holy Mothers, the Wakecliffs didn't have
clear right to it if you look closely. Ezra Wakecliff was
supposed to deliver the title deeds of twelve crown properties to the church during the Prinmae War for safekeeping, and she delivered eleven. The bitch stole it,
and because her brother was married to our great-great-
grandmothers, she was never called on it. We have as
much a right to it as any of those women out there."

"She stole it?" Lylia asked.

Odelia nodded. "That's what the whole children's
rhyme is about, the 'Wakecliff in the corner, eyeing
queenly pies.' The title deeds were inside pies, to disguise them in case Wakecliff was stopped by the
enemy." Odelia made a rolling motion with her hand,
indicating that the rhyme continued to be quite literal.
"The 'plum' was a plum piece of property."

" 'You know in whose bed her brother lies,' " Lylia
finished. "Oh, I see. Her brother was prince consort."

"Well, it's time for us to take back what is ours." Ren
rapped for a vote. "Agree."

"Agree," Lylia said, eyes glowing.

"Agree," Trini murmured.

"Agree," Odelia said.

"Once we separate Elpern Bank from the rest of the
estate, we'll decide who gets the rest."

"I have found a young man who delights me." Ren
had rehearsed the speech for hours and days. She now
faced her Mother Elder, alone at last, in the privacy of
the queen's wing—weak-kneed for the first time in years.
"He is warm, loving, intelligent, strong of character yet
biddable, chaste, and very beautiful. I wish to marry
him."

After a moment of pleased surprise, the Queen

Mother Elder put aside the book she had been reading with a slight, worried frown. "Yet you say nothing of breeding. After the adventure you've told us, I doubt you've met anyone of acceptable breeding."

"His breeding is odd." Ren wished she could leave the whole of it out, but knew eventually her mother would dig out the truth, then hold it against her for omitting it. "His grandmothers were conceived in the Order of the Sword's cribs. Blacklisted from the army due to their Mother Elder's crimes, they joined the Sisterhood of the Night. Wellsbury employed them in the war as spies. They won the Queen Elder Cross of Victory, were knighted, and retired to a land grant."

"That would make him the very lowest of landed gentry I've heard tale of, Rennsellaer."

"During the siege of Tastledae, his grandmothers kidnapped Prince Alannon, and after they were knighted, they married him."

The clock ticked off the silence between them. In one of the many specimen jars that lined her mother's desk, a cotton weevil scratched on the glass wall of its prison. Ren felt a sudden sympathy with it.

"Yes, odd breeding," Queen Elder finally murmured. "Are you sure of their claims?"

"He wears the Emerald Hart."

"Which has been faked in the past."

"I believe their claim." Ren handed her mother the copy of Wellsbury's memoirs. "Wellsbury herself reports sending the Whistlers into Castle Tastledae during the time that Prince Alannon vanished. Trained thieves, desperate for a husband, and a missing prince—I don't know why no one has ever connected the two before now."

Her mother opened the book where Ren had placed a marker, scanned the page, and caught where Ren had underlined the name of Whistler, then skipped on to a passage Ren had purposely not underlined. " 'As I hoped,' " she read, " 'the Whistlers have found ways to come and go unobserved into the castle. Their intelligence indicates that we will not be able to take the castle by honorable siege, but will have to resort to mayhem. Fortunately, the Whistlers excel at mayhem.' "

Ren had chosen to ignore the passage. Acknowledging it could only make things worse. "I visited the wall of sorrow this morning. The Whistlers all bear a striking resemblance to Prince Alannon."

"I see." Her mother set the memoirs down beside her own book. It was titled, Ren noticed now, *Breeding for the Success of Pest Resistance—a Study in Genetics.* Had her mother picked up this passion for breeding before or after the princesses' marriage to Keifer? Most likely before—whatever her mother thought of Keifer, she couldn't fault his breeding. "I suppose one could argue that knighthood and a royal husband eliminate all black marks against a family."

Ren struggled to find the thread of the argument she had hammered out over the last five days. "His family has maintained the status of landed gentry since the war. Their farm is well ordered and bountiful."

"No crimes, lapses into thievery, or joining the army?"

Ren was not sure if this was a truthful question or a sarcastic comment on the Whistlers' background. "No." She returned to her planned discussion. "He is one of four sons, and has three uncles."

"Seven males in two generations?" her mother asked with sudden, sharp attention.

"I've checked the best one can, and his three uncles and one set of split-off aunts all have sons, somewhere between a confirmed two and a rumored five."

"You argue your case well."

"He has thirty-one sisters and brothers, all healthy as horses, sharp-eyed, quick-witted—sound teeth—pretty enough to put most of the peers to shame, hardworking, polite—"

"Enough, enough." Queen Elder held up her hand. "You said 'chaste' earlier. Are you sure?"

"Perhaps it is my vanity speaking, Mother, but I cannot imagine him refusing me after accepting another woman." She caught her mother's look, and found herself blushing hotly. "I wanted him, and pressed him close. He allowed kisses—no—he delighted in kisses, but for his family's sake held the line on further pursuits."

"Dear, how many times have I told you? Don't dabble before marriage, or you'll be blinded by your heart. As Eldest, you have to be the clear thinker now."

"He was very sweet. With his father gone, he tends the babies as if they were his own, and he is gentle, firm, and loving with them. He understands honor, pride, and loyalty. He can withstand the pressure of a wanton princess when he is but poor landed gentry." She found herself scrambling for more, for her mother's look was hardening. "He is the one that went down to the creek and carried Odelia home because his younger sisters left him and his baby sisters alone."

"And you're already in love with him." The look was stone-cold now.

Ren closed her eyes, hoping her mother would not deny the suit based on that alone. "Yes, I believe so."

"And what does Odelia think of this wonderment? Did she meet him? Kiss him?"

"She lay in bed an extra day in hopes he would come nurse her through. I don't think she managed to obtain a kiss; I think she would have gone on at great length if she had."

"I see."

"Please, Mother, let us consider him. He is almost sure to throw healthy children with good chances for a boy or two. He would certainly be a good father. His royal blood balances the thieving soldiers turned landed gentry. He seems to have the strength of will to be the royal husband—he can resist temptation and do the right thing. He is beautiful—very, very beautiful."

"Let me consider."

With the statement, Ren fell silent. Any further arguing would only damage her cause. After that royal decree, one could only retreat, wait, and hope.

Queen Mother Elder gave her verdict later that night. "If your sisters agree, you can marry him. I will send for him, on pretense of a reward for saving your sister. There is no need to taunt his family with hopes of a match that might not come about."

"Thank you, Mother."

Chapter 6

"Rider! There's a rider coming in!"

The call echoed over the farm. Jerin came to the kitchen door to see the solitary rider coming up the lane. His youngest sisters and little brothers stopped their game of "recon" to stare out toward the road. Middle and elder sisters came drifting out of the barns and outbuildings. Before the rider had reached the bottom of the hill, Heria picked up Kai, took Liam by the hand, and started toward Jerin. Doric followed reluctantly, throwing curious glances over his shoulder. Eldest went into the house via the front door and came back out wearing her pistols.

Princess Ren's captain of the guard, Raven Tern, cantered her horse up to the beaten dirt of the barnyard. She pulled her horse to a halt before Eldest. "Eldest Whistler, greetings to you."

"Greetings to you, Captain."

"I carry a message to you and your sisters from the Queens."

Eldest took the message with a trembling hand, broke the seal, and read it. When she reached the end, she took a deep breath, and tension went from her. "I'll have to talk to my sisters about this. Birdie will help you stable your horse. You're welcome to dinner and to spend the night."

"Thank you. I'd like that." Captain Tern dismounted. "If you decide to accept, I'm to provide escort."

Eldest looked surprised, then schooled her emotion.
"That would be an honor." Eldest signaled to Corelle.
"Show her where she can put her things, and get washed
up for dinner."

Corelle led Captain Tern off, clearly annoyed that
she'd be the last to learn what the Queens' letter had
to say. No sooner than Captain Tern was out of sight
did the rest of the family gather around Eldest.

"What does it say? What does it say? Are we getting
knighted?" The youngest bounced in place from
excitement.

Jerin clasped his hands together hard in order not to
tear the letter from Eldest. The letter was good news—
that much was clear from Eldest's relief—and Captain
Tern was going to act as an escort, so someone was
going to Mayfair. Suddenly his heart was like a caged
wild bird, beating madly against his ribs, crying, "Ren!
Ren! Ren!"

Eldest held up her hand, signaling for silence. "The
Queens send thanks for saving the princess Odelia's
life," she started, once her gathered family fell quiet,
"and as a token of their thanks, they've invited us to
bring Jerin out at the capital. Jerin and I, and one or
two others, would stay at the palace and be sponsored
by the Queens." Eldest was shouting now to be heard.
"It would allow us to meet the most influential families
in Queensland, and thus make the best possible trade
of brothers."

As his sisters whooped and hollered, Jerin stood,
stunned silent, hands clasped so tight they were white.

Eldest caught sight of him, and sobered. "Get ready
for dinner," she told everyone. "Remember we've got
company. Go on!" As she spoke, she caught Jerin's
shoulder and guided him away. "Are you all right?"

"I don't know." Jerin felt a strange hollowness in his
chest, as if that wild bird of his heart had burst out,
leaving nothing behind. "For a minute there, I thought
that maybe Princess Ren was sending for me."

Eldest cursed softly. "Oh, Jerin." She looked down at the letter still in her hand. "This is a shining coin, Jerin. You'd be presented as an equal to all the nobles in the land. We could never match this again. If we refuse this, we only have common country bumpkins, the likes of the Brindles, to choose from."

"Holy Mothers, no!" Then, fearing she misunderstood, he caught her wrist and said as clearly as possible, "I do not want to marry the Brindles! I hate them! They're like rabid dogs!"

"I wouldn't give you up to someone who would hurt you."

"They might not turn on me, but it's nearly a sure thing that I'd have to watch my children grow up to be just as mean. People are saying Balin tumbled his mothers to father his sisters. It's not like the Brindles would tell us, if it was the truth; we'd have to wait until after the marriages to know for sure, and then it would be too late, at least for me. Besides, they say apples only come from apple trees; the family might have practiced incest for generations now. They all could be inbred monsters."

A smile quirked onto Eldest's mouth. "Well, it would explain why they're all so gods-awful ugly."

"Eldest, please, please, don't make me marry them!"

"I'm not asking you to. We're invited to the palace, remember?" Eldest rumpled his hair. "Quite frankly, Jerin, I'd rather marry a pig than Balin Brindle. I don't understand what Corelle sees in him. He's a smug, ugly little thing, and his sisters have always made my skin crawl. I'd hate to have a houseful of children that looked like them."

Jerin giggled.

Eldest held up the Queens' letter. "Will you do this?"

"It's not like I don't want to marry. I just want to be picky!" He winced as he realized he was whining. He tried a more adult tone. "I want a family of clean breeding, one that doesn't fight, well, at least no more than we do, and—and ten to fifteen wives at the most. None of this thirty wives or more! Mothers above, I'd feel like a whore! I'd have a different woman every night for a month mounting me."

She laughed a moment, then gazed sadly at him. "I hadn't thought of the Brindles in quite that way. I'm glad that we're able to afford more than one husband. I'd hate it if I had to wait a whole month for one night of pleasure, and only twelve chances a year to catch a baby. Years go quickly when measured in twelve days. I don't have many years left before my time of change comes."

"I didn't think you'd like having babies."

Eldest shrugged. "I'd like to have at least one, to see what it was like. Our mothers seemed so miserable pregnant—puking in the morning, bloated up like something dead left in the sun too long, and waddling around like a force-fed goose." After the birth of thirty siblings, Eldest could mimic the walk quite well, making Jerin giggle. "I don't know why anyone would want to live through it. Yet, at times, it seems like that's when they were the happiest. They'd get that smug, satisfied smile, and practically glow." She reflected a moment, and then nodded. "I think one baby will be enough to leave me content, more than happy for my sisters to bear the rest."

They fell silent.

Eldest took out the letter and read it silently once more. "It's a shining coin, tossed up in the air for us, and all we have to do is reach out and catch it."

"Let's catch it, then."

Surprisingly, Captain Tern came down for dinner in her dress uniform, boots polished to a gleam, her chest covered with medals. Tucked under one arm, she carried a long leather case that the Whistlers had missed in their excitement for the letter.

She spoke quietly with Eldest, who nodded soberly, then called the family to standing attention.

"Heria." Eldest motioned for her to come forward.

"Me?" Heria startled and, with a worried frown, pushed back her chair to come around the table to where Eldest and Raven stood.

Captain Tern snapped open the catches of the case, opened the lid, and held it out to Heria. "Their Royal Majesties, Queen Mother Elder and her royal sisters, have charged me this duty. As a duly appointed representative of their royal will, I present this gift to you in thanks for saving Princess Odelia. Please accept this honor for your selfless courage."

"Holy Mothers!" Heria's eyes went round in surprise, and she whispered, "They're beautiful!"

She took the case and turned so her family could see. An engraved rifle and matching pistols lay in the case, each in a compartment lined with velvet. There was a moment of stunned silence, and then a roar of approval.

After several minutes, Eldest called for order, had Heria put up the gun case, and commanded the family to dinner. Everyone sat, but, with the exception of baby Kai and little Liam, ignored the food, gazing expectantly at Eldest and Raven.

Eldest broached the subject as it became apparent that no one was going to eat until the course of the future was plotted. "I've talked to my sisters. We're going to accept the Queens' offer. We haven't decided who will go."

This triggered cries of "Take me, take me" from all the youngest. The middle sisters looked silently wistful, except for a sullen Corelle, who was still in extreme disfavor and unlikely to go.

"We haven't decided," Eldest repeated firmly. "We expect our mothers any day. I would feel better if they were here before I left with any of my sisters. I'm leery of leaving the farm shorthanded of adults."

Captain Tern nodded. "I have business in Heron Landing. We're still trying to find the Prophets. I'm checking back with the Queens Justice to see if any more information has surfaced on the thieves." Raven glanced meaningfully to Jerin. "I thought you would need a few days before sending your brother out to be married."

With a sudden ring of silver on china, Doric dropped his fork on his plate. "Jerin won't be coming back, will he? Once he goes off to get married?"

"I'll be back," Jerin said with careful cheerfulness. "It will be just like our cousins. You'll see me from time to time."

"I don't want Jerin to go away like Papa did!" Bunny, the littlest of the youngest sisters, suddenly wailed.

"Papa died, honey." Jerin reached across the table to pat her. "I'm not going to die. I'm just going to live at someone else's house."

"No!" Bunny cried, ducked under the table, and scrambled up into his lap. "I don't want you to go!"

It triggered a wave of crying little girls. Most of the youngest over five years old managed to contain themselves. The three- and four-year-olds, though, could not be consoled.

He hugged them, four and five to an armful, rocking them. "Hush, hush, this is a wonderful day for the Whistlers. We shouldn't be crying. We should be happy and celebrating." The words were like ash in his mouth, but to show his own pain would only make his little sisters unhappier. "I know—let's forget about dinner and make ice cream and cake."

"Ice cream?"

"Cake?"

"Maple ice cream and pound cake," Jerin said firmly. "Come on, let's go into the kitchen and start making them."

"You'll have to excuse the family," Eldest murmured to Captain Tern as Jerin herded the sniffling girls toward the kitchen. "We lost our father early this spring, and our mothers have been gone several weeks. The little ones are fragile at the moment."

Captain Tern waved away the apology as unnecessary. "They're just babies. They seem to love their brother well."

"Jerin has lots of patience with them," Eldest said.

"Patience is invaluable in a husband," Captain Tern said. "Children need a nurturing hand to grow them into strong women. His wives will be lucky. Tell me, how did your father die so young? Heart failure?"

"No, no, it was an accident." Eldest sighed. "He slipped on icy steps and fell. He struck his head. . . ."

Jerin was glad when the kitchen door swung closed, shutting off that quiet conversation. Tonight would not be a good time for him to have those wounds opened by the recounting of their father's prolonged death.

Captain Tern rode out after a breakfast of dinner leftovers, promising to return at dusk. Jerin waited until his youngest sisters were deeply entrenched in their morning chores before he started to pack; there was no need to give them fresh reminders that he was leaving.

His wedding chest would go with him. He took everything out and repacked it carefully for the trip, mindful it would be shifted and possibly dropped. He used his wedding linens to pad the bone china tea set his mothers had bought for him on his twelfth birthday. There would be no way to foretell the quality and wealth of his future wives, his mothers had stated as he'd unwrapped the expensive gift, but his children should be raised with manners befitting the blood of the Queens. At that time, his grandfather, Prince Alannon, and two of his thieving spies of grandmothers were still alive, and they laughed until tears came to their eyes.

He kept out three of the silver engraved spoons stolen from the Castle Tastledae, and three of four tintypes he had of Prince Alannon. These he divvied into his younger brothers' wedding chests so they each would have something from their royal grandfather. Another generation or two, and there would be nothing to share out but memories.

He took only his best clothes, leaving behind his work clothes for Doric. Lastly he packed the items about his room that he wanted to keep, leaving only his quilt out, to be added on the day he left.

He sat staring at the now stark room. What was he forgetting?

His birth certificate!

The family records box sat in the corner of the parlor, firmly locked against little fingers. The key was kept on the high trim piece of the window beside it. Jerin no longer had to stretch to reach the key, which surprised him.

The first piece of paper was the death certificate for their father. Jerin set it quickly aside. Under it was baby Kai's birth certificate, which Jerin lingered over to erase the jolt of pain that the death certificate had put through him.

Kai Whistler, male child born to Bliss Whistler and fathered by husband Tullen Beadwater from Bowling Green. Grandchild of Nida Whistler and husband Alannon (ancestry documented but uncertified). Great-grandchild of Kei Whistler & Order of the Sword crib captive named Gerard, #458. Great-great-grandchild of Allysen Whistler & Order of the Sword crib captive Kyle, number unknown. No other lineage known.

A family copy, it was stamped and sealed with reference numbers of where the original was stored. Also indicated was where the marriage records for their mothers and grandmothers could be found.

Jerin leafed down through the birth certificates, layered youngest to oldest, till he came to his own.

Jerin Whistler, male child born to Mother Elder
Whistler and fathered by husband Tullen Beadwater from Bowling Green. Grandchild of Tea
Whistler and husband Alannon (ancestry documented but uncertified). Great-grandchild of Jo
Whistler & Order of the Sword crib captive named
Harrid, number unknown. Great-great-grandchild
of Mother Elder Whistler & Order of the Sword
crib captive, name and number unknown: tattoo
initial of *T*. No other lineage known.

If not for their father and grandfather, Jerin suddenly
realized, he wouldn't be blood related to Kai at all. He
thumbed through the others, noticing for the first time
how odd his family was once all the bloodlines were
assembled. His ten grandmothers were divided among
five crib fathers, and no two shared the same birth
mother. None of his great-grandmothers represented by
their surviving daughters even shared the same crib fathers; they seemed to be nine strangers sharing a family name.

Lifting out the records of his mothers' generation, he
studied his grandmothers' papers underneath. They were
dog-eared, much folded, and largely incomplete. One
even had an elaborate map inked on its back. The birth
certificates recorded birth mother and father, and most
had a birth grandmother named. Often for grandfather,
the records stated, "Order of the Sword crib captive,
initial designation," and this varied from grandmother
to grandmother, and then a general time period of years
was noted.

Among the grandmothers' papers was one crisp sheet,
obviously carefully protected. It declared that the ten
Whistler sisters married one Alannon, pedigree lines
waived as the groom was war plunder and verbal questioning indicated no crossbreeding.

Too bad he hadn't thought to show Princess Rennsellaer this. She seemed interested in his grandfather. Bit-

ing his lip on bitter thoughts that wanted to crowd in, he placed all the documents back into the box, and locked it tight.

Their twelve mothers arrived after lunch, while middle sisters tended the back pasture fence. The youngest reached their mothers first and shouted news at the top of their lungs. Even from the kitchen where he was kneading bread, Jerin could hear cries of "Heria got a rifle from the Queens!" and "Jerin and Eldest are going to Mayfair! Can I go too?" Jerin covered the dough to rise, washed his hands, and went out to welcome them home.

Mother Elder was sitting up on the buckboard's seat, stranded there by a wailing Bunny on her lap, trying to listen to all her children at once. "Quiet! Hush! Eldest, what in Mothers' name is going on?"

"Princess Rennsellaer's Captain Tern came to stay yesterday," Eldest said, reaching up to free Mother Elder of Bunny. Eldest passed the little girl to Mother Dia, and then gave Mother Elder a hand down. Mother Elder had been with their father the night before his accident. When she left for Annaboro, she hadn't realized that she was pregnant, thinking her weight gain had signaled the start of menopause. Even without her letter from Annaboro, however, there was no missing the pregnancy now. The buttons of her shirt, stretched over her swollen belly, were threatening to pop, and she had a satisfied smile and glow.

"She's at Heron Landing today," Eldest said of Captain Tern. "But she'll be back for dinner. The Queens sent an expensive custom rifle and pistols for Heria. They also offered to sponsor Jerin's coming out in Mayfair. We've accepted. Captain Tern is to escort us back to the palace. We haven't decided who will all go."

"I want to go! I want to go!" the youngest chorused.

"Hush! None of the youngest will go!" Mother Elder

said firmly. "Marriage is business only for elder and middle sisters. They'll be the only ones going."

This was greeted with groans of disappointment.

"Now, now, we've been riding for hours to see you, so no long faces, or no one gets their presents from Annaboro."

The horses were cared for, the supplies carried into the house, and the presents distributed, all in record time. With the youngest shooed out into the play yard with their new treasures, Jerin, his elder sisters, and their mothers settled down to discuss who would go with Eldest to Mayfair.

"It says 'with as many sisters you wish to also attend.'" Eldest tapped the Queens' letter, folded stiff, on the table. "Harvest will start soon; we'll need almost everyone here. With Captain Tern escorting us downriver, and then us staying at the palace proper, I can't see needing to take more than two others. Which two?"

"I think we should take Summer," Jerin said quietly.

"Summer?" Eldest looked and sounded surprised. "Why?"

Jerin blushed, ducking his head from his elder sisters' confused scrutiny. "We're not going just to get me wives, but you a husband too. It'd be a shame to pass up the chance to make an influential marriage both ways. And, well, I don't mean to slight anyone, but Summer's the prettiest."

"What does that have to do with anything?" Birdie asked.

"Well," Jerin said, "if your husband has any say in who he marries, then we should take the prettiest sister with us. Right?"

There was reluctant agreement from his sisters.

"Then we'll take Summer," Eldest stated. "And who else?"

"Corelle," Mother Elder stated.

"Corelle?" Jerin yelped in surprise as the others murmured their agreement with Mother Elder. "She's been taking favors from Balin Brindle and she left the farm unprotected. Take her? After the way she's been?"

"Especially after the way she's been," Mother Elder said quietly. "She hasn't seen enough of the world, what she's giving up if she settles for Balin Brindle."

"But Mother Elder!" Jerin cried. "It would be like rewarding her for being bad! I don't know why you let Corelle get away with things."

"Jerin, we have four sons," Mother Elder said, taking his hands. "We could easily split the family four ways, though we probably won't, but we certainly will be splitting at least once. Either Corelle, Heria, or Blush will be Mother Elder for the younger sisters. You can't make good decisions as an adult if you were never allowed to make any decisions while you were a child. Now is the time for Corelle to learn from her mistakes."

"Couldn't you split the family so Summer is Mother Elder?" Jerin grumbled.

"Summer isn't strong enough. Where Corelle leads, the others follow. We only need to teach her to lead wisely."

The middle sisters rode in shortly before dinner. Eldest met them at the paddock, pulled Summer and Corelle aside, and told them that they would be going to Mayfair. The others could hear Corelle scream from all the way in the kitchen, sounding like someone was murdering her with a rusty knife.

"What did Corelle do this time?" Blush asked.

"What's Eldest doing to her?" Leia peered out the kitchen window. From there they could see Corelle, leaping up and down in the paddock, still screaming.

Heria glanced out the window and made a noise of disgust. "Corelle's going with Jerin and Eldest to Mayfair. Eldest just told her."

"Lucky dog," Blush muttered.

After a sleepless night that seemed to go on forever, dawn came. Jerin dressed in his loose, dun-colored walking robe, folded up his quilt, placed it in his wedding chest, and locked it tight shut. When he came down to breakfast, Eldest and Birdie went up to carry his chest out to the buckboard. Eldest, Corelle, and Summer stacked their bags on top of it.

Breakfast was quiet and solemn. Afterward, he hugged and kissed his mothers, sisters, and brothers good-bye. He gazed one last time at the solid stone farmhouse, the well-kept barns, the sprawling fields. Then he left home, forever.

Chapter 7

They planned on being early to Heron Landing so there'd be no chance of missing the packet that arrived at noon. Three-quarters of a mile from the house, the Whistlers' lane joined the common road; there, Eldest was able to whip the horses into a smooth trot. Captain Tern rode outrider on her big black, easily keeping pace, her eyes sharp for danger.

While they traveled, they discussed what to buy at the mercantile in town. Mother Elder started the discussion by clucking over the condition of Jerin's traveling hat, and stated that he couldn't board the packet without a new one. Summer had promised all those left behind to buy stick candy and send it home with the wagon. Eldest wanted ammo for their pistols, which, in Mayfair, would be their principal weapons. Jerin needed cream for his hands, as they were hopelessly callused and chapped by his chores, but he wouldn't give Corelle the satisfaction of hearing him say it aloud. Corelle, of course, had no money, so it came as no surprise when she declared that she would stand guard on their luggage with Mother Erica.

By Eldest's pocket watch, they arrived in town a good two hours before the packet was due. She pulled the wagon up to the mercantile's hitching post and swung down to tie the horses off. Captain Tern tied her black alongside, then came to give Jerin a hand down. Eldest frowned but said nothing; she was used to him scrambling up and down on his own, but then normally he wore trousers.

The mercantile was the largest building in town, with twin mullioned bay windows bracing the door. A wooden sidewalk ran the length of the front, and the hitching posts were cast iron. The Picker sisters had run the store for as long as anyone could remember. The tiny old women had frightened Jerin when he was small; compared to his tall, lean grandmothers and mothers, the merchant sisters seemed like something out of a fairy tale.

The bell over the door announced the Whistlers' entrance. They scattered among the bins and tall shelving: Captain Tern followed Jerin to the hand creams near the back counter, and watched without comment as he studied the selection. Apparently only men used hand cream. The bottles showed simplified pictures of hands, flowers or fruit, and perfect little mounds of cream; one chose by scent. Lilac. Rose. Jasmine. Apple. Peach. Vanilla. Jerin wondered which scent Rennsellaer liked the most; he wished he had the nerve to ask Captain Tern. Then again, would the captain of the guard even know?

He chose vanilla and took it to Eldest so she could buy it for him. She stood at the back counter, box of ammo in hand, watching with interest as one of the Picker sisters painted a sign. Jerin couldn't tell the sisters, with their faces wrinkled up like dried-apple dolls, apart; Eldest, who did most of the family purchasing, could.

"What's this, Meg?" Eldest tapped the painted sign. "You're selling the place?"

"Yup," the wizened old woman said. "The store, the outbuildings, and all of the goods. We're getting too old to run the place. Haddie fell and broke her hip last night; she's the youngest of us Picker girls and we depended on her to do all the heavy work. We've talked for years about putting this place on the market. Last night just decided it for us."

"Your family has been here for ages," Eldest said.

"One hundred and thirty-three years," Meg said proudly. "Mothers to daughters for"—the old woman paused to count on her fingers—"five generations. My great-great-grandmothers came upriver with a boatload of goods in 1534 and bought two acres of land from the crown. But we've always had bad luck with the menfolk. Not like you Whistlers."

Another Picker sister had come up the aisle to brush past Jerin. She came only to his chest and stood child-sized next to his sister. She gazed toward Mother Elder with sharp, envious eyes. "Rumor has it that you've got another on the way."

"Don't jinx us, Wilma Picker," Eldest growled. "It's unlucky to talk about a child still in the womb."

"Gods love the boy children—that's why they call so many back before they can be born." Meg used the most popular belief for the cause of miscarriages.

"Our mothers had twenty-six miscarriages," Wilma sighed. "And Mother Ami had one little boy stillborn, perfect down to his fingernails yet blue and cold as the sky. The grief of it nearly killed her."

"Hush, you ninnies." Eldest Picker hobbled out of the back room, hunched nearly double with a widow's hump, leaning heavily on a cane. She paused to poke threateningly at her younger sisters. "Decent women don't talk that way in front of menfolk, especially the young ones."

The younger Picker sisters skittered away, leaving Eldest Picker frowning in their wake. "Can't whack them like I used to."

"I'm sure you can still deliver a good thumping, Picker." Jerin's sister nodded in greeting, Eldest to Eldest.

"I can hit just as hard as I used to, Whistler!" Eldest Picker snapped. "It's them! They break too easy now. I got to pull my hits!"

Eldest Whistler ran her tongue along the inside of her cheek, trying not to grin. "Well, now, that's a problem."

"I'm too old to be learning how to curb my temper,"

the old woman snapped. "Especially with this pack of ninnies! I swear they're all getting senile."

"How much you asking?" Eldest Whistler tapped the For Sale sign again.

"Two thousand crowns," Picker stated firmly.

Eldest whistled at the price.

"It's worth it," Picker snapped, then added softer, "We're willing to listen to offers, though. We need enough to live on until the last of us die."

"A shame you don't have children to take it on," Eldest said.

"It's a tasteless stew, but it's all we have to eat." The old woman shrugged. "Our mothers mortgaged everything to buy Papa, and he died without giving us a brother. We could have paid the mortgages, or paid for visits to a crib. If we hadn't paid the mortgages, we'd be out on the street now, so old the first winter storm would put a period to us all."

Meg returned to fetch wet paintbrushes. "We should have took in a stray or two, adopted them as our own."

"And broken the laws of gods, Queens, and good common sense?" Picker snapped. "It's been thirty years, for gods' sake. Can't you shut up about that?"

Meg wrinkled up her face more. "We wouldn't be selling this business to strangers if we had."

"No, we'd be giving it to them instead!" Picker said. "The prophets say adoption is a hidden evil. It only encourages the idiots to overproduce in vain hopes of a boy. Look at those Brindles. They got the boy sleeping with his mothers in search of another son to sell off. Like someone would buy the inbred monster. Idiots! They're struggling to feed thirty children and all the while producing more that no one would want their brother to marry. I'm sure, if they thought they could get away with it, they would be littering the countryside with dead girl babies."

"You shouldn't slander the customers," Meg muttered.

"They won't be mine for much longer!" Picker snapped. "If I could have gotten my hands on good solid stock like the Whistlers here, I would have said yes to you thirty years ago—but people like them don't give up their little ones. It's the lazy ones that overbreed because it's easy to do, pleasant to do. Breed with a man, eat like a pig while increasing, and if the baby is born the wrong sex, just toss it away to start again. I tell you, if we'd adopted your 'strays,' we'd be up to our armpits in lazy children. Breeding tells, I say. It tells every time."

The old woman had wound down as she talked till this last was a slow, soft mutter. She took a deep breath, glanced at Jerin, and frowned fiercely at her sister. "Now, look what you've made me do. Talk coarse in front of this pretty little thing. My pardon, Eldest Whistler."

"No harm done." Eldest grinned. "I'm pleased to know our neighbors think of us as good solid stock."

"Aye, we do," Picker said. "You're not drunks, wastrels, smugglers, thieves, or idiots. You're honest in your business, and no one begrudges you thirty-two children when four of them are boys. People wonder that you didn't try for more."

Eldest threw a look where Mother Elder was still looking at the hats. "Now is not the time for counting children."

"Sorry. I forgot." Eldest Picker reached back without looking and selected a thin cigar and offered it as an apology.

"Thank you." Eldest put it in her mouth, reached for her matches, and then, glancing to Mother Elder, dropped the matchbox back into her pocket. "Later," she murmured around the cigar, not adding that the smell would make their pregnant mother nauseous. "Two thousand." Eldest studied the store with narrowed eyes. "It's worth it."

"You thinking of buying?" Jerin asked her, surprised. He didn't think his family had that much cash.

"Your brother's price, even without going to Mayfair, could reach two thousand crowns."

"I thought you wanted a husband." He tried not to whine. What he left unsaid was *I thought you were going to swap me.* Swapped families were always closer because cousins sharing both bloodlines were more like sisters than true cousins.

"I do." Eldest shook her head. "But this is a shining coin, Jerin, and it's up for grabs now. If we don't snatch it up, it's going to be gone."

"What if I don't bring two thousand crowns?"

"Don't underrate yourself, Jerin." Mother Elder came up holding a wide-brimmed straw hat. She put the hat firmly on his head, then studied him, head cocked in speculation. "Remember who your grandfather was. I think we might be able to do both: buy the shop and afford a husband of good breeding."

"You're giving yourself airs, Elder," Picker said. "I could see two thousand with your family's breeding record for boys—but three or four?"

"Nobility, they say, pays dearly for good breeding."

"Mama!" Jerin blushed hotly, partly for their discussing him like a prize stallion, partly for the idea that he could command two or three times the normal amount of a brother's price.

"Bah!" Picker scoffed.

"The Queens are sponsoring Jerin's coming out," Summer said quietly as she came up with the front of her shirt filled with stick candy. She counted the sticks out onto the battered wood counter into two uneven piles. "Thirty-six pieces." A silver gil joined the candy on the counter.

"The Queens?" Picker humphed, taking the gil and counting Summer her three quince change. With the ease of lifetime practice, she tore a perfect length of brown paper from a bolt, wrapped the larger pile of candy into a neat package, and tied it off with cord. "You want the rest wrapped?"

"Nope," Summer said, picking up the seven remaining sticks. She held them out to Jerin. "Pick two."

He took a black anise and a brown maple. Summer offered one each to Mother Elder and Eldest, then, shyly, one to Captain Tern.

"You think the Queens' goodwill is worth two thousand crowns?" Picker asked.

"Not so much the Queens' goodwill as the peers' opinion of their own worth," Mother Elder explained. "Downriver, they say if you want a noblewoman to pay for a drink of river water, you say it's a medical tonic brewed for the Queens and charge her a gil."

"So," Picker said dryly, "that's what your sisters sell in that fancy Annaboro store of theirs? River water?"

Mother Elder scowled at the barb, then controlled her irritation. "We'll need a length of veiling to go with the hat. White lace, I would think." She took the hat off of Jerin and measured a length of blue ribbon around the rim. "What a bind. If we wait for Jerin to marry, we have the money without worries. But by waiting, someone might beat us to the purchase."

"We're willing to work with you," Picker said. "Agree to meet our price and sign a contract, help us run the store until you have the full purchase amount, and we'll hold the store off the market until your boy's birthday. If you get your fancy price in Mayfair, then use it to buy the store. If not, you back out of the deal, paying a penalty."

"We're leaving within an hour," Jerin protested, aghast that his family future suddenly hung on the moment.

"What penalty?" Eldest asked.

"Ten percent," Picker stated.

Jerin gasped. Two hundred crowns just to back out of the deal!

"One percent," Mother Elder countered.

"Five," Picker said. "No less."

"One hundred crowns?" Mother Elder glanced at Eldest Whistler and Summer. "It's your brother's price."

"It's a shining coin," Eldest murmured to Summer.

Summer glanced about the store, considering, then nodded. "A wonderful golden shining coin."

"Deal," Eldest Whistler said, and shook hands with the old woman. "Let's go to the Queens' Witness and have the papers drawn up."

Mother Elder gave a silver gil to Summer with instructions to buy the hat, the ribbon, and the lace. Eldest added her ammo, Jerin's cream, and coin for both. With a stern reminder for Summer to guard Jerin, they went off to make the deal permanently legal. Jerin stared after them, slightly stunned. He was not sure how many Picker sisters tended the store, but forty-four Whistlers just had their lives utterly changed. When his sisters split the family, only half would stay on the farm. He would definitely wed on his birthday. If he fetched only two thousand crowns, Eldest and the others would have to wait until Doric was of age to get a husband. Six years would put Eldest into her thirties. If he didn't fetch two thousand crowns, his family would have to pay one hundred crowns to back out of the deal. A heinous amount of money to throw away, but a small price to pay if the worst happened.

Jerin added extra of the blue ribbon to their purchases; it would be pretty braided in his hair. He would need to look his best at Mayfair to fetch a high brother's price; his family was counting on him.

At least an hour remained before the packet arrived. Summer, Captain Tern, and Jerin went out to join Mother Erica and Corelle. They moved the wagon down to the village green and set out a light picnic lunch. Jerin got out his sewing kit and tacked the veil to his new hat between bites of his sandwich.

Corelle and Summer were both pleased with the idea

of becoming shopkeepers. The older sisters would take the store, they reasoned, because it would need minding right away.

"No more getting up before dawn!" Corelle cried happily. "No more fighting with stock in the middle of snowstorms. No more watering fields during droughts using endless buckets of water. No more plowing, and planting, and seeding."

Mother Erica laughed at their logic, saying it made more sense for their aging, wiser mothers to mind the store, moving the younger sisters to the city to learn storekeeping as they grew up.

"We at least have worked at our sisters' store in Annaboro," Mother Erica reminded them. "Besides, your baby sisters aren't big enough to take on all that brute work, and your mothers can't tend the farm alone. You know that it takes at least twenty able bodies to manage planting and harvest."

Summer frowned. "But there are only eleven of us. How are we going to work this?"

"We'll manage." Mother Erica smiled. "There are so few opportunities like this. Unless a family ends like the Pickers, or loses everything in some disaster of bad judgment, farms and businesses just aren't sold. Your aunts had to travel to Annaboro to find a business to buy."

"Look!" Summer stood and pointed upriver. A trail of gray smoke drifted above the treetops. A deep-throated whistle sounded, far off and echoing. "The packet is coming."

"Eldest will have to eat on the boat," Mother Erica said, repacking the basket.

The packet rounded the bend as they reached the sloped cobblestone of the landing. It was a triple-decked stern-wheeler with twin smokestacks. Now in sight of the landing, it blasted its whistle again, a deafening howl of near discord. The stevedores caught the mooring ropes and looped them about great pilings set into the stonework of the levy, tying the stern-wheeler off by bow and stern. The swinging landing stage, fixed with ropes at the bow of the boat, was dropped down to form a gangplank up to the main deck.

The smooth and practiced docking complete, the huge boat was suddenly laid still beside the stone landing, dwarfing all structures in town. Jerin stood in awe, though he had seen it many times before. What great works woman could create!

Jerin recognized one of the women waiting to board, a small hill of bandboxes and steamer trunks beside her. Miss Abie Skinner taught the one-room schoolhouse that his school-aged sisters attended at the intersection of Whistler, Brindle, Fisher, and Brown land. She had been kind enough over the years to extend the classroom to Jerin and Doric by sending homework back with their sisters. Occasionally, she even came to the house to teach. Reed-thin, she dressed with the same artistic flair of her handwriting. When Jerin was very young, he had been madly in love with her. He recognized signs of it in Doric now. Their infatuation came, he decided, as a side effect of her being the only female they closely associated with who wasn't blood related.

"Miss Skinner." He greeted her with a smile. "You're going to be on this boat too?"

His teacher turned in surprise, smiled with pleasure to see him, then frowned. "Master Whistler, you know that a proper young man never starts a conversation with a woman outside of his family when in public."

Jerin recoiled, hurt. "But I've talked to you lots of times."

"I know, lad, but I shouldn't have let you. 'Once' leads to 'always.' You're leaving Heron Landing, where everyone knows not to mess with your sisters, and your sisters know where they live."

Jerin nodded. "I know not to talk to strangers, but you're Miss Skinner."

Abie Skinner smiled. "Thank you, Master Whistler."

"So, you're going to be on this boat?"

She tried not to grin, then shook her head and laughed. "Yes, Master Whistler. I'm going home."

"For a visit?"

"No, for good. I got a letter from Eldest." She patted her pocket, and a paper crinkled under the pat. "My scattered sisters and I have finally accrued enough money to purchase a husband of modest breeding."

"How wonderful!" Then the implication sank in. "You're not coming back?"

"No." She grinned widely. "Someone else will have to force basic figures and reading onto willful young minds."

"My sisters will miss you." He could think only that Doric would be crushed.

"Some of them. I will miss those ones."

They had two cabins on the second deck. Jerin would share a cabin with one of his sisters. Captain Tern would sleep in the other cabin. They worked out a schedule where at all times at least two of the women would be awake while the other two slept. One of his sleeping sisters would always be in the bunk under the window while he slept. It was as safe as they could make the trip.

That afternoon he took a stroll on the sundeck with Summer and Corelle. He had stepped out of his room intending to pull down his veil. The unobstructed sight of the sunshine on the water checked him. He climbed the stairs to the sundeck with his sisters trailing him.

Jerin expected Corelle or Summer to say something about his veil being up, but they didn't. Feeling someplace between guilty and free, he walked the sundeck, more interested in the fellow passengers. They gave him wide smiles and nods of greeting, but, with quick looks at his armed sisters, didn't speak to him.

At the stern, over the churning paddle wheel, he met Miss Skinner.

"*Tch,* Mr. Whistler, what are you doing?" Miss Skinner reached up and tugged down the veil. "There are people on this boat not to be trusted. If they thought you were an ugly thing behind that veil, they might leave you alone. Don't tempt them by showing them how stunningly beautiful you are."

"I'm not stunningly beautiful."

"Most women only see a few men in their lives. Their father. Perhaps their grandfather. If they are lucky, a brother and their husband. Any other men they see are always veiled. To them, anything with both eyes and sound teeth is a handsome man. My family are portrait painters. My hand is not as good as my sisters', so I decided to teach instead, to see a bit of the world. Before I left, though, I had seen an extraordinary number of men and paintings of men. You, Mr. Jerin Whistler, are the most stunningly beautiful man I have ever seen."

"Me?"

"Yes, you." She twitched the veil, artfully arranging the fold at his neck. "So don't tempt the scruffy lot on this boat more than your mere presence already does."

"Yes, Miss Skinner."

The next morning it was raining. Captain Tern was guarding him while his sisters slept. Miss Skinner came to the door, bearing a gift.

"Here, I have something for you to look at." It was a large book, almost three feet square. She set it down on the table and opened it to reveal maps done in gorgeous color. "This is an atlas. It has maps of all of the countries of the world."

"I wish I could have gone to school," Jerin murmured.

"*Tch,* I wouldn't have wanted the responsibility of keeping you safe, Mr. Whistler. It would have been too easy for someone to steal you away, and then where would I be? All alone in Heron Landing with the Whistler girls out for my blood."

"Are you happy about getting married?" Jerin asked.

"To tell the truth, I'm giddy as a girl."

"Even though you don't know your husband at all?"

"Honestly"—she blushed—"I haven't thought much about him, just the babies. We had a brother, who was killed a year before we would have swapped him for a husband. Maybe if we hadn't grown up so sure we would be married, it wouldn't have mattered so much. Some days, it's all I can think about, having children of our own."

"Really?"

She nodded unhappily. "The first day of school and the last are always the hardest. The seven-year-olds come in that first day, oh so little and darling. You just want to cuddle them. You try to keep your distance, but at the end of the year, when it's going to be months before you see them again—it just breaks my heart."

"I'm sorry."

"It's not your fault," she scolded.

"I mean—well, I guess I mean that I feel sorry for you."

"Don't. I'm getting married. We'll have baskets and bushels of babies and get as blasé about them as everyone else."

"Blasé?" he asked, unsure what the word meant.

"Casual. Careless." She defined the word using ones he did know. "Ever been to a social function and watch the mothers with their babies? Oh, you can't hold the little boys—no one but family gets to hold the boys— but they pass the baby girls off like sacks of wheat. Anyone can hold them as long as they want. And they sigh over the fact that the baby girls weren't born boys. You want to scream at them how lucky they are, and how they shouldn't take these healthy babies so lightly. And at least once a week you wonder if you're still young enough to carry a healthy child to term and survive delivering it, or maybe you should avoid all the risk, even though the thought of not being pregnant at least once is like putting a gun to your head and—"

She shuddered to a stop, and wiped tears from her cheeks. "I'm sorry. I shouldn't say things like that to you. I'm happy. I truly am."

He reached out and covered her hand. "I'm sure things will be fine."

"Indeed. Holy Mothers are kind." She sniffed, and forced herself to smile. "Well, I'll leave this with you to study. Eldest can drop it at my cabin later."

With that, she withdrew.

"She should have gone to a crib," Raven murmured after Miss Skinner's footsteps had faded away. "Got herself pregnant before this. It's warped her."

He could not help but feel that she was right. "Are you married, Captain Tern?"

"No. Don't particularly want to be. I don't get along well with my sisters, so I try to stay away from home. Not everyone fits the molds of society."

"Do you want children?"

Captain Tern considered the question and finally shrugged. "I don't like small children. Their noise—that high-pitched squealing—and energy level grate on my nerves. You can't reason with them. If you try bribing them, then they get spoiled and throw fits. My baby sisters drove me out of my home. I couldn't stand them. I certainly don't have a desire to raise any of my own. Still, I can't imagine not having a family. I send part of my paycheck home every week, and visit when I get lonely."

The first deck of the steamboat had a dining room. They had avoided it the first night, eating instead from the food hamper. For breakfast and lunch of the next day, one of his sisters carried sandwiches back to their cabins to supplement the dwindling cache. By the second night, the food was gone. Reluctantly, they went down for dinner.

Round tables, with chairs to sit ten, crowded into the space, lit by chandeliers of oil lamps. Eldest chose a table with easy access to the doors. She and Captain Tern sat on either side of Jerin, Summer and Corelle flanking them. Jerin was the only one able to sit and eat in peace.

Most women approaching the unoccupied chairs veered away after one hard look from Captain Tern and Eldest. When they were almost through with dinner, however, a family of four sisters sat down, ignoring the pointed stares.

"We have a hundred crowns," the oldest-looking of the sisters stated.

"So?" Eldest looked as mystified as Jerin felt.

"We're the Turners," the oldest Turner said. "We were going to Suttons Ferry. There's supposedly a clean-run crib there. But we heard the talk since you've boarded. Four boys in your family, and you're taking this one to market."

Captain Tern put down her silverware and slowly slid back her chair, her hands dropping down to her gun belt.

Eldest growled softly. "Shut your mouth! My brother isn't livestock."

A younger Turner sister leaned in. "What my sister is saying is that your family throws lots of boys. We were going to spend ten crown a night for one of us, probably Jolie here, to try for a baby." She indicated the youngest, a mere teenager. "We're too poor to afford a husband, so we're doing it by tens, as they say."

"My brother isn't for sale," Eldest said.

Younger Turner said, "We're offering twice the crib price, twenty crowns, because he's of good lines and sure to be clean!"

"No!" Eldest shouted, drawing looks.

"Jolie is a virgin," older Turner pressed. "She's clean. It would be a hundred crowns in only five nights!"

"My brother's price is four thousand and not a crown less," Eldest said through clenched teeth.

Their jaws dropped.

"Four—four thousand?" older Turner finally stuttered, apparently torn between being angry and laughing. "You're insane!"

"We're landed gentry with royal bloodlines and throw boys," Eldest snapped. "That's worth four thousand to a peer!"

"But you can't be sure," younger Turner said. "This is money in hand. It's not like you can tell when a man is a virgin or not."

"No," Eldest said quietly.

"No one would know," younger Turner said.

"I would know," Captain Tern stated.

"And who are you?" older Turner asked.

"Raven Tern, Captain of the Royal Guard, serving as escort to Master Whistler by order of Queens. The Queens are sponsoring Mr. Whistler's coming out and it would reflect poorly on them to present used goods."

Jolie Turner laughed, which earned her a hard cuff from her older sister.

"They're not joking, Jolie," older Turner snapped, and stood. "My apologies, Captain. We won't be bothering you again."

They watched the Turners make their way back out of the dining room.

"We're done eating," Eldest announced, although Jerin was the only one finished. "Let's go back to the cabins."

It was Eldest's turn to sleep while Captain Tern guarded the door. Eldest went into the cabin, but Jerin held back, pretending to look out over the railing at the moon shimmering on the water, the star-studded sky, and the black ribbon of shore between the two.

"Captain Tern," Jerin whispered so Eldest wouldn't hear.

"Call me Raven." Captain Tern's low voice came out of the darkness that cloaked her.

"Raven, can I ask you a question?"

Beside him, Raven moved, and he took it to be a nod.

Wetting his mouth, he asked quietly, "Do nobles actually pay as much as four thousand crowns for a brother's price?"

"Yes. The princesses paid nearly five thousand for their husband, Lord Keifer."

He felt as if Raven had thrust a sword into his chest. His throat constricted around that formless blade. "Ren—Princesses Rennsellaer and Odelia are married?"

Raven moved as if startled. "The prince consort was killed six years ago! Enemies of the crown had filled the basement of Durham Theater with gunpowder and set it off while the royal family were attending a play."

He turned away, ashamed that Raven might see the relief in his face even in the dark. *Horrible man*, he thought. *Her family dead, and you're relieved. You know she's too far above you. You're only landed gentry. Your grandmothers were thieves, spies, common line soldiers, and kidnappers.*

"Master Whistler?" Raven touched his shoulder, then quickly took her hand away. "I thought you knew. Half the royal princesses were killed. It was all anyone would talk about for months. It was on the front page of all—" She cut her sentence short as she remembered the normal limits placed on his sex. "As a man, you couldn't have read the papers. I'm sorry. I didn't consider."

"I was only ten." Back then all he wanted to read from the newspapers were the serial stories—adventures of steamboat captains, river pirates, and card sharks. "My family might have told me, but it would have mattered little to me. Children are so self-centered."

"Some adults too," Raven added quietly. Jerin glanced at her, wondering if she meant him. As if sensing his expression, she said, "No, not you. You strike me as bravely selfless. Your family is putting you in a difficult position, and yet you're not complaining."

"If I knew they were wrong, I'd complain," Jerin said.

"Their reasoning, though, seems sound. One of our neighbors might be able to afford a brother's price of two thousand. Surely a noble could afford twice that. One hears how wealthy the nobility are. Their estates encompass over a hundred thousand acres. Their houses contain ballrooms, gaslights, and indoor necessities. They eat fresh fruit in the winter off of plates made of gold."

Jerin reached out and caught Raven's wrist. "Is it true? Are they that rich? Is there a hope that my family can get the price they want? The price they need?"

"Some noble families are richer than you can ever imagine, little one," Raven said. "Some are poorer than your family. Some of them will look at you and see what a good, beautiful young man you are. Some will only see you as the grandson of common line soldiers. There will be families where the Eldest is free to choose any man she desires, and in other families the mothers will have to approve of you first."

"So it's all 'maybe' and 'it depends.' "

"Yes."

Jerin let go of her wrist, knowing she told him the truth, wishing she had lied. "A simple 'yes' would have been kinder."

"No, it wouldn't have," Raven said. "Much rides on how you and your family present yourself. To get what you want, you can't be careless in your actions."

"I see."

They stood in silence, absorbed in their own thoughts, as the dark river murmured far below.

"Tell me," Raven said after a few minutes, "what does your family mean when they say 'a shining coin'?"

"It's a long story."

"We have time."

"My great-great-grandmothers were first-generation line soldiers. We don't know what drove them to enlist. Maybe it was that or starve."

"For many it is."

"They won their way into the Order of the Sword, giving them access to the military cribs. Many families chose only one man to father all their children, to maintain the illusion of normalcy, I guess. My great-great-grandmothers hadn't, and it showed. My great-grandmothers were a very motley crew."

Raven rubbed the Order of the Sword tattoo on the back on her hand. "It sounds like me and my sisters."

"Their mutt breeding, though, was what saved them. Apparently just looking at them lined up at the court-martial inspired the judges to believe my great-grandmother Elder acted alone when she committed treason."

Raven laughed softly.

"Still, they were discharged, stripped of pensions, and all their daughters were barred from service. They didn't know anything but soldiering, and they started to starve to death. Grandma Tea ended up in charge of the family, and she managed to force the Sisters of the Night to take them in, train them as thieves, but she wasn't happy. No retirement, no pension, no crib, no future except to dance at the end of a rope."

"They still tell stories of Tea Whistler. She was a force to be reckoned with."

"One day, all the luck of the Whistlers changed. Grandma Tea had gone to her Mother Elder's grave and made a bargain with her."

Raven snorted but said nothing.

"She told her mother that she didn't blame her for what she had done—being a soldier of the line wasn't a wonderful thing. Tea's mothers had no husband of their own, lost sisters to diseases caught in the crib, lost sisters for causes they didn't understand, and lost daughters to the wet and cold and hardship of following the drum. It was a slow and steady grind. Many think it is taking them uphill when it is only wearing them down."

"Unless a sister makes it to officer grade, yes, the army eats families."

"Grandmother Tea recognized that her Mother Elder

had made a desperate gamble to better their lot, and lost—she grabbed for a coin tossed in the air and missed. If she had caught the coin, her sisters and daughters would have praised her. Instead they cursed her name and spit on her memory.

"So Grandmother Tea made a bargain. She needed an opportunity, that golden moment, where playing loose and wild and reckless, like her Mother Elder had, gave her the slimmest chance to win. She pledged that if her mother gave her the opportunity, just set the coin flying into the air, even if she didn't catch it, they'd honor her memory."

Raven shook her head. "And she got a shining coin?"

Jerin nodded. "The day she was caught while thieving by Wellsbury. She convinced the general that trained thieves would make excellent spies. That led to being knighted and given the farm, and kidnapping Grandpa. Our family hasn't been poor and starving since then."

Eldest was still awake when he came into their cabin. He should have known that she wouldn't sleep until he was safe in the room. She sat cross-legged on her bed, cleaning her revolvers.

"Be sure to secure the door," she said without looking up. The shutter on the cabin window was already latched and a piece of lumber wedged in the frame to reinforce the shutter.

Jerin locked the door and then propped the cabin's chair under the door handle. He wondered how much of his conversation with Captain Tern Eldest had heard. He felt vaguely guilty about talking to someone outside the family about his fears—but none of his sisters could have answered his questions about nobility. What Captain Tern told him, however, hadn't settled his fears. He changed into his sleeping shirt, and then sat on his bed, chin on his knees.

Eldest eyed him, reloading her revolvers without looking. "What's wrong, Jerin?"

"I'm worried," he whispered. "What if we don't get more than two thousand for me? What are we going to do?"

"Don't worry." She spun the cylinder on each gun, double-checking she had a full load. "If things come to worse, we could sell futures on Doric's brother price."

"Futures?" Jerin asked.

"Like grain futures." Eldest slid her pistols into their holster, hanging from her headboard. "A lot of farmers sell their crops in the summer at a set price before the harvest. It helps them tide money over, but it's risky. Basically, it's a loan, and you put your farm up as collateral on the loan. People that don't look at it as a loan usually lose the family farm."

Jerin picked nervously at his sheets. "What if the market price of your crops goes higher than the set price?"

"That's what the women that bought your crop are hoping for," Eldest said. "You don't see the profit; they do. That's why the Whistlers don't sell futures. We don't work to make other people rich."

"Why don't you use my brother's price?" Jerin asked.

Eldest smiled, and hugged him suddenly. "Because I want a husband, silly, not the money."

Three days later they arrived at Mayfair. The city seemed to go on forever, stunning even his sisters into silence. Eldest took firm hold of his arm with her left hand, keeping her right free to draw a gun, and didn't let go.

"Stay here." Raven went down the canted stage to the crowded landing. The ship's calliope started up, drowning out all normal levels of conversation with bright loud music. Jerin watched the captain's broad back as she pushed through the milling crowds. Partway to the cobbled street, an odd thing happened. A woman in a wide-brimmed hat coming down the street glanced at Raven as they passed each other. The stranger started as if recognizing the captain, then ducked her face away. Raven, intent on the wagon, seemed not to notice.

"Did you see that?" Jerin shouted at Eldest, standing beside him, as he kept watch on the mystery woman. The woman had turned to watch Raven's retreating back, and Jerin had a momentary stab of fear for the captain.

"What?"

"The woman. Did you see her?" Jerin pointed at the only figure that seemed to be standing still in the crowd.

"I can't hear what you're saying, Jerin! Who do you see?"

He took his eyes away only for a moment, to turn and shout into Eldest's ear. "That woman is acting oddly."

"Which one?"

He glanced back, and found her gone. "She's gone now."

Eldest scanned the crowd. "Was she armed?"

He shook his head, and shouted back, "I don't know!"

"Here comes Raven!" Eldest pointed out the captain.

Raven waded back through the crowd, signaling that they were to join her. Eldest took his arm above the elbow to escort him down the stage. Raven met them at the foot.

"I've got a hackney hired," Raven shouted to Eldest. "Take Jerin over and I'll bring the luggage."

Eldest nodded, not bothering to shout back. Eldest turned, apparently spotted Corelle and Summer, and flashed hand signals for them to get the gear and follow.

"We'll get your stuff loaded and go straight up to the palace," Raven told Jerin, pointing.

Jerin gasped. The city ran back to sandstone cliffs, which leaped skyward in walls of rich tan. Crowning the bluffs, with windows glistening like diamonds, sat an immense building. It was an architectural sprawl of turrets and wings, gables and dormers, slate roofs and copper cladding, gray stone veiled with ivy, and windows—

hundreds and thousands of mullioned windows. Too
huge, too impressive, too noble to be anything but the
royal palace.

"I've never seen anything so big," Jerin breathed.

His words fell in a moment of silence as the calliope
paused between songs.

"It's where you'll be living for—for the next few
weeks," Raven said, then patted him on the shoulder.
"Go on to the hackney. You can gawk through the
window."

He and Eldest pushed their way through the crowd to
the closed carriage. While he climbed into the hackney,
Eldest waited outside for Summer and Corelle to catch
up. He scooted across the battered horsehair-stuffed seat
to stare up at the palace. Ren and Odelia's home. He
remembered Ren, standing in the Whistlers' kitchen,
watching him cook. How poor and lowborn he must
have seemed to her.

He was aware of someone staring at him, and he
looked down.

The young woman with the wide-brimmed hat stood
before him, shielded from Eldest and the others by the
hackney. She looked at him with neither envy nor the
open speculation that he had grown used to during the
trip, that "I wish I had him" or "Can I get him without
being caught?" She seemed, instead, stunned by some
surprising news.

Jerin gazed at her, wondering why she sought him
out, what was so surprising about himself. He could find
nothing familiar about her face, no hint that he might
have known her long ago. True, the silvery line of a scar
ran from the corner of her left eye down the line of her
chin to the edge of her mouth. The skin lay smooth; the
healing had been perfect despite the fact she had nearly
lost her left eye with the wound. The scar, thus, did not
disfigure her beyond recognition.

In fact, he would not say it disfigured her at all. At
one time, her face had been a harvested field under a

winter sky: barren of good features, containing no bad. Plain. Neither beautiful nor ugly. It had existed.

The scar gave her plainness character, like a thick choker, or a large bold earring. It spoke to Jerin of strength and determination.

The woman had tensed when their gazes met, a look like fear going through her eyes. He had thought Raven might be the cause for her alarm, but then the woman didn't glance to see where the captain was, or what Raven was doing. Instead her eyes widened slightly, and Jerin realized she had been somehow afraid of him, and now she wasn't.

She stepped forward, reached out, and lifted his veil.

Time stopped.

They froze there. He half leaned out the window of the hired coach. She held the veil up with both hands. Her eyes were green, green and changing as summer wheat, one moment dark as velvet, next light as silk, with long thick dark eyelashes. Gorgeous eyes. How could he have thought her plain with such eyes?

She gasped, as if surprised, and then kissed him.

He hadn't expected it, and sat stunned during the touch of warm lips, the fleeting exploration of her sweet cinnamon tongue, the brief touch of fingertips on his check.

Then she was gone, his veil drifting down, the calliope blasting forth into the silence that had surrounded them.

The hackney rocked, and Summer climbed in beside him. She leaned against him to look out and up at the palace on the cliff. "To think, after all these years, the Whistlers are going to be guests there."

Chapter 8

The hackney cab jostled and swayed through town, and climbed the cliff road. At the palace gate, Raven leaned out to have them passed through. All the while, Jerin found himself pressing his hand to his mouth, feeling again and again the kiss of the stranger on his lips. What was wrong with him? Why did he let a stranger kiss him? True, he had not expected the kiss, but still, once it started, once he was aware it was happening, he should have stopped it. Was he in truth a slut, unable to resist any woman's advances? Certainly, prior to Ren, he never *had* to resist a woman; his sisters kept all comers at bay. Ren certainly hadn't taught him anything in the way of resistance.

All this time he thought—actually, he still believed— he was in love with Ren. If he loved her, why had he let that woman kiss him? Gods above, he didn't even know the woman's name!

Eldest finally noticed his silence, the hand pressed to his mouth. "Are you sick?"

Sick? Well, mental illness would explain his actions. "Perhaps."

"Should we stop and let you throw up in the gardens?" Eldest asked. "It would be better than spilling your accounts in the palace proper."

"If he goes, I go." Summer looked slightly green from the jostling.

"Ah, Whistlers at their finest hour." Corelle earned a cuff from Eldest.

"I'll be fine," Jerin muttered, blushing. Certainly with his family pressed so close, he would be able to resist the next woman who tried to kiss him.

The cab came to a stop before the palace in a vast paved courtyard and they spilled hastily out into the fresh air. Women in the livery of the Queens unloaded the wagon as Raven paid the cab driver. The servants were of similar coloring and height, making Jerin suspect they were sisters.

"This is the Queens' majordomo, Barnes." Raven indicated the woman supervising the others, polished in dress, face passive, but eyes deeply curious.

"I'm at your service," Barnes said in greeting, giving a half bow. "The Queen Mother Elder wishes to meet you immediately. I must insist, however, that no weapons be kept in the palace. Anything you surrender will be returned to you at the end of your stay."

"There are rifles in our luggage," Eldest stated, undoing her gun belt.

Jerin froze, unsure what to do. His mothers always stressed that he should never go unarmed among strangers.

Summer carried only the six-shooter but had three knives. Corelle wore two six-shooters and a derringer, but no knives. Eldest matched Summer with knives, Corelle for guns, and then added two pairs of brass knuckles and a wire garrote. Barnes and Raven took the weapons without comment or surprise. Jerin was amazed Eldest surrendered all her stash weapons, but apparently she judged the risk of being caught with them in the presence of the Queens too high to warrant keeping them on her.

Which probably meant he should give up his weapons. He gave Eldest a questioning look, and she nodded. Reaching into his pocket, he produced his derringer.

Barnes startled visibly. "Holy Mothers above."

Raven raised one eyebrow and accepted it. "You know how to use this?"

Jerin nodded, blushing at the thought of taking his knife off. Eldest rescued him by kneeling at his feet, reaching under the hem of his walking robe, and undoing the shin sheath. She made no move, thankfully, to retrieve his lock picks; if she had, he would have discovered if it was possible to die of embarrassment.

Raven accepted the knife with a slight, unexpected smile.

Barnes gave Raven an unreadable look, then turned to the Whistlers. "Thank you for your cooperation. Come this way."

Barnes led them through a portcullis and down a graveled path to a deep porch overlooking the gardens. Wicker chairs sat in a loose circle, facing one another. A tall stately woman sat waiting for them. She wore a green silk shirt, high-collared with long, narrow sleeves that matched her deep green eyes. A gold circlet over her short, gray-tinged red hair proclaimed her as Queen Mother Elder. Besides the green eyes and red hair, she shared her daughters' deceivingly delicate features and fair skin.

Barnes announced them, waited until the Queen Elder dismissed her with a wave of fingers, and bowed out.

Queen Elder considered Jerin with a cock of her head and slightly pursed lips. After long minutes of study, she indicated that they should sit. A servant moved forward to pour tea, then faded into the background.

The Queen Elder addressed Eldest. "I was one of seventeen sisters. There are only five of us left. Illness, war, childbirth, and assassins have weeded us down. We had twenty daughters, which are now ten. It matters much to us that the count is not nine. We are indebted that you put a brother to risk providing aid to our daughter."

"We merely followed the law," Eldest said quietly, choosing to ignore the fact she hadn't been present to consult on the matter. The law usually held the entire family responsible for one sister's action. A family could otherwise engage in wanton lawbreaking, sacrificing one sister to save the rest if they were caught. The inverse, Jerin decided, must be that they were held accountable for good deeds too.

"Unfortunately," the Queen Elder said, "when it comes to men, our people tend not to be law-abiding. Finding a stranger on their land, most women would have let their fear for their menfolk rule their actions. In part, by rewarding you, I lift you up as an example. If we're to stand against our neighboring nations, we cannot be fighting so between ourselves. This was why the husband raids were outlawed. This was why blood feuds are forbidden. This is why the traveler's-aid law was created. Our people must be made to understand that their neighbors are their sisters."

The Queen Elder sipped her tea and they sat in silence, unsure what to say.

Eldest finally cleared her throat and said into the silence, "My grandmothers were line soldiers before they were knighted. We are just landed gentry. We're aware of the benefits from bringing Jerin out with your sponsorship—but we're not sure what this all entails."

"Wisely said." The Queen Elder smiled. "In the next three months there will be nightly social events to attend. Actually there will be several on any given night; one picks and chooses—and one is picked and chosen, as they are all by invitation only. Normally, landed gentry such as yourself would field only invitations from the lower strata of the Peerage. With the sponsorship of the Queens, all who wish to curry our favor will invite you. There are dances, musicales, dinners, and picnics—window dressing for the true event—bringing Eldests together with brothers in tow. Offers are made, negotiations follow, and hopefully, by the end of the season all will be happily married."

"It sounds like extended fairs."

"I'm sure the Season grew out of fairs. Unfortunately, in my view, things have gotten out of hand. I'm afraid that members of the Peerage put too much importance on dress. It is a sign of how rich they are that they can sink so much money into an outfit, then never wear it again. We have not invited you here to bankrupt your family by keeping up appearances, nor to be humiliated unfairly because you're wise not to waste your resources. As our guests, we intend to provide a modest wardrobe to your family."

"The costs are truly prohibitive?" Eldest asked.

"Fifty crowns." She gave a number that made Eldest startle, and then added, "For each outfit."

"Each?" Eldest asked.

"Each."

Jerin blanched. One hundred for Eldest and himself to be made a single set of outfits. Two hundred if Summer and Corelle were included. Multiply that by three or four. The numbers staggered him. His entire brother's price could be swallowed by the cost of the clothes.

His sisters exchanged a look.

"We will have to depend on your generosity," Eldest murmured.

"Good," the Queen Mother Elder said. "The best tailors in Mayfair were put on notice. A runner has been sent to their shop with news of your arrival. You will see them this afternoon."

"Yes, Your Majesty," Eldest said, bowing her head.

The answer pleased the Queen for some reason. She offered cakes and they accepted, using their best manners to negotiate getting the rich flaky pastry from the delicate china plates to their mouths using only the silver dessert forks. Jerin remembered without prompting that *he* was the senior ranked male at the table, and thus responsible for refills. He filled everyone's cup without spilling a drop or trailing his sleeves in the liquid, all the while grateful that their grandfather had drilled table manners into the family. They even managed polite small talk, answering questions on the trip down and the health of the sisters and mothers they'd left behind.

"Your family seems blessed with strong, healthy, beautiful children. Any birth defects?"

"None," Eldest said proudly. "Our family has always kept itself clean of inbreeding. If a family can't pin down a male from the time the first daughter is born until the last daughter hits menopause, some forty or fifty years, then the family shouldn't reproduce in the first place."

The Queen Elder laughed for a moment, then sobered. "There is much to do, and time is growing shorter. Barnes will show you to your apartment."

Barnes led them up a curving flight of stairs and down a long carpeted hall to a set of double doors. These she opened to reveal a spacious parlor, done in pale yellow damask-velvet wallpaper and cheery yellow silk drapes and matching settees. On the left-hand wall, two doors led to bedrooms. Jerin's wedding chest sat untouched in the small corner bedroom with a large four-poster bed. Barnes called this bedroom the men's quarters. His sisters' luggage had been unpacked into the richly carved mahogany wardrobes of the much larger bedroom, which contained six elegant sleigh beds.

"Will you be wanting baths?" Barnes asked Eldest.

"If it can be arranged," Eldest said.

Barnes signaled a younger woman with a family resemblance to her standing at the parlor door. "Two hip baths, hot water, and towels will be brought up. It will be removed while you are at dinner."

She showed them how the double parlor doors could be barred at night. She went on to quietly point out that the parlor and women's room isolated Jerin's bedroom from the rest of the palace. She demonstrated how one of the parlor settees could be wheeled to block his bedroom door and used as a bed. Surely even the most paranoid of sisters would feel safe with their brother in this apartment.

Jerin recalled that in his sisters' adventure novels, there were always secret passages to the men's quarters. The daring heroines used them to save their true loves from heartless mothers, cruel sisters, abusive wives, and vile kidnappers. He sighed over the banks of windows, evidence that no secret passage could open into his bedroom; Ren wouldn't be visiting him late at night.

A squad of servants, obviously younger sisters of the majordomo, brought up two copper bathtubs. They set one in his bedroom, the other in his sisters' room to share, and poured buckets of steaming water into them. All the while, the women sent curious glances his way. It made Jerin blush—these strangers preparing a place that he'd step naked into.

"The Queens have commissioned tailors for you," Barnes was saying. "They'll be here in an hour." The tub filled, the servants filed out. Barnes followed them to the door, then turned, indicating a length of tapestry fabric hanging from a loop in the ceiling. "This is the bellpull here. Ring if you need anything."

Jerin glanced to his sister and saw the slight frown Eldest wore when irritated. Was she as baffled as he was but too proud to ask? Summer and Corelle studiously ignored Barnes, which probably meant they were also ignorant. Luckily men were expected to be naïve. He cleared his throat and asked quietly, "I don't understand. Ring what?"

Barnes looked surprised. "The bellpull. You pull on this, and it rings one of the bells down in the kitchens to let us know you want something."

"Really?" Summer exclaimed. "How does it do that?"

"There are cables on small pulleys run through the walls, going down to a rack of numbered bells. You pull here, and your bell in the kitchen rings. If you want anything, just ring."

Jerin nodded, wondering what "anything" constituted. With a tub, towels, and chamber pot at hand, he could not guess what more they could want.

"The Queens keep country hours, so dressing gong is at six and dinner gong is at seven," Barnes continued.

"Dressing gong?" Jerin asked.

Again the startled look from Barnes. "It's like a bell sound, deep and not so sweet. Brassy, one could say, kind of like hitting a slipper against a big kettle lid."

"What's it for?" Jerin pressed on.

"So you know it's time to dress for dinner," Barnes said.

"You expect us to take that long to bathe?" Summer half laughed, nervous that things were vastly different with the nobility.

Barnes worked her mouth, considering words carefully before saying, "Dress in one's dinner clothes as opposed to one's daily wear."

That stunned all the Whistlers speechless.

"Will that be all?" Barnes asked after a moment.

"Yes," Eldest murmured finally. "Thank you."

Barnes backed out of the room, apparently a habit from serving royalty, and closed the door. The Whistlers stared at the shut door in silence.

"Dinner clothes." Eldest crossed to bar the door. "They have clothes just for eating?"

"Apparently," Corelle said.

"Daily clothes. Dinner clothes. Party clothes." Eldest counted on her fingers, squinting. "I think we should have asked for the reward in money and stayed home. We could have bought the store and a husband for the cost of these clothes."

"A good husband is worth it," Summer murmured. "Besides, we can resell the clothes in our new store later for at least half their cost."

Jerin glanced at his wedding chest, thinking of the clothes within. What would he wear for dinner?

"We've got an hour before the tailors come," Eldest said. "Let's hurry with the baths."

The tailors were a family of at least seven women, with a goodly chance of many more not in attendance.

The eldest was a small, bird-boned woman with sharp features and a bright chirpy voice. Her salt-and-pepper hair was twirled up into a bun by way of a charcoal pencil, joined by a hemming guide and a pattern roller. A flock of younger sisters followed in her wake, carrying colorful ribbons and swatches of fabric. It was obvious by the way they migrated about the room, emitting pleased twitters over the rich appointments, that it was the first time the younger sisters visited the palace.

"My, my, my, what a pretty little brother you have here." The eldest tailor circled Jerin. "Certainly makes my job more pleasant. Nothing is worse than trying to make an ugly toad of a boy into something someone would want in their bed."

"Someone bedded their mothers," Eldest said.

"Fathers are bought, not mothers." The tailor grinned at her own wit. "I'll enjoy making this one radiant. I could even use him to set the next rage."

"Rage?" Eldest asked.

"The most popular fashion at the moment," the tailor explained. "They're started by the powerful or the beautiful. The rage this season is to dress the family in a theme, say a dark blue silk." She snapped her fingers. One of the younger sisters thumbed through her stack of fabric swatches to select out several shimmering blues. "A shirt for the boy, a vest for the Eldest, trousers for the Mother Elder—that sort of thing. In a glance, you can see who belongs to who."

"If this season is just starting," Summer asked, "how do you know what is the rage?"

A chorus of twittering laughter broke out from the flock of younger tailors, silenced by a look from their eldest. "Oh, orders for clothes start as early as the end of last season." She took the blue silks, and examined each carefully in turn. "Normally a rage starts the last week or so of a season and hits full force at the beginning weeks of the next season. The ladies of Avonar started the family-theme rage the last season while courting for a husband, and one could not have asked for a better starter of a rage. Powerful and beautiful in one package."

"You recommend a blue?" Eldest asked.

"This one would be perfect." The tailor held a swatch of cobalt-blue silk stamped with a shimmering design to Jerin's chest. The intimate touch of a complete stranger made him blush, especially with so many people watching. "To bring out his eyes, not that they don't jump out and grab you already. Landed gentry you might be, but I think you'll find no end to offers."

Eldest also seemed bothered by the tailor's encroachment. She rested a hand on Jerin's back. Jerin more felt than saw the gaze his older sister directed over his shoulder at the tailor.

Summer drifted closer. "Are there ever brothers stolen?"

"Oh, yes." The tailor backed off unhurriedly, perhaps well used to possessive sisters. "Not out from under the Queens' eyes, I would think, but a number of boys are snatched each season. Oh, it's not the peers you have to watch; they aren't the desperate ones. It's those poor of resources: street vendors, house guards, maids—"

"Tailors," Summer added to the list.

The tailor laughed, unembarrassed. "Yes, there was at least one case of such." She sobered then, and looked levelly at Eldest. "Some boys end up in a crib, whored out to father children for the desperate. Disease runs rampant in those houses; there's a reason the gods forbid us from sharing our husband with the less fortunate. Even if you find the boy and free him, most families won't run the risk of a disease taking out wives and children in the future. Guard this little sweetie well."

"We always have." Eldest glowered at the tailor.

"Well"—the tailor turned away—"there is much to do, so let us start. It will take several days to prepare a wardrobe for your family; until then, you will need something suitable. Princess Odelia advised us on your build, and we've brought some clothes that should fit with some alterations. The peers of the realm—" She shook her head. "They order clothes and then change their mind, usually after they see the bill. Funny thing is, money is never the reason for them. No, no, the color is wrong, or the cut, or the fit; they're always too proud to say they cannot afford our clothes."

Raven waited for Ren at the palace stable.

Ren swung down off her horse, and threw her reins to her groom as a grin bloomed on her face. *He's here! Jerin's finally here!*

"I wish I could believe that smile was for me." Raven nodded in greeting to Ren.

"I'm glad to see you too." Ren swatted at Raven. "How is he?"

"He's fine. The trip went well. No attempted kidnappings and only one offer to stud him out—which was politely but firmly refused. You might be interested to know that they're planning to hold out for four thousand crowns."

Ren paused. "They know we're going to offer?"

"Actually, I don't think they have a clue. Sometimes they're refreshingly naïve about the whole thing. They reason if they can get two thousand out of landed gentry, they should be able to get four thousand out of nobility."

Ren shrugged, said, "Not unreasonable," and headed for the palace in long strides. The city clocks had rung five o'clock during her ride up—she had missed the dressing gong, and dinner would be soon. "I'm willing to pay four thousand. He's worth it."

"More the point of their plan," Raven said, falling in step with her, "is that it lets them afford a husband of good breeding, and the mercantile at Heron Landing."

"The one run by those tiny old ladies? What was the name? Picker?"

"The same."

Ren started to strip off her sweat-stained clothes as soon as she entered her bedroom. Raven leaned against the mantel, looking entirely pleased with herself.

"So what do you think of him," Ren asked, "now that you've had a chance to spend time with him?"

It was Raven's turn to shrug. "Keep in mind that I have known only three men in my life. Your father, Keifer, and your cousin Cullen."

Interesting, she doesn't consider Keifer as my husband, Ren thought, washing off dirt and sweat.

"Of the three," Raven continued, "I would say Jerin is most like your father, but only in the way apples are like oranges."

"What does that mean?"

Raven looked annoyed at her own analogy. "Forget I said that."

"Tell me." Ren toweled dry. A middle Barnes sister had laid out her dinner clothes, knowing Ren liked privacy for discussing matters with Raven before dinner.

"Jerin is stronger of character than your father. I don't think Jerin would have let Keifer rule the roost like your father did. He certainly wouldn't have let what happened to Trini occur in the next bedroom."

Ren froze in the act of reaching for her shirt. "Don't say that."

"Keifer was poison for your family. Worse yet, Eldest and the others took it willingly. No one would put their foot down, so he got away with everything."

Ren forced herself to continue dressing, her fingers suddenly seeming too thick to deal with the buttons. "True, but that's over; Keifer is dead, and Jerin's nothing like him."

Raven considered, her eyes distant. "The more time I spend with Mr. Whistler, the more I like him," she finally admitted. "I think he's a good man, but I could be wrong. I've only known three men in my life, Ren, and only one of them was a responsible, reasonable human being. If I am wrong, Jerin could be far more dangerous than Keifer."

"Meaning?" Ren tried not to let panic in. It was her captain's job to be paranoid, to seek danger where it might not be found.

Raven reached into her coat and took out a small pistol that she sat on the mantel beside her. A long slim knife joined the pistol. "Keifer was never this well armed, and certainly never trained by thieves, spies, and assassins."

Ren sighed, thinking not of how dangerous Jerin might be, but of how her mothers would react to such news. "Does anyone else know he was armed?"

"Barnes."

Which meant her mothers knew. She cursed softly. "Have any of my mothers met the Whistlers yet, or will dinner be their first exposure to them?"

"Queen Mother Elder gave them a private audience. She wanted to appraise their social skills—to see if tutors would need to be hired prior to them meeting polite society. I'm told it went well. Your sisters-in-law dine with the family tonight, as will the Whistlers."

Out with the old and in with the new.

Ren pulled on fresh boots as she considered how to put a positive face on the situation. Nothing came to mind until she went to comb her hair in the mirror. "Raven, drop a tale into Barnes's ear. Tell her about finding Egan Wainwright raped and killed. Stress the fact that the Whistlers witnessed it all, knowing that Jerin had been alone less than a mile from these rapist killers."

"And you'll tell the same to your mothers?"

"Not at dinner, but as soon as I can."

The dinner gong sounded, muffled by the floors between it and them. Ren shrugged into her dinner coat, realizing belatedly she had spent the entire briefing on Jerin without a word said about the cannons.

"Did you learn anything about the thieves?" Ren asked as Raven followed her out into the hall.

"Not yet, but Jerin gave me an interesting idea. So far the thieves have killed everyone that might be witness to them, including that cruelty to Egan Wainwright. I have my staff checking to see if any ship on our list recently had part or all of its crew killed off. I should have a report by tomorrow."

"Jerin?"

"He's a man of surprising intelligence."

A Barnes sister directed Ren to the blue salon, where she found her in-laws, the ladies of Avonar, and her mothers gathered. Her youngest sisters still hadn't graduated to formal dining parties. Odelia was late, as usual. Trini was absent and sent a sketchy apology, complaining of a migraine; truth was, she refused to deal with their in-laws. Lylia, Ren was informed, had gone to escort their cousins, the Moorlands, upriver. The Whistlers were the only ones unaccounted for.

Ren poured herself a brandy and then sought Barnes out.

"The tailors only finished altering the premade clothes a short while ago," Barnes said in reply to her questioning. "A youngest sister will be guiding them down as soon as they are dressed."

As Barnes bowed off, Kij Porter drifted to Ren's side. "Did I hear Barnes mention newly arrived palace houseguests? Who rates that special honor? Your cousins?"

Ren covered her wince by taking a sip of her brandy; the Porters were not the ones she would have chosen as first contact for Jerin's family. As close a friend as Kij was, "pompous ass" still defined the Porter family as a whole. Families of old blood tended to be that way, due, perhaps, to inbreeding. She suspected that the Porters were among the worst because, along with their name, they retained the taint of common blood. "The Whistlers. They're the ones that saved Odelia from drowning upland. My mothers are sponsoring their brother this season."

Kij made the polite noise of understanding. "A charity case?"

I'm going to marry him. Ren restrained the impulse to say it aloud; she didn't want Jerin hurt if she couldn't clear all the hurdles between them. She nodded slightly, giving a tight smile over the rim of her glass.

"How very kind of your—" Kij paused, her eyes focusing over Ren's shoulder. "Well, I see that the task will not be an odious one."

Jerin! Ren turned, locking down on a smile that wanted to blaze across her face. At the sight of him, only that control kept her jaw from clicking open. They had swathed him in layers of silk: a short-sleeved undertunic of deep blue that showed off his tanned, muscular forearms; fashionably snug britches of the same shade; and a richly embroidered waistcoat that came to mid-thigh to make the britches more modest, and yet accentuated his wide shoulders. His silken raven hair was gathered into graceful falls and small loose braids woven through with ribbons.

His sisters wore deep blue, high-collared silk shirts, and black silk dining jackets and slacks. Clean, carefully groomed, and formally dressed, the women were nearly as striking as Jerin. Eldest Whistler led, Jerin on her arm, the younger sisters trailing behind in flanking positions. The Whistler family entered the room with the feral grace of hunting wolves.

"They don't look like farmers to me," Kij murmured as Eldest correctly approached Queen Mother Elder first to pay respects.

"Their grandmothers were knights," Ren told her simply. The less said about what else the Whistlers' grandmothers had been, the better. "The title reverted after their deaths, of course, but the family remains gentry."

"Just barely," Kij murmured. "Too bad—he's quite pretty. I'm sure someone who doesn't mind adding a little common stock into the line will be quick to snap him up."

Pompous ass.

Ren knew that the Whistlers had never been before royalty, and doubted that they had ever been to a formal dinner, yet she watched with awe as they greeted each of her mothers with regal calm. After bowing to Ren's youngest mother, Milain, the Whistler party turned, and Jerin saw her for the first time. His smile was warm, shy—and stunning as a blow from a giant mallet.

Kij drifted off, no doubt to warn her sisters that the pretty stranger wasn't up to the Porter level of breeding. Ren crossed to the Whistlers. Her mothers, bless them all, hung back so she had their visitors to herself.

"Whistler." She nodded to Eldest. There was a dark look that wasn't there before. *Drat, they know what I did with their little brother!*

With that in mind, she cooled her greeting to Jerin to all that was proper. It was almost maddening, though, to be so close as to feel the heat of his body, be able to catch his light scent, and yet be unable to touch him.

She scrambled to find a neutral subject to talk about, finally settling on, "I hope you had a good trip."

"Uneventful, which is always good," Eldest said.

Queen Mother Elder called for attention. "Our esteemed daughters-in-law, ladies of Avonar, welcome again to our dinner table. May we introduce you to our guests in our home this summer, the family Whistler."

As her Mother Elder named members of each family, Ren wondered if this was in some way a subtle cut on her mothers' part. The Porters had been almost shameless in their pursuit of a royal marriage, making sure Keifer was always in Princess Eldest's eye, and allowing Eldest to take discreet liberties with their brother. The Porters succeeded in their campaign, and reaped the rewards of being in-laws to the crown, but Keifer had been a bitter disappointment. If Ren had her way, the Porters would soon lose their coveted position.

Queen Mother Elder had finished explaining the Whistlers' tie to Prince Alannon and his royal bloodline when Odelia appeared in the doorway. She smiled brilliantly at Jerin and hurried to his side.

"Whistler." Odelia gave a quick nod to Eldest, and then she caught Jerin's free hand in hers. "Jerin! It's good to see you here!"

"You look well." Jerin reached out to brush back Odelia's bangs, away from where she had been struck. "Hardly a scar. No one could ever tell."

"Thanks to you." Odelia beamed, looking more radiant than Ren had ever seen her. "Come, they're sitting for dinner." She swept him away without a glance at his sisters. "I'm sure no one will mind if you sit beside me."

As Ren gazed after Odelia in stunned amazement, Corelle whispered overloud to her sister, "I don't know, Eldest—I think we better find some mighty big sticks, and soon."

"Yup," Eldest Whistler murmured low enough so only Ren and her sisters could hear, and made a motion with her hand. The younger Whistlers nodded to their Eldest and hurried after Odelia and Jerin. Corelle cut off a middle Porter sister to claim the chair beside Jerin, and Summer flanked Odelia.

Ren suspected if their guests had been anyone but the Porters, her mothers would have set the sitting arrangements back to the original plan. Since the Porters were their in-laws, however, the dinner could be considered "only family." Whatever the reason, their mothers made no move to correct things. Perhaps Odelia had even counted on that; Ren could never understand the inner workings of Odelia's mind.

Ren took advantage of the change and sat Eldest Whistler beside her, wanting a chance to mend their friendship. They were, hopefully, going to be sisters-in-law.

Kij Porter took the chair to Ren's other side. As the first remove made its rounds, Kij leaned close and whispered, "Is it true? Their grandmothers married Alannon?"

"Go look at his portrait upstairs after dinner and compare."

Kij made a noise of disgust. "That proves nothing."

"There's a paper trail. Do you think we wouldn't check? Besides, it's not as if they came forward with the claim. Our paths happened to cross when Odelia was attacked, and the story came out."

Kij gazed down the table at Jerin. "He is certainly a pretty one. We were thinking of offering for Dirich Dunwood, but maybe we'll go for royal blood instead."

Ren covered her dismay. She'd forgotten that her sisters-in-law had been quietly searching for a husband. She shot a glance at her Mother Elder. Were the Porters here not as a subtle dig at them, but to provide a way to marry Jerin off before Ren could get her sisters' approval?

After dinner they retired to the blue salon. There, Odelia and the Porter sisters vied for Jerin's affection. Ren did not have the heart to press him, so she stood back and watched as Jerin flustered under the close attention. He flashed shy smiles at their compliments and witty remarks, but grew quieter and quieter.

"Jerin's had a long day," Ren finally murmured to Eldest Whistler. "And he's not used to this mobbing. Why not send him up to your suite?"

"I'll take him up."

Ren rested a hand on Eldest Whistler's shoulder to keep her from going. "I'd like to talk to you. Have— can Summer and Corelle take care of him?"

Eldest studied her with ice-blue calm, then nodded. "We should talk."

Good-nights were said, the younger Whistlers went off to their rooms, and Ren led Eldest to her study. Ren poured out brandy, offered good cigars, and then said, "You seem angry at me."

Eldest Whistler spoke slowly, obviously choosing her words carefully. "Shall I say that I was disappointed when I learned what liberties you had taken with my brother?"

"Corelle saw us, then," Ren guessed.

Eldest nodded. "And told the first moment it was useful to her to do so."

"I'm sorry," Ren murmured.

"This sponsoring of Jerin. It's your idea, to make amends?"

"In part." Ren considered and decided. "I love Jerin. It would make me happy to marry him. If I had been born Eldest to another family, I wouldn't have left your farm without a marriage contract."

"But we're too far beneath the princesses of the realm," Eldest said bitterly, almost spitting the word "princesses." "Except for a quick dalliance."

"Perhaps not."

Eldest looked up sharply, and then frowned. "You toy with me."

"No. My first husband was politically a good choice. Keifer was also a spoiled, self-centered, manipulative brat. He played my sisters against one another to get his way. He threw fits, threw food, threw dishes, pouted, cried, and withheld sexual services. The public appearance at the theater was typical of his refusal to listen to common sense."

"I would have spanked him," Eldest murmured.

"I wished my sister had, often. Perhaps she would be alive today." Ren sighed. "Keifer was everything that Jerin is not, including a bloodline that traced back twenty generations. I have asked my mothers to allow a marriage between our families. To be frank, without Prince Alannon's blood, they would have never agreed to consider Jerin. I don't know if it's enough, though, for them to decide in favor of a marriage."

"I see," Eldest Whistler said, face controlled against any emotion that she might have been feeling. A soldier's face. How many generations before that military stamp would breed out?

"My mothers thought it would be unfair to raise your hopes for a royal match," Ren said. "I thought you should know, so you can keep it in mind when the offers for Jerin come in."

A trace of a smile flitted across Eldest's face. "You don't want us to accept any offer before you can make yours."

"Yes."

Eldest stood swirling the brandy in her glass, considering, and finally sighed. "And how long must we wait?"

Ren hesitated before saying, truthfully, "I don't know. I know your family made a good first impression. I know that my mothers are now convinced of your royal bloodline. I know that I love Jerin, and that Odelia is most likely favorable to a match. Lylia is just old enough to marry, and anxious for her wedding night. She'll be swayed by Jerin's beauty alone, I think. Trini suffered at Keifer's hands, and will probably not endorse any man, which my mothers well know. Halley—if she's to be found, if she's alive—she'll be the difficult one to sway; she was not happy with our first marriage."

"So the rumors are true; Princess Halley is missing."

"For months." Ren sighed. "She has never dealt well with the murder of my sisters. At midwinter she said not to worry about her, that she'd be gone for a while, then vanished."

"Can you make an offer without her?"

Ren shook her head. "I don't think I can. Halley is much better Eldest material than I, and so her word carries much weight with my mothers. They might decide to wait for her to reappear."

Eldest Whistler sighed, and was long silent. "We will

let you know of any offers we receive, and give you a
chance to counter them, but we can't wait forever. We
need Jerin's brother's price a week after his birthday.
We've made arrangements to buy the mercantile at
Heron Landing from the Picker sisters, and they've given
us only until then to buy it, else we pay a penalty."

Two months. Ren nodded, feeling sick. Halley had
been gone for eight months. Sixty spare days did not
seem enough time.

"Excuse me," Eldest murmured, "but I should go and
tend my family. They're still unsettled, this being a new
place and all."

"Of course," Ren said. "Good night, Whistler."

"Your Highness." And Eldest Whistler left with a
bow that was hardly more than a nod.

"Gods above, Halley," Ren murmured to the fire.
"Where are you? Are you even still alive?"

Chapter 9

It had been a night of nightmares and Ren jolted awake at dawn. A light rain during the night had dampened the fireplace ashpit, and the ghost of winter fires lingered in the room. Ren tumbled from her bed still half asleep and flung open the windows. After a couple of deep breaths of clear summer morning air, she sat on the window seat, staring as the sun turned the river molten, letting the glitter fill her eyes and blot out the night images. Her nightmare had been twisted by fears of losing Jerin. Halley was missing in a burning building, while the dwarflike shopkeepers from Heron Landing were carrying Jerin off to marry a stranger. No, it wasn't difficult to tell what had triggered her nightmare.

Where had Halley gone? More importantly, how could they get her back in time?

While Halley hadn't said where she was going, it hadn't been hard to guess why she left. More than any of them, Halley had been marked body and soul by the explosion that killed their sisters and husband.

Typical of Odelia's luck, Odelia had not gone to the theater that night. Ren could never remember why, except a hazy notion that it came as punishment for some small crime. Trini, fortunately, had not gone either—she was still recovering from Keifer's unnaturally vicious treatment of her. Lylia and the youngest sisters, of course, were too young to take to the theater. With their husband, Keifer, all ten oldest princesses, however, and two of the middle princesses made a rare appearance at a public performance.

After six years, odd memories remained crystal clear. A virgin layer of snow had covered the city, not yet touched by the omnipresent soot of deep winter. They arrived late, delayed by another fit of anger from Keifer, and the great arching windows sent pillars of light into the night. Ren and Halley came through the doors a step behind Lieutenant Raven, and the music struck them all of a sudden, as if they had been deaf up to that moment. Behind them, Eldest ignored Raven's older sister Hawk as she explained that they hadn't vetted the building yet due to the sudden plans and pleaded for the royal family to wait in the coaches. They swept up the stairs to the Porters' private box, where a handful of ancient Porter mothers already waited. In the next box over, their middle Moorland cousins acknowledged the princesses with slightly cool nods—they were still angry with Keifer for slapping Cullen.

The opera was *Barren Winter,* which had been banned for two generations. The princesses settled into the Porters' box as the opera's opening lines reminded the audience that Ren's great-grandmothers had split their royal daughters into two families. Ren's grandmothers married Michael and took rule of Queensland. The younger sisters took Rafael as a husband and were given the newly annexed island of Southland to rule.

Ren started out bored. She knew the story well, the events having triggered the War of the False Eldest, and the repetitive nature of the lyrics annoyed her. Ann Kinsen, however, gave a brilliant performance as Michael, her powerful alto sweeping Ren up in the story of a man's sterility destroying his family and country. As the younger sisters grew more strident in their demands that their children be considered heirs of the childless elder sisters, the more tortured Michael became by his affliction.

It was Queen Titia, however, who made the opera

painfully real and personal. Nana Titia had been a woman forever undecided. To wear the red shawl or the blue one. To sit next to the fire, or near the lamp. To take the fish, or eat the lamb. She wavered on the smallest of details, always with a twittering laugh to cover her awareness of her own weakness.

There on the stage, with her embarrassed polite laugh, Titia dithered about delivering a secret offer to share a noble husband, an option that would have saved Eldest from visiting the disease-ridden cribs in a desperate attempt to produce an heir. Titia hesitated when action would have prevented pregnant Beatrice's murder and thus the entire war. She wavered as Michael begged for divorce, which would have allowed him to escape the sense of responsibility for the growing tragedy that ultimately led to his suicide. She vacillated instead of stopping Cida's bloody revenge at the war's end, letting their imprisoned youngest sisters and nieces—including the infants—to be beheaded in one gory afternoon. With a downcast look and a soft laugh, she refused to make any decision that would have saved her sisters, her husband, and a full score of innocent children—girls that could have been Ren's mothers if they had lived.

In a stunned moment, Ren realized that the true source of tragedy hadn't been Michael's sterility, but Titia's indecision. Ren thought of her nana, how rarely she smiled, how she often stared out the windows of the palace crying, how she lived into her nineties knowing she destroyed almost everything she loved. For her poor heartbroken nana, for the grandmothers she never knew, for her might-have-been mothers that had been killed in anger, Ren wept.

Ren's elder sisters and husband heard her crying. They shot cold looks at her—silent orders for her to cease her sobbing. Finally, Keifer leaned against Eldest and whispered his displeasure. A hard look, a flick of his fingers, and she was bundled up to be taken home.

Oh, she hated them so that night, for not weeping, for

not being touched by this horrible tragedy that happened to *their* family, for scolding her with their silent disapproval, for sending her home like a screaming infant. She stood on the front steps, weeping openly now, waiting with a guard for the royal coach to be brought around.

She would get back at them somehow. She would make them pay. Only Halley would she spare, for Halley followed her outside to find out why she was crying.

"They should have spared the children," Ren said as she took the handkerchief that Halley offered. "If they hadn't split the family, those would have been their own children that they killed. The children would have been our mothers."

"Their mothers and father had been executed." Halley scowled at her. "Do you think you could take that hatred to suckle at your breast?"

"They had done nothing wrong!"

"If we had aunts that executed our mothers for fighting over a just cause, would we calmly accept them as our new mothers, or would we rebel?"

"Merrilee was just seven months old."

"And Livi was seven, and Wren was seventeen. Which ones do you spare? Where do you draw the line?"

"It wasn't right," Ren insisted, hunching her shoulders.

They fell into silence, recognizing that they couldn't agree on this issue. It snowed in huge, slowly drifting clumps, like goose down falling to earth. The coach appeared at the corner. Halley nodded to her and started back up the stairs.

At the theater door Halley stopped, and bluntly announced, "I hate him."

"So do I." Ren knew she meant Keifer.

"I don't want to be married to him."

Ren scoffed, "We don't have a choice. The royal family is never going to split, not after last time."

Halley glared at her.

In the silence between them rose Michael's poignant aria lamenting the death of innocent children.

There was a muffled noise, like a distant cannon being fired. Then a roar of noise and light whiting out her senses as the explosion smashed Ren down the steps. She landed in slush, bitter cold on her face and hands, flames already furnace-hot across her back.

Six years later, a memory, broken free by her nightmares, suddenly surfaced. The moment before the explosion, Halley broke the silence and said with heartfelt spite, "I wish Keifer was dead."

The murder of their sisters held them all prisoner. Trini wore the scars of Keifer's cruelty as if they were still fresh. Lylia rushed to be an adult, to fill the void that their sisters' deaths created. Odelia retreated in the opposite direction, trying to dodge the responsibility that made them targets. Ren resisted all suggestions of marriage—until she met Jerin.

Halley, though, had been consumed. She abandoned everything to find their sisters' killers. It had mystified them all, the way she devoted herself to the search.

Sitting on the window seat, trying to forget her nightmare, Ren remembered Halley's last words, and realized the truth. Halley'd wished Keifer dead, and in that instant, he died—and with him, all their sisters.

Halley was searching for someone other than herself to blame.

"You're thinking of the bombing." Raven had knocked, and entered at Ren's call, finding her on the window seat, still stunned by the insight to Halley's soul.

"Yes. I think I finally realized why Halley vanished."

"Any idea as to *where*?"

Ren shook her head. "No, and if I'm going to offer for Jerin, I need to find her soon."

Raven looked pessimistic. "I have been searching for her, discreetly, not that any of my people could bring her home against her will if they found her."

Ren snarled a curse, getting up to cross the room to the washbasin. "I can't offer for Jerin without Halley. I can't put word out to Halley that I need her back to make an offer; if I did, the world would know."

"It might be the only thing to make her surface."

The newspaper story of the attack on Odelia should have brought her running. Ren could think of only one reason why Halley hadn't reappeared when Odelia was wounded.

"It would add fuel to fire the rumors about her." Ren splashed cold water onto her face; it dampened old tears that burned anew. She leaned over the bowl, water dripping from her face, blinking away the salt fire in her eyes. "Plus our enemies will then know that she is traveling without royal guard."

Raven held out the hand towel. "I'll set more people on finding her. Quietly."

Ren scrubbed dry her face. "Would it put you short on finding the Prophets?"

"Oh, yes, the cannons. We found the ship they used to transport them from Heron Landing. The *Onward*. The cannons were unloaded, here in Mayfair, the night before we arrived."

Ren started to smile, then remembered Raven's theory on how they could find the ship. "The crew is dead?"

"The thieves included two kegs of ale, heavily laced with arsenic, with their payment. The captain and eight of her sisters are dead. Six more are not expected to live."

Ren jolted at the name of the poison. "Did any survive to talk?"

"None that interacted with the thieves directly," Raven said. "Those who did survive told us the captain was hired in Heron Landing to pick up ten heavy crates downriver, and give passage to the gentry family riding herd on the cargo."

"What made them think the women were gentry?"

"Cut of the clothes they wore, the way they talked. There were eight to ten of them in their late teens and twenties, fair of coloring, average height and weight."

So the cannons were here nearly ten days ago. Most of the witnesses were dead. Dozens of ships had come and gone during that time.

"So our haystack grows again."

"They only had a few hours to hide the cannons before my orders to check all incoming and outgoing cargo arrived in Mayfair. There's hope we can run them to ground. We also have a lead."

Raven reached into her vest pocket and pulled out a folded piece of paper. It was a leaf of common foolscap, cheap in quality, the fool grinning at her in the watermark. With a light hand, someone had covered one side of the paper with pencil shading, revealing a series of crude pictures marching across the paper like letters.

"What's this?"

"A trick I picked up. If someone has written on the top sheet of a pile of papers, the next sheet down retains an impression of the writing. You can capture the impression by shading the page with a graphite pencil." Raven grinned smugly. "The drawings are written thieves' cant. Apparently the thieves wanted the cannons elsewhere. During the trip, they tried to talk the captain into changing the scheduled stops and couldn't. They also tried to hire the ship out once they arrived at Mayfair, but didn't want to wait for the two-day layover that the *Onward* had planned. They borrowed paper to write out this note and sent it by runner. A short time later a woman showed up with some roustabouts and wagons to unload the cannons. Lucky for us, the gentry returned the unused paper."

Ren gazed at the crude drawings. "Can you read it?"

Raven's mouth gathered into a chagrined smile. "No.

I'm trying to track down someone who can read it and yet would be unlikely to be involved in this case. I don't want to tip off our thieves."

Ren stripped out of her sleeping shirt and started to dress in the clothes laid out for her. The idea of waiting chafed. The longer they waited, the less chance they had of finding these murderers. She was buttoning her slacks when an idea came to her. "I wonder—do you think the Whistlers still know their thieves' cant?"

Raven shrugged. "Can't hurt to ask."

Eldest Whistler nodded through their explanation as she wordlessly studied the paper. When it was clear that they had no more to say, she shook her head. "It isn't cant. It looks like cant, but it isn't."

"Are you sure?" Raven tapped a square with two wheel-like circles at the bottom of it. "This is *wagon*. Everyone knows that much cant."

"Yes, that's *wagon*." Eldest went on to name a few other words that even Ren could make out just by the pictures. "There's lots of commonly known cant in it, but the rest—it's like someone made up pictures for the words they didn't know."

"Are you sure the cant hasn't changed since your grandmothers knew it?" Ren asked, since it had been over fifty years since the Whistlers were part of the Sisters of the Night.

Eldest shook her head. "The Sisterhood assumes that anyone can learn enough cant to fake a message, so cant has a second level which acts like a security check. There are things like the number of pictures per line, and a certain set of words that have to appear at least once in the message. Sometimes there's a series of items listed—like five gil, two pistols, and seven quinces—where the items aren't important, only that all but the last number add up to the last number. Five and two are seven. Written cant started out as a way to communicate with illiterate members of the Sisterhood, but it evolved into a means to do business without having to worry about the authenticity of the message."

"So someone is throwing suspicion on the Sisters of the Night."

"Or just stealing a good idea," Eldest said. "Part of this is a set of directions on where to take the cargo. Mill on Dunning Street. I can't read the rest, though this part might be a woman's cant name: Black Hat."

Eldest Whistler and Corelle volunteered to join Ren in the pursuit of the cannons, reclaiming their weapons with great enthusiasm. As they rode down off the palace's high bluff, listening to Raven outline her plan to storm the mill, however, their eagerness faded into distaste.

"If it's not to your satisfaction, Whistler," Raven finally said in her blunt way, "what would you suggest?"

Eldest shot the captain a cold look, and then shrugged. "You're doing the best with what you have. Troops, though, are best for fighting big noisy wars on battlefields. Hours before you manage to push those troops through city traffic, the thieves are going to know you're coming. Not only could this get very messy, but there's a chance they could slip the cannons out in the confusion."

"And?" Raven said with the air of not hearing anything she didn't know.

Eldest shrugged again. "If you had a smaller force of women, doing what my grandmothers did under Wellsbury, they could move through the West End without notice, scout the mill, and take out the thieves with much less fuss."

"Unfortunately, I don't have such a force," Raven said. "Your grandmothers were singular in their training."

"Not quite. They trained us."

Ren saw where this was going and started to shake her head. "No, I'm not going to put you at risk! These women have killed everyone who has crossed their path." *Jerin would hate me if I got you two killed.*

"And there's only two of you," Raven added. "The reports put twenty roustabouts in the employ of ten gentry. You would need a miracle to eliminate that many by yourselves."

Eldest shook her head. "I wasn't talking about taking them out. We could scout the mill, find out what your troops will be marching into, and make sure the Prophets aren't slipped out."

"Your Highness?" Raven turned to Ren with a clear look of "They will be your sisters-in-law."

"Whistler honor." Eldest held up her hand in pledge. "We won't run unnecessary risks. We'll be fine."

How could Ren keep them safe and yet keep them as equals? In truth, she couldn't do both. And equals they had to be in her eyes or there would be no hope of the Whistlers being considered peers by the nobility. She would release a noblewoman on her word of honor, and so she must let the Whistlers take their risks.

"I seal you to your word—no unnecessary risks."

Ren worried as they rode to the barracks, gathered the troops, and marched them into the city with the rattle of drums and the incessant call of "Make way! Make way!" The narrow city streets required the column to be four abreast, twenty-five rows stringing out to create a scarlet centipede stamping its way through West End. A narcissistic young lieutenant by the name of Cowley rode at the head of the column on a showy white mare. Raven kept shadow-close to Ren and her guard in the rear.

Many of West End's streets were meandering tracks, following what once were footpaths through a wood of live oaks. Dunning Street, however, turned out to be a long straightaway, narrowing slowly in degrees, ending at the doors of the mill.

Ren scanned the crowds of onlookers as they made their way down the street, looking for the Whistlers. What had happened to them?

Cowley called for a halt, and the drums rattled and

dropped silent. Over the heads of the infantry women, Ren could see Cowley dismount to try the tall, wide mill doors. The lieutenant obviously found them locked as she moved off to one side and motioned the first rank in position to force them open.

Suddenly gunshots, muffled by the walls of the mill and distance, echoed up the street. A single shot, then a score, sounding like a string of firecrackers.

The women in the front line ducked out of habit, but didn't move to return fire—obviously the shots weren't aimed at them.

The Whistlers! Ren cursed hotly. "Get the door open! Get inside!"

The shooting continued as Cowley barked out orders and the second line crowded up beside the first, shoulders to the door. The drummer took up a beat to coordinate their efforts.

Come on! Come on!

A long sharp whistle from a nearby rooftop caught Ren's attention. She glanced up and saw Eldest Whistler crouched beside a chimney. Eldest pointed down the street to the doors, shouting something unheard over the wind and the rattle of the drum. She made a hard chopping motion with her hand, made a fist, and let it fly open, then pointed urgently to the shop door beside Ren. She started to repeat the whole sequence when Ren recognized the first hand signal.

Trap!

But what kind of trap did you lay for an army? Ren gasped as the second signal became clear. Grapeshot! The thieves had the cannons loaded with grapeshot and pointed them down the street.

"Ambush!" Ren shouted, throwing herself off her horse. "Get to cover!"

"Take cover!" Raven repeated, though it wasn't clear if she had seen Eldest herself or just took up the cry. "Take cover!"

There was a muffled thud and a flash of fire from the

mouth of the street. Out of the corner of her eye as she raced for the shop door, Ren saw the mill doors flying outward on a plume of fire, blown off by small explosives set at their hinges. Flame and smoke engulfed Cowley and the front line, as the great doors skipped and jumped down the street on the force of the explosion.

The tableau beyond the blasted doorway stamped itself on Ren's vision. Two cannons, the cyclopean eyes of their barrels pointed straight down the street, sat in temporary cradles behind a wall of sandbags. Like so many cornered river rats, twenty women in dirty ragged clothes crouched around the cannons, two already lowering the burning wand of a fuse lighter.

"Take cover!" Raven shouted again, somewhere behind Ren.

The cannons roared, spitting out flame and screaming grapeshot.

Ren flung herself through the shop door. She had an instant impression of heat and fresh bread—it was a bakery. Then, through the open door behind her, like a sharp hailstorm of death, the grapeshot blasted up the street, shredding everything in its path. Women shouted in horror and screamed in pain; some of their cries cutting off abruptly. The abandoned horses went down, great bloody slashes laying them open.

And then there was silence.

"Return fire!" Ren shouted, scrambling back to the shop door, hoping that someone was alive to hear her. "Stop the next volley! Return fire!"

The street reeked of blood and viscera. Her troops had tucked themselves into every alcove and doorway. Her yelled commands shook them out of their shell shock, and they returned fire in a thunderous volley.

Where the hell is Raven? Has she been killed?

Half the thieves were reloading the cannons, ignoring the rain of bullets, while the other half kept the royal troops at bay. If they managed to reload and fire, her troops would be cut to ribbons.

"Set bayonets and charge! Engage in hand-to-hand!" Ren shouted, working her way down the street from niche to niche, tearing her voice ragged in an attempt to be heard. "Charge!"

They heard her and obeyed, probably out of fear of facing the cannons once more. More than half her women lay dead in the street, but the remaining ones surged forward. Forty trained soldiers against fewer than twenty river trash. The fight was bloody but quick.

Silence fell again, broken only by the moans of the wounded.

"Take a horse," Ren said to a private, a young girl who looked barely sixteen. "Return to the barracks. Tell the commander we need wagons for the wounded, and more troops to clean up this mess."

The girl nodded repeatedly, eyes wide, as if she had seen too much today.

Ren set the remaining survivors to searching for the cannons and thieves. She also gave them descriptions of the Whistlers and instructions that they shouldn't be harmed. Raven still hadn't made an appearance, so Ren stumbled back up the street, heartsick, looking for the captain's body among the dead. Her other bodyguards had been from the palace guard, a rotating handful from nearly two hundred women. Raven, though, had been with her for over ten years, had been there on the night of the explosion, had been her captain since that night. To lose Raven would be like losing a sister.

She made it back to the bakery shop without a sign of her captain.

"Hoy! Princess."

Ren looked up at the call and found Corelle Whistler, leaning against the doorway of the bakery, splattered with blood, looking pale but smug. "Corelle!" Ren cried. "Where's Eldest? Have you seen Raven?"

"We found the captain out cold. Eldest is patching her up. I'm afraid that any others you're missing are dead."

Ren nodded, too relieved to care now. She'd mourn

later. She brushed past Corelle, anxious to see Raven with her own eyes.

"You're alive," Eldest said, glancing up when Ren entered. Raven slumped in a wooden armchair, face pale under a stain of blood, eyes closed, coat off, and blood-soaked shirtsleeve cut away. A strip of white bandaging was wrapped about her temple, a spot of red growing on it as Ren watched with concern. "We thought with so many trigger-happy regulars, we should keep out from underfoot."

"How is she?" Ren asked, torn between staying out of Eldest's way and wanting to reassure herself with a touch.

"I'm not sure." Eldest mummified Raven's shoulder, her hands and the bandaging blood-tainted from Raven's wound. "I don't have my grandmothers' experience with battle wounds. Head wounds always bleed a lot, and the shoulder looks shallow to me. You'll want someone who knows what they're doing to look at her, though."

"I'm—I'm fine," Raven muttered, her eyes fluttering open. She eyed the shop as if seeing it for the first time. "Ren, Your Highness, were you hit?"

"No." Ren reached out to grip Raven's unhurt shoulder. "I'm fine." She thought then to inspect the Whistlers. They looked as if they had been dragged down a bloody street behind a wagon, but there were no visible bullet wounds. "Thanks for the warning. Are you two all right? What happened? We heard shots."

"It's why we came along." Eldest shrugged, then looked sheepish. "We had worked our way into the mill. When we realized they were laying a trap for you and tried to pull out, they spotted us. It might have been trickier for us if your people hadn't started beating on the doors. It kind of spooked them."

"What happened with the cannons?" Raven asked.

"There were only the two to be seen," Eldest explained. "But the others might still be in the city. They had coal wagons and buckets of coal. I think they were loading cannons on the wagons, then spreading coal on top of the cannons. It's an old trick."

Raven started to nod, and then winced. She reached up with trembling fingers to explore her bandage, but Eldest caught her hand before she could.

"Eh, eh," Eldest scolded. "It's almost stopped bleeding. Touch it, and you'll start it going again." After she was sure Raven listened to her, Eldest continued her story. "There were five door guards and fifteen more women inside playing cards, sleeping, and waiting. There were three women that seemed to be running things: walking rounds to the guards, keeping the others quiet, and such. Soon after we heard the drums start, two gentry rode up."

"Gentry?" Ren asked.

"They were all spit and polish," Corelle said. "High boots, tan leather riding britches, and broadcloth coats, neat as new. The three in charge all bowed and said 'yes, madam' to them."

Eldest nodded. "As Corelle said, nothing flashy but good-quality riding clothes, both about five foot seven, maybe about fourteen stones. Same build, same walk, like they were sisters. They rode up on bloodstock, a trim bay mare with four white socks, and a black mare."

"They wore executioner's hoods," Corelle added. "One in black silk and the other in red."

"They were still adjusting the hoods, so they must have pulled them on just as they rode up, before we noticed them," Eldest said. "They came in snapping orders, not like they were scared, just in a hurry. At first I didn't see the rhyme and reason to what they were doing." Eldest frowned, apparently angry at her own lack of understanding. "And then you were nearly on the street and we were hemmed in. We backed out quietly as we could, but they spotted us and we exchanged fire."

Ren offered up a prayer of thanks that neither one of them had been killed.

"I hit the one with the red hood," Corelle boasted. "Grandmas told us to always aim for the commanders—you do more damage per bullet that way. I think I nailed her fairly good."

"Remind me to keep you on our side," Raven said dryly.

Ren leaned outside and called one of the troops to her. "Spread the word. One of the wounded or dead thieves was wearing a red executioner's hood. I want her found."

The soldier saluted and hurried off. The Whistlers continued recounting their adventure, in greater detail. They had found the doors all guarded, but found a broken, unguarded window on the second story. They had moved quietly to a place where they could view the thieves. When the gentry arrived, the action shifted to in front of the doors, out of sight from their original position.

Telling Corelle to stay put, Eldest had worked around to where she could see them.

"Even then, there was a wagon blocking my view of the cannons themselves, or I would have figged to their plans immediately. When I heard them discussing the grapeshot, I realized it was a trap." Eldest's eyes went winter cold. "We'd given you our word not to take them on single-handed, or I would have tried to nail them. It felt wrong to just cut and run."

Corelle took over the explanation. "They spotted Eldest and started to shoot. I laid down some cover for her, taking out one of the commanders to throw them into confusion. After she was clear, I made myself scarce."

Eldest put out a hand and squeezed her sister's shoulder. "You did good." She turned back to Ren. "I came across the rooftops to warn you, Highness. I wish we could have done more."

"You saved myself and a goodly number of my women," Ren said. "Thank you both."

A soldier appeared at the door with the news that the dead red-hooded thief had been found.

The woman wasn't lying where she had been hit. A trail of heel marks and blood showed where she had been dragged to a back corner of the mill, beside a trapdoor. The red silk executioner's hood had been peeled back, revealing a smashed pulp of flesh and bone framed by short gold curls. A fist-sized hole had been punched through her chest, leaving her fine clothes a soggy red mass of cloth. Her silk-lined pockets were turned inside out, coins littering the ground like bright tears.

Eldest shifted the woman onto her side, grunting at the deadweight. A small neat hole marked the entrance of the bullet that had caused the massive chest wound. "She was shot in the back, then in the face."

"I hit her in the back," Corelle said, and then added defensively, "She was facing away from me, shooting at Eldest."

"You did right," Raven murmured.

"She was shot in the face so she couldn't be recognized," Ren growled. "Her sister searched her pockets, left the money, but took anything that would reveal her identity."

Eldest examined the trapdoor, then, satisfied that it was safe, flipped it up. A short drop into gurgling darkness. "Access to the river."

"So it's a dead end," Corelle grumbled.

"Well, depends." Eldest shrugged. "A dead sister is something. We hurt them, if nothing else." Eldest glanced at Ren. "How long do you think a noble family could disguise the fact they're down by one?"

"Forever," Ren muttered, rubbing the bridge of her nose. "Most families have shipping interests. They could say their missing sister is taking a prolonged trip until she's lost at sea."

Chapter 10

It had been a fine morning for Jerin, one with the dawn sun pouring rich golden light into the yellow silk parlor. A youngest Barnes brought a tray of hot melted chocolate, triangles of toasted bread anointed with fresh butter and little cups of fruit jams, and the promise of another bath. Jerin rose from his feathered bed with silk-soft sheets, sat in the sunshine, ate of a breakfast he hadn't prepared, and felt royally pampered.

Did nobles live every day of their life like this? Did they wake like him, reveling in the comfort? Did it fade in time? Perhaps, he considered, if they lived their whole life this way, they couldn't find the same level of pleasure in it. Surely you had to get up at dawn and cook for forty people to realize the luxury of having the food brought to you.

Barnes came to the door then, saying Princess Rennsellaer wished an audience with Eldest Whistler. Eldest returned a short time later for Corelle, saying that they were riding out with Ren. Summer followed them out into the hall for a short murmured conversation about their plans.

Jerin had raised a cup to his mouth, unconcerned, when thoughts came together in his mind. The royal summons. The cannon thieves leaving a trail of dead behind them. His sister suddenly keeping things from him.

A cloud passed in front of the sun, and he lowered the teacup as the shadow slid over him.

Summer came in quietly, avoiding his eyes.

"Where are they going?" Jerin put the cup down harder than he intended.

"Just out for a ride. Princess Rennsellaer thought they would enjoy a ride," Summer said too lightly, too quickly. "The tailors will be here shortly."

Summer was a terrible liar. Jerin wished, for once, she was better at it. Since she had obviously been instructed not to tell him, it would have been more comforting if he had been able to believe her.

The tailors arrived. While they pinned and poked, Summer stood at the window, looking out over the city. Shortly before lunch, there was an odd double clap of thunder.

"Is it going to rain?" the eldest tailor asked, frowning in concern at the window, where clouds raced on the wind.

Summer turned toward her, an odd expression on her face. "Perhaps."

"I hope not. Rain would ruin this fabric," the tailor muttered around a mouth of silver pins.

Thunder or cannons? Jerin stepped off the fitting stool and toward the window, only to be stabbed by a thousand tiny sharp prickles as the tailor cried out in shrill dismay.

"No, no, no!" The tailor pushed him back, losing her mouth of pins. "Stay put! This fabric costs a fortune, so we must be right the first time."

"A fortune?" He froze in place, his voice breaking in nervousness. He lifted an arm draped with the flimsy, shimmering cobalt blue fabric. It was like being wrapped in cool air and nothing else.

"A crown a yard." She gathered up the dropped pins, tucking them between her lips again. "Now," she murmured, "stand still."

Summer paced for the rest of the fitting session, stopping often to look out over the city. When the tailors finished, she impatiently herded them out.

"What is it?" Finally free, Jerin hurried to the window. All of the city was laid out below them, running to the river, an endless jumble of buildings cut by streets seething with people. "Was it the cannons? What did you see?"

"Nothing," Summer said, pulling on her coat.

"Where are you going? What did you see?"

"Nothing, Jerin, just nothing. I'm going out. I'll be back shortly. You lock the door after me and let no one in, understand? No one."

"What do I do if someone tries to break in?"

"Ring for help." Summer opened the door.

"What if one of the Barneses is the one trying to break in?"

Summer stopped with a cry of anger and frustration. "Barnes isn't going to break in! They're the Queens' most trusted servants. Just lock the door and ring if there's trouble!"

Summer fled. Jerin threw the bolt with trembling hands and went back to stare down at the city. What had happened? What had Summer seen? He scanned the city, still unable to pick out what had set his sister racing out of the room. Frowning, he tried a more methodical search, slowly examining the city block by block, moving east to west. Time stopped as he pressed against the glass, searching without knowing what he looked for.

There was a slight noise from his sisters' bedroom. At first he ignored it; then, with a spike of cold fear, he realized he was supposed to be alone. He turned and saw a shadow, cast from his sisters' window, on the floor of the parlor—the outline of someone climbing through the window. He snatched up the fireplace poker, hefting it high, and edged sideways toward the bellpull.

The path to the bellpull, however, took him in front

of the bedroom door. He saw, for the first time, that it was a boy climbing through the window. Jerin froze, confused.

The boy looked about sixteen, with dirty blond hair and square, plain features. While cut from fine cloth, his light woolen kilt of green was gathered high about his waist with a horse-blanket pin. One knee bled slightly, while the other sported a scab from previous outings. He started at seeing Jerin, his green eyes going wide in surprise. "Oh! There you are! You gave me a start! Quick, hide me!"

Jerin considered. If a strange woman appeared in his quarters, he knew what to do: flee, fight, or shout for help. But what about a strange man? The boy seemed to lack any malice, and Jerin hadn't seen another man outside his family since the harvest fair. "Um, you can hide in—in my room."

The boy needed no further directions. He beamed a happy "Thanks!" and darted off to Jerin's bedroom. Jerin returned the poker to the fireplace and followed, still confused but now unalarmed.

"What are you running from?" Jerin asked.

"My sisters. Stupid rules. Complete and total boredom." The boy threw himself onto Jerin's bed. " 'Sit up straight. Smile. Don't sit with your legs open. Don't slouch. Don't talk. Don't think.' I'm bored, and lonely, and now I'm whining. Sorry."

"I don't mind," Jerin said. "I didn't know there was another man in the palace."

"We got in last night. The Queens invited us to stay. I think to give you someone to show you the ropes without getting your sisters' hackles raised. But, of course, every time I asked when we were going to meet, it's 'later,' and 'in good time' and 'when there's time.' All I have is time! I've been sitting sewing wedding linens all morning, with tiny invisible stitches, and no one even offered for me yet."

"And you are?"

"Cullen Moorland." A brilliant smile. "I'm the Queens' nephew."

Jerin considered what he knew of the royal family. "I didn't think the Queens had a brother."

Cullen laughed. "You don't know who I am? I'm hurt! But I forgive you, since you don't know better. My mothers are—were sisters to the Queens' consort, the princesses' father. We're old blood, very tah, tah and all that, but we didn't have much clout until the royal wedding brought us up in the world. Got anything to eat?"

"We could ring for tea," Jerin stated, and then marveled at how naturally it came to him, as if he always had tea delivered at the ring of a bellpull.

"Then they'll know I'm here."

"And you shouldn't be?"

"Oh, it's just that it's more fun them not knowing. It makes being here feel like I'm doing what I shouldn't be doing." Cullen took a deep breath. "The air even smells better when I decide where to be."

"You could stay in here when the tray comes."

Cullen flashed another brilliant smile. "You're a great gun! Ring away."

Jerin went back to the parlor and pulled the bell cord. A tap on the door announced a Barnes sister. Jerin unbarred the door and asked for a tea tray, adding that he felt very hungry, and that his sisters might return in time to join him, so could she make it a generous tray with at least four sets of cups? The Barnes youngest nodded, impassive as always. Was she totally unaware of Cullen, or was she humoring Jerin like a child?

When Jerin returned to his bedroom, he found Cullen kneeling beside the nightstand, jiggling the open drawer.

"This is the best suite in the palace." Cullen lifted out the drawer and set it on the bed. "We usually have it when we stay here. It put my sisters' noses out of joint to find you were put up here instead. I don't know why—we've had to give it up before. A case of speaking before thinking, to be sure."

Cullen reached into the empty drawer hole and fished out a bundle of papers. "My secret stash. Look at these."

Still kneeling beside the bed, he untied the bundle and spread seven tintypes out onto the bedspread.

Jerin looked at the pictures, then looked quickly away, blushing. "Where did you get those?"

"Lylia gave them to me. Of course my sisters would have a fit if they knew she was corrupting me."

Jerrin frowned. He thought at first Lylia was one of Cullen's sisters, but now it didn't sound like it. Who else would have access to a noble male? A servant? "Who's Lylia?"

"Gosh, you are an innocent! My cousin, Her Royal Highness, Lylia." Cullen rooted two cigars out of his bundle and handed one to Jerin. "She doesn't see the point of keeping boys ignorant. Accident of birth does not make us less human or less intelligent. We've got a vow that whichever of us has sex first, we'll tell the other everything. One time"—he dropped his voice to a whisper—"we practiced kissing." He shrugged, propping one elbow on the bed and resting his chin in the palm. "But it was like kissing your sister. Well, your *own* sister. I'm sure kissing *your* sister wouldn't be the same."

Kissing Lylia's sister certainly hadn't been the same. Jerin picked up one of the tintypes and found himself burning with embarrassment. He had done the pictured act with Ren.

Cullen put a finger on the top of the picture and tipped it down so he could see. "I always wonder why you would want to put your mouth there."

Luckily, there was a knock on the door. Cullen dived down behind the bed. Jerin dashed toward the door, slammed to a stop halfway, ran back, and swept the pictures from the bed to snow down on Cullen. He ran back and jerked the door open. The Barnes sister stood with the tea cart.

It wasn't until Jerin barred the door after the Barnes

had left that he realized that he had the cigar still in hand. He collapsed into the chair beside the cart, giggling. "You can come out."

Cullen peeked over the edge of the bed. "What are you laughing about?"

Jerin waved the cigar. "I forgot about this."

Cullen laughed and vanished behind the bed. "One last thing." He popped up holding a bottle. "Wine!"

"Lylia?"

Cullen nodded, breaking the seal. "A truer cousin is not to be found." He produced a cork puller and fumbled through the opening of the bottle. He made a show of splashing wine into the dainty teacups. "A toast! To Lylia!"

"Lylia." Jerin picked up the cup and raised it high.

"And to our friendship, may our sisters allow it to prosper!"

The tea had come with sandwiches of roast turkey with spiced mustard, slices of chilled cucumber in a dill vinaigrette, and raspberry tarts.

They talked as they ate, sounding out each other. They compared sisters first. Cullen had far fewer in number, partly due to an outbreak of yellow fever. His father, a young brother-in-law, and five out of ten elder sisters died then. His middle sisters died in the same blast that killed the princesses. His youngest sisters ranged from late teens to early twenties, making Cullen the baby of the Moorland family.

"Actually, I was born after my father died," Cullen admitted. "My mothers married him in the olden days, when men were only thirteen when they wed, something they thank the gods about every chance they get, since he died so young. Personally, I'm glad I didn't have to act the blood stallion at thirteen. What?"

Jerin had bitten his tongue on the news that his Mother Elder would also bear a child after his father had died. It would be unlucky to talk about that before the baby was born. Cullen still looked at him, so he volunteered a different family secret. "I have three younger brothers."

Cullen's eyes went wide. "You're joshing! Four boys?"

Jerin nodded, slightly embarrassed by Cullen's impressed reaction. He, himself, had done nothing toward the feat except be born.

"What's it like," Cullen asked, "having other men in the house?"

Jerin had never considered this. "It's—nice. A lot of time, it's no different than having girls around. Well, at least with my little brothers, except everyone's more careful with them. I loved it when my father was alive. He had to shave his face with a razor every day, or he would grow whiskers. His voice was deep; when he was in another room, he rumbled like a distant storm. He was always patient, but he never talked to me like I was a child, like my elder sisters do. He would say, 'You're almost a full-grown man. You need to act like it.' He told me all sorts of stuff about being married, like how to make sure your wives aren't jealous of each other."

"How?" Cullen asked, his eyes bright with curiosity.

"Well, you never tell any of them that they're your favorite, even if they are. He said you should always try to act equally happy to be with any one of them, and to always stick to a service schedule, Eldest to youngest, without skipping anyone for any reason."

"Ugh. That doesn't sound like fun. What if that night's wife is sick?"

"Wait a day and sleep alone," Jerin said after a moment of recalling his father's advice. "Father was a youngest child, and his elder sisters married a man who was obvious in which wives he liked the most. It caused all sorts of fighting between the sisters. One sister even left to join the Sisters of Hera."

"Sounds like Keifer, only Keifer kept changing his mind."

Jerin's heart skipped a beat at the mention of Ren's dead husband. "What was he like?"

"Keifer? Oh, I hated him. He used to lie to me and make me cry. I was only nine or ten at the time. He told me that my you-know-what would fall off because I ate too many cookies. Then one day he smacked me, I forget why—actually, I'm not sure there was even a reason why—but we didn't come back to the palace again until after he was killed."

"Oh." Jerin fiddled with a raspberry tart, saddened that Ren had had such a terrible marriage. At least she was out of it, able to marry someone better for her and Odelia and the others.

Cullen chattered on. "I suppose, though, he wasn't any older than we are now. You know, I don't feel old enough to get married and father children."

"My father said you never feel old enough."

"Oh, rats."

The conversation drifted off onto other subjects. Neither one of them liked to sew, or had any interest in clothes. However, they shared a love of horses. Jerin made the mistake of complaining that his sister would let him ride only the older, gentler mares who rarely would do anything more than a easy canter.

"They let you ride! Good gods, Jerin, I would kill to be able to ride! My family won't let me near horses. I had some great-great-grandfart that got kicked in the head and died. Lylia will sneak me out to the stable, but even she won't let me do more than pet them over the stable wall."

There was a bang at the door, followed by Eldest calling, "Jerin? Jerin? Come open the door!"

Jerin jerked up in surprise, and then all the worry he felt earlier came flooding back, chased by guilt that he'd forgotten about his fears. He rushed the door, unbolted it, and flung it open without a thought about Cullen. His sisters stood waiting in the hall—Eldest and Corelle in strange ill-fitting clothes for some reason—safe and sound. With a cry of happiness, he hugged Eldest.

"Where have you been?" he asked. "What happened to you?"

"Nothing happened," Eldest laughed, lifting him up in a bear hug and walking him back through the doors.

"Then what happened to your clothes?"

He had never seen Eldest blush before.

"You've been pinched!" Summer grinned at Eldest, using the cant word for "discovered" or "apprehended." Jerin wondered what he'd caught Eldest doing, and why it had been necessary for her and Corelle to change their clothes. Summer's smile faded as she spotted the table set with four cups and a host of dirty plates. "Jerin, who did you have tea with?"

Eldest came to attention, moving Jerin behind her as she put him down. "You're not alone?"

"Ummm." Jerin peered over Eldest's shoulder to discover the parlor was empty. "Cullen?"

For a moment, he thought maybe Cullen had climbed back out the window. Then Cullen peeked around the doorway of Jerin's bedroom. He had taken out the horse-blanket pin so his kilt fell to its proper length.

"This is Cullen Moorland," Jerin said.

"My cousin Cullen, who shouldn't be in guest quarters by himself," a female voice behind Eldest clarified. The voice belonged to a girl in her mid-teens, with hair the color of a new copper coin and a rash of sun-darkened freckles. "And I'm Princess Lylia." Lylia, the supplier of wine, cigars, and naughty pictures. She held out her hand to Eldest and they shook like equals. "I'm Cullen's escort, when I can catch up with him. I was hoping to find him here."

"I'm a boy, not a baby." Cullen pouted.

Eldest ignored the comment. She introduced herself, Corelle and Summer, and Jerin.

Lylia gave Jerin a long measuring look and smiled at what she saw. "A pleasure."

Cullen *tsk*ed as Jerin blushed. "No, no, you tilt up

your chin, raise one eyebrow calmly, and state, 'I know.'"

"Oh, but I like the blush," Lylia said.

"If he keeps blushing like that, you'll have to use a pry bar to get the women off him," Cullen said. "Arrogance. It's the only way to have a moment's peace."

"As if you had practice," Lylia said, tugging on Cullen's braid.

Cullen tweaked her cheek. "I'll have you know that there are families out there that are willing to overlook a small streak of headstrongness."

"Small? Ha!" Lylia rolled her eyes. "I was going to suggest a walk in the gardens." She tilted her head in the direction of the door. "Just the six of us."

"A pleasure," Eldest murmured.

Lylia did not take Cullen's arm, as Jerin expected her to do, but let her cousin lead the way. Summer and Eldest fell into step with Cullen, flanking him. On a hand signal from Eldest, Corelle took Jerin's arm with a sigh of the long-suffering, and Lylia walked beside them.

"There are actually several gardens inside the palace walls," Lylia explained as they strolled down a flight of stairs and several hallways to the porch where the Queen Mother Elder had first met with them. "The family is mad about puttering about in the muck, bending nature to their will. I don't have the madness, so I don't quite understand it, but Trini and, strangely enough, Odelia are both crazy about it."

The gardens were a riot of color, in full bloom with early-summer flowers. Paths of pea gravel meandered through drifts of peonies to archways leading to other gardens.

"The back wall is sixteen feet tall and is patrolled night and day. The gardens are as safe as the house." Lylia pointed out the wall a few hundred feet away. "We can walk around without fear in here."

"My favorite area is down here." Cullen led the way to a well-shaded grotto, where water spilled over a waterfall into a deep, rock-lined pool. "The cliff was built here for my uncle. If you look carefully, you can see the individual slabs of stone they fitted together to make it."

Jerin studied the wall several minutes before finding the finger-wide joints of the very natural-looking cliff face.

"The water is pumped by that windmill." Lylia pointed to a picturesque structure, its sailcloth arms creaking in the stiff wind.

"Oh." Pieces of Jerin's education came together in his mind. "We're at the top of a sandstone cliff. The ground is probably too porous to keep water up here."

His reasoning seemed to please the princess for some reason. Lylia grinned widely at him. "Exactly!"

Beyond the grotto, there were lily pools and a hedge maze. They strolled on, he and Lylia falling behind the others, frightening hidden frogs into the water with a soft *plop, plop*.

"Does the windmill pump all the water for everything, or just the gardens?"

"There are several water supplies. Specially lined cisterns collect the rainwater; plus there are several wells. If you look up there, on the roof, there are tanks that the windmill fills. In the family wing, there are indoor privies with running water. Mothers had them installed when I was little."

"My aunts needed to build a new wing to their home, so they designed their house to have a indoor privy," Jerin said. "It's very clever."

"It's just a tank of water high over a piss pot with a hole in it," Lylia said, grinning as if she enjoyed the innocent rudeness of the conversation.

"It's that the tank fills itself to exactly full and stops that I think is amazing. A human would know that the tank is empty and could fill it and then stop when it was full. It's like they made it intelligent, yet inside the tank are only little pieces of metal and cork."

She covered her mouth on a laugh. "Oh, please, you'll

make me nervous to sit with my pants around my ankles with these 'intelligent' tanks of water above my head."

He laughed. Lylia surprised him by taking his hands in hers and looking up at him.

"Kiss me," she demanded.

"What?" Jerin blinked in amazement.

"Kiss me."

Jerin glanced around to see if anyone was about to observe them. Where had his sisters and Cullen gone? "Would it be proper?"

Lylia seemed to consider for a moment, or maybe it was just an act of considering. "Proper enough. It's not like I'm asking to mount you."

"No," he admitted uneasily, "but one seems to follow the other."

She giggled, and then leaned forward—pressing her body full against his, wetting her lips before whispering again, "Kiss me."

He supposed this was why the sisters were princesses. They commanded and everyone else was helpless not to obey. Certainly he also was helpless not to enjoy. Her lips were warm, moist velvet, her taste of apples, and her scent of cinnamon. She put her arms about his neck, ran her fingers down his braid, and tugged at the end. A moment later his braid uncoiled and his hair cascaded forward, a waterfall of silky black. She ran fingers through his hair.

"Lylia," Ren said from behind her sister.

The younger princess broke the kiss. "I'm behaving." She skipped backward, grinning, until she collided with Ren. She rolled her head back on Ren's shoulder to look up at her older, taller sister. "He's dreamy."

"You're supposed to be escorting your cousin." Ren lifted her arm to point back up the path. "Go!"

"I'm gone." She spun to duck under Ren's arm and cantered off.

"Um." Jerin ran his thumb across his forehead, gathering up his hair and pulling it out of his face. "I'm not sure how to say no to you princesses."

"I suppose not," Ren said quietly. "Our society can't allow men to learn how to say no; it's too important they say yes to so many women. Maybe if there were one man for every five women, or every three women, we could afford for men to say no."

"What if there were five men for every woman?"

Ren studied a cloud as she considered. "Interesting question. Five sisters can share one man because each of them is individually rewarded with a child. Five men *could* share one woman, and be individually rewarded, but only if the woman was careful in allotting her pregnancies. It seems to run against human nature, though. Waiting five nights for one's turn is not the same as waiting almost five years. Allowing your husband to impregnate your sister is not on the same level of commitment and risk as letting your wife carry and give birth to a child for your brother. Plus, any midwife can tell you, space the babies too close together, and each subsequent child is unhealthier than the previous one. Which brother gets to go first? Which brother has to be last?"

"It would seem that the power would remain with the woman," Jerin said.

"It does indeed. The very nature of intercourse—an act to produce a pregnancy—and the risks to the woman's health as such, I think will always make the choice of yes or no the woman's."

"So the man can never say no."

"Actually," she said as she gathered up his hair into a ponytail, "you can always say no. I suppose I sound the hypocrite, but you have the right to choose who does what to your body."

"Even though I belong to my sisters, as much as a chair or a table belongs to them, and they can sell me to whoever they want, despite my wishes?"

"I have never believed that to be right and good."

She began to rework his hair into a braid. "Nowhere in the holy book does it say that a sister has the right to treat her brother as something less than human. Sometime, somehow, simple human greed worked its way into the law. The greed says, I will not give up something I have without getting something in return, even for someone I should love dearly."

"But if you are giving up the only male you have, you're giving up the ability to have children, even if only by means of incest. No babies to love, no daughters to tend you when you are old, no descendants to honor your memory."

She picked up his ribbon from where her sister had dropped it and tied the end of his braid. "If it didn't cost you to gain a husband, you wouldn't have to sell your brother. The ability to sell a brother leads to circumstances such as your uncle's, who was sold to finance a trading house."

"My mothers allowed him to choose his wives. He loves them dearly."

"Your mothers are particularly noble, then, compared to stories I have heard at court. The most pitiful ones are widows suing their husband's sisters because he committed suicide after the money was exchanged."

He nodded slowly. "It is hard knowing I won't be going back home, that I'll only see my youngest sisters and little brothers again if my wives allow it."

"That, unfortunately, is the nature of marriage and not an evil that can be banished by law. The husband has to go live with his wives."

"I suppose it's because a man's little sisters will grow up and become women with a husband to fill their thoughts, run their house, and raise their children. In his wives' home, a man's wives and children will always need him."

"You are wise beyond your years." Her eyes sung his praises.

He suddenly realized that he was wasting this moment

alone with her, maybe the last he would have. Perhaps it wouldn't be wise of him to kiss her, but he had been wanting to since she left the farm. He stepped closer to her, leaning awkwardly forward, torn between wanting to close his eyes and knowing that he'd probably miss her mouth if he did shut them.

For a moment he thought he was horribly wrong in trying to kiss her, because the slight smile on her face faded. But then she was pulling him close, her lips pressed to his in unmistakable desire.

I love you! I love you! But he was afraid to speak the words aloud, because if she didn't crush him down with some cruel remark, he knew that his feelings would grow. Even now he found great comfort in her returning his kisses as if she was as starved for his touch as he was for hers. When the edge of their mutual hunger was dulled to bearable, they stood, foreheads gently touching, his arms about her neck, her hands on his hips, holding him to her. She would exhale, and he would inhale her warm breath, feeling at one with her.

He finally whispered much safer words that those that shouted in his heart. "I've missed you. I've dreamed of you."

"And I, you," Ren breathed.

Lest his empty mouth fill up with the dangerous words, he trailed kisses down the tan, graceful curve of her neck, desire filling him, blotting out common sense. The memory of her breasts, replayed almost every night since that night in the kitchen, lured him downward. Her fingers moved in front of his advance, opening the line of attack. He moved his lips across skin silken as flower petals. Ren arched her back, making a small sound of pleasure. His right hand found the buttons of her trousers, worried them open, and slid down her flat stomach.

His universe became her; she filled all his senses and thoughts. The murmur of falling water, the birdsong, and the drone of bees faded till he heard only her breath, her soft sighs. She guided his mouth to hers, demanding his lips, and they breathed as one. And when she finally clung to him, shuddering, it was as if they were a single being, filling all of reality. They stood entwined—mouth to mouth, heart to heart, hip to hip.

"I envy my ancestors," Ren murmured against his lips. "I think I would give anything to be able to just take what I wanted."

"Does that include me?"

Ren laughed softly. "At the moment, you're the only thing I want—your sisters, my sisters, my mothers, the whole queendom be damned."

Jerin jerked away from her with a hiss and a curse. "My sisters! Oh, gods, if they caught us, they'd kill me!"

"They would kill me." Ren hurriedly refastened her trousers. "And Cullen's sisters would kill Lylia if they knew what she did."

"Lylia?" Jerin glanced around for the others. "What did she do?"

Ren laughed, buttoning her shirt. "She used Cullen to distract your sisters, to get you alone, the little minx."

Jerin winced, remembering Lylia's sweet stolen kisses. How many men had the young princess lured out and kissed before him? "They do this often?"

Ren grinned, cupping his chin with a warm hand and running a callused thumb along his cheek. "No, which is quite encouraging in all regards." She glanced down the path as sounds of the others reached them. "Here they come."

Cullen wore a crown of flowers, and looked extremely tousled, and pleased. Eldest had a slightly smug expression, which made Jerin wonder what exactly had taken place before—and perhaps even after—Lylia had caught up with them. The young princess grinned at her older sister, as if well satisfied with the whole affair.

"The dressing gong will sound soon," Ren said, making a show of pulling out her pocket watch and checking the time. "We should retire to get decent."

*   *   *

Clearly, it was ambush.

Lylia and Odelia lazed in Ren's study, idly bouncing a ball between them, as if they had nothing better to do. Odelia, on the divan, gave a nonchalant, "Hoy." Lylia, sideways in the leather armchair with her booted feet on the antique cherry end table, feigned a look of surprise. Plainly, they had been waiting for her, joining sides to do gory battle, but over what?

"Well?" Ren pushed Lylia's feet off of the end table.

"Well, what?" Lylia put on her doe-eyed innocent look, perfected and much abused over the years. It worked well with people outside the family, but Ren had witnessed too many of Lylia's maneuverings to believe it.

"What are you two here for?" Ren asked.

Odelia smirked at Lylia. "Told you she would know."

Lylia stuck out her tongue at Odelia, then addressed Ren levelly. "What are you doing about Trini and Halley?"

"Trini?" Ren could understand their worrying about Halley's prolonged absence, but they'd worked alongside Trini that very morning. "What's wrong with Trini?"

"She's taken a tray in her rooms every meal since Jerin arrived," Lylia groused. "She's refusing to meet him. She's still saying it's too soon to get married."

Ren jerked in surprise at the word "married." She hadn't talked to her sisters about a possible marriage in hopes of staving off any negative reactions before they had a chance to meet Jerin personally. Apparently Lylia, Odelia, and, unfortunately, Trini all knew why the Whistlers had been invited to the palace.

"Completely pigheaded," Odelia added, hopefully meaning Trini. Odelia lay back on the divan, tossing the ball upward until it nearly touched the ceiling and catching it when it dropped.

"This is a perfect opportunity, and she's letting it slip away." Lylia launched herself out of her seat to rove through Ren's study with restless energy. "Every noble-man available for us to marry has been raised like a vacuous songbird. Other than ignoring traditions and marrying Cullen, quite frankly, I don't see another alter-native on the market."

" 'Vacuous.' Is that really a word?" Odelia asked as the ball rose again in another orbit.

Ren settled herself on the edge of her desk, trying to smother a smile. Obviously both of them were for mar-rying Jerin—but then, she had figured they would be. "We can't marry Cullen."

"There's precedent for royal cousins marrying," Lylia stated firmly.

Ren shook her head. "The parents weren't full siblings in those cases. The bloodlines are too close with us and Cullen. I checked it one time—his mother was full sister to Father."

Odelia caught the ball and sat up in one smooth mo-tion. "You two are serious! Cullen? Holy Mothers, you're both as bad as Trini."

"What's wrong with Cullen?" Lylia asked, jerking up her chin.

"Besides being more like our brother than our cousin?" Odelia scoffed. Then, apparently realizing that she about to fall into full warfare with Lylia, she threw up her hands. "Forget I said anything. We're here to talk about Jerin and Trini and Halley."

Lylia swallowed her attack, and nodded. "Trini can't be allowed to get away with this. It would be one thing if she met Jerin and found fault with him, but she's being completely irrational. We need to get married. She has to be reasonable."

Odelia snorted. "Trini is never going to be reasonable when the subject is men."

"What Keifer did to her couldn't have been that bad!" Lylia snapped, then glanced to them, uncertain. "Could it?"

This is going to hurt a little, right, Keifer? Oh, no, Ren, it's going to hurt a lot! Ren flinched at the memory. At the time she believed the pain had been unavoidable. Since then, she had grown sure that Keifer had enjoyed inflicting much more pain than necessary.

"Oh, don't do that!" Lylia snapped at their carefully blanked faces. "Since I was ten, every time I ask about this, everyone gets quiet and then they change the subject. I'm an adult now! I'm a royal princess of the realm. I have a right and a duty to know what happened."

Ren sighed. Lylia was right. "You might not remember, but Keifer was very beautiful. Eldest and the others fell in love with his beauty, and didn't care that he wasn't very intelligent."

"I've seen dogs smarter than him," Odelia muttered, then added wistfully, "But he was beautiful."

"Trini was only thirteen," Ren continued. "She wasn't interested in men yet, and I think she saw him more clearly than the rest of us. She saw that he was stupid, spoiled, and ill-tempered. She called him a breeding bull. She tried to block the marriage, but she wasn't an adult yet, and she was vastly outnumbered."

"Back then, she was much like you, Lylia." Sorrow tinged Odelia's voice. "She had a sharp tongue and she was fearless in using it. She could get him so mad."

In the beginning, it would take several minutes of cutting remarks before Keifer would react. Toward the end, a single facial expression from Trini could make Keifer explode. Trini played it as a game, even taking bets that she could get Keifer to throw things at the dinner table or scream in public.

"So, what happened?" Lylia asked. "What did Keifer *do*?"

Ren swallowed old anger and disgust. "He hit her in the head with a paperweight and, while she was stunned, dragged her to his bed and tied her there. He beat her, and—and serviced her, and everything else he could think of to hurt her."

Odelia cataloged the injuries. "He broke her nose and

blackened her eyes. He broke two of her fingers, and burned her on one hip, like a cattle brand, for calling him a cow. He was threatening to cut her face when Eldest showed up."

Lylia look horrified. "And we didn't send him back to his sisters?"

"Eldest got Trini cleaned up and half convinced it was all her fault before our mothers saw her." Ren swallowed the rage again that her Eldest acted not in the best interest of their sister, but for her own desire to keep Keifer as a husband. "Keifer turned all sweet on Eldest, said he was sorry and that he really didn't mean to do it, that Trini drove him to it. Eldest was blindly in love with him."

"Obviously," Lylia murmured.

"So what do we do about Trini?" Odelia flopped back onto the divan. "She's going to think we're just like Eldest, in love with a pretty face."

"And you're not?" Ren asked as Odelia tossed her ball skyward again.

Odelia threw her a surprised look and nearly missed her ball. "No! Well, Jerin's beautiful, but he's also very gentle and sweet and caring. After I was attacked, Jerin was like a father comforting his little one. Me! I wasn't a princess of the realm to him. I was just a stranger he found half dead in a stream."

Lylia sighed. "If Trini would only talk to him. He's so intelligent for a man."

Ren caught herself before she, too, sang Jerin's praises. "We're in complete agreement that Jerin isn't like Keifer and would make an excellent husband. How do we convince Trini?"

"We don't," Odelia said, flinging her ball skyward. "Jerin does. She won't believe anything *we* say anyhow."

Chapter 11

On the morning of the Season's opening ball, a hip bath-tub and buckets of warm, scented water were delivered to the suite. After the Whistlers had bathed, dried off, dressed, and eaten a light brunch, a horde of women descended on the suite.

A manicurist family arrived first, corralling all the Whistlers into having the dirt scraped out from under their nails and their ragged edges trimmed and filed. Eldest, Corelle, and Summer got off with a quick ten-digit service. Jerin found himself propped in a semire-clined position, each limb in the command of a separate plump-cheeked woman. They trimmed, shaped, and ran a pencil of white chalk underneath his finger- and toe-nails to give them a lasting "freshly bathed" appearance. The manicurists voiced dismay that he had gone bare-foot when he was younger, leaving ghost calluses on the bottom of his feet. They also *tsk*ed over the condition of his hands, and discussed at length the benefits of full-length gloves.

Eldest vetoed the suggestion of gloves, looking dis-gusted at the fuss over Jerin's feet, and chased them out. The hairdressers, however, were waiting in the hall. Since his sisters trimmed their military-style short hair every morning, Eldest elected to retreat with Summer, leaving Corelle to watch over Jerin's suffering.

The hairdressers undid his braid, combed out his long hair, trimmed it to an even length, and then washed it.

Normally his hair took hours to dry. The hairdressers blotted individually coiled sections, again and again, working through a stack of forty or fifty towels. It left his hair slightly damp to the touch. He was reclined once more, his hair carefully arranged on a drying rack, and the hairdresser sisters blew air down over the hair via a crank-driven machine with teardrop-shaped revolving blades. It made him nervous and slightly dizzy to stare up at the spinning blades, and the sound was thunderous.

It took an hour of cranking the machine before his hair was dry. He had to admit, as they combed it out, that it had never lain so silky straight before. They braided it then, in loose coils woven through with ribbons, strings of small glass beads, and tiny blue flowers.

He was allowed tea. Apparently noblemen ran toward being heavyset—and considering how little activity they were allowed, it was small wonder. Perhaps with this in mind, someone had tried to change what had become Jerin's normal tea to just dry muffins. Corelle sent a youngest Barnes off for a true tea with sandwiches made of chicken and a sweet pickle relish, and little cakes of sweet cream topped with fresh raspberries.

Lastly came the tailors with his formal ball clothes. At all the fittings, they had allowed him to wear undergarments. He was dismayed when they explained that the clothes were to be worn without underclothes.

"It's the fashion," the tailor murmured, carefully keeping her face averted as she held out the leggings. "With underwear on, you won't . . . settle . . . properly into the codpiece. Just slip off your underwear, and into the leggings, and we'll sew them shut."

Jerin balked. "I'll feel naked. I'll look naked."

"I'm sorry, sweetheart, but women like to see what they're buying. You'll be fine. All the other men will be wearing leggings just like these. I should know—we've made a goodly quarter of them."

Corelle scolded him impatiently. "Oh, Jerin, don't be a crybaby."

Jerin supposed this was what Captain Tern had meant when she said their success was riding on his conduct. If he refused to wear the most fashionable clothing, it would be unlikely he'd catch the eye of a well-to-do family.

I wish I could marry Ren.

He bit his lip on that thought. No one would want to look at a boy with eyes full of tears. So he stripped out of his underwear, stepped into the leggings, and tried not to pout as they explained how to tuck himself into the codpiece's pouch, and then sewed the fabric shut. The shirt had padded shoulders, curiously shaped sleeves that managed to leave his forearms bare while draping fabric almost to the floor, and a collar open to midchest. At least they let him wear riding boots, with cuffs that faired up around the knee.

A slight gasp made him look up. Eldest stood in the doorway, looking stunned.

"Holy Mothers," Eldest finally murmured. "You're beautiful."

Jerin ducked his head at the praise. "I feel like a midwinter tree with beaded strings and glittering ornaments. All that's missing are the gingerbread angels."

"Jerin!" Eldest came across the room and gave him a quick hug, careful not to muss his hair or crinkle his shirt. "Don't be a ninny."

"I've got bells on," he said, taking a few steps to illustrate his point. The tiny bells sewn into the long sleeves rang as he walked, a faint shimmering sound.

Eldest shook her head. "I don't know if I should let you out of this room dressed like that."

"I look silly."

"You look sensual, beautiful, and erotic. We'll be beating women off of you."

He blushed and went back to the mirror to consider

his image. His reflection barely seemed to be him, but did look like someone who could command a brother's price of four thousand crowns.

He had been prepared for a fair: women in work clothes, men clustered together for the rare chance to talk to someone of their own sex, children moving like schools of minnows, all contained in a meeting hall, a tent, or a rough dance floor under the stars. Potluck dishes. Amateur musicians mostly playing together.

He thought it would be like a country fair, just on a grander scale.

They came down a dim hallway and out a side door to the brightly lit foyer. Stairs cascaded down in vivid red velvet into a ballroom, a shifting sea of the most beautifully dressed people he could imagine. Great crystal chandeliers hung overhead, thousands of candles setting fire to the glittering glass prisms. Every person was arrayed in silks and satins, diamonds and rubies.

There were no children. There was no food in evidence. The few men were scattered and closely guarded. Music came from a small orchestra, in tune and on beat.

Jerin froze at the top of the stairs, wanting to turn and escape back to their rooms.

Eldest checked at the sight of the whirling dancers, then, hooking her arm with his, led him down the stairs, murmuring, "We've got the blood of Queens in us. We're just as good as they are."

Corelle and Summer trailed wordlessly behind, Summer wide-eyed and Corelle looking sour, as if it all was putting a bad taste in her mouth.

Behind them, Barnes announced loudly, "Miss Eldest Whistler, Master Jerin Whistler, Misses Summer and Corelle Whistler."

A handful of women turned at the announcement, glancing up at the Whistlers as they descended the stairs. The women's gazes flicked over Eldest, then settled on Jerin and stayed. In ones and twos, others glanced their direction and didn't look away, until dozens of eyes were focused on him.

"They're staring," Jerin whispered.

Eldest tightened her grip on him. "Of course they are. You're beautiful. Smile. It's not like they're going to eat you."

"How can you be sure?"

"I'll rip the heart out of anyone that lifts a fork to you," Eldest said so only he could hear, all the while giving a tight smile to those looking in their direction.

"Holy Mothers!" Summer gasped. "Cullen!"

Jerin missed Cullen at first, expecting to see the boy that climbed in through his window. After a minute of futilely scanning the crowd, he realized that the young man standing demurely behind Eldest Moorland was Cullen. His muddy blond hair had been dyed to a deep rich honey, interwoven with strands of gem-encrusted gold threads, and gathered in loose falls by green silk bows. Eyes down, head slightly bowed, hands clasped before him, his clothes falling in elegant unwrinkled lines, it seemed as if all of what was Cullen had been stripped away and a soulless doll stood in his place.

Then Cullen lifted his head slightly to peep around, noticed Eldest Moorland was distracted, and saw them watching. He made a face, sticking out his tongue and rolling his eyes, then ducked his head again. His fingers, though, wiggled, indicating that they should join him.

"Scamp," Eldest Whistler's tight grin relaxed into a true smile. "Let's rescue him from his family."

"Ah, a husband raid," Jerin whispered. "What us Whistlers do best."

Eldest Moorland greeted them with a nod. "Whistler."

Cullen flashed a grin at them and then returned to his demure mask.

"Moorland." Eldest Whistler started the social dance. It had been explained to them that by protocol, any woman that wanted to speak to a man had to talk first to his sister. Cullen and Lylia had gone over the acceptable topics for the conversation, and the length needed prior to addressing the brother.

Luckily, there were no limits set on conversation between men.

"What happened to you?" Jerin whispered to Cullen.

"Eldest heard about our walk in the garden and gave me a blistering with her tongue," Cullen whispered back. "She called me a Dru Hightower. Ha!"

"A what?"

Cullen risked glancing up to scan the room, then pointed out an elegant-looking young man, slightly older than the two of them. "In the east corner, in white—as if wrapping dirt up in clean linen could save face."

"He was caught kissing a girl?"

"Worse. He was caught tumbling his betrothed wives' servants during the betrothal period. It was a huge scandal—not that anyone really blamed him. His betrothed are all bloated toads, warts and all, but his betrothal contract had been signed, his brother's price paid, so his betrothed had possession of him and everything. All the deal needed was the wedding—and a massive one had been planned. His betrothed hauled him back to his sisters and demanded a repayment."

"Did they get it?"

"Of course. Damaged goods! No way to prove he was clean before the betrothal, and certainly they didn't want to risk infecting the whole family. They say that one of the servants had been to a crib and caught something other than a baby. They say on his first night with one of his actual betrothed, his Eldest wife discovered sores all over his you-know-what."

"Really?"

Cullen shrugged. "Who knows? People start making stuff up after a while."

"I didn't know wives could demand a repayment."

"Happens all the time."

Eldest Whistler turned to Cullen. "Your sister has given me permission for this dance." She held out her hand, palm up. Cullen brightened and reached out to rest his fingertips on hers. They went out onto the dance floor, where other couples were gathering. How odd that the only time a woman and a man could be completely alone was in front of so many watchful eyes.

"Jerin," a woman's voice said, making him turn. Kij Porter stood beside him, smiling. She indicated Summer with her chin as she extended her hand. "Your sister has given me permission for this dance."

He glanced to Summer, surprised. Summer gave him a helpless look, as if the older, politically savvy woman had outmaneuvered her. Corelle was nowhere in sight, apparently scouting out the rest of the men.

Jerin rested his hand on Kij's warm fingertips and allowed himself be led out onto the dance floor. She took him to the opposite end from where Eldest Whistler waited with Cullen for the music to start. They were deep in conversation, and didn't notice him joining the dancers.

"Do you remember your grandfather Prince Alannon?" Kij asked.

"Yes." Out of habit, he avoided giving out too much family information.

Kij seemed annoyed by the evasive answer. "He lived to be very old?"

"Nearly seventy." Jerin reminded himself this wasn't a country fair; it would be safe to discuss family here. "He was fifteen when my grandmothers . . ." He swallowed the word "kidnapped." With the Queens' coaching, they had come up with a "sweeter" version of his family's history. He substituted in the word ". . . found him. We lost him to a fever three years ago."

It was an important breeding point that none of his family had died of a weak heart, stroke, or other inherited illness. Only disease and accident had winnowed their ranks.

"I see," Kij said. "Why didn't he ever try to contact the Queens?"

"After the public executions of his mothers and sisters, he didn't see any point."

"Ah. Yet you saved Princess Odelia's life. Wasn't that a betrayal to his loss?"

Jerin blinked in surprise. "Betrayal? No."

"He was said to be trained in the ways of *k'lamour*," Kij said.

Jerin blushed and ducked his head.

"You know what that means?" Kij asked.

"It's not really a proper thing to talk about," Jerin murmured, glancing to see where Eldest was in the shifting couples.

"He passed this to you?" Kij pressed.

"The paths of pleasure?" Jerin whispered, to quiet her. The music was coming to an end, and he didn't want be overheard. "Yes, he and my father told me. Please, talking about sexual union isn't the proper thing to do."

"On the contrary. A woman should know what she's getting," Kij all but purred, taking firmer hold of his hand.

The dance, though, ended with bows. He spotted Corelle coming toward them to claim him back. He gave Kij a false smile, tugged free his hand, and met Corelle halfway. Kij, infuriatingly, trailed alongside him.

"I would dance with Jerin again," Kij stated, putting out her hand to him.

Corelle took Jerin's right hand with her own, blocking any move to claim him. "I'm sorry, but we need to spend Jerin's time wisely. A second dance would be impossible."

"I don't know if you realize, little mushroom, how important my family is and how much you would gain by courting us."

"Your family of old controlled the portage over Hera's Step," Corelle said in a bored tone. "Your grandmothers bankrupted your family building the lock to replace the portage when it was destroyed by sabotage during the war. Through marriage and other means, you've reclaimed a controlling interest in the lock. Second to the royal family, you are the oldest recorded family, noted when a brother was married to the second generation of the royal princesses. You are not considered, however, the oldest noble family, as you gained your title through service to the crown—lending money—and not by marriage. In fact, you are one of the few noble families that never married a royal prince." Corelle flashed a grin. "Unlike ours. Good day."

With that, Corelle turned Jerin away from Kij and led him across the room.

"That was rude," Jerin whispered after he got over his shock.

Corelle still smiled smugly. "Perhaps. I'm not going to have any sisters-in-law looking down their noses at us. They'll see as equals, or not at all."

"We're not going to get four thousand crowns if you insult everyone that dances with me."

"Perhaps."

"How did you know all that, anyhow?"

"Her sister Alissa told me most of it. She went on and on like I cared. Eldest and I asked around to dig out the dirt."

"It was still rude." Jerin bowed his head in embarrassment.

"Yes, but I thought you might want to dance with someone else." Corelle came to a stop, loosing her hold on Jerin's hand. "Your Highness, you asked for a dance?"

Jerin looked up in surprise at Ren's smiling face.

"Your sister has given me permission for this dance," Ren said.

Jerin ducked his head again, this time to hide the grin that bloomed uncontrollably across his face. He slipped his hand into the princess's, and she squeezed it slightly before leading him out onto the floor, where Summer was partnered with Cullen.

*   *   *

There would be, Jerin reflected, a profound lack of things to do in his new life. True, they had slept in after a late night dancing, but after brunch, as rain started to drizzle down, there was nothing to do. No dishes to clean up. No dinner to get ready. No clothes to wash. No knitting or mending to be done. No children to keep entertained.

The suite had several musical instruments, none of which they played. It was also devoid of reading materials, except the newspaper and a score of books on profoundly dry subjects such as *Land Improvement via Introduction of Fertilizer,* and *Primer of Livestock Breeding Practices.* Either the royal family didn't know about the existence of novels, or had formed an undeservedly high opinion of the Whistlers' intelligence level.

The siblings took turns swapping newspaper pages between them, occasionally murmuring, "Did you see here that it says . . .?" and getting their fingers black from the ink. One by one, they finished the newspaper and then hunted through the loose pages, hoping for something they'd missed, something more to read.

Jerin was beginning to understand why Cullen had been so bored.

They had hunted out writing paper to play code breaker, devising quick cryptograms and handing them off to the next person to break. Corelle had just won the first round, as usual, when a knock at the door provided a welcome distraction. It proved even more welcome when it turned out to be Cullen and Lylia.

"We're bored," Jerin told them. "We just read the *Herald* to death."

"Yes, yes, that's a dead newspaper." Lylia nudged a rumpled page aside with her foot. "You can read? How wonderful. I've tried to teach Cullen in the past, but he refuses to learn."

"You're a lousy teacher." Cullen pouted. "Besides, what's the point? My wives probably won't let me read."

"Why not?" Eldest asked. "Whistler men all read—doesn't make them cross-eyed or sterile or anything."

Lylia shrugged. "I guess it's like the poor who don't want their daughters going to school. The girls make more money by working alongside their mothers."

"Oh, like you see noblemen out weeding fields every day," Cullen said.

"I didn't say it made sense," Lylia murmured, tweaking him gently with her thumb and forefinger. She turned back to the Whistlers and gave them a bright smile. "How about a tour of the palace?"

The palace proved to be more rambling than Jerin had imagined. The tour ended in a suite of rooms that his youngest sisters would kill for. Called the nursery, it held a room of fanciful beds, a well-stocked schoolroom, and a playroom. One wall of the playroom contained windows, and the rest of the walls had shelves to the high ceiling, filled with toys. Baby toys were put up, and the floor was now littered with toy soldiers. Tiny cannons, a fleet of warships on a blue painted river, even supply wagons, accompanied the soldiers to war. The five red-haired, youngest princesses, Zelie, Quin, Selina, Nora, and Mira, were just settling down to battle.

Lylia introduced Jerin to the five, and then went off to chaperone Cullen in the schoolroom with Jerin's sisters.

Zelie was the leader of the youngest princesses. With a regality that fitted her position, she announced, "We're reenacting the battle of Nettle's Run."

Jerin smiled. The soldiers might be tin instead of wood, the cannons might articulate and fire, but it was one of the same battles his sisters engaged in on long winter afternoons. He glanced over the troops. "Where's Peatfield?"

"What do you know about playing with soldiers?" Mira, the obvious baby of the sisters, asked.

"My grandmothers were under Wellsbury," Jerin explained, pointing to the mounted general flanked by her younger sisters. "My sisters and I have re-created this battle, just like this."

"But you're a boy," Princess Zelie said with puzzlement tinged with contempt.

"Yes. I find it depressing sometimes," Jerin admitted.

"Why?" Quin, or perhaps Nora, asked. The two looked very similar and all the girls had shifted since he'd been introduced to them.

"There's lots of things I would like to do that I'm not allowed," Jerin said.

"Do you want to play?" the other of the two asked.

"We've already picked troops," Zelie reminded the others.

"You don't have Peatfield," Jerin pointed out. "She was held in reserve for most of the battle. I could play her troops."

They consented after a quick check with their history books to confirm Peatfield's existence and the strength of her troops. Almost seventy-five thousand women clashed in the woods alongside the Bright River, leaving nearly ten thousand dead or wounded. It was attributed as a brilliant win for Wellsbury, but luck had played a large part in the victory—Smythe's misunderstanding her orders and withdrawing just as Wellsbury attacked, for instance. Though in truth, the garbled message she received hadn't been the true orders issued. Peatfield's orders too had been waylaid, and thus her reserve troops never entered the battle.

When played without the sleet, the exhaustion, the lack of food, the poor visibility, the sniper attacks, and the Whistlers confusing enemy orders, the outcome favored the False Eldest's forces. It surprised him, thus, that the royal sisters kept to the same attacks and retreats of the original battle.

After watching for several minutes, he faked a retreat up Granny Creek, crossed over Blue Knob, and took out the overextended left flank of Wellsbury's force. Zelie shrieked with dismay and literally had the army fly to protect her tin general.

"No, no, no, you can't do that." Jerin laughed as he caught a tin soldier that was flying miles across the landscape to land in his path.

"Yes, I can." Zelie pushed his hand away to thump the soldier down. "I just did!"

"No, you can't." Jerin struggled to stop laughing. "That's against the rules."

"You can't talk to me that way!"

"Good heavens, why not?"

"I am a princess of the realm," Zelie explained in perfect princess tones.

Jerin covered his mouth to hold in a crow of laughter. She was so delightful using the adult deadpan. "Your Highness, the point of the rules is to mimic battle, so you can learn how to fight one without getting everyone killed on your first charge. Your tin soldiers can only do what real soldiers do, because you must learn what your real armies can do. If you cheat, then you're not only cheating on me; you're cheating yourself out of a chance to learn, and you're risking the life of every woman you'll ever command."

"But you cheated!" Zelie cried.

"Oh, there is cheating and then there's cheating. What I did, real soldiers could do, that is, pretend to run away and then attack elsewhere. Real soldiers, however, cannot fly across the battle, willy-nilly."

Five serious faces considered him. "So it's all right to cheat sometimes?"

Oh, dear, Ren probably wouldn't be happy if he perverted her youngest sisters. Still, Whistlers never found a little cheating to be harmful.

"My mothers always said," Jerin said carefully, "that those who are completely forthright are often at the disadvantage of those who are corrupt. Here." He picked up three of the earthen cups that held the cannonballs, passed the cannonballs out to the princesses, and turned the cups upside down. He picked up a marble and showed it to them. "We're going to pretend your cannonballs are coins. I'm going to put this marble under one of the cups, and shuffle them around. You bet your 'coins' on which cup that you think the marble is under. If the marble is under the cup, then I'll match the number of 'coins' you bet. If the marble isn't under the cup, then I get to keep the 'coins' you bet."

He made a show of placing the marble, palmed it, and allowed them to win the first pass by palming it under the cup they chose. After that, he left the marble pocketed and began winning all their cannonballs. Eventually, one of them remembered what had started the game.

"Wait!" Selina squealed with surprise and dismay. "You're cheating! Aren't you?"

"Oh, yes. See?" He overturned all the cups. "The marble isn't under any of them. There's no way you can win."

"How did you do that?" Zelie asked, chewing on one long lock of hair. "We saw you put it under one of them."

So he showed how he could palm the marble, using misdirection and sleight of hand. "The point is, you could have lost all your money, because you thought I was being honest, and you were playing fair. The more you know how people can cheat you, the less likely you'll be cheated."

"So it's all right to cheat?" Mira asked slowly, obviously struggling with the concept.

He shook his head. "Lying and cheating is like playing with guns. When it's real, it's very dangerous. You have to be very careful, but we Whistlers always thought it was a good thing to know how to do it well, and more importantly, how to tell when someone else is doing it."

Jerin realized that someone else was in the room. He glanced up to meet the gaze of a young woman leaning against the door, watching them. Judging by her auburn hair, fair skin, and delicate features, she could be none other than the mysterious Princess Trini. Her look was a mix of amusement and dismay.

Lylia wandered back into the room. "Trini, there you are! You haven't met the Whistlers yet. This is Jerin."

Princess Trini straightened up with a scowl at her younger sister. "Well met, Master Whistler, but if you'll excuse me, I have better things to do than to play with toy soldiers."

The others, minus Eldest Whistler, returned to the playroom. Barnes, they said, had fetched Eldest to meet with a visitor. The Whistlers showed off their skills at sleight of hand for the youngest princesses, making coins and balls disappear and reappear. The children and Cullen picked up most of the basic moves, but Lylia, laughing at her own fumble-fingeredness, couldn't get it.

"Finally," Cullen gloated, "something I can do that you can't!"

The young princesses' tutor arrived, announced playtime was over, and shooed the visitors away. The group decided to troop back to the Whistler suite for tea. They reversed their normal marching order, with Lylia and Jerin leading, while Summer and Corelle, flanking Cullen, trailed behind.

Reaching the suite first, Lylia opened the door and halted.

Eldest Whistler and Kij Porter stood in the room, the tension almost visible between them. If Kij and Eldest Whistler had been armed, surely both would have hands resting on their weapons. Seeing them standing thus, it struck Jerin for the first time that the Porters were built much like his sisters—tall, lean, and broad in the shoulders.

"You'll have to give us time to decide." Eldest's voice was carefully flat, void of any emotion. "I won't be pressured into a snap decision."

"I don't see what there is to decide," Kij said lightly,

though her eyes were narrowed in something that might be anger. "We're willing to offer twice the amount you'd get from commoners. We're a powerful family with ancient noble lines. There isn't a family greater than ours in all of Queensland."

Jerin's heart quaked in his chest. Offer? The Porters?

The two women realized that he stood in the doorway. They turned toward him, Eldest with a flash of irritation, Kij Porter with a look close to greed.

"We'll talk about this later," Eldest stated firmly; it was unclear if she spoke to Kij or Jerin.

"Jerin!" Kij came to claim his hands, squeezing them possessively. "You're more beautiful every time I see you."

"It's the clothes," he murmured, ducking his head shyly, but then glancing up to study her. Did he want Kij as a wife? Kij and her sisters were handsome women—stronger in features than the delicate royal princesses, which some would say was a bonus. Certainly they did not tend toward freckling like Lylia. Kij's eyes were the hard blue of sapphires.

Jerin could not find a single spark of warmth for Kij. Was it because he had given his heart totally to Ren already? Was it just a lack of knowing Kij?

She leaned toward him. A month ago, he would have missed the warning signs. Thanks to his experience with the royal princesses, however, he realized she was going to try to kiss him. He stepped backward with no conscious thought in the action, not even aware he'd avoided her until she straightened with a slight frown.

"Come, what's the harm in a simple kiss? A sample of what I'm buying?"

"My brother is not a horse, nor a whore." Eldest's voice was toneless with her controlled anger. "We'll need a contract and brother's price in hand, a secure betrothal, before anyone can *try* for a sample."

Not counting royal princesses, of course. Jerin studied

his feet as his face burned. *Hopefully that comment won't blow up in our face.*

Kij didn't seem put off in the least. She chuckled softly and murmured, "Ah, I do enjoy taming a spirited colt before mounting and riding."

"Good day, Porter," Eldest snapped.

Kij nodded to them and went out.

"I don't like her, Eldest," Corelle muttered.

"You said he wasn't a horse," Summer growled.

"Corelle. Summer," Eldest snapped. "We don't discuss family business in public."

Lylia and Cullen! Jerin turned around and found the two hovering by the door, looking paler than any of his sisters.

"This is not a good time," Lylia said, blinking rapidly. "We'll leave you to discuss this."

She went without seeing if Cullen followed. Cullen opened his mouth, closed it again, and hurried after his cousin. The Whistlers stood in silence, the younger siblings waiting out of habit for Eldest to speak.

"Well?" Corelle finally asked. "What do we do?"

"We wait," Eldest stated firmly, leaving no room for discussion. "This is only our first offer. We have time. We wait."

Ren was in her office in town when Lylia came in like a firestorm.

"Where is she? Barnes said she came to the offices, and her office said she mentioned she was coming here! Was she here?"

"She, who?"

"Trini!" Lylia shouted. "That cold, self-centered bitch of our sister!"

"Lylia!" Ren snapped. "You will not use that language when speaking about one of our family."

"Kij offered for Jerin!" Lylia wailed. "And that— that—Trini refused even to meet him!"

Ren sat. She had no choice as her legs wouldn't support her. "Whistler didn't accept?"

"She said they would need time to think, thank gods. It worked just like I planned. I got Jerin and Trini both to the playroom, and just as Odelia predicted, he was terrific with the youngest—I've never seen them so good. But all she did was stand at the door and sulk. Then—then!—to top everything off, she insulted him!"

"She didn't!" Ren suddenly felt like calling Trini a few choice names herself. "What did she say?"

"Oh, nothing really bad. Just that she had better things to do with her time than play with soldiers." Lylia deflated slightly at a look from Ren. "Oh, okay, it wasn't really an insult. It just seemed like a slap in the face to me, after Jerin was so nice. He's such a sweetie. He can do magic!"

"Magic?" Ren could think of only one thing magiclike that Jerin did—and she hoped that he hadn't done it in front of the youngest.

"He can make coins and little balls disappear. He's so clever with his hands."

Ren recalled Jerin being clever with his hands and her body pulsed with a sudden need to be with him again. Had he done magic on Lylia too? The kiss she interrupted seemed mild compared with the embraces she had shared with Jerin.

"What do we do?" Lylia asked, drawing Ren out of her air dreams.

"I'll order Trini to spend time with Jerin, let her get to know him, and then push the issue. We've got to get married, and we want our husband to be Jerin."

Eldest Whistler was waiting for Ren in the princess's study at the palace.

"I've heard," Ren said.

"No you haven't." Eldest held up an envelope addressed in thin spidery writing. "Eldest Picker has died. Meg is now head of the Picker family. Someone approached her with a better offer. She's going to hold us strictly to the terms of our contract. Payment for the store will have to be on the contracted date, or she'll sell it to the other party."

"I thought you had an exclusive contract."

"We do, until Jerin's birthday, which we were assuming would be his betrothal day. We had hoped for some traveling time beyond that, but Meg Picker's disallowed it. We need to be back to Heron Landing by that date. If we don't hand the Picker sisters their money on that day, then we owe them the penalty and they are free to sell to the other buyer."

Ren did the math. Once Eldest accepted an offer, she would need four or five days for the betrothal contract to be written, all prenuptial tests run on Jerin, and then the actual signing. Add another five days for traveling, and the Whistlers actually needed to accept an offer two weeks prior to Jerin's birthday. "So you only have thirty days or so to decide."

Eldest nodded. "Have you heard from your sister?"

Ren shook her head. Raven's people had found no trace of Halley.

"If it was a straight choice between you and the Porters," Eldest said, "it would be a simple pick. Jerin's happiness matters much to me, and any fool could see that my brother is in love with you. If I was sure that your family would eventually come around to favoring the match, we could wait financially. We have different options, but they're not as simple to access as the brother's price on Jerin, and not without risks." Eldest looked at Ren with frank honesty. "But I'm not sure. Princess Halley may show up and want nothing to do with us. Or she might not show, and yet your mothers could continue to deny the match. Much as I love my brother, I have to do what is best for my sisters. I can give you until thirty days, and then I must accept Kij's offer."

"I understand."

Ren would face Trini and make her see the facts. If

four of the five elder sisters agreed on Jerin, perhaps her mothers would allow the marriage without Halley's presence.

Trini managed to mostly avoid Ren for a week. Their duties precluded her from avoiding Ren completely, but she slipped into court minutes before the first case was called, and then darted out the moment the last case was settled. Unwilling to estrange Trini from Jerin completely, Ren settled on giving a rare command as Eldest, ordering Trini to eat with the family. It was almost comical to see Trini try to avoid Ren, Odelia, Lylia, and Jerin at dinner.

Aware of the days slipping by, Ren finally cornered Trini deadheading her prize roses. "We need to talk."

"No, we don't." Trini snipped viciously at the innocent flowers. "I know what Lylia tried to pull. I know what you're trying to do. I'm not going to be roped into marriage again so soon. We're young. We can wait."

"No, we can't!" Ren snapped. "Do you want it to end here, with us? After twenty generations, our family ends with us? The entire country thrown into the same chaos of Wakecliff's estate, with no clear heirs?"

"You're being melodramatic, Ren."

"I am not. We're only ten in number. If something happened to any one of us, our daughters could be even fewer. We have to marry and start having children."

"Why not this violent outcry last year? Or the year before? Or any time in the last six years?"

"Halley hadn't gone missing last year. Odelia hadn't been attacked last year. I hadn't had a few narrow calls myself. And yes, this opportunity hadn't presented itself."

"Opportunity? Let's call things as they are. You've met a pretty boy and you want to be serviced like a cat in heat. This is no different than with Eldest and Keifer."

"Jerin is nothing like Keifer. This isn't like our first

marriage. The Porters poured a fortune into Keifer's dress; they kept him under our elder sisters' nose, and gave full liberties to him prior to the wedding."

"And this differs how from the Whistlers? It seems he's here, under our noses, well dressed, and, from what Barnes tells me, well tousled."

"If Odelia and I hadn't gone north, we would have never met them. I caught Jerin alone at night and seduced him. I brought the Whistlers here. And if I hadn't begged Eldest Whistler to wait for our offer, they would have already accepted Kij Porter's generous offer a week ago and left."

Trini whirled around. "What? No one's told the Whistlers what a monster Keifer was?"

"Kij is not her brother." Ren waved it tiredly aside. "Besides, it would seem as if we were just poisoning the well to keep the water for ourselves."

"All bad apples come from apple trees."

"You can't say Keifer is a fair representation of his sisters, any more than Cullen is like his sisters."

"I find Cullen exactly like his sisters—intelligent, fairminded, openhearted, charming, and headstrong. I wouldn't mind marrying Cullen."

"Cullen is too close in blood." Ren rubbed at the bridge of her nose. "I like him too. He would be a safe choice; we know him well and there'd be no surprises, but we can't marry him."

"I know. I know."

"Trini, do you remember how Keifer was with you and Lylia? He could barely be civil even with Eldest watching. I've seen Jerin with his youngest sisters while trying to cook for forty people. There's no way he could have faked being so patient, gentle, and caring with them."

"I've seen Jerin with Zelie and the youngest," Trini admitted. "He seemed very good with them, but it could have been an act. All of it could be an act."

"If you don't trust him, at least trust me to know .

the difference between genuine goodness and fake. I've resisted a second marriage this long because Keifer hurt me too. Of all the men paraded before us, Jerin's the only one I've trusted."

Trini stared out over the rosebushes for several minutes. "And if we don't take Jerin, Kij gets him?"

"Most likely."

"I wouldn't give a dog to the Porters," Trini growled.

Was it too soon to ask for her support? Ren hesitated, afraid that Trini might construe the next question as her being bullied into a decision. But it made no sense to avoid the issue after pushing it to a head. "Can I tell Mother Elder that you support a marriage to Jerin?"

Several minutes passed, and then, quietly, Trini murmured, "Yes."

Ren went to her Mother Elder. "The Porters have offered for Jerin. Let me make an offer too."

"Have you spoken with your sisters about this?" Mother Elder asked quietly.

"Odelia and Lylia are eager for the marriage. Trini has agreed."

"And Halley?"

Ren bit down on a bolt of anger. She mustn't lose her temper. "There hasn't been any word from Halley, Mother. I am beginning to doubt she is alive; I would have expected her to surface when the *Herald* reported the attack on Odelia. In that light, I do not think it's reasonable to wait for her. We have a majority."

"With another man, a brother of a well-established noble house, I would agree with you. While Jerin is a charming man, there will be many objections to him fathering the next generation of rulers. We are the daughters of the Holy Mothers, unsullied by common blood for twenty generations."

"All the noble houses were commoners at one time, from the Keepers on down."

"With the exception of the Porters, the nobles have all taken royal princes as husbands."

"If the Porters were acceptable, why not the Whistlers? They at least married a royal prince. In fact, in many ways, they are more noble than all the noble houses, since their royal blood has been less diluted by successive generations."

"Truly, Ren, how can you compare the Porters, landowners for twenty generations, to thieves fathered out of cribs?"

"Landowners? The Porters were not much more than river pirates cutting the throats of those who failed to pay for portage around the falls. They claimed to be neutral during the War of the False Eldest, but everyone knew they played both sides, and yet we married them. "

"This is not about the Porters; it's about the Whistlers."

Ren realized that her mother was going to hold to her impossible demand. "If you hadn't planned on giving your permission all along, why did you allow me to hope? You've made losing him all the more bitter now."

Her mother shook her head. "I told you that you shouldn't engage your heart."

Ren stood, feeling hollow, betrayed.

Her mother reached out and took her hand. "Ren, I was willing to allow the marriage if Halley agreed to it. In such an unequal marriage, you're asking your sisters to take a huge risk, a risk a normal marriage wouldn't entail. If you wished to marry the brother of a noble family, a majority would be enough. This isn't the case. You must *all* be willing to take Jerin as husband."

"Halley is dead!" Ren snapped. "Dead! She went out and got herself quietly killed!"

Her mother slapped her hard. "Shut your mouth! Until her body is buried in the family crypt, she is alive! The answer is no. You cannot marry without Halley's agreement. That was the case from the very start. Do not whine, child. It does not become you."

"I am not whining. I believe your grief has made you unreasonable. Even if Halley is alive, she's passed all responsibilities of her duties to us, her sisters. Choosing a husband is just one more duty she's neglecting. We have not stopped the courts. We have not stopped the balls. We will not stop choosing a husband."

"You will! I am still the Queen Mother Elder. You are my subject. I say you will not marry Jerin Whistler without your sister's approval. Push me any further Ren, and I will refuse the marriage totally."

Ren clenched her teeth together, balling her hands into fists, trying to keep her anger in. Her mother meant it. It had been years since she'd heard such a decree, since she had lost favorite toys and been barred from outings as a child with such rulings.

"I'm sorry you've set your heart on this boy," her mother said in a softer tone. "But our line can ill afford discord between husband and wife again. Trini tried to block the marriage to Keifer, and no one listened. This time, we will listen to everyone."

Eldest Moorland cracked the door to Ren's study and peered in. "Have you seen Cullen?"

Ren waved her in. "He's usually either with Lylia or Jerin."

Ren's cousin sat, shaking her head and sighing. "The younger Whistlers are in the billiard room with Lylia and Odelia. Eldest Whistler is apparently trying to track me down, so I assume it's safe to say that he's not with her."

An unmarried Eldest sister looking for the Eldest sister of a marriageable man—it wasn't difficult to guess what Whistler wanted. "What are you going to say?"

Moorland sighed again. "Are you going to offer for Jerin? It makes a difference for us."

In other words, would the Whistlers continue to be poor landed gentry or would they be sisters-in-law to the princesses? Commoners might sell their brothers to the highest monetary bidder, but noble brothers went to the most powerful political tie.

Ren sighed. She owed it to her cousin to be truthful on the matter. In sketchy details, she told Moorland where negotiations stood. "Not a word of this, though, should leave this room. I don't want to raise Jerin's hopes, only to disappoint him. If he has to marry some-one else, I would rather he be ignorant that we love him."

"So that's the way the wind blows? Well, yes, let him start with his wives with a clean slate, so to speak."

Ren flinched at the idea of another family being Jer-in's wives. A knock at the door saved her from having to reply. "Yes?"

Eldest Whistler opened the door and stood in the doorway. "Eldest Moorland, I would like to speak with you."

Moorland made a gesture to indicate that now was as good a time as any. "It would spare me having to repeat it all to my cousin anyhow."

"We wish to marry Cullen."

There was a shout from behind the heavy drapes and Cullen tumbled out from his velvet hiding spot. He gave another whoop of delight and flung himself into Eldest Whistler's arms. Whistler shook her head, smil-ing indulgently, and was soundly kissed. Ren had never thought of Cullen as a sexual creature—in that moment of frank passion, she realized he was as mature in that matter as Jerin. Her heart went out to Eldest Whistler and Cullen.

"Cullen!" Moorland growled. "We haven't accepted. We haven't even heard terms."

"I want to marry them! Things will work out for Ren. I know they will. It's not like any of those other fusspots would ever offer for me, anyhow. They want a biddable, beautiful man."

"You are beautiful." Whistler didn't address biddable, but Ren had no doubt that Eldest Whistler could keep

Cullen in line. "But Moorland is right. We need to discuss terms. We're not nobles with deep pockets. We might not be able to afford your brother's price."

Cullen clung to Whistler, throwing his sister a tragic, pleading look. "I want to marry them. They would be good to me; I've seen them with Jerin. They have little brothers; I'd have other men around. They would teach me how to ri—" Cullen broke off at the word "ride" before it escaped completely, and changed it to "—write and read."

"We can only afford two thousand crowns for the scamp," Eldest Whistler said. "Payable on Jerin's betrothal. We might be able to work up more, but we'll have to take futures out on our little brothers. It would take time to raise more money."

Moorland looked from Cullen to Eldest Whistler and then to Ren. The woman who loved her brother warred with the woman responsible for her family's best interests. Ren could offer nothing, and waited, sure that Cullen would lose out.

Amazingly, though, Moorland said, "You won't have to work up more. We'll settle on the two thousand. It doesn't pay to beggar your sisters-in-law."

Whistler had been braced for a no and looked as stunned as Ren felt. Shouting, Cullen leaped to hug his sister, then mauled Ren in a hasty, exuberant hug, kissed Eldest Whistler again, and dragged her off in search of Lylia, Jerin, and the others to break the news.

The office seemed bare after they were gone, like someone had plucked the sun from the sky, leaving vast emptiness behind.

"Why did you say yes?" Ren asked Moorland. "You know it's unlikely we'll be able to marry Jerin."

"Mother calls your father her sacrificial lamb sometimes. He bought us a lot of power, at the cost of being poisoned at the age of thirty-five. I don't want to spend the rest of my life with the same guilt my mother carries."

* * *

Ren woke the next morning from another night of horrific dreams. The worst nightmare started in the garden, where she talked to Trini as her sister deadheaded the roses. Ren realized suddenly that the wilted flowers had Halley's face, and the cut stems seeped blood. Ren pulled up the rosebushes to find Halley buried underneath, but then her mothers wouldn't come to the garden to see the body. Every time she gripped their hands, they would slide away like a bar of wet soap. She woke in the dark, crying in frustration and fear. Other dreams plagued her after she went back to sleep, none as vivid, but all filled with pain and the sense of loss.

She was still in bed when Raven came in.

"I received this via regular post." Raven held out a battered envelope.

Ren took it. It was addressed to "R. Tern" at Raven's town house address; the captain had torn the canceled stamps in opening the envelope. Inside was a common sheet of foolscap, folded once. Ren pulled it free, and the word "Eldest" in Halley's bold script made her catch her breath.

> So you've lost your heart to the son of landed gentry? Well done. No need for a formal meeting for me. I approve your choice. Proceed with the wedding plans. I'll be there. Now, call off the dogs!
> Your little sister.

Ren turned the paper, knowing that there was no more, but feeling as if there should be. "Where is she? How does she know about Jerin? Why hasn't she put any names on this? Why address it to you?"

"She sent it to me so only you and I would see it, instead of the whole palace staff. By the amount of the postage, I'd say she's close by, though."

"And no names so if someone was to see it, they'd be none the wiser of who it was from and who it was for."

"Aye," Raven said.

Ren sighed, and then, as reality dawned on her, smiled. "She's approved of Jerin! We can make an offer! She's approved!"

Chapter 12

Jerin's face was starting to hurt from smiling so much, but he couldn't stop.

I'm betrothed to Ren and Odelia and Lylia.

All was not perfect, of course.

Princess Trini stayed on the edges of his awareness, watching him, wary like a horse broken with a heavy hand and now distrustful. Princess Halley remained a complete unknown; no one seemed willing even to talk about her. All he knew about her was that she, like all her sisters, was red-haired and strong-willed.

Summer sulked because, with Jerin fetching the hoped-for four thousand crowns, the family would definitely split at Corelle. Cullen would be the older sisters' husband. Eldest and Corelle had already fought often over using futures on Doric to purchase a husband for the middle sisters. Worst of all, once Jerin's brother's price was in their hands, his sisters needed to buy Cullen and leave immediately; they had tickets for passage upriver on a boat that left at noon.

Still, he couldn't stop smiling.

It was decided to sign both contracts at the same time. Ren came in the morning, while he was still damp from his bath, for the prenuptial inspection. It was difficult to tell which of them was more embarrassed—Ren, he, or Eldest. Despite her blush, Ren's eyes glowed with an excitement that sent his heart racing and other parts of his body reacting.

"I'm satisfied." With a grin, Ren picked up his dressing gown and helped him into it. "Everything seems to be in good working order."

"But you knew that," Eldest said.

"I would not be so cavalier," Ren warned. "You have Cullen's inspection yet, and you are more guilty of dalliance than I am."

Eldest faked innocence. "Oh, I was talking about the sperm test."

That only made Ren smile wider and Jerin blush more. Cullen's report indicated that Jerin's elder sisters could expect the normal number of boys from their new husband. The doctor hand-delivered Jerin's report, fortunately hours later, just to see "the amazing specimen of male virility" herself. His sisters had been exceedingly smug about the report; one would think they had filled the small glass jar themselves. Cullen, thankfully, did not take it as a personal slight on himself.

Ren apparently already had all the originals noted on his birth certificate researched and double-checked, so this visual check for inbred deformities was the last formality.

Betrothals are for women; marriages are for gods. While solemn, there was no mistaking the betrothal for anything but what it was: a purchase. Ren handed over Jerin's brother's price in four small strongboxes, and signed the betrothal contract. Eldest Whistler counted through the boxes separately, verifying that each contained a thousand crowns, then countersigned the contract. Eldest took Jerin's hand, led him to Ren's side, and gave his hand over to the princess. Ren clasped his hand tight, taking ownership.

Then it was time for Cullen's betrothal. The Moorlands received two of the four boxes. Eldest Whistler and Eldest Moorland signed as the heads of their families. Eldest Moorland gave Eldest Whistler Cullen's hand.

It was done. Cullen's wedding would be in a month at Heron Landing. Jerin's royal marriage would need an additional two months to plan. Hopefully, Princess Halley would reappear in time for the wedding.

They had a betrothal lunch, and then, with lots of hugging and kissing, Cullen and the Whistlers said good-bye.

"Take good care of my little brother," Moorland said.

"We will," Whistler promised.

"These are the husbands' quarters," Ren said, unlocking the doors and pushing them open.

His new family stood around him, waiting for his reaction, and Jerin could only gasp. All previous splendor of the palace paled to this. His first impression was of vaulting ceilings, the flood of sunlight from a wall of windows across the room, the soft murmur of water, the smell of roses, a splash of cool green to his far left.

"Go on." Lylia slipped around to the front to tug his hand gently. "From the balcony you can see forever."

He entered the room, not sure where to look first, feeling doll-sized against the scale of the room. There was a fireplace he could stand inside. A massive grand piano sat dwarfed in one corner. Settees and lounges that would have crowded any room in the Whistler home littered the room like chains of islands, surrounded by great expanses of polished marble and shoals of carpets.

"There's a private rose garden with a fountain," Trini murmured from behind him.

"Over there is the bedroom!" Odelia pointed out double doors opened to expose another vast chamber and a huge bed on a raised dais.

"If there is anything you don't like, we can have it changed," Ren stated, unlocking the door to the balcony. It was deceiving, that door. Wrought iron twisting and curling, painted white, backed by glass. It looked bright and open, but it could keep out an army.

The sunbaked balcony of dressed stone looked out

over the cliffs—in essence, protected by the sheer drop. Below, the sprawling city, the glittering river, and then the green roll of fields went out as far as the eye could see. He stared out, feeling suddenly small and lost.

Ren sensed his distress, and touched his shoulder, concern in her eyes. He reached out for comfort and she came into his arms.

"I'm sorry," she whispered for his ears alone. "I know it's confining after the freedom of your farm, but it's to keep us all safe."

"When we were little," Odelia called, oblivious to his distress, skipping and hopping on the wide paving stone, "we ate breakfast with Papa out here, and then played hopscotch. This is the best place for hopscotch in the whole palace."

Jerin turned his back on the open sky and found the vast room transformed by the very presence of his new family. The Queen Mothers had followed them into the room, but stopped midway, taking up residence on the settees. His child brides darted about the room, exploring, laughing, and calling to one another. The huge room contained them comfortably, keeping them together without making them feel in each other's way.

Ren gave him a sad smile, so he hugged her.

"Was this a good place when your father was alive?" Jerin asked.

"It was my favorite part of the palace."

"I'll have to work on making it so again."

The husbands' quarters were very much a place of history. The rooms had been cleaned and aired, but layers and layers of the generations remained. A cabinet of board games. A jeweled collection of kaleidoscopes. A sewing stand filled with musty supplies. A knitting basket with a half-finished baby blanket. A collection of music boxes. Even the massive wardrobes in the dressing room brimmed with clothes.

"After our husband was killed," Queen Mother Elder said with slight bitterness, "Keifer wanted some of his nicer clothes. Then, after the explosion, none of us could stand the thought of dealing with them. We should have removed them before today."

Jerin lifted down one floral dressing gown, the silk floating in his hands. "It seems a shame. They're beautiful."

"Many of them have memories attached," Ren said, taking the gown from him. "Not all of them good."

Even the good ones, Jerin reflected, could be painful. "What will you do with them?"

"Sell them to a ragpicker," Odelia said.

"I'd rather see them burned," Ren said, "than to have strangers going over Papa's things."

An idea occurred to Jerin, and he started to speak without thinking it through. "We could—" And then the thought reached its logical end. He was about to suggest sending the clothes to Cullen; his sisters could never provide such a rich wardrobe. Then he remembered the fate of the fine clothes the Queens had provided to his sisters; they were to be sold on the racks of his sisters' new store. He winced at the realization that his sisters would be equal to ragpickers.

"We could what?" Ren asked.

He considered saying, "Nothing," but in truth, he couldn't be sure that his sisters would sell them at the store. "We could send them to Cullen. My sisters could never afford the type of clothes he is used to."

Odelia laughed. "Cullen is probably withholding sexual services until he's allowed to ride horses. These are barely clothes you could wear outside."

"You could make holiday shirts for the little ones out of these," Jerin pointed out. "Or curtains, or slipcovers for chairs."

Odelia and Lylia laughed.

Trini frowned at them. "Jerin's right. It would be a

horrible waste to burn them. There's hundreds of crowns here in silk. The cost of one outfit probably could feed a poor family for a month."

More likely a year, but Jerin didn't correct her. He smiled instead at the stray thought that one obscure corner of Queensland was going to be suddenly much more gaily dressed.

"We'll pack them up and send them," Ren said.

"Really?" Jerin asked.

Ren touched his face softly. "For another smile like that last one, I'd send my clothes too."

He could do naught but kiss her. Odelia and Lylia then claimed their share of his affection, so it was quite a while before they moved on. The bed, dressed in goose down and layers of softest linen, proved to be able to hold them all at once—blushing husband, affectionate wives, and giggling child brides. The Queen Mothers looked on, smiling indulgently, while the youngest princesses romped innocently on the bed. Jerin wondered what the Queens were thinking. Did they recall a similar moment from their marriage on the same bed? Or were they remembering how these laughing girls were conceived between these sheets? Or were they looking forward to grandchildren yet to be born?

The dinner gong tumbled them out of the bed. The youngest claimed him first, all but dragging him away, until Trini rescued him. She freed him, shooed the girls on, then shyly took his hand.

"Betrothed."

The single word shot a bolt of happiness through him. He smiled, giving her hand a squeeze. "Betrothed," he said.

He's charmed Trini. Ren nearly cheered. She put a hand over her mouth to cover the huge grin on her face. Her mothers had noticed the exchange; Mother Elder waited to walk with her down to dinner.

"What do you say now?" Ren struggled not to be smug.

Mother Elder tilted her head, considering. "He'll be good for this family, Eldest."

Eldest. The title sobered Ren. There seemed to be something implied in the straightforward comment. "But?"

"The common people barely grasp how this family suffered since your father died; Keifer wreaked such damage, alive and dead. With Jerin's background, perhaps it will be wise to educate them."

Let the tarnished truth be known. Ren nodded, feeling guilty for agreeing. It seemed a betrayal to let the world know how badly Eldest had chosen their first husband. Surely she had chosen more wisely than her older sister, or was she just as blinded by love? No, Mother Elder agreed that Jerin was a better man. But if Ren questioned her own judgment, then there could be no doubt that others would question it too.

It would be a delicate path to walk.

Later that night, Ren realized that she had forgotten about the bolt-hole. She was so used to Raven handling security issues that the secret hiding space and passage out of the palace had slipped her mind. The husbands' quarters, however, were off-limits to the entire palace staff, Raven included. It was up to Ren, as Eldest wife, to make sure the passage was clear, the doors worked, and that Jerin and her adult sisters knew all its finer points.

If by showing Jerin his secret escape route, she also received some late-night cuddling, then all the better. She stripped off her shirt, did a sketchy sponge bath, changed into a clean shirt, and tried for a casual stroll down the hall to the husbands' quarters. The door guard came to attention as she walked up, but kept their faces carefully emotionless as she nodded to them and rapped on the door.

The second rap got a "Who is it?" muffled by the iron-reinforced door.

"It's Rennsellaer, Jerin. Let me in."

With various clicks and clangs, the door was unlocked and Jerin cracked it open to peer at her, his eyes stunningly blue.

"Should you be here?" he asked.

"Yes." She slipped into the room and locked the door behind her.

"I need to show you the bolt-hole. I didn't show you while the little ones were here this afternoon; they don't know not to talk about such things. When they're older, we'll tell them."

He smiled shyly. "I like the sound of 'we.' "

So did she. He wore a sheer nightshirt, a deep blue that caught the color of his eyes, the silky fabric warm with his heat. After several minutes of bliss she managed to restrain herself and lead him to the dressing room.

"It's in here so that both bedrooms have access to it," she explained.

"I didn't notice the smaller bedroom this afternoon. It surprised me when I found it tonight. Was it Keifer's room?"

"While Papa was alive. Keifer moved into the larger bedroom after Papa was killed."

She saw his curiosity and his reluctance to ask. Because it seemed unfair to keep him ignorant of what even the baby sisters knew, because his reluctance reflected his hesitancy to hurt her, because she loved him, she opened herself to the pain that talking about her father's death always brought. "Papa was poisoned about six months before the explosion. It was a beautiful summer day, and we decided to take carriages out into the country for a picnic." Keifer decided, and they were already learning it was easier to give in than to fight with him. Easier. Deadlier. "Papa was barely thirty-five at the time. The five youngest were learning to walk, and he was so happy. Later than night, when Mother Elder came to him for services, he was vomiting, dizzy, and weak. Within minutes, he collapsed into a coma and died. They say he died of arsenic poisoning—but we don't know what the poison had been in."

"I'm sorry," Jerin whispered, hugging her, wrapping her in his warm comfort.

She held him, finding peace within his arms. "At the time, we were so bitter about his death that we never thought how lucky we were that he was the only one killed. The explosion at the theater taught us to count the small blessings."

They stood for a while, hugged close. Finally, she resolutely set him aside. He had to know how to keep himself safe. She showed him how the dressing room doors bolted. The locks were simple bolts, but disguised within elaborate woodcarvings to hide the function of the room.

"Keep the doorways clear of clothing or chairs." She recalled the instructions her sister had given her six years ago when she was judged old enough to know the family secrets. "You might want to keep the smaller bedroom's door bolted at all times. This is the bolt-hole's door here, behind this wood paneling, so you want to keep this clear too." She showed him the catch hidden in the carved trim, and had him trigger it himself.

The door creaked open; the chamber beyond was musty from disuse. "The dressing room doors give you time to get here and shut this door after you. There's a lamp here with a box of matches." She grimaced as the cobwebs on the lamp clung to her hand when she set the glass chimney aside. "Don't waste time lighting them until you've got the door barred solid. There's a light well here, so during the day you'll see even with the door closed and locked."

He nodded, so solemn. Locks of hair were escaping his braid, spilling onto his face, and he brushed them back absently. Distracted by him, she dropped the matchbox after lighting the lamp.

"Oops!" She bent down, lantern in hand, to scan the floor for the box. It sat on a pile of burned discards. She frowned at the blackened matchsticks, picked up the matchbox, and glanced into it. Five lone matches rattled about the box, while their spent sisters lay on the floor, covered with dust. The lamp, she noticed now, was almost empty too, the chimney black with soot, the wick badly trimmed.

She, Halley, and Odelia had been shown the bolt-hole shortly before her father's death. Eldest made them spend the day taking care of the secret route—a rite of passage, Eldest called it. Together, they secretly cleared the outside door, swept the floor clean, counted the crowns in the emergency purse, and replaced the unused matches and lamp with new. Trini would have been the next to do maintenance on the passage, but by the time she turned sixteen, Keifer was dead.

There had been no attacks on the palace. No attempted kidnappings. The lamp should be clean and full. The matches unused.

Keifer had used the bolt-hole.

Cursing, barely aware of Jerin now, she hurried down the secret passageway. A straight shot back, down a tight flight of stairs, and through a series of sharp turns, she hit the end.

The door was bolted, but dropping down with the lamp, she could read old evidence of a betrayal that went beyond words. Tracked in from a muddy garden, dusted now with six years of disuse, footprints of various sizes led in toward the sanctity of the husband quarters.

"Oh, Gods, how could he have done this?" she moaned, sick, sick. She fumbled with the door, stumbled out, and threw up in the sweet, sharp profusion of roses. Jerin followed her out, held her head as she was sick.

"What is it? What's wrong?"

"Keifer! Gods damn the crib bait slut! He was bringing women into our husbands' quarters! Oh, gods, night after night, he turned us out, refusing us sexual services while he was whoring himself with someone else."

"Who?"

"I don't know." She thought of all the spent matchsticks, far outnumbering the number normally found in a box of that size. "Perhaps half the guard by the count I can figure."

He nodded, then glanced about the garden. "We should go in, before we give away the door."

The door is given away, she almost snapped, but swallowed it. He was right. She followed him back inside and bolted the exit carefully shut. Jerin was silent the whole trip back. It wasn't until they were in the dressing room that she realized he was holding something back from her.

"What is it?"

He refused to look at her. "Ren, you were with Keifer, weren't you?"

"Yes." She was puzzled.

"Odelia too?"

"Yes."

He whispered so softly, she almost didn't hear him. "Ren, you two should be checked, before the marriage, so if Keifer passed—if Keifer had—who knows if his lovers were clean? We should be sure. For the youngest's sake, for Lylia's sake, we should be sure."

"Ren! What's wrong?" Queen Mother Elder asked as Ren stumbled into her room and collapsed into the chair before the fire.

"Keifer betrayed us." Ren gazed numbly at the fire. Had Keifer died instantly in the explosion, or had he been pinned and burned alive? "When he was refusing Eldest and others services, he was servicing strangers he brought in through the bolt-hole. Jerin—Jerin thinks it would be wise if Odelia and I were checked, since we can't be sure we're clean."

"Oh, dear gods in the heavens," Mother Elder whispered.

"Halley will have to be checked, if we ever run her to earth. And Trini—sweet Mothers—he could have infected her too." She pressed a trembling hand to her eyes as she realized the true depth of the danger. "I don't know about these diseases, Mother, how intimate you need to be to pass them. I might have already infected Jerin. There was no joining, but otherwise, we were extremely intimate."

Ren stared numbly at the fire, trying not to think of all the horrible ramifications. Keifer had died six years ago. Surely, if they were infected, at least one of them would have fallen sick by now.

Gods, she hoped Keifer hadn't been killed immediately by the explosion. She hoped he burned slowly.

The doctor was a thin, old woman, part of a family that had treated Ren through sore throats and broken arms. She examined Ren with dry, cold, dispassionate fingers, then asked a myriad of questions, reminding Ren often to think carefully and to hold nothing back. With a growing sense of relief, Ren could truthfully say that she never had a sore on her vagina or rectum. She had never lost patches of hair. Her eyebrows had never thinned. She never had rashes on her body, and especially not on the bottoms of her feet or the palms of her hands.

"You know if you're lying, you'll give any child you conceive this awful disease while it's still in the womb. It will be born dead, or so damaged you'll wish it had been."

"No. I'm not lying. It would be stupid to lie," Ren said.

"Yes, but it never seems to stop people from doing it," the doctor said. "It would be helpful to have Princess Halley here as well, but so far, I see no sign of disease. Recently, they've developed a test. A device has been invented that allows one to see things so small they're invisible. We actually have small organisms living in our blood."

"I know. I've worked with a microscope."

"Oh. Well, they couldn't see syphilis for a while.

Turns out it's white. On a normal slide, you can't see it. Recently, they found a way to examine things on a black background. The syphilis shows up. It still isn't very accurate in the early stages of the disease, but if you were exposed six years ago, it should be fairly simple to spot."

"How soon can we have it done?"

"I'll come back in an hour or so with equipment to take your blood and have it tested."

Jerin attacked the mystery of Keifer's lovers. Surely, somewhere in the husband quarters, well secured and untouched these last six years, there had to be clues. No one outside the family, not even the Barneses, were allowed into the husband quarters. Once Ren's father died, Keifer could have kept lovers' mementos with no fear of discovery. Since Keifer died suddenly, any damning evidence should have remained.

Jerin tore through the accumulation of the ages. He carried armfuls of objects out to the balcony, examining each piece carefully before setting it aside. When shelves, dressers, and closets were empty, and the balcony was overflowing, he attacked the furniture itself.

The massive bed in his bedroom yielded up an earring, a bold hoop of gold, with strands of golden hair caught fast in it. Had the earring been Keifer's? Certainly the rest of the Porters were blond. He checked the well-stocked jewelry boxes and found no mate; in fact there were no earrings at all. Keifer, it seemed, didn't follow the recent fashion of men's piercing their ears. Jerin placed the earring carefully in the center of a piece of paper, and then tackled the smaller bedroom.

Tucked up under the support boards of the bed, he found a box wedged onto the shelf made by the bracing. He pulled it out. It was six inches square, and locked.

Resisting the urge to beat it open, he got his lockpicks and sat tailor-fashion, amid the wreckage he'd caused, to tweak it open. At first his find seemed disappointing, a handmade book, containing hundreds of small yet in-

credibly detailed pictures. The first pictures were por-
traits of the Queens, then women that must have been
Ren's older sisters, and finally Ren and the others, the
surviving sisters, almost unrecognizable in their youth.
Detailed drawings of palace rooms followed. As he
reached abstract pictures—a dining table set for dinner,
a ballroom filled with dancers, a theater with actors on
the stage and a crowd of people watching—he noticed
the cant. Beside each detailed drawing was a small cant
symbol. The dining table was represented by a circle in
a rectangle, crude knife, fork, and spoon. Two stick figures with a line joining them indicated a ball. Jerin
flipped back to the beginning. A crown and a counter
marked the Queens. A crown under a bar and a counter
ticked off princesses.

It was a lexicon, he realized, of someone's personal
cant. Keifer's lovers must have given it to him so they
could communicate with him. Under the book, little
scraps of folded paper contained Keifer's secret
messages.

Jerin unfolded one: a ball, Heraday, a cant name, talk.
Despite the unknown symbol, the meaning was fairly
clear. *At the ball on Heraday, talk to cant-named person.*

The second message sickened Jerin: Claireday, a clock
showing midnight, a simple drawing of a bed, a key unlocking a door. *Unlock the door to your bedroom Claireday at midnight.*

The third message sent Jerin to the lexicon for the
first symbol. *Picnic.* *Food* was the second word, though
he checked the lexicon to be sure. The third symbol
couldn't be found in the lexicon. Jerin's grandmothers,
though, had carefully taught it to him: an *X* with an oval
drawn over it—to stand for skull and crossbones. *Poison.*

The husband quarters looked like Keifer still lived
there, throwing his fits, wreaking his anger on anything
at hand. Ren stopped just inside the door, shocked.

Surely Jerin wasn't like Keifer! Surely Jerin didn't turn his anger on everything and anything.

The rooms were strangely quiet. No howls of anger. No screams of ugly, yet childishly simple names. Was Jerin even here?

She walked to the bedrooms, noting with some relief that nothing seemed broken. No shards of glass. No splintered, battered furniture. In fact, there seemed to be a strange order to the chaos.

Jerin wasn't in the big bedroom, with the bed stripped down to the frame, nor the dressing room, where not a stitch of clothing remained. It was the stark emptiness of the dressing room that turned her annoyance to concern. This was far too orderly and systematic to be compared to Keifer's random acts of destruction.

Jerin sat tailor-style on the floor of the little bedroom. He sat silent, statue-still, a box and a book both open on his lap, a scrap of paper dangling in his hand, nearly slipping from his fingers.

"Jerin?"

He looked up, pale, his eyes wide with shock. He gazed at her, seemingly too stunned to move or speak.

"Jerin? What's wrong?"

"I—I thought I might find out who Keifer's lovers were." He held up the paper and book to her. "I was searching for clues."

It was thieves' cant, written out on a piece of good stationery. Three neat symbols. There was also a lexicon for translating it, the simplified symbols expanded into pictures a child could understand.

"Keifer's stupid, Ren. He's a cow!" Trini had sneered her contempt of their husband. *"I know you don't marry men for their brains, but there's a limit!"*

Keifer's lover had apparently known his mental limits as well as Trini had. The book left little chance for misunderstanding. Ren looked at the quality of the stationery and the lexicon with its careful renderings of the

palace, its occupants, and the daily life of gentle society
and realized the truth. "This isn't thieves' cant. This is
the personalized cant of the cannon-stealing gentry that
nearly killed Odelia."

The color drained out of Jerin's face. "The ones that
killed Egan Wainwright?"

Ren flinched in memory of the mutilated, raped man.
Had Jerin's sisters told him about that? "Yes. Them."

"How could they get into the gardens to get to the
bolt-hole door?"

Ren knew that the gardens weren't perfectly secure
despite the wall and the guards. It was unlikely, however,
that such a vast number of women scaling the wall could
go unnoticed. The Barneses? They had access to the
gardens. No. The Barneses never left the palace in any
large number—they couldn't have been the ten women
escorting the cannons on the *Onward*. Nor had one of
the Barneses vanished mysteriously when the red-
hooded thief had been killed.

Only palace guests could have been in the garden
unobserved.

And the only women invited to the palace, prior to
the Whistlers, were from noble families. During Keifer's
short time in the palace, the royal family entertained
often. He liked parties where he was the focus of powerful women. Keifer flirted with everyone; those who had
the decency not to return the attention were never
asked back.

Ren flipped through the lexicon, hoping for a clue
to the family's identity. There was the picture of the
executioner's hood, and a translation for colors, but
nothing as damning as a woman's face with "black hat"
transcribed beside it. She cast the book angrily aside and
looked into the nearly empty lockbox. All that remained
was a small square of fine white paper, folded carefully
into an envelope, as you might receive from an apothecary. Powder shifted inside the envelope, creating sand
dune shadows as she held it up to the light. A circle

overlaid an X to obscurely label the substance. Ren
started to unfold the envelope, only to have Jerin catch
hold of her hands with a yelp, squeezing until she stilled
her fingers.

"It's poison!" Jerin cried. "Don't open it! It could kill
you if you breathed it in or got it into your eyes."

She froze. "Poison? How can you tell?"

"The cant. It's marked poison. Skull and crossbones."

"What was Keifer doing with poison?"

Jerin picked up one of the abandoned slips of paper.
"Ren, I think he killed your father."

She found Kij and flung the note into her face. "Look
at this!"

Kij took the note, unfolded it, gazed at it for a long
time, and then asked carefully, "Am I supposed to understand this?"

"This is the note that *your brother* received along with
a packet of arsenic to kill my father!"

Kij forced a hollow laugh. "Oh, be serious. Keifer
would never do anything like that!"

"Keifer was a whoring, murdering slut!" Ren snarled.
"After murdering my father, he fucked women in our
wedding bed!"

In a flat, emotionless voice, Kij asked, "Are you
sure?"

"Yes! The evidence is everywhere, once you start
looking!"

Kij sat still, controlled. "What do you want me to
say, Ren? 'I'm sorry' does not seem to be large enough
for this."

"You can tell me who!" Ren shouted. "Who killed
my father? Who laid waste to the Wainwrights, nearly
murdered Odelia, and butchered forty of my troops with
grapeshot? Who was fucking your brother?"

"I don't know!" Kij cried, spreading her hands. "He
flirted with everyone. I don't know who could have seduced him to that level. Even if Eldest knew that he

was being unfaithful, which I'm sure she didn't, who could have guessed that anyone was using him for treason? Keifer? He wasn't intelligent, Ren!"

Intelligent, no, but cunning, yes. He should have been on that stage that night. What a performance he wove for such a young man. During the courtship, he pretended to be blindly in love with Eldest. He fooled the Queens into thinking he would make their daughters a fine husband. His fits of anger were just illusions to cover his infidelity.

"I need to know who was using him, Kij. He might be dead, but they're continuing their treason."

"I don't know. It was six years ago, Ren, and I wasn't Eldest at the time. I tended family business. I was always either on the *Destiny* or at Avonar. Eldest stayed here in Mayfair, but she couldn't have known. Do you think she would let him chance destroying our connection with the crown? We gained so much influence when we became your sisters-in-law; we'd have lost it all if you returned him to us."

Ren sighed. If Keifer had kept his secrets from her own sisters, right under their noses, she supposed that his sisters could have been just as fooled. They would have seen him only at social functions and occasional joint family dinners. "Raven will be by to interview your staff and sisters. I'm sorry, but we'll have to make this public in hopes of information surfacing. We need to track down my father's killers."

Kij frowned. "Is that truly wise? There will be rumors that Keifer picked up something and spread it to you. I know what that's like, Ren. People don't want you sitting on their chairs, afraid they'll catch something."

"If rumors are all I have to deal with, Kij, I'll be happy. It has yet to be seen if Keifer has left death behind him. But I *will* find these women, and then, heads will roll."

* * *

The thunderstorm started with the longest thunder Jerin had ever heard, as the cloud boiled off the plateau and struck the river valley. It went on and on, and finally died. He went to the window and watched as the thunderclouds claimed the sky until only the farthest horizon remained clear, a slice of gold in a sky of rolling gray. Raindrops began to fall on the gray flagstone of the balcony, a splattering of dark spots. And then the rain started in earnest, in driving sheets.

I was so happy. Jerin opened the door and walked out into the pounding rain. *It was too good to be true. Keifer was probably diseased. Ren and Odelia and Trini are going to die.*

If they did, he couldn't bear going on too. It would be more than just the grief of losing them. No one would think him clean, not even his own family, who knew of his indiscretions with Ren. Everything balanced on an edge of cascading disaster. If Ren was infected, the Queens couldn't allow him to marry Lylia and the younger princesses. If his family had to give back the four thousand, they would lose the mercantile, and would have to pay the penalty.

His sisters had planned to stop in Annaboro for a few days before going on to Heron Landing. With a quick boat, the Moorlands could fetch back Cullen with his reputation fairly intact. With four brothers, why would his sisters need to visit a crib? The public opinion would be that, unlike Ren, his sisters were clean and thus Cullen was safe, regardless of any dalliance.

But Jerin's brother's price would be worthless forever. The betrothal notice had gone to the newspaper before his sisters left. His return to his sisters—and the reason why—would be equally public. Returning the four thousand crowns would be a crippling blow to his family. Much as his sisters loved him, they would have no choice but to set him up in a crib, servicing strangers for ten crowns a night.

He stared down at the bleak drop below the balcony, a storm of dark emotions raging through him. *My life has been ruined by a man already dead.*

"Jerin!" Ren dashed out into the cold pounding rain and caught his arm. "What are you doing out here?"

"If he was alive, I would hunt him down and cut out his heart!" Jerin trembled with the desire to do violence. Never before had he wanted to hold on to someone—preferably by the throat—and squeeze the very life out of him. Nothing would be slow and painful enough to ease the pain inside himself. "Why did he do this? He had everything!"

"Jerin, we're clean!" Ren shouted over the roll of thunder. "If Keifer had anything, he didn't pass it to me or the others!"

He blinked the cold rain and the hot tears out his eyes. "Clean?"

Ren smiled at him, oblivious to the rain. "There's not a single trace of anything! Keifer's noble lovers must have been clean. Nobles don't visit cribs!"

It sounded so sane and reasonable. Of course, nobles were never pushed to desperation—they had money to buy the pretty son of a poor farmer if they had to bend that low. Surely if the women slept with Keifer, it was part and parcel of using him to commit treason. Had sex and the lure of doing something forbidden been simply an easy leash to control Keifer with?

The darkest and bleakest of Jerin's emotions drained away, leaving him feeling bruised.

"Come on." Ren tugged him back toward the suite. "Come out of the rain, and take off those wet things before you catch a cold."

Numbly he followed. She pulled his nightshirt up over his head. She was soaked to the skin and shivering herself.

"You need to get dry too." He reached for the buttons of her shirt.

Ren toweled his hair as he undid her clothes, dropping

them into damp piles at their feet. All at once, it seemed, they were naked, pressed close together, kissing. All the fear and anger and hurt twisted into a desperate, consuming need to be together.

Two steps, and they were on the bed. Ren reached between them, took hold of him, and guided him into her. One smooth warm stroke, and they were joined as one.

"We shouldn't have done that," Jerin murmured much later. "Not yet."

"We're wife and husband minus a large circus act called a royal wedding. It's only a show for the common folk. The betrothal contracts are the true binding word, and those are all signed and legal."

"We're married," he whispered, barely believing it. A few weeks ago he was a simple landed gentry's son, without a title, in an obscure part of the realm. "I'm Prince Consort."

"Yes, my love, you are."

"You love me?"

"With all my heart."

"I wanted to tell you, before you left the Whistler home, that I loved you, but there didn't seem to be a way. I never dreamed you would want me for a husband."

"A hundred years ago, and I would have carried you off that first night, Odelia and your sisters be damned."

She brought a basin and a towel to the nightstand. Dampening the towel, she washed him clean, the warm nubby fabric rubbing gently against him.

"That's nice," he said sleepily.

"Go to sleep," she murmured, drying him. "You'll need the rest."

He fell sound asleep, wondering what she meant by her remark, and woke to find Odelia joining him in the bed. Under the loose wrap, Odelia wore nothing. She was fuller in the chest than Ren, broader of hip, and wanted to try positions she had read about. Like Ren, she washed him before tucking him in.

"I wore you out," she laughed as he yawned.

"I didn't get much sleep last night."

"They should make it a tradition. No one ever waits for the wedding night."

"Someone must."

Trini woke him with a tray of food and a session that was mostly eating, talking, and tentative cuddling. He thought that they wouldn't consummate their marriage until later, but then Trini, in sudden silent resolve, held him down and mounted him from the top. Afterward, she lay on top of him, listening to his heartbeat until they both fell asleep.

Lylia woke them, impatiently scooted her older sister out, and allowed him to clean himself for her. She was nervous, awkward, curious, and eager. He felt like a mountain range, being explored, climbed, and conquered. Yet when she fell asleep tangled in his arms and sheets, he watched her breath, her so-kissable lips parted slightly, and felt deep, moving love for her. He loved them all. Ren's strength. Odelia's whimsy. Trini's passion despite her shyness. Lylia's determined struggle for justice.

He kissed Lylia's lips, and cuddled her close, and fell asleep happy.

Chapter 13

Jerin's father liked to say, "Over. Done. Gone." It settled many fights between his siblings, with no lasting hard feelings. They all struggled to meet their father's high expectations. With maturity Jerin realized that you needed that release from anger, to put it behind you, in order to work ahead. As children, his parents forced them to put the hurt aside. As an adult, he had to find the power to decide he had raged long enough, that his anger had served its purpose, and move on.

The news that Keifer's infidelity had left no lasting harm helped. And the serial prenuptial sex worked wonders. So the next morning, at a cheerful breakfast with his wives on the balcony, he decided it was time.

The novelty of the husband quarters was wearing off, and he noticed now how shabby they were. The carpets were threadbare. The divans were battered from the princesses' roughhousing on them. Sun rot and moths tattered the drapes. The ceiling needed paint where damage from roof leaks had been repaired. Some of the ivory had been picked off the keys on the grand piano. Even the wallpaper was worse for wear, grubby from tiny hands as high as a child might reach, and peeling at the very top at every point the water damage had reached. What surprised him most was that Keifer hadn't made any changes.

Odelia shrugged it aside when he mentioned it. "He was lazy."

"He liked to make himself pretty," Trini said. "He didn't care about how the room looked."

Lylia pointed out, "Father didn't want the fuss of redecorating, and Keifer died only a few months after Father."

"Keifer came up with some plans before he died," Ren said. "It would have bankrupted the country. He wanted to gold leaf the ceiling." She took a bite from her toast, thinking for a moment before continuing. "And to tear out the floor and put new marble in—and mirrors over the beds. He and Eldest would have screaming fights over it, and he'd lock her out of the quarters."

"So he could be with his lovers" echoed between them without being said.

"If you make a list of what needs to be done," Ren said, "and give it to Barnes, she'll line up the workers."

"It would be expensive," Jerin said.

"Don't plan on gilding the ceiling, leave the floors be, and I'm sure it will be a reasonable amount. It needs to be done, love."

Jerin gazed through the windows to the massive set of rooms. "Are we going to do all the work ourselves?"

"Good gods, no!" Ren laughed. "The workers will be closely supervised, though, and you'll have to stay someplace else. It would take forever if we tried to do it on top of our other work."

"I can paint—" he started to offer, but Ren put fingers over his lips.

"I don't want you up on the tall ladders it would take to paint the ceiling or hang the wallpaper. Besides, with a crew of ten or twenty women, the work would be done shortly. Think like a commander, love, not a private."

He kissed her fingers. "I'll try."

Barnes knocked on the door an hour later. He looked out the spy hole, saw her and the guards that bracketed his door, and undid the lock.

"I just finished," he told Barnes while they stood in

the doorway. "I think it would be nice to go with the yellow silk, like in the guest room. It's very cheerful. That wallpaper wouldn't stand up to children well, though, so I was wondering, could we put in wainscoting?"

Barnes looked puzzled a moment, then nodded. "Ah, refurbishing the suite. Yes, wainscot is certainly doable."

"The drapes could be the yellow silk, but the divans and carpets should be something darker, so they don't show dirt. I was thinking green."

"I could have samples sent up for you to choose from."

Jerin winced. He was hoping to avoid anything that resembled his time with the tailor, looking at dozens of fabrics that all seemed fine to him, and needing to chose one. "If I must."

"I will try to make it as painless as possible," Barnes assured him.

"Let me get the list." He left her at the door to fetch his list. Their conversation had already covered most of the main points. "The piano needs work. I—I would like to learn how to play it."

"You don't play?" Barnes seemed surprised, then looked as if she regretted letting it show.

"We didn't own a piano," Jerin told her quietly.

"I see. Arrangements can be made, with the Highnesses' permission." Barnes slipped an envelope out of her coat's breast pocket. "A letter came for you from your sisters."

Jerin took the letter quickly. "Thank you, Barnes. That will be all." He ducked back into his quarters, blushing hotly. He had written his sisters shortly after the true depth of Keifer's betrayal came to light, but before Ren's announcement of being disease free. Initially he meant it to be a short, politely worded warning that he might be returned to them. His anger and fears, however, had spilled out onto the paper, all the sordid details. It ended with *"Damn Keifer, damn him, damn him,"* which, he later realized, might seem deranged. When he gave the letter to Ren to post, even its haphazardly folded, ink-splattered appearance seemed slightly maniacal.

The letter back from his sisters looked so sane and unremarkable compared with what he had mailed out. Its looks, he discovered, were purposely deceiving.

Burn this, it started,

> *once you have read it. You and your wives are in grave danger. We researched the Porters when they offered for you, and came across a piece of information that did not make sense until your letter. Eldest Porter and Kij were born to a husband who died a month after the wedding. The rest of the family was fathered by the Tibler husband. Tiblers apparently have a genetic quirk of eleven toes. According to their birth certificates, half the Porter daughters born to the Tibler line have this quirk. The Porter mothers and, of course, Kij do not. Kij's daughter, however, has eleven toes. She could only be fathered by a Tibler. The second husband died two years prior to the birth of Kij's daughter. Kij must have been Keifer's blonde lover. If the princesses are digging for new information, pushing to find this lover, then the Porters must act. Tell this information to your wives in private. Warn them to be careful. The Porters have proved to be extremely dangerous, and they are being backed into a corner. Do not underestimate them! Do not let the Porters know that you have this information until they can be safely taken into custody! Do not trust the palace guard or even the Barneses with this information; anyone can be bribed. We are coming as quickly as possible. If you need anything before we reach you, remember your aunts are as close as Annaboro. BURN THIS LETTER!*
> *Eldest.*

He stood, shocked still, his eyes dragged back to the line "Kij must have been Keifer's lover." Vividly in his imagination, he saw them in the royal wedding bed, twin blond heads bent close together, Kij's arms and legs clinging to her brother's humping body, Keifer's incestuous seed spilling into his sister's womb.

Cullen had told Jerin about Kij's daughter, supposedly a product of a grief-triggered visit to a crib. Did Kij's sisters know the truth? Had Keifer slept with his other sisters too, with only Kij becoming pregnant? As a younger sister, Kij could have carried a child without anyone outside the family being any the wiser. As Eldest, however, she would be in the public eye, and her pregnancy had to be explained.

And she had explained it well—no one until now even questioned the daughter's parentage. How well Kij must lie, to baldly claim not to know the identity of her daughter's father. *To claim not to know who was Keifer's lover!*

The letter in Jerin's hand trembled violently. Ren had told Kij that they knew Keifer had taken a lover! She told Kij that they wouldn't rest until the lover was found! If Keifer's lover was head of the cannon thieves, then Kij was quite capable of murder. Jerin reeled then, realizing that Kij had murdered the entire Wainwright family, and the crew of the *Onward,* and all the troops shot down with grapeshot in Mayfair's streets.

Murderous Kij knew that Ren was looking for her! Surely Kij would strike first!

He flung down the letter and rushed to the door, throwing the single lock he normally kept looked, and jerked the door open. The guard turned with surprise.

"I need to speak with Princess Rennsellaer!"

"She's at court," the guard said.

"Send a messenger. Tell her I need to see her immediately. It's urgent!"

"She'll be back within a few hours."

"This is critical, I must talk—"

"Surely anything you require could wait until she returns."

"If you won't send a messenger, then I'll go myself!"

That struck home. "Sir, a messenger will be sent."

Jerin shut the door and carefully threw the entire series of heavy bolts, feeling safer with every clank. After the betrothal, Ren had returned all of the Whistlers' weapons, including Jerin's, as a gesture of goodwill. He had put his in his wedding chest, thinking then that neither he nor any son he fathered would ever have need of them. He retrieved them now, checking over them out of habit. He had unloaded and cleaned the palm-sized derringer when he stored it. After double-checking that the pistol was unloaded, he tested the hammer, trigger, and firing pin. Satisfied it was in perfect working order, he loaded it.

Afterward, he sat on his wedding chest, heart pounding as if he had run a race. Why was he so scared? He was perfectly safe. It was his wives who were in danger. *Am I,* he asked himself, *or am I not a Whistler?* He might be a man, but he was also trained by the best spies the country had ever known. If his wives were in danger, he had to act. If Ren took his summons no more seriously than the door guard, then she might put off her return for hours. Surely every minute he delayed gave Kij Porter a minute to act without suspicion.

And if he waited for Ren to ride to the palace, hear what he had to say, and act upon his news, then Odelia, Trini, and Lylia—still at the courthouse—would remain in danger.

He had to go to Ren himself, and tell her about Kij.

The royal tailors had made him a walking coat to replace his old brown robe. However, it was nearly as revealing as the formfitting trousers he currently wore. Nor did it have any pockets. He changed quickly into his old walking robe, and slipped the derringer into the pocket designed to hide the pistol's bulk. His stash pouch, with lockpicks, matches, money, and other emergency needs, he strapped up under his robe, snug to his waist. Only the most thorough of searches would find it. He also strapped the shin sheath to his right leg, fluffing his robe so it would resettle around his ankles, hiding the knife. He stood looking at his deceptive reflection, a picture of mildness.

He started for the door, and then spotted Eldest's letter lying open on his writing desk. What an idiot! Kij had defiled the sanctity of the husbands' quarters once. If she or one of her agents found the letter, all was lost. He burned it, crouching before the fireplace.

It was the slightest noise that made him look up.

A strange woman stood in his bedroom door.

Their eyes locked in mutual surprise, and then the sharp, weasel-faced woman gave a smile full of evil promises, and came at him at a run.

Jerin yelped in surprise and terror, and half scuttled, half stumbled back and up.

There were other strangers, not one a Porter sister, coming out of the bedrooms. Five, all running toward him.

He shouted as he ran for the entry door. As he fumbled with the locks, he heard his guards calling on the other side of the door. Then the weasel-faced woman caught him by the hair, jerking him backward, out of reach of the locks. It felt like his scalp would rip from his skull. He screamed in pain, and spun. The woman wasn't expecting him to fight, and went down to his punch.

The others, however, took him like a flood.

Ren had dithered.

It would shame her to the end of her days, that the man she loved had sent for her, and she hadn't hurried to him, almost ignored his message completely.

Ren found the palace in chaos, the guard bristling with

weapons, charging across the grounds. Barnes hurried out to meet her as she dismounted, pain filling the old woman's face.

"Your Highness, I'm sorry. I'm so sorry. We tried. We could hear him calling for help, but we couldn't get through the door. I'm sorry."

Ren stared at her in horror, trying to understand, but it was like hearing a foreign language; the words wouldn't take meaning. "What?"

"We broke the door down, but by then—" Barnes spread her hands helplessly. "We were too late."

"No." Nothing could have happened to Jerin. She just saw him this morning. She was coming to talk to him. "No."

Then her legs started to run, taking her racing through the palace before she even knew where she was headed. She was calling his name.

The door to the husband quarters lay on the floor, the doorframe in splinters where the hinges had been pulled out. She paused in the doorway, suddenly fearful of what she'd find. The room was tomb silent. An overturned divan was the only sign of violence.

Footsteps ran up behind her. "Your Highness."

"Where is he?" she whispered.

"They took him." Barnes's voice cracked, and she worried her hands together. "They must have come in through the bolt-hole, caught him, and taken him out. I delivered a letter from his sisters around ten. A few minutes later he sent for you. The messenger had no more than ridden off when he started to cry for help. The guard heard other voices in with him. We broke down the doors—but it was too late."

"He's not dead!" She clutched at that. It was nearly one now—he had been gone for less than three hours.

"They've gotten clean away. We've sent messengers to the Queens Justice. We're starting a citywide search."

Ren dashed to Jerin's bedroom and the dressing room

beyond. "The gardens. The bolt-hole comes out in the gardens."

"We've searched the grounds." Barnes stayed at the door out of habit. "There were eight or nine in all. They split up. Half went over the back wall with him. The rest decoyed the guard away. We were able to kill one. River trash! Common river trash!"

The bolt-hole door stood open. Ren stopped at the sight of it. Surely the guards already checked the passage. Black handprints surrounded the door, as if someone with soot-covered hands had struggled to keep the door closed. Jerin? But why the soot? She looked carefully at the marks. Among the many handprints, the word "Kij" had been hastily written, sooty fingerprints dotting the *i* and *j*.

Kij? Kij had taken Jerin? The *Destiny* had steamed out of Mayfair yesterday, and the palace guards knew her former sisters-in-law on sight.

The consort has something urgent to tell you.

"Barnes?"

"Yes, Your Highness?"

"You said a letter came from his sisters?"

"Yes. I handed it to him personally."

"And a few minutes later, he sent for me?"

"Yes."

In the fire pit, she found the remains of the letter; a single piece of curled blackened paper remained intact. Very little remained legible. *. . . fathered by a Tibler . . . pushing to find this lover, then the Porters must act. Tell this information to your wives in private. Warn them to be careful. The Porters have proved to be extremely dangerous. . . . Remember your aunts are as close as Annaboro.*

Kij? With sickening clarity, she knew then. The Porters had lured the princesses into marriage, and then used Keifer to deal them death. He poisoned her father. He had been the one who demanded they go to a theater filled with explosives. He had been the one who delayed their arrival, preventing any search for danger. The royal family never suspected the Porters—too many of them had died that night too. Thinking back, now knowing Kij's ruthlessness, Ren realized that only the feeblest of the Porter mothers had been at the box. Had Keifer known that he had been walking into a death trap? Or had Kij kept him ignorant of it all?

No, Ren couldn't believe Keifer was innocent. He took too much pleasure in hurting her and her sisters. Keifer's and Eldest Porter's deaths must have been an accident—perhaps Keifer misunderstood the Porters' instructions and wasn't supposed to go himself. Certainly the Porters never tried to explain why Eldest Porter had arrived so late, or used the back entrance. Had she been rushing to save Keifer, who wasn't where they planned him to be?

If Keifer hadn't died in the theater, who would have been next on the Porters' list? Her mothers and all the adult princesses, leaving the Porters regent to the youngest? The entire family?

Yes, the entire family. Sisters-in-law inherit an orphaned estate. They were an ancient and powerful family, lacking only a royal marriage, thus Jerin's kidnapping.

If the Porters planned to marry Jerin, then there was hope. They would keep him alive, and hopefully clean. Logic suggested that they would take him to the *Destiny,* and from there, upriver to above Hera's Step to the ducal seat, Avonar. She needed only to catch up with them before they could force the marriage.

And then she had vengeance to wreak.

Jerin woke to female voices arguing. For a moment of complete disorientation, he thought he was home with his sisters squabbling as usual. Then he remembered the attack at the palace, the desperate struggle to leave a warning for Ren as they dragged him from his rooms, the entry door booming like a great drum as the guard tried to force their way in. His attackers had been hampered by the fact that they wanted him unharmed—if they had wanted him dead, he would have never been able to fight free long enough to write his message on the wall.

At one point, though, one of them had whined, "Give it to him, already!" and a needle had jabbed into him like a wasp's sting. Everything went weird and dreamy after that. A race down a dark tunnel. The garden from an upside-down perspective. A wagon ride with wheels rumbling like unending thunder. It seemed as if the true him had been shrunk down, caught like a butterfly in a glass jar, and was riding in the large shell of his body. That tiny him, unable to act, watched with helpless alarm as they slipped out of the city and took to the Queens highway before sleep finally spared him the agony of witnessing his own abduction.

"Just tell us straight—how did ya know it was us that nabbed the royal mount?" a woman was saying as he woke up.

"I guessed," a second woman answered in a cultured alto that seemed familiar, as if Jerin had talked to her before. "Anyone with two ears and two eyes could see that the Hats tapped you for something big, and then this turns up."

There was a rustle of newspaper.

"Ya know we can't read, Miss High-and-mighty," a third female speaker growled.

"Well, Bert, if you could read anything but Hat cant, you'd see that you now have what the entire Queensland is looking for," Miss High-and-mighty stated in her strangely familiar voice. "The Hats told you to take him, Fen? Or you just figured to do a little husband raiding while you were in the palace?"

"We did exactly what we were supposed ta do. Take the boy." Fen proved to be the first speaker. "Iffen ya want ta know more, ya can ask the Hats when they come for him."

"What do they want with him?"

A short nasty laugh, and a fourth woman said, "I expect what any healthy woman would want with a man that pretty."

In the general laughter that followed, Jerin picked out at least seven separate female voices. Seven strangers! Oh, merciful gods, he was lost. He wished he could sink back into oblivion, but now that he was awake, his body was making demands on him. He needed to pee and his stomach was queasy, like he'd eaten too many sweets.

He blinked open his eyes. They were in a shack, large enough for two good-sized rooms with a door between them, but river-trash poor in quality. The walls lacked plaster and whitewash, and were made of roughhewn lumber nailed to framing timbers. Sod covered the roof, pale fingers of grass roots prying at the cracks between the overhead boards. One paneless window, its outside shutters latched tight, a shipping crate standing in as bedside table, a lit oil lamp, and the bed he lay on made up the furnishings of the room he was in. The voices spilled through the open door from the next room; shadows cast by a second lamp moved menacingly across the rough walls. A girl, filthy-faced and feral-eyed, stood in the doorway, a finger digging into her nose.

"He's awake," the girl intoned with the same disinterest a kettle of boiling water might raise.

"Get away from him, Dossy," Miss High-and-mighty said.

"Ya ain't my sister." Dossy stared on at him.

"If I was, I would wallop you good for not listening." Miss High-and-mighty walked closer. "I told you to stay away from him."

"I ain't ever seen a man before," Dossy said.

A hand reached into the room, caught the girl by the scruff, and jerked her back into the other room, out of sight. Miss High-and-mighty muttered softly, "With any luck, you'll never see another one." She stepped into the room, a chair in hand. With a hollow thunk, the chair was set beside the bed he lay on, and a black-haired woman sat down on it. She gazed at him with infinite sadness on her face.

Jerin blinked at Miss High-and-mighty a few moments, recognizing the woman but not knowing from where. Then he remembered. She had been at the landing when they arrived at the summer palace. She had stolen a kiss from him. Did this time she steal more than a kiss? "What have you done to me?"

"You haven't been touched." Miss High-and-mighty reached out a hand and he flinched away. "Easy, easy, it's just a towel." When he held still, she dabbed at his forehead with the damp rag. "Nobody is going to touch you. I promise you."

"Don't go giving promises ya can't keep!" Bert called from the next room, and there was snickering.

Anger flared in Miss High-and-mighty's eyes, the muscles in her jaw jumping as she gritted her teeth. She didn't speak, only continued to carefully clean his face with the gentleness of a mother.

His left hand was caught somehow above his head, the back of his wrist pressed against the cold bars of the brass bed. Twisting his head up, he saw that iron manacles shackled him to the bed. He stared at them with sick dread.

"Easy," High-and-mighty murmured again. When he glanced at her, she was glaring at the manacles, the anger in her green eyes at odds with her soft murmur of, "Everything will be fine."

"Who are you?" Jerin asked, shifting slightly until he felt the comforting lump of his emergency stash.

She looked troubled and busied herself at refolding the rag to a clean corner. "Cira."

"If you take me back to the palace, my wives will pay twice what the Hats offered you." Jerin struggled to keep his voice firm and authoritative.

"Fen?" Cira raised her voice without turning. "It's a good offer."

"The Hats are paying us in hard cash and land," Fen

called from the next room. "Them bitches in Mayfair will just string us up to dance by our necks."

Jerin scrambled for a better offer. "Then to Annaboro, I have kin there. They can get you three times what the Hats offer without my wives in the deal. You can buy your own land with it."

The sister or mother of the girl came to lean against the doorframe. She worked a wad of chewing tobacco between her back teeth. "Boy." By her voice, he knew her to be Fen. "I'm no fool. No one has that kind of money just sitting around except the nobles, and yer just poor gentry. Everyone says so."

"They can borrow the money from the bank when it opens. They've got a mercantile that they can take a loan against. My wives will pay them back."

Fen spat on the floor. "Mercantiles? Nah, they won't beggar themselves on the hopes yer royal bitches will have you back. Everyone knows that those sluts nearly turned ya out once 'cause they thought one of *them* caught something riding the wrong horse."

The truth of her words hit him like a hard slap. Much as Ren might love him, she wouldn't dare take him back without being sure he was clean. He had to get away from these women, quickly.

"Cira. I have to wee-wee." He used the baby word and tried to look helpless.

"Who has the key to these manacles?" Cira said.

"He's a man!" Fen shrugged. "He doesn't have to get up to piss."

"What if he has to void?" Cira said.

Fen spit on the floor. "If he has to shit, he's got room to move around some. I saw to it myself."

Jerin noted that the loop of steel latched to the bed could indeed ride the bar from straight over his head down to the bed rails. He could get out of the bed, stand, and reach the length of his outstretched arms. He kept himself from experimenting—no need to let them know how mobile he was.

"This isn't decent," Cira growled. "You don't treat menfolk like this."

"I really need to wee-wee and poo." Jerin added the second to buy himself more time. He had to get free before one of them decided to rape him.

"There's the piss pot." Fen spit into it to point it out.

"For gods' sake, give him privacy." Cira brushed past Fen and went into the next room.

"Fine with me." Fen caught the loop of rope serving as a doorknob on the crude door. "We were told not to touch him. That's what they're paying well for, and I'm not going to nick this deal by not giving them what they want."

As the door shut, Cira said, "If we take him now, straight from the palace to his aunts' store, then everyone can count on their fingers and know that there wasn't time for rides on the side."

Jerin held still, waiting for the answer.

"We?" Fen's voice was muffled now, but he could tell that she had brushed off the suggestion without giving it any serious thought. "There's no 'we' here. There's us and you. Don't come crowding in here, after the work is done, with yer hand outstretched."

Jerin lifted the loop of metal, ran it down the headboard to its farthest reach, and slipped out of the bed. He relieved himself in the chamber pot.

"Who got you out of that mess in Sarahs Bend?" Cira countered. "You would have been hung if I hadn't bribed the Queens Justice."

"That's the only reason," Bert said, "that I didn't plug ya dead when ya waltzed in here unannounced like."

"I've seen you shoot," Cira drawled. "I wasn't in any danger."

As the women laughed like baying dogs, Jerin slipped his lockpick out of his stash pack, stabbed the stiff wires into the keyhole, and fished about carefully, while his heart hammered in his chest. All the winter days he and his sisters spent playing thieves, hiding in the shadows, seeing who could pick locks the fastest, and he never dreamed he'd have need for the skill.

"Iffen we're doing this sister thing," a new speaker said, making the count of women to be eight, "maybe we should count Cira in too. We could use someone with book learning and smarts like her."

There was a moment of silence from the other room. The click of the lock springing open seemed loud as thunder. Jerin paused, listening, poised to fall back into the bed and pretend helpless innocence.

"Sister thing?" Cira asked.

"When we git this land," Dossy said, "we're going ta tell folks that we're sisters."

"You seven?" Cira's voice was full of disbelief.

"Mothers did it by tens." Fen meant that they would claim that their "mothers" had visited cribs to explain how they were all sisters. "Been done before. You interested?"

Jerin stepped quietly to the bedroom window. The shack stood on pier footings, a stone's throw from the river. A barn loomed against the night sky, some fifty feet away; the soft noises of restless horses came from it.

Cira said, without any real excitement, "Perhaps."

"We're not making this offer to everyone," Fen said. "Greddy's right, though—yer a sharp one, through and through."

Jerin wavered at the window. He'd be running blind in an area they knew well. If he just slipped away, the moment they realized he was gone, they'd be on him like a pack of dogs. He might not get any farther than the barn. He needed to throw them into confusion. He turned back to the room.

"You'll be the Eldest?" Cira was asking.

"Ah," Fen replied. "So that's it—ya want to be Eldest? Greedy little bitch."

"I've done second in line," Cira said. "It doesn't work too well."

"Ha!" Bert cried. "Ya got thrown out for back talking to your Eldest?"

"Let's just say," Cira said, "that some of the parties involved thought I was usurping my sister's authority and it would be best that I leave."

As the women howled in laughter, Jerin shoved the limp pillows under the ratty blanket. He unscrewed the top of the lamp and poured its oil out onto the bed. Plucking the hot chimney free of the tines on top that kept the glass from shifting, he carefully he laid the top—lit wick and all—down on the cover. Hopefully the wick would act as a fuse. He was lowering himself out the window when the bed went up in a soft muffled *whoof*.

He landed with a jolt that went up his right leg. He folded to the ground with pain, clutching his ankle. Light and smoke spilled out the window above him. Steeling himself against the pain, he limped as fast as he could to the barn. It leaned precariously, the roof was sway-backed, and the air inside was rank with rotting hay. A dozen horses stood waiting in box stalls, their bridles hanging from pegs. He unlatched all the stall doors and tossed all but one bridle into the dark corners. Back at the shack, the window framed a brilliant blaze—how had they not noticed the fire yet?

Returning to the first stall, he slipped in beside the horse there with the last bridle in hand. Then his escape, which had been going so smoothly, stuttered, as he fumbled with the straps of leather and pieces of metal in the dark.

"Come on. Come on," he whispered.

A shout went up from the house. The fire had been discovered. Desperate now, he urged the bit into the horse's mouth and tried to fit the headpiece over its ears, only to discover he had the bridle upside down. Jerin removed the bit, flipped the bridle around, and coaxed the bit back into the horse's mouth. As he pulled the headpiece into place, someone stumbled into the stable.

The horse startled forward, forcing Jerin to step backward. Pain flared up his leg. He bit down on a gasp, but not quickly enough.

Cira's voice came out of the darkness. "Who's there?"

"I've got a gun." Jerin tried to keep his voice calm as he pulled out his pistol and leveled it at her. It was so heavy for something so small. "I know how to use it. I will use it."

"Jerin!" Cira cried, and launched herself at him.

If it had been one of the other women, he would have pulled the trigger. He was sure he would have. He tried to tighten his finger, to pull the trigger, to kill her, but he couldn't, he just couldn't. Her acts of respect and kindness flashed through his mind, freezing him in place.

She caught hold of him in a crushing hug, pressing a damp cheek to his. "Oh, thank the gods, oh, thank the gods, oh, thank the gods," she breathed like a mantra into his ear. Then she was kissing him, a desperate hungry kiss.

He jerked out of her hold, whimpering in pain as he put weight on his bad ankle again. "I've got a gun. I know how to use it. Please, don't make me."

"I'm not part of them, Jerin." The flame from the shack gleamed on her pale face. "On my word. I came to save you."

"I can save myself."

"I can see that." Her tone almost seemed like admiration. "Let me help you."

"I don't trust you!"

They stood, facing each other, as the fire crept through the shack's ceiling to feast on the dried sod roof.

"You're not going to believe anything I say, are you?" she said quietly.

"No." He motioned with his gun. "Back up."

She backed up, giving him plenty of room to run. He swung up onto the smooth back of the horse and took it.

Chapter 14

It was almost a royal brawl on the landing of Mayfair. Despite Ren's orders for Odelia, Lylia, and Trini to be escorted back to the palace, they met her on the cobbled landing.

"Look at this!" Lylia cried, thrusting a copy of the *Herald* at Ren. "Is it true? Is he gone?"

Ren took the paper and scanned it. The *Herald*, always willing to blare out rumors, hearsay, and outright lies, blasted the story of Jerin's kidnapping across the front page. The *Herald* went on to decry the royal security, lamenting that losing an innocent from the palace was a sign of supreme incompetence. Worse, the story begged someone, anyone, to save the poor royal-blooded boy before it was too late. Read carefully, it hinted darkly that such saviors could expect to keep their spoils. After such an article, the public would look softer at Kij for keeping Jerin after "rescuing" him from the river trash. Kij was already juggling madly to make her marriage to Jerin respectable. The news of Jerin's kidnapping must have reached the *Herald*'s office long before it reached Ren. Or—she gritted her teeth in sudden anger—even before Jerin had even been kidnapped!

"Well?" Trini asked quietly.

"Yes, he's gone," Ren admitted, crushing the newspaper, wishing it was Kij's throat. "They came in through the bolt-hole and kidnapped him, just like the paper says."

"What are we doing just standing here, then?" Odelia cried.

"Raven is securing a boat," Ren told them, beating her palm with the crumpled paper. Jerin's kidnapping wasn't an impromptu grab and run. Kij had planned it in greater detail than Ren had initially given her credit for. What other plans were set? Did Kij count on their chasing after her?

Ren uncrumpled the paper and scanned the story. Not surprisingly, there were no mentions of cribs; Kij would want to keep Jerin's reputation clean of that rumor. Otherwise, though, the text ran close to hysterical over the possible dangers that Jerin faced. Surely, upon reading the story, even the most coldhearted of women would rush after their betrothed. "Where did you get this, Lylia?"

Lylia was standing on tiptoe, looking over their guard's heads for Raven. "One of the clerks at the courthouse brought it around. She was concerned that we didn't know what had happened." Kij was concerned that they didn't know. "There's Raven now!"

"Good! We can get moving!" Odelia started toward Raven.

Ren caught Odelia by the elbow and pulled her back. "No. You three aren't going anywhere."

"What?" they cried in dismayed chorus.

Lylia recovered first. "I'm going after Jerin!"

"Me too!" Odelia tried to shake loose from Ren's hold.

"It's a wife's duty to guard and protect her husband," Trini stated firmly. "You can't stop me from doing so."

"The Porters are behind this! They killed Eldest and the others. They want the throne," Ren told them. She added in what she knew, and then what she only suspected. "Kij wants us to chase after her. She has some trap in store."

"Surely you're not suggesting letting *them* keep Jerin!" Trini growled, her eyes narrowed in anger. "Not after all they have done to us!"

"No!" Ren cried, hurt that they would think her capable of that. "I'm saying that only one of us should go!"

"Kij doesn't know that we know it's her!" Odelia pointed out. "We'll be on our guard!"

Ren shook her head. "She can't trust her luck that we haven't guessed. She's in too deep. She has to be sure that when she strikes this time, she gets us all. She's taken our husband, printed this damn story, and left a trail to follow. It's a trap!"

"And we're supposed to sit back and let you ride off to get killed, and do nothing?" Lylia asked.

"You're supposed to stay here and make sure our little sisters are safe, or have you forgotten that they're between the Porters and the throne too?"

Her sisters exchanged guilty looks.

"You think Kij is going to lure us upriver and then attack here?" Trini asked.

"Quite possibly," Ren said. "Our mothers might be mostly retired, but they're still a force to fear. If Kij kills us upriver, unless she counterblows here too, against the palace, then she'll be facing a very angry Queen Mother Elder."

"Go upriver," Trini said quietly. "We'll guard against the Porters here."

Raven broke her silence. "It would be best if none of you go. I can take a boat and fetch Jerin back."

Ren shook her head. "Much as we love Jerin, he figures in this only as bait, and as a royal husband for whoever comes out alive. I need to go upriver and nail Kij to the nearest tree."

"You can't arrest a duchess on her ducal grounds, Captain," Trini added. "You don't have the power."

Raven's mouth quirked into a grin. "It might be fun to try, though. She wouldn't be suspecting it—a common arrest is much below her own sense of self-importance."

"I don't want her warned," Ren said. "I have a feeling that we'll have only one shot to get her. I want to make the most of it. Raven, take the boat you just commandeered to Sparrows Point. Get the *Red Dog*. Bring it back. I'll ready a platoon of marines here."

Raven eyes widened. She controlled a grin, and then bowed slightly. "Yes, Your Highness."

As Raven hurried off, Lylia crowed with delight. "A gunboat? Ren, that's truly evil! Blow that bitch out of the water!"

Ren grinned, and swatted Odelia with the newspaper. "You! You're eldest while I'm gone, unless Halley shows her face, which she may once she sees this paper! Kij has done us a favor there. Send troops to the *Herald,* find Kij's mole there, and root her out. I don't want any more articles that smell—ever so mildly—of treason."

Odelia gulped at the promotion, and nodded, eyes huge.

"Trini, have a fast messenger go on to Annaboro and let Jerin's family there know what's happened. I'll send one on to Heron Landing once I get upriver. Send word to our cousins—Kij might try to eliminate them too. Send out messengers to the Queens Justice for news on Jerin—Kij will be expecting us to do that, and we don't want to disappoint her."

Trini nodded solemnly.

Ren turned last to Lylia. "Call in troops; fortify the palace. The youngest aren't to go out. Keep our mothers in, if you can. Remember that Kij's favorite weapon is poison."

Lylia nodded, and then suddenly hugged Ren tight. "Take care of yourself. Get Jerin back!"

Ren blinked back sudden tears. "I will. Go on, now. Kij has her plan in motion. We've got to get ours going too."

Jerin wasn't aware Cira was following until her big roan muscled beside his. She reached out, caught him by the waist just as he registered her presence, and jerked him sideways onto her horse. Taken by surprise, he was left with the choice of falling between the horses, perhaps to be trampled, or letting her settle him onto the saddle in front of her.

To his shame, his body chose the latter, clinging tightly to her.

"Where the hell did you learn to ride?" Cira growled, reining her horse sharply and turning suddenly down a side track. His horse raced on without him. She held him tight with one arm, and stripped the pistol from his belt. "You certainly have pluck, I have to say that!"

"Let me go!" He swung at her awkwardly with his free hand, but she dodged the blow.

"What a little lion cub." Cira laughed at him. "Hush! Quiet as you can! Here they come!"

The shack was a torch in the night behind them. She had tucked her horse into a thick grove of sumac, screening them from the road he had been racing along. Horses were coming, a rolling thunder.

Jerin stopped fighting Cira to be quiet. She held him close, stroking his hair. Her heart pounded under his cheek.

The river trash rode past, dark forms moving through night, hooves drumming on the dry earth.

"It's okay. We're safe now." Cira lowered him to the ground but kept hold of his forearm. "Get on behind me. I can get you back to the palace without so much as a blemish on your reputation. It will get all hushed up, no one the wiser."

He hesitated, not sure what to do. A throbbing pain in his ankle reminded him that running on foot wasn't an option.

Cira tightened her hold on him. "Alone, you'd be at the mercy of every woman that sees you."

She was right. If he didn't run afoul of a family desperate for a husband, then there were the women that would use him to establish a crib. Much as he didn't trust Cira, his chances were better with her.

He scrambled up behind her. "Where are we?"

"Halfway to Hera's Step." Cira clucked to her roan

and guided it out of their hiding space. "This is the main road into Sparrows Point. If we stay on it, we'll be caught between them and the damn hat-wearing bitches that hired them."

"How do I know you're not lying to me?"

Cira chuckled. "I'll try not to push my credibility with you. Fen and her women went that way; we'll go this way. How about that?"

"Will it take us downriver to Mayfair?"

"We can't go downriver. We have to cut across a dozen fields and get upriver."

"Why?"

"We're just north of Snake Run, and it's all white water and deep fast pools. We can't ford it. We'll have to go all the way to Queens Highway for a bridge across. With us riding double, those river rats would catch us before we could get to where we could buy fresh horses."

"It would have been better if you left me on my horse."

"I'm hoping they think you were thrown. I don't know many women that could have kept their seat through that. If they believe you've been thrown, they'll have to be searching for you to be on foot, or unconscious, in the dark."

For a plan conceived at a full gallop, it seemed sound enough.

Jerin pointed out the one flaw. "But won't they think you've caught up with me, like you have?"

Cira's shoulder lifted under his chin. "I tried to give the impression that I thought everything was a lost cause, and started out in the opposite direction. Whether they believed any of it, is another thing."

They went as quickly as they could, crossing open fields in reckless bursts and carefully picking their way through cave-black woodlots and windbreaks. With the gray of predawn came a thick fog, whiting out the landscape. Steamboat whistles echoed from the distant river like cries of great hunting beasts.

The roan, lathered and winded, couldn't go any farther. They dismounted and found that Jerin's ankle was weak, but he could limp.

"We're almost to Sarahs Bend," Cira said as she helped Jerin to a hay barn standing like an island in the fog. "It's just a half mile down the road. The Queens Justice here is corrupt. I think the Hats have the lieutenant in their pocket. Fen might think I pulled wonders getting her and her women free, but all I had to do was mention the Hats and drop a few crowns, and someone forgot to lock their cell door."

"I'm supposed to believe you're not one of them after comments like that?" Jerin asked.

The barn was in good repair, with no windows and a door padlocked against passing river trash.

Cira tested the heavy lock with a tug. "Fen was a means to something bigger."

"And I'm just a means to something bigger too?"

Cira gave him a hurt look and then turned away, studying the barn for another entrance. "I've been hunting the Hats for over a year. Fen is getting me closer to knowing who they are."

"They're the Porters: Kij and her sisters. We found proof."

Cira jerked around to face him. *"What?"*

Jerin backed away from her. "We found the proof in the husband quarters."

Cira caught his hand, keeping him from bolting away. "Honey, I'm not angry at you. Just tell me what you found."

"Kij was sleeping with Keifer, even after he was married." Jerin slipped out his lockpick and tackled the padlock to distract himself. "Keifer poisoned the princesses' father. And then, after the princesses' father was dead, every time Keifer acted angry, it was so he could let Kij into the husband quarters. We didn't know at first that

Kij was his lover, though, and Ren went to Kij and showed her what we found."

"Oh, bloody hell." Cira started to pace. "This all makes sense. They're after the throne. You're Prince Alannon's grandson; marrying you would give them legitimacy."

"But I have male cousins nearly my age—they could have made an offer. . . ."

"You're the one who's been verified by the Queens themselves."

The padlock clicked open and Jerin unlatched the door.

Cira eyed the lock with surprise. "So that's how you got free from that bed. An interesting talent for a prince consort."

Jerin limped inside to collapse onto the fresh hay. Cira led in her roan and tied it outside reach of the hay, so it couldn't eat itself to death, and then found grain and water for it.

"Three daily packets stop in town," Cira said as she returned Jerin's pistol to him. "I think the first packet comes through town before noon. I'll get tickets so we can board at the last moment and go straight to a cabin. Once we're on the river, we'll be safe until we hit Mayfair."

Somehow sharing a cabin with Cira didn't seem like a "safe" option. Nor did Jerin like the idea of waiting here, trusting Cira while she could be selling him to the highest bidder.

"And your plan is for me to sit here quietly until you come back?"

"Sweetie, I'll just be more river trash, but you're a man, one that the entire Queensland is looking for. If the Queens Justice is in town, they might have drawings of you." Cira took his hand and clasped it tight. "And I know you have no reason to trust me, but just because they're soldiers doesn't make them infallible."

As his own family history would attest to.

He sighed and pulled his hand free. "I'll wait here. Can you bring me something to eat? My stomach is still queasy."

She gave him a slight smile, pulled her Stetson down low to throw a shadow across her scarred face, and left. He waited as the bells of the nearby town rang five o'clock. Once he was fairly sure she was gone, Jerin unbuckled her saddlebag and carried it to the hay mound to look through it.

On top was a silver flask. He unscrewed its lid, sniffed its contents. Brandy—and fairly expensive if he judged it correctly. He had expected to find corn whiskey, the standard smuggler drink.

He put the flask aside and continued unloading the saddlebag. A turtle shell comb. A bottle of black liquid he couldn't identify. A small book tied shut with a piece of ribbon.

Untying the ribbon, he found the book was a journal written in code. He worried at his bottom lip. While his grandmothers had taught him code breaking, nevertheless, it could take him hours to crack it and translate the book. He didn't have hours. He flipped through the pages, checking if anything had not been written in code. Between the back pages, he discovered three newspaper clippings. The first was headlined FORTY DEAD IN WEAPON SHOP FIRE. The second story looked like it had been torn out instead of clipped; while it was missing the headline, he recognized it as the *Herald*'s story about the attack on Odelia. In the same handwriting as the journal were names and numbers written in the margin. "*Osprey* 6/4 Dusk. *Frontier* 6/5 Dawn. *Enterprise* 6/4 Midnight." Ship names and times, he realized. Where had she gone? The *"Osprey"* had been underlined, seeming to indicate a need for speed.

The third story had been carefully clipped, neatly folded and refolded, and was well-worn from being handled.

QUEENS SPONSOR PRINCE ALANNON'S GRANDSON

After decades of mystery, the fate of the vanished Prince Alannon has been finally revealed. A report issued from the palace today stated that the prince married Queensland knights Sirs Whistler and retired to their up-country land grant. In an amazing twist of fate, Master Jerin Whistler, the grandson of Prince Alannon, has been named as Princess Odelia's recent savior. As a reward for his selfless bravery, the Queens will be sponsoring Master Whistler for the upcoming Season. Sources close to the crown state that the young man has been installed at the palace and bears a striking resemblance to the beautiful missing prince. . . .

The story would have appeared after he met her on the Mayfair landing—after she kissed him. He supposed it was understandable she would want a keepsake of such an event. Kissing was something only husbands and wives were allowed to do. His sister Summer would keep a newspaper story of a boy she kissed. That Cira was like his sister helped calm his nerves.

He could glean nothing more from the journal. He returned the clippings, closed the book, and tied it shut. He dug deeper into the saddlebag. A can opener. A tin pan with a screw-on handle that could be stored inside the pan. He marveled at the ingeniousness of the pan and then started to set it aside. It struck him then, the quality of the items Cira owned. The journal had not been showy, but was well bound with a stamped leather cover. The tin pan was cunningly made. The saddlebag itself was a sturdy and handsome item. The fine roan horse she rode. Even the brandy in the flask had been quality.

Cira was a rich woman, though she did not show it. It was, in fact, as if she was trying to hide the fact.

The other women at the shack, though, seemed to be

river trash. The shack. The two or three of them he saw. The language that the others used. Dirt-poor and willing—no, needing—to steal to survive.

Cira hadn't been one of them. Considering the newspaper clipping, it even seemed likely that she had been there only to rescue him. Still, he could not afford to trust her. Trust had led to betrayal too often, too recently.

A short time after the town bells rang six, Cira reappeared.

"There's no sign of Fen and her women," she told him as she sat down on the hay beside him. She had two small loaves of fresh bread. "This was all that could be had this early in the morning. I would have brought you ginger if the apothecary was open. Most likely it's the drugs that Fen gave you that upset your stomach, but it might be because you haven't eaten for a full day."

He ate the bread cautiously; it seemed to help settle his queasy stomach.

"The first packet is at nine." Cira tore her loaf of bread in two and gave him the larger piece. "And the Queens Justice is in town. If I'd had the coin, I'd have bought fresh horses. I don't like this sitting and waiting, but we don't have much of a choice."

She started to unload her pockets, producing a small ceramic crock, rhinestone hair combs, a bright red silk scarf, and a white-feathered boa. "I thought that one way to slip you past the Queens Justice is to hide you in the open."

"What do you mean?" Jerin opened the crock, hoping for something to eat. It contained a bright red cream. "What is this?"

"That's lip paint," Cira said, dipping one finger into red. "Purse your lips and hold still."

"Makeup?"

Cira blushed, a first for her. "It's a disguise. Everyone is looking for a man; they might not look twice at a whore."

He knew some women pleasured others for money, but his mothers and sisters kept him innocent of the details. "Whores are women, aren't they?"

"In body, but not always in appearance. Many dress as men, the manlier, the better." Cira glided her fingertip over his lips in a way that was at once intimate and erotic.

Jerin scrambled to take his mind away from her fingers. "Don't they lack certain vital equipment?"

"There are artificial devices." Cira dipped her finger into the crock again, and rouged his cheeks, her breath on his face as she blended color out. "They call them bones because they're made out of ivory. They strap on. Whores carry them sheathed to their leg, here, to look more manly."

She put her hand on him, and found him excited. She smiled, stroking him gently, her eyes full of lust.

"Wh-wh-why red on the lips?" he asked.

"To advertise they know how to use their mouth." She ran the tip of her tongue over her lips, moistening them, drawing a slight gasp from him. "It feels very, very good."

He understood then what she was referring to—his wives claimed he was very good at it. He couldn't believe he had anything in common with a whore. Maybe she was just repeating a rumor. "You—have you ever—you know—been with a whore?"

"I had a lover, a beautiful young officer, whose mother had been a whore." Her voice turned bitter as she draped the scarf about his neck, trying to cover his man's apple. "She should have been a whore herself. She was well suited for it: ambitious, heartless, and very talented. She could make you feel like you were about to turn inside out."

"What happened to her?"

She caught his hand and pressed it to her scar. "This happened to her. After I was scarred she couldn't bear to touch me, look me in the face."

"Why?" He traced the scar on her face. "It's like an exotic piece of jewelry. It becomes you."

In a sudden angry move, she pulled her shirt off and turned her back to him, revealing a mass of puckered skin and silvery scars. At some point she had been badly burned. "Look at me! I'm repulsive!"

He ran a hand over the wounded skin. His fingertips reported only warm flesh and solid muscle, the ugliness of the burn invisible to the touch. "No. You're not repulsive."

She turned—her eyes luminescent with unshed tears—and kissed him. Apples flavored her mouth. He retreated. She advanced. They ended sprawled in the hay, no more room for him to retreat, and she on top of him, her groin pressed against him instead of her hand, rocking suggestively. They fitted together as if molded from one flesh, only her trousers and his walking robe and underclothes between their bare skin.

"Show me," she whispered against his mouth. "Show me how beautiful I am."

"No!" He pushed at her shoulders. "You're taking me back to my wives. You promised. I won't be unfaithful to them."

She laughed, seemed about to say something, and then shook her head. "I won't push you, my love. This will all be over soon, and you'll see that you can trust me."

He snorted as she retreated then, drawing her shirt back on.

"We'll pad the front of your shirt a little, to make it look like you're hiding breasts." Cira glanced at him and laughed. "And we'll have to put the lip paint back on again too."

Three hours later, they started into the town of Sarahs Bend. Cira would have liked to wait until they heard the steam whistle of the packet docking at the landing, but was afraid they might miss the boat. A weak sun had burned off part of the fog, revealing the edge of town within rifle shot; Cira still insisted that he ride the big roan while she led it.

Sarahs Bend was much larger than his hometown of Heron Landing. There were several blocks of paved streets flanked with tall, narrow but deep, brick buildings. The first floors were storefronts, while the upper floors were obviously residences of the store owners. Some of the buildings were four stories tall, casting shadows onto the cobblestones. The edges of their roofs sparkled oddly in the sunlight.

"City people hang laundry on their roofs," Cira explained when Jerin asked about it. "People embed broken bottles into the roof parapets, to discourage husband raids."

He noticed then that the storefronts also had cast-iron gates that could be padlocked shut at night.

It surprised him how many types of stores there were. Besides two mercantiles, there were stores for apothecaries, books, dry goods, shoes, tailors, watchmakers, and more. Each carried the name of the family that ran it and then symbolic signage for the illiterate; he recognized all but one.

"What do they sell there?" Jerin pointed to a gas lamp with three blue glass globes. The stone building lacked the glass front of the rest; while the front door stood open, heavily armed women guarded the entrance. Customers came and went, but they carried items neither in nor out. "Is it a bank?"

"Hush, don't point," Cira murmured, and then clucked the roan to speed them past the store.

"What is it?" Jerin whispered.

"Pay it no mind."

He'd heard that tone enough in his life to realize it was a crib. He looked back to study the fortresslike building. He never thought such a thing would be on a Main Street corner, its gas lamp bright in the overcast morning so it couldn't be missed. How many men were inside? A dozen narrow windows cut into the thick stone of the first story. One window per man? Iron bars covered the larger windows of the second story. A short railing lined the roof with sharpened iron points. He knew that they were there to keep out women, but they would work to keep men in. The trickle of women in and out of the building was constant—each representing a forced coupling.

His breakfast churned in his stomach. "Cira, I think I'm going to be sick."

"Now?" Whatever she saw on his face convinced her. She guided the roan into a narrow alley.

His breakfast came up while Cira kept his hair and clothes out of the way.

"That's where I'm going to end up." He moaned. "In a place just like that. Locked in and drugged."

"That is not going to happen to you. You're getting home and it will be just like nothing happened."

"Ren won't be able to take me back. No one is ever going to believe that nothing happened to me."

More bread came up, and then his stomach was empty, but his body continued to heave.

Cira rubbed his back soothingly, patiently waiting for him to recover. "Ren will believe you. If she loves you, she will trust you and believe what you tell her to be the truth, even if you were gone for years."

He shook his head. "Her mothers wouldn't let her offer for me for weeks—they might force her to give me back to my sisters."

"Jerin." Cira straightened him up and wiped his face. "I swear to you, you will never be in a crib. I can guarantee that you're clean. I might seem like a river trash, but I come from a powerful, old family. The Queens will take my word."

He thought of all the fine belongings in her saddlebag, everything that indicated that she was much more than what she seemed. "Really?"

"And I am not poor either. If need be, I have the money to pay your brother's price and marry you."

"All by yourself?"

"We can start a new trend. One wife per husband."

He laughed at the ridiculousness of her plan.

The loud roar of the packet's whistle came from the river.

"Come on. Dry your tears and put on a smile. We're almost home free. Just a little more, and we'll be safe on the river."

It was odd to be among people and not be the center of attention. He and Cira moved through the crowd waiting on the landing without anyone noticing them. Amazingly, the flimsy disguise was working. Women would glance his direction, see the bright boa that Cira had him wave lazily about, gather in the lack of veil and the painted face, and lose interest in him.

They almost made it.

A few feet from the gangplank, Cira took a sudden deep breath, and hands caught Jerin tight from behind.

"Not a word!" growled a familiar voice. "A single noise, missy, and we'll pop you where you stand."

"Ya should pop her anyhow, stealing 'im away like that!" Dossy whined.

He swung about. They had a revolver tight to Cira's spine. "Don't you dare hurt her!"

"Or what, little boy?" Bert sneered. "Ya cry?"

"I'll tell your bosses that you raped me. Oh, it was awful! You dirty, infected crib sleaze took me again and again. They're paying for clean and untouched. I'll be sure to convince them you're pulling a double cross. Selling used goods!"

"Shut ya mouth!" Bert jerked her gun back, swinging the butt around to strike him with it.

"Bert!" Fen snapped, catching her hand. "Don't you dare, shithead! Unharmed and untouched, they said!"

"So what do we do?" Bert asked.

"Give them both to the bosses. Let them work it out," Fen said.

Jerin glanced around them. The other women on the landing looked on but made no move to interfere. Guns were already in the mix. From their faces, he realized that they still saw him as a whore having trouble with river trash. If he appealed to them as a man, once they rescued him, would they try to keep him?

"Come quietly," Fen said. "Or we *will* pop Miss High-and-mighty here and now."

He let himself be dragged to an alley where horses waited. Since none of his counteroffers had worked, he tried a new ploy. The Porters had left no witnesses behind them—surely they wouldn't allow Fen and her women to live, knowing their darkest secrets.

"The Hats are a noble family planning to marry me to claim the throne," he told them. "You'll know as soon as the marriage is announced which noble family is the Hats. You're the only ones that can testify they're one and the same. They've—"

Fen cocked her hand in warning. "Hush your mouth, or I'll knock you silly enough you can't talk, and blame it on Miss High-and-mighty."

He wanted to stay conscious, so he kept his suspicions to himself.

The side-wheeler *Destiny* sat waiting for them, tied off to massive oaks on a secluded bend in the river, its stage lowered to the desolate shore.

Kij and her sisters came down to greet them in the woods, six-guns holstered on their hips. Kij smiled at Jerin, then noticed Cira and frowned. "So, you make an appearance, finally."

"Gods, your soul must be black," Cira growled.

Kij waved the insult away. "Faith is for the well-to-do. My grandmothers left us too destitute for that nonsense."

"But Keifer, and your Eldest, and your mothers?" Cira asked.

"Our family doesn't age well," Kij said lightly, as if

she were talking about spilling cheap wine and not her family's blood. "Our mothers had long slipped into senility, and babbled family secrets right and left. They made a useful sacrifice—one last service to the family. Keifer, dearly as I loved him, was an idiot. He was to get himself to the first-floor bathroom. We picked that theater primarily for a place he could survive the blast. The walls reinforced by the plumbing would have protected him. He never showed. Eldest went to fetch him, but then— they weren't supposed to be killed."

"Ahhh, too bad. So now a husband raid?" Cira asked.

"Oh, *we* didn't raid for a husband," Kij cried, pressing her left hand to her chest, looking wounded. "The royal guard can testify without influence from us that not a single Porter sister took Jerin from the palace."

Kij's right hand flashed downward, drawing her pistol.

Jerin had been watching for the move; he stepped in front of Cira, shielding her. "Kij, no!"

The Porters' revolvers fired in thunderous rounds. Fen, Bert, little Dossy, and the others went down in a hail of bullets, the Porter sisters emptying their six-guns into the hapless river trash.

Birds startled up out of the trees and winged away as the echoes returned from the far shore. Gun smoke wreathed them. The smell of blood grew as the river trash's lives poured out into the dirt around them.

"There's an interesting law that applies here," Kij calmly explained as she reloaded her pistol. "It's similar to war plunder. It says that if an unmarried man is kidnapped by party A and rescued by party B, then he belongs to party B. Losers weepers, finders keepers." She spun the chamber on her pistol. "Step out of the way, Jerin."

"No." Jerin was pleased that he sounded more firm than he felt.

"Sisters, please, get our new husband out of harm's way."

"If I were you," Cira called out to Kij from behind

him, "I'd think long and hard before you walk down that road."

"It's a road we've walked before." Kij raised her revolver. "A few more miles, and Queensland is ours."

"Kill her and I will never be your husband!" Jerin growled. "You'll have to keep me chained to a wall, because I'll escape you every chance I get. I'll tell anyone I see of the crimes you committed. You'll have to rape me for my seed! You'll have to raise our children alone."

"Jerin, hush." Cira caught his shoulders and started to push him aside. "Don't give them cause to hurt you."

Jerin dug in his heels, refusing to move out of the way. "Let her live, and I marry you willingly. I'll stay by your side. I'll pleasure you in bed, and I'll take joy in our children. My word of honor."

"She knows too much," Kij explained to him gently, then made a shooing motion with her gun. "Move aside, Jerin."

"Kij!" Kij's sister Meza hissed. "Not in front of him. Frankly, I want a husband with a tongue."

"Let's keep our options open," their sister Alissa added.

Kij stared at him and then lowered her pistol. "You win for now, beloved." She turned away. "I don't want him haring off over the countryside again. Search them both, Alissa, and handcuff them in my cabin. We'll do a rotating guard on them."

"Search them both?" Alissa quirked up an eyebrow.

Kij holstered her pistol. "He may be gently born, but his family were knights of valor. Unless I miss my guess, they'll arm anything that can hold a gun."

They found his derringer and knife, which made them search up under his robe, teasing and touching him rudely. He covered his face, and hid his fierce attention to which pocket Alissa dropped his stuff into. When Meza found his stash pouch, Cira winced. Obviously she had hoped he would free himself a second time.

"I can't believe you're turning against the Queens," Jerin said to cover his turning, watching Meza as she frowned at the jumble of items in his pouch and then slipped it into her own pocket.

"You can't?" Kij took his hand, pleading understanding with her eyes. "Did you think we gave a fuck which princess was Eldest? Either one would have been the same to us! So an idiotic war we cared nothing about was waged, and our entire livelihood was blown away!"

"That doesn't give you the right to murder the royal family!" Jerin cried.

"They destroyed our family!"

Cira gave a bitter laugh. "How do you figure that? No Porter was killed in the war, and you received reparations for the damage to the locks!"

"We received chicken feed! We could only rebuild half the system on what we received, and half is worthless! We had to mortgage everything to scrape up the money, and still it wasn't enough! So we started smuggling and stealing and murdering to make ends meet. We lost our honor. We lost mothers and sisters overseeing the dangerous construction and smuggling ring. I had to shoot my own sister in the face so she couldn't be identified! The indignities we've suffered—all because the royal family couldn't settle who would be Eldest. Well, never again. We're taking the thrones."

Jerin exaggerated his limp, and as he came off the stage, stumbled against Alissa. She caught him out of reflex, and as she righted him, he dipped his hand down into her coat pocket. His fingers closed on the cold, welcome grip of his derringer. Lightly, he lifted the small pistol out, his heart hammering fit to break, and slipped it into his robe pocket. There was no outcry from her sisters and Alissa smiled as she took the opportunity to grope him. Even Cira, who was watching him with concern, seemed unaware. He limped forward, faked another stumble into Meza Porter, and retrieved his stash pouch. He didn't even want to try for his knife—it was so awkward a shape he was sure to be caught. Instead he meekly allowed himself to be led to Kij's cabin.

Kij's cabin was on the second deck, in the corner farthest from the great churning paddle wheel. Jerin balked at the door, for here was surely a den of seduction. A huge bed dominated the room, covered with a thick feather mattress, sheets of silk, and drapes of brocades and dark green velvets. Cherry paneling and stained glass on the portholes darkened the room. Alissa, entering before him, took a match to the oil lamps, and the warm glow of their flames reflected on gold leaf and brass.

Alissa looked at the bed and then at him, nostrils flaring. "On the bed, love."

Conscious of the four armed Porter sisters behind him, Jerin limped to the bed and sat on the very edge.

"Chain her to the foot like a dog," Alissa said, eyes locked on him. "She can watch while I tumble him."

With a great deal of laughing, they handcuffed Cira to the foot of the bed. Jerin braced himself. Against the five of them, there was nothing he could do except act as if he would honor his vow. Thankfully Alissa made no attempt to undress him. She merely pushed him back onto the bed. He twisted his robe as he fell so his pistol and stash were under him as Alissa sprawled on top of him. She writhed against him as she raped his mouth.

"Really, Alissa," Cira said in a tone near boredom. "Taking Diva from me hurt me more than anything you can do with him."

Alissa laughed, tossing her head to flip her gold hair out of her eyes, and slunk up, catlike, until she sat astride Jerin. "She was a delightful little bitch. You had her trained well. Tell me," she said as she ran her finger over Jerin's painted lips, "is he as talented with his mouth?"

"Why would you think I would know?" Cira drawled. "You know my tastes. You've eaten my leftovers."

Alissa glared at Cira, eyes narrowing, Jerin all but forgotten below her. "If you are so disinterested, why are you riding herd on him?"

"What better bait for wolves than the sacrificial lamb?"

Alissa made a sound of disgust and climbed off of Jerin. "Leave you to take the fun out of it. Meza, gag the bitch." She handcuffed Jerin firmly to the headboard. "You'll have first watch, Meza."

Meza gagged Cira tightly, settled at the paper-strewn desk, and reached for a pen. "Good, I can get caught up with these invoices."

I made the right decision. I made the right decision.

Ren clung to the mantra, though as the sun moved across the sky, she sank into utter misery. Runners bringing her updates from her sisters did nothing to shake the soundness of her decision, or give hope that Jerin would be restored to them. The ever-so-polite raid on the *Herald* ferreted out the Porter mole and a wealth of information. Recent deliveries of cooking goods to the barracks turned up enough poison to lay waste to the Fifth Battalion. Incensed by their close call, the troops marched the street, arresting all loiterers, turning up scores of heavily armed river trash.

The *Red Dog* steamed into port, low and sleek as a hunter, the late afternoon sun glinting off the crimson-painted wood shields enclosing her decks. As women and supplies were loaded at frantic speed, Raven reported that orders had been sent downriver as far as the mouth for the *Red Dog*'s sister ships to join in the hunt.

Wait, was Raven's unvoiced appeal.

Ren shook her head. All afternoon, the image of raped, mutilated, and murdered Egan Wainwright seared through her memory. Gods have mercy, her sweet beautiful Jerin was in the hands of women that had done that to a man! If the Porters meant to marry Jerin for his royal bloodline, then he would be spared that fate. But what if she had been wrong about the Porters? What if they had taken Jerin as disposable bait?

She wouldn't delay any longer. She signaled that they were to steam out immediately. "What armaments do we have?"

The corner of Raven's mouth dipped in worried disapproval. "The *Red Dog* is only lightly armed. Two eight-inch guns, one forward, the other aft, behind iron shutters. True, their twenty-pound balls will put a hole in just about anything, but you've got to be pointed in the right direction first. The bow is reinforced as a ram. And we've got the marines—a hundred rifles is nothing to sneer at."

"Hopefully more than what Kij has."

"One hopes."

Chapter 15

Jerin never considered he'd fall asleep, not with the stress and fear of his situation. If he had thought it possible, he would have guarded against it. The day's rigors, however, combined with the warm, soft bed, put him fully asleep before he realized the danger.

He woke to Kij's voice, coming from across the room, asking softly, "Is he still sleeping?"

"Like a babe," Meza whispered in reply. There was a rustle of paper. "Sign here, and here."

"We're through the last lock. We're going ashore here. See that he gets well cared for—something to eat, a chance to relieve himself. You'll reach home within a few hours. Install him in the husband quarters—quietly. No one but family is to see him. We'll have to handle this carefully for it to work."

"And if it doesn't?" Meza asked.

"The last fifty years have proved us cleverer than all. We'll weasel out and land on our feet. Have we not time and time again?"

"We've never pushed our luck this close before."

"This will work. It goes faster than I planned, but a nudge here, a nudge there, and everything will fall right. Trust me, Meza."

There was a slight, tired sound from Meza. "I do. Please, be careful. I'd rather not have Alissa as Eldest."

With a laugh, Kij said her good-bye and went out the

door. Jerin lay with his eyes closed and forced his breathing to stay deep.

The duchy of Avonar lay upriver of Hera's Step. Kij said they were through the last lock, so they were now above the great waterfall. He recalled the small town that supplied boats with coal, food, and entertainment while they waited their turn to move through the locks. The town was crowded with ship crews and passengers, people he could hide among and perhaps find aid from. While there were towns north of the falls, he would be a lone stranger in a place loyal to the Porters.

Now was the ideal time to escape. If he was to free himself, though, he needed to get rid of Meza. Considering Kij's orders, asking for food and water might force Meza to fetch it herself. If not, she'd at least undo his hands so he could eat.

He stirred then, making a show of waking and stretching, blinking with sleep befuddlement. Did Meza believe his act? She glanced up from her paperwork, fingers ink-stained, looking more an accountant than a murderous smuggler. Cira, on the other hand, glancing over the rim of the footboard, had murder in her eyes. Was that look of anger for him, for falling asleep, or just anger at the situation?

Trying to ignore the hate on Cira's face, he whined, "I'm hungry, and thirsty, and I have to wee-wee."

"I'm not surprised," Meza said, methodically cleaning her pens and putting the desk aright before standing. "You've been asleep for hours."

He felt a flare of guilt at her words. He should have tried to escape hours ago, gotten free and back to his wives. Every minute he spent away from them, the less likely he could ever return to them.

Meza came and unshackled his wrists. Holding firmly to his elbow, she steered him to the corner where there was a chamber pot built into a dresser to make an indoor privy. She kept hold of him while he relieved himself, though she averted her eyes. He chanced much, moving his stash pouch from his pocket to his loosely gathered sleeve.

Afterward, Meza led him back and handcuffed him to the bed again. "I'll go get you something to eat."

Even as she shut the door behind her, he slipped the pouch out, fingered through it, and pulled the lockpick free. From the foot of the bed, Cira's eyes went large.

Minutes later, when he undid her gag, she whispered fiercely, "You have to be the slipperiest prince consort in history! I saw them take that from you. How did you get it back?"

"I picked Meza's pocket," he whispered, tempted to gag her again. "I wanted to be free of them before they decided that they wanted to be serviced."

"What about your word of honor?"

"I lied." Jerin struggled with her handcuff. "You meet people at their level, or the liars and murderers of this world will drag you under."

Cira smothered a laugh. "I can't believe you! Did Queen Mother Elder really agree for you to marry her daughters?"

"I don't see how being raped would be preferable to lying."

The cuffs came undone and she rose, rubbing her wrists.

"What should we do now?" he started to ask, but she caught him and kissed him. Her mouth was warm and sweet, and he realized that he was half in love with her.

"Why did you do that?" To his shame, he wanted to do it again.

"You're teaching me never to give up."

He wasn't sure if this was a good thing. He pulled himself free, needing to put distance between them before he gave in to kissing her again. "So what do we do?"

"Get in the bed," she said with a grin.

His heart leaped and a flame of arousal went through him. "What?"

"Pretend like you're still handcuffed. I will too." She glanced about, then picked up a heavy stone paperweight, and gave him an evil grin.

He sat down, put his hands back above his head, and tried to be calm. Cira settled at the foot of the bed, her eyes glittering with contained excitement. Minutes stretched out until they seemed unbearable. Then finally Meza stepped through the door.

She carried a glass of lemonade and a bowl of biscuits covered with sausage gravy. Jerin's stomach growled at the smell. In tense silence, he and Cira watched as Meza came across the room, unaware of the danger to her, intent on not spilling the nearly full bowl. As she set the food on the table beside the bed, Cira rose, drawing back the paperweight.

Meza must have caught the motion in the corner of her eye. She started to turn, and Jerin lunged out, grabbing hold of her hands. Her eyes went wide in shock, and then Cira struck her. It was a hollow noise. Meza's eyes rolled back, showing their whites before they closed, and her knees folded.

Jerin jerked his hands away from her as she crumpled, and covered his mouth to hold in the dismayed cry that was trying to escape. Cira bent over Meza, quickly and ruthlessly binding the woman. When Jerin trusted himself, he took his hands from his mouth and whispered, "Is she dead?"

Cira glanced up and her eyes saddened. "No! No. I'm sorry, honey, I would do anything to spare you this." Cira undid Meza's gun belt and strapped the six-gun to her waist, tying it down low for a fast draw, and then checked the pistol. "Let's get out of here."

The *Destiny* was steaming directly up the center of the massive Bright River, making it nearly a quarter mile on either side to the shore. The sun was in the final throes of setting, and the river reflected all its vivid blood reds and fire yellows.

Holding Jerin's hand tight, Cira guided him through a maze of cotton bales and crates stacked on the *Destiny*'s decks to the railing. There they crouched in the growing shadows.

"Can you swim?" Cira asked him.

Jerin looked uneasily out over the quickly moving water. "Some. I—I don't think I could get to the shore. It's too far and the current's too strong."

Cira nodded as if this was a fair assessment. "Truthfully, I don't think I could either. We'll have to get up to the pilothouse and take control of the ship there. I wish I knew how many women Kij left on board."

"Why do you think Kij got off?"

"I'm afraid to guess, honey." Cira patted his hand absently.

Waved ashore by the Queens Justice late the morning after she left Mayfair, Ren heard her first news of Jerin. A whore matching Jerin's description and a scarred woman had been taken from the docks at gunpoint earlier that day. Investigating gunshots, the Queens Justice had found the kidnappers freshly murdered. There were signs at the murder site that a paddle wheel had tied off there, and the *Destiny* had been one of four ships spotted that morning. Seven women dead, river trash, used and disposed of.

Raven asked questions of her own, but Ren stood numb, barely hearing the replies. She knew everything that mattered. Jerin wasn't one of the dead, the Porters had recaptured him, and the *Destiny* had several hours' lead on them.

"She was riding high and fast, full steam," the region captain of the Queens Justice shouted as the *Red Dog* made to cast off. "You can burst your boiler and still not catch her."

"This just gets worse and worse," Raven growled beside her. "I pray to the gods that Kij does not murder Halley out of hand."

Ren swung around to face Raven. "What? When did Halley enter into this?"

Raven lifted an eyebrow. "Jerin was with a scarred woman." Raven ran a finger down her face. "Pearl-handled six-guns, riding a big roan."

Ren gasped. "Halley! How in the gods did she free Jerin?"

Raven lifted her shoulders. "If she's been tracking your sisters' killers, then she might have infiltrated part of Kij's networks. She wasn't one of the dead. Kij must have both of them."

Ren cursed quietly. Marines packed the gunboat, allowing her no room to vent anger or fear. "The *Destiny* is the safest place for Kij to commit this treason. It's a floating island, easy to defend. I doubt she'll be taking them off until they reach Avonar. We're hours behind them, but they'll have to stop for the locks."

"Kij most likely has things set so the *Destiny* won't have to wait for the queue."

"Even Kij has to wait for the locks to fill with water. It takes several hours to work through the locks. On horseback, we could reach the end of the locks before the *Destiny* steams out."

"Your Highness." Raven used her title like a whip. "Kij knows that's when she's most vulnerable and where you're most likely to catch up with her. She'll have the trap there."

"She has Halley and Jerin!"

"If you get yourself killed, Your Highness, no one will be able to rescue them. You've got the gunboat. Put it to best use!"

Ren let out her breath in a long sigh. "You're right. You're always right. We'll keep to the gunboat." *Halley! Jerin! Sweets gods above, protect them!*

*   *   *

The pilothouse sat on the topmost deck of the *Destiny,* a shack perched at the center of the vast flat space. A lone Porter sister stood at the wheel, gazing out over the bow of the ship as Jerin and Cira crept from the stern. As planned, Jerin crouched outside, hidden behind the half wall. Cira drew her pistol, quietly worked the door latch, and then stepped inside.

Instantly things went wrong. There were multiple startled cries, a crash and splintering of wood, and a gun went off, the bullet whining into the night. Jerin risked a glance over the wall.

There had been a second, unseen Porter in the room, apparently lying on the back bench. She had rushed Cira, knocking the pistol from her hand. The two now grappled in the tiny room, smashing back and forth. The pilot gripped a hand to her arm, blood seeping between her fingers.

As Cira and the other crashed through the door, the pilot lifted a flap on a wall-mounted tube. "Koura! Mitzy! Get up here! We've got trouble!"

From the tube, a tiny startled voice queried urgently. The engine crew shoveling coal had been alerted!

The pilot awkwardly drew her pistol and hurried out after Cira and her sister.

"Cira, watch out!" Jerin shouted, standing up.

The pilot turned, bringing up the pistol, then recognized him and froze. Cira twisted suddenly, the Porter sister's pistol in hand, and fired. In the gathering dark, the muzzle flare bloomed bright again and again. The report echoed, bank to bank, repeating up the river hollow.

He and Cira faced each other, gun smoke swept off by the stiff wind. A moment of silence passed between them, and then Jerin said, "The engine crew is coming."

"Everyone on the ship is coming." Cira snapped into motion. Holstering the pistol, she muscled the younger Porter sister up and over the railing edge. There was a distant splash. "We have to steer the ship to shore."

But the wheel was broken, smashed in the fight. Cira swore. The great paddle wheel was slowing down, the untended engines were dying, and the thud of heavy boots thundered up the many flights of stairs toward them.

"We're going to have to swim anyhow." Cira caught his hand and they headed for the stairs, hoping to beat the oncoming crowd. Two coal-blackened women appeared at the top of the stairs. Cira wheeled in front of them, racing back toward the pilothouse, cursing softly.

Like black wolves the women came, splitting up to run them down. One snatched up Jerin, lifting him from the ground, while the second tackled Cira to the floor. Jerin struggled in his capturer's grasp, reaching over his head to try to gouge out her eyes. She jerked her head back from his questing fingers, and shifted him into a choke hold. As grayness rushed in, he heard a splash, and then Cira was there, pistol in hand.

If the woman had thought, she could have kept him as a shield. She threw him, instead, at Cira. Cira caught him with her left arm, firing as soon as she was sure he was clear of the gun. His ears rang from the retort, and he clung to Cira, trembling. Cira panted, nose running with blood. She swiped the back of her hand across her mouth, clearing the blood, wincing at the pain.

"Are you all right?" she asked.

Jerin nodded.

"I'm out of bullets with this gun." Cira tossed the pistol aside. "Let's get Meza's pistol—I dropped it in the pilothouse—and get out of here."

Jerin nodded.

Cira led him back to the small structure and hunted through the wreckage to find the pistol. Jerin saw a flicker of shadows and called out a warning too late. Alissa Porter struck Cira with a short pole. Cira fell, unmoving.

"You!" She pointed at Jerin with the pole. "You, I'll deal with later." She switched the pole to her left hand, freeing her right hand to pull a long knife. "Right now I have a serious mistake on Kij's part to correct."

"No!" Jerin scrambled to the pistol on the floor. His hand closed on the gun and he started to bring it up when Alissa backhanded him with the pole. The pistol went clattering across the floor.

"I will kill you if you don't stay put!" Alissa shouted, bringing up the knife in warning.

"Leave her alone!"

"Stay out of this!" She moved toward Cira, eyes on him.

Jerin remembered then the derringer in his hidden pocket. He scrambled backward, out of her striking range, clawing for the tiny gun. "Leave her alone!" he shouted again, pulling it out and aiming at Alissa.

Alissa's eyes went wide at the sight of the pistol. "How the hell—put it down!"

"Get away from her!"

"Put it down!"

"Get away from her!"

Alissa made a sudden motion, one he recognized as the start of throwing her knife, and he pulled the trigger. In the small enclosed space, the tiny gun sounded like a cannon. Blood sprayed the glass behind her. She looked at him, surprised, made a slight mewling sound, then collapsed.

Suddenly the night seemed too still, too empty. Jerin stood, a wisp of smoke coming from the derringer's barrel.

I've killed her.

For several minutes he stood, unable to move, the violence of his action shocking him to his core. Then, desperately, he wanted to go home.

He glanced about the room, filled with unconscious and dead bodies, guns, knives, and broken ship parts. The wheel spun freely, the boat giving no indication that it connected to anything anymore. If they couldn't turn to follow the river as it wound its way through the hills, they would crash on the shore.

Jerin looked out through the pilothouse windows. They were drifting downriver, stern first. The stern lantern marked the back of the boat. The water shimmered black, reflecting faint starlight. A thicker black marked the trees on the right and left banks. The boat rode roughly in the center of the river. Downriver, he could make out nothing but a faint frill of white cutting across the darkness ahead of him.

He stared at the line for a minute before he realized what he was looking at. It dawned on him that there was no horizon. No hills. No trees. As if the world suddenly ended a mile downstream—and he was rushing toward that edge. Like a sleepwalker, he opened the wheelhouse door and heard the deep endless roar.

The waterfall!

He glanced again to his left, downstream this time. Glimmering on the shore like evening stars, the lights of the lock and the town of Hera's Step shone at once dangerously near and yet unreachably far.

"Oh, Holy Mothers," he breathed as the thunder grew louder.

His mind raced from point to point on a straight line. There was no one in the engine room who could start the paddle wheel turning. The current was taking them downriver. The steering wheel was broken. The ship was going over the falls. He and Cira had to get off the ship.

He knelt and shook her. "Cira! Cira, get up! Get up!"

"What is it?" Cira asked groggily, getting to her knees.

"We've got to get off the ship. It's Hera's Step! We're going over the falls!"

Cira stared out at the lifting spray, and then glanced to the shore. "We'll never make it in time. The current will take us over before we swim ashore."

"We have to try!"

"It will be safer to go over with the ship." She caught hold of the whistle cord and pulled. "Find something to weigh this down!" she shouted over the howl. "We need to bleed off steam before we go over, or we might be scalded before we're drowned!"

He tugged the coat off of Alissa, tied one sleeve to the dead woman's wrist, and then stretched the other sleeve up to tie the whistle cord down. Cira gave him an odd look, then nodded. Then they hurried out of the pilothouse to the center of the two-hundred-foot boat, opposite the great side wheel. Cira shouted something, unheard over the endless howl of the steam whistle.

"What?" Jerin shouted.

Cira pulled him close and shouted directly at his ear. "It will go stern first, but then it will spin toward the side wheel! Hold tight to the rail, but let go toward the bottom! Don't let yourself be trapped under the boat as it flips over! Do you understand?" When he nodded, she hugged him fiercely. "Jerin, I love you!"

And there was no time for anything more. The roar of the waterfall drowned out even the howl of the steam whistle. The spray enveloped them like a cold rain. The stern speared out over the vast empty darkness, and then, as Cira had predicted, the weight of the great paddle wheel slued the boat sideways. The deck canted as the whole ship tipped, and they hung from the railing as if from an overhead tree branch. For a moment, they dangled over the chasm, the foaming water at the foot of the falls hundreds of feet down, and then the ship dropped.

For almost a minute it seemed they fell, weightless, the river's roar louder than their own screams. Then, with a brutal smash, they hit the cold darkness. Jerin tumbled over and over in the freezing black water with no sense of up, his lungs aching. Finally he broke surface. There were stars above, so he wasn't under the *Destiny*. Huge forms glided around him, parts of the boat rushing with him downriver in disjointed confusion.

"Cira!" he shouted, flailing and striking wood. "Cira!"

In front of him, something had caught fire, and flames danced liquid down to the waterline. He realized the blaze was growing larger, that it was caught on the rocks or something, and that he was rushing toward it with all the mass of the *Destiny* behind him.

Dusk was falling as the *Red Dog* made its way the last few miles toward Hera's Step. The banks rose until the gunboat steamed through the gorge cut by the waterfall into the escarpment over thousands of years. Slowly the river narrowed, and seemed to change to a place of menace, the granite cliffs throwing shadows over the boat, and huge boulders, lining the shores, blocked any landing. Amplified by the towering gorge walls, the low rumble from the distant waterfall sounded like the roar of a great beast.

Ren paced the top deck at the edge of the pilothouse shielding. "We'll close with the first ship in the lock queue and use it to unload half the marines, then back off to safety." She nervously covered the plans they'd laid, looking for a weakness. "The marines will cross to shore and take control of the locks. When they give the clear signal, we move into the locks."

It would, however, be full night when they arrived at the locks. The marines faced a battle on unfamiliar ground in the dark. More of Kij's damnable luck and careful planning, no doubt.

"Ship to starboard! Ship to starboard!" The shout was followed by a deep boom and the scream of grapeshot.

Ren ducked behind the wood shielding. The sharp metal tore open a marine beyond the shielding, her blood spraying the wood decking.

There were shouts of dismay. Ren risked a look over the wood shield. A gunboat steamed out of the shadowed creek mouth, a wall of woven tree branches screening it from casual glance. A gout of black smoke rose from the ambusher's smokestacks, indicating Kij'd banked her fires to hide her trap, and now was frantically stoking up her boilers. Black, low, nearly featureless, the Porter gunboat glided like death toward them. It was an ironclad gunboat, its decks and hull covered with iron plates several inches thick. Ren had seen one only on paper, and now realized her own gullibility and naïveté. Kij had talked her out of building the ironclads, said they were a waste of money in a time of peace. In all the speculation of what Kij had prepared as a trap, Ren had not once recalled the conversation, not even after the attempt to steal the heavy naval guns.

In the massive gunports, the barrels of the Prophets looked like oversized rifles. It would be a close battle—Ren without heavy armor, Kij without heavy guns.

"Hard to starboard! Bring the forward cannon to bear! Sink the bloody bitch!" Ren shouted.

The forward gunners ran out the bow cannon even as the ironclad spat another screaming round of grapeshot. Their distance was such that the grapeshot had time to spread over a wide pattern before striking. It peppered the decks, chewing away planking where the wood thinned. Screams of pain came from all quarters, mixing with the moans of those already wounded.

With a thunder that vibrated to Ren's very core, the forward cannon fired. On a column of smoke and fire, the ball hurtled the gap and struck a glancing blow along the ironclad's stern.

"We'll have to hit them dead on to punch through their plating!" Raven shouted.

"Lieutenant!" Ren called to the marines' commander, then paused as grapeshot roared from the other ship. Kij was firing her cannons in series, trying to keep Ren's soldiers from sharp shooting the gunnery crews. "Have your women fire at will!" Ren shouted into the relative silence. "Aim for the gunports!"

It was a slaughter, her women trying to sharp shoot in the deadly hail, dying before they could get their shots off. The aft gun was useless. As the fore gun was run out to fire, the ironclad turned, forcing them to take another glancing shot. The ball careened off the thick plating. Beside Ren, the pilot fought the fast current to try and close with the ironclad while keeping clear of the boulder-strewn shores. They circled, wary as knife fighters, moving upriver as they cut each other with cannon fire.

"There's the Portage River mouth!" the pilot shouted. "But I can't get past her! She's forcing us up the Bright River, toward the falls. It runs shallow from here on up! Either we'll run aground or we'll be forced under the falls!"

Ren swore. The ironclad's steep side offered no purchase for her marines to board, and closing with Kij's ship would only increase the damage that the grapeshot would do. They were running out of river, though, and soon would be at the foot of the falls itself.

"Do you hear something?" Raven shouted.

How can you hear anything over this hellish noise? Ren tried anyhow. Over the thunder of the cannons and the endless roar of the waterfall, there was a high-pitched sound, ceaseless, growing louder. A steam whistle, she recognized suddenly, blowing without stop, and coming closer.

"Where is that coming from?" Ren asked.

"Look!" A marine on the deck suddenly cried, pointing upriver toward the white curtain of water. "The falls!"

Half a mile upriver, and hundreds of feet up, the underbelly of a boat speared out over the edge of the falls. It came and came, unending, its steam whistle screaming a death keen that was now being caught and echoed back by the granite cliffs of the gorge. A hundred feet of hull showed before the side wheel appeared at the brink, and the whole mass pivoted on its weight. Sluing sideways, the boat started to fall, and the cannon fire picked out the lettering on its side wheel. *Destiny.*

Ren shouted in wordless protest. *Jerin! Halley!*

With a curse, the pilot swung the wheel hard, turning suddenly without regard to the ironclad. "If that hits us after it comes over the falls, it'll take us under!"

The ironclad too was turning, trying to escape the massive ship now tumbling over the falls.

"No!" Ren caught the wheel and jerked it back. "Kij's giving us her broadside! Ram the bitch! End it here! Kill her now!"

The pilot threw her a panicked look, and then shouted into the tubes, "Full speed ahead! Full speed!"

The *Red Dog* leaped forward, its bow arrowing through the dark waters. Ren ducked down low behind the shield, bracing for the impact. They struck with a great splintering crack, the braced bow of the *Red Dog* cleaving deep into the ironclad. Ren was slammed forward into the shielding, striking her head, eclipsing the world with a flash of dark and pain. Then the fore gun fired, more felt than heard, the muzzle apparently buried in the guts of the ironclad. The ball punctured one of the boiler engines of the ironclad, and the shriek of escaping steam and screaming women joined with the crack of rifles.

Raven had her by the arm then, and was hefting her up, crying, "It's going to hit us!"

Ren turned, and saw the shattered decks of the *Destiny* rolling toward them, out of the night, tumbled by the fast shallow rapids. Her mind only understood flashes of what she saw: a railing here, an open doorway there, a hanging flight of stairs breaking off in mid-tumble.

Raven dragged her backward, back along the *Red Dog*'s top deck to the stern gun. There Raven pushed Ren down and caught her by the foot. "Strip! Get your boots off! We're going to have to swim for it! The nearest Queens Justice is Annaboro. When you get to shore, stay low. Kij might have backup troops!"

They went into the dark, fast water then, Ren stripped to only a shirt while Raven was still fully dressed.

Caught in the icy current, Ren struggled to keep afloat. She looked back. The water was littered with bodies, some thrashing, some still. The wreckage of the *Destiny* struck where the two ships were joined, and the river forced it up, rearing above the gunboats. Borne down by the weight of its plating and the water filling its bowels, the ironclad sank quickly. The *Red Dog,* still caught by its ram, rolled as the ironclad sank, the *Destiny* toppling over its dipping bow.

Oh, Jerin, love, I'm sorry. I'm sorry that I took you away from your mothers' farm where you were safe. I'm sorry I let Kij take you as bait. I'm so very sorry that I've gotten you killed.

Ren came ashore downriver of the Portage River confluence, teeth chattering from the cold, bone weary and heartsick. Raven had vanished into the waters, and Ren could not remember if her captain even knew how to swim. Two guards kept faithfully to her. The sergeant, Buckley, apparently swam like a fish and had helped Ren keep her bearings as they struggled for shore. The other was a young private whose face Ren could not recall, and in the dark could not see, by the name of Cherry. For miles the fast current had carried them, and they could only keep their heads above water. Then the river turned, and in that bend, the water deepened and slowed and they thrashed ashore.

The wind had kicked up, tossing the trees and cutting cold as sharp as knives through their wet clothes. Buckley knew approximately where they were, and knew too of a nearby mansion laid to ruin in the last war. It would give cover and shelter well away from the exposed riverbank. Ren wanted only to lie in the mud and grieve, but dragged herself up anyhow. She couldn't give up until she was sure Kij was as dead as her father, her elder sisters, Halley, and Jerin. She had to be sure Kij paid.

They were past the escarpment, and the land was flat here, smoothed by countless floods. They kept to the cave-black shadows of the windbreaks, hedging fields of freshly cut hay. The night was full of distant cracks of rifles, faint echoes of shouting, and the rolling thunder of racing horses. The gray of false dawn touched the sky as they reached the mansion sitting alone on a hill, the short summer night fleeing before the sun. In the silence before dawn, the dark, broken structure, surrounded by shorn fields, seemed ominous.

They paused in the windbreak at the foot of the hill, shivering, scanning the fields.

"How close is Annaboro?" Ren asked.

"Another ten miles south, Your Highness," Buckley murmured, then cocked her head, listening intently. "Riders are coming."

Ren swore. In their white shirts and red uniform pants, they stood out in the scanty cover of the windbreak. "Let's try for the mansion."

They ran. The sharp stems of the cut hay stabbed like a thousand needles in their bare feet as they raced for cover. The riders broke out of a woodlot behind them, and came sweeping toward them. A glance was enough to show the riders weren't the Queens Justice. Even as Ren and the others reached the old front yard of the mansion, the riders cut them off, looping around them in a rough circle of lathered, blowing horses.

Kij looked worse for wear, at least. Her beautiful face was cut and bruised. Part of her shirt had been torn off, and a bloody bandage showed beneath. But she was alive, damn her soul, when everyone else was dead.

"Don't you know when to die?" Ren asked her.

"I could say the same for you. I've been trying to kill you for six years," Kij growled.

"So, how did you find me?" Ren asked, wondering how she had ever thought this woman to be her good friend.

"You washed up where all the dead bodies come to shore." Kij gave a bitter laugh. "You just don't have the decency to realize you're dead."

"Give it up, Kij. Killing me will only dig your grave

deeper. My sisters know of your crimes. I've blocked all your plots in Mayfair. I've sunk your gunboat and your cannons. The *Destiny* is gone, and Jerin with her, damn you. Shooting me will get you nothing."

"It will make me feel better." Kij raised her pistol.

"Don't even think about it!" a woman shouted from high above them.

Ren glanced over her shoulder, startled.

From the mansion's second-story balcony, a shooter stood mostly hidden behind a support column, a sniper rifle aimed down at Kij. "Drop your guns!"

"Who the hell?" Kij shouted.

"I'm Eldest Whistler!" the woman shouted back. "Unlike you nobles, 'sisters-in-law' means something to us. We Whistlers have an unbreakable rule—you mess with one of us, you mess with us all!"

Like thorns growing from a rose, the long slender barrels of rifles emerged out of the broken windows of the mansion.

"Now, put down your guns!" Eldest shouted. "Or we'll be finding out who gets the orphaned estate of Avonar!"

The moment froze in time, and then Kij made a show of dropping her pistol. "Put them down," she commanded her sisters. "We'll live to fight another day."

Don't count on that, Ren thought savagely, but held her tongue.

The other Porters threw down their weapons. A lone Whistler came out of the mansion to collect the guns while her sisters covered her. Ren recognized the black hair, and the blue-eyed, steel-jawed look of the woman, but not her individually. The reason why became apparent as the other Whistlers stalked out of the mansion once the weapons were secured. Ren picked out Eldest, Summer, and Corelle easily, then Jerin's other elder and middle sisters too, leaving a whole host of Whistlers she had never seen before. They were, she realized, Jerin's cousins, the Annaboro Whistlers.

"Your Highness." Eldest nodded to Ren as she flashed hand signals to her family. "It's mighty hard to hold a wedding when you half drown most of the wedding party."

"What?"

"We spent half the night plucking people out of the river. We would really like it if you took better care with our brother from here on in. He doesn't swim all that well."

"You've found Jerin! Alive?"

Eldest grinned. "Aye. We fished Princess Halley and Captain Tern out too."

"They all are all right?"

Eldest sobered. "We sent Jerin home with my aunts. He's chilled to the bone, addled, and took in lots of water. He should be fine, with bed rest. Captain Tern has a broken leg, else she'd be here. Your sister—we had to all but sit on her to keep her back where things are safer. A hard thing to do with a royal princess."

Ren laughed. "And how did you find me?"

"Oh, we just followed Kij."

The Whistlers secured the Porters and then escorted Ren back to the river to wait for a hastily commandeered steamer to pick them up. Halley arrived with a guard of four Whistler cousins. Despite the six months and the night of hardship, Halley looked younger than Ren remembered, bruised but grinning. She had stained her red hair black, but the night in the river had washed much of it out, leaving only her roots dark.

Ren hugged her hard, glad to finally see her alive and well. Releasing her younger sister, Ren swatted her on the shoulder. "Don't ever do that again!"

"What, go over Hera's Step? I won't, I promise! Once was enough!"

Ren blinked at the answer. This was the Halley she remembered from years ago, not the solemn woman who'd haunted the palace for the last six years and stolen away eight months ago. "I meant disappearing. You're more important to me than petty revenge."

"It wasn't just revenge, Ren. It was the fact that everyone kept looking to me to be the Eldest when I wasn't. Six years, and Barnes would still come to me five times out of ten. I thought if I disappeared for a while, people would look to you like they should."

Ren felt a flare of anger at all the worry and trouble she had dealt with since Halley had vanished. "Don't you think, as Eldest, I should have decided how to handle it?"

It was Halley's turn to look startled, and then she grinned. "Well, I don't think eight months ago you would have thought it was your due."

Perhaps.

By unspoken agreement, they turned away from their escort and walked along the river.

"I've been worried sick about you," Ren said. "You could have written more often. My nightmares started back up after you vanished."

"Ah! Sorry." Halley stooped to pick up a handful of stones, then hurled one into the river, grunting. "I suspected someone close to us, even the Barneses. I wasn't thinking high enough. I didn't dare write."

"They fooled us all."

Halley flung another stone and, while watching it skip away, asked, "So, what do we do about Eldie?"

In all the confusion, Ren had forgotten about her niece. "What do you mean?"

"We can't let her live." Halley flung another stone, but it sank on the first skip.

"What?" Ren felt like she'd been punched.

"Holy Mothers, Ren." Halley picked up another handful of stones, avoiding her startled gaze. "We're going to execute her mothers and grandmothers. They killed our father, our sisters, and stole our husband. We can't let them walk away from this."

"What the hell does that have to do with killing Eldie?"

"Face the truth, Ren. She's the incestuous fruit of the man who poisoned the prince consort and the woman who blew up half the royal princesses! Do you think any of even her most remote noble relations are going to take her? Do you think *we're* going to take her? You would ask our youngest to be raised with her? Her father murdered ours. Do you think our babies would be safe around her once she realized that we executed her mothers and grandmothers?"

Ren shuddered at the image of a smothered infant, a baby "accidentally" dropped, a killer lurking amid all the dangers a young child narrowly missed, from the fireplace to the fishpond. Still, she recoiled at the thought of executing the golden-haired five-year-old so proud of her missing front teeth. "She's just a child."

"Now she's a child. In eleven short years, she'll be the age Keifer was when he killed Papa. Kij and Keifer had no good reason to hate you and me, except for deeds of our grandmothers. Do you really want their child, with better reasons for hating us, anywhere near our children?"

"Stop it, Halley! This is our niece. This is Eldie!"

"She isn't our niece," Halley said coldly. "Keifer didn't father any children on us, thank the gods, and he died before she was born—severing any connection between our families."

"I have spent five years thinking of her as my niece, Halley. I can't think of her in any other manner."

"If we don't take her, she'll have nowhere to go. She'll have to make her way like the river trash. Do you think that's kinder to a child her age?"

"We could take her," someone said behind them.

Ren and Halley turned, surprised, as Eldest Whistler came out of the darkness.

"We could take Eldie," Eldest said. "Our great-grandmother Elder was executed for treason. The judges, though, were merciful. They let the rest of the family live. Our grandmothers could have been bitter, but they had been raised knowing you made your choices and paid for them when you were wrong. Twenty of my thirty grandmothers gave their lives in the War of the False Eldest, fighting for the very people who put their Mother Elder to death. There is redemption for the innocent."

"I don't understand why you'd offer," Ren said, though she was glad for it.

Eldest shrugged. "You're marrying my brother. That makes us sisters. It sort of makes her our niece. She's not yet six, and since your youngest were her only playmates, the Porters couldn't leak any poison into her heart. She's not even really incestuous fruit—Kij and Keifer had different fathers and mothers, which normally would have made them cousins at most. It would be a shame to shoulder her with her parents' blame."

"You'll raise her like a sister?" Halley asked, obviously surprised.

"I've got fourteen youngest sisters under the age of ten; what's one more?"

"What happens when they marry?" Halley pushed. "How could you expect them to share their husband with her?"

"It will be up to them to decide. After looking at my family records, I suspect that my family started when a group of women banded together and called themselves sisters. We're not ones to worry about bloodlines. If you're willing to run the risk, we'd be willing to raise her."

Ren glanced to Halley, saw her willing, and nodded. "Have someone go now, though, and get her away from the Porters. I don't want them to have a chance to plant any murderous thoughts in her before we execute them."

Jerin woke in a strange bed, in a strange room, wearing a strange nightgown. He sat upright, panicked. Someone had taken off all his clothes to put new ones on him! Who? What else had they done to him? His head ached; there was a bandage on his head and the flesh underneath felt tender. Snatches of his adventure swam up through his memory, but nothing was complete or sensible. He had been kidnapped, had been on the *Destiny,* and had been in the river. If he had been on the *Destiny,* why had he been in the river? Had Kij thrown him overboard? Where was he now?

He threw back the sheets and swung his bare feet out of the bed. A quick check showed his stash pouch was missing, and so was his derringer. There was a wardrobe beside the bed. He opened it to find men's clothing, good in quality, in his size, and vaguely familiar. He fingered them, then looked about the room again. He knew this place. Relief poured in as he realized where he was. Annaboro. His aunts' house. His cousin Dail's room.

The door swung open; almost as if summoned by his name, Dail came in, a slightly younger reflection of Jerin, carrying a load of folded towels. "Oh, good, you're up!"

"Dail!" Jerin caught his cousin in a hard hug. "Oh, merciful Mothers! I didn't know where I was!"

Dail laughed, patting him on the back. "You're safe! Mothers brought you home last night, looking like a drowned cat. Eeeew, you still stink like river water. I'll have to change my sheets before tonight."

"What happened? How did I get here?"

Dail shrugged, nonchalant. "I don't know. No one tells me anything. Aunt Erica, Cousin Eldest, and the others showed up on lathered horses yesterday just as a royal messenger did too. There was a big war council, without us men, and then everyone but Lissia and Kaylie and my youngest saddled up on fresh horses and rode out. A few hours before dawn, some of my mothers showed up with you, looking like they'd fished you out of the river. I was told to keep an eye on you since Papa's busy with the babies and see that you had a bath once you woke up, if you felt up to it."

"I feel up to it," Jerin said, while his mind raced. Eldest had written that they were coming. Apparently a messenger from Ren had reached Annaboro at the same time his family did. They had come looking for him, and found him in the river.

His aunts had a bathhouse much the same as his mothers'. Dail led him down to it, chattering on about meeting Cullen. Jerin's sisters had stopped on their way home in order to lay plans for their wedding. With only eight months before his sixteenth birthday, Dail was starting to consider wives. Apparently Cullen thought a Whistler cousin married to his sisters was as good as a Whistler brother.

"It would be a step up. Cullen says they have servants and he's never had to cook before." Dail rolled his eyes. "Cullen's looking forward to cooking—can you imagine? He says having servants do everything is boring. I think once he has to wash diapers for seven babies at once, he'll be wanting a servant! You're so lucky to be marrying into a wealthy family. Here are towels—I've got to go help with dinner. We eat in a hour."

With that, Dail left him to ponder his missing memories and his future. Would he actually be able to marry Ren and the others? Disturbing memories were starting to rise. Cira holding him close. Cira kissing him. Cira taking off her shirt. Cira lying on top of him, grinding against him. What had happened? Had Cira taken him? If she had, how could he return to his wives?

He bathed in agony over the lost memories, trying to scrub away the feeling of being used and ruined. If he had been ruined, though, he couldn't return to his wives. He had no way of knowing what diseases Cira might carry; he couldn't subject them to those risks.

He was toweling his hair dry when Dail came running down the hall.

"Jerin! Your wives are here! Princesses Rennsellaer, Halley, and Odelia! Three of the royal princesses, here!"

His heart sank. From what he could remember, there

was little chance that he was still fit to marry. He would have to tell Ren the truth, and worse, tell her in front of a stranger, Halley. He dressed slowly, and went down to the parlor, shaking. He cracked the door and peered inside. Odelia sat in a chair, leaned over her knees, worrying at her thumbnail. Ren absently turned her hat in her hands. Halley, the missing princess, stood looking out the window, her back to the door, the sun in her royal red hair.

Ren noticed the opened door and went still. Soundlessly, she lifted her hand to him, entreating him with her eyes. There was such pain in them that Jerin couldn't deny her. He slipped quietly inside, for it seemed making a sound would trigger words, and with words, he would have to confess, and it would all come to an end.

He clung to her, reveling in her softness one last time.

"I'm so sorry," Ren whispered finally. "I never wanted for you to be a target."

So it ends. "I'm the one that's sorry, Ren. I don't think I'm clean anymore. I think I slept with another woman. She helped me get away from the river rats, and we were alone in a barn together—I—I—don't remember what happened. I'm so sorry. I failed you."

"If that was your idea of sleeping with a woman," a familiar alto voice drawled, "then we're going to have problems coming up with babies."

He jerked out of Ren's arms to stare at the familiar scarred face, surrounded by a nimbus of flame red hair. "Cira?"

"Halley, actually." She grinned as she came to join Ren and him. "Your wife. Cira was just a name I used to get close to those river trash, so I could get my pretty new husband back."

Jerin could only stare as the events of the last few days turned themselves onto their heads. All at once he recognized the Moorland stamp on Cira's—Halley's—features; no one had ever told him that Halley alone took after their father.

"Personally, I would hit her," Odelia said, "but then I'm not a boy."

"Why didn't you tell me?" Jerin asked.

Halley spread her hands. "I tried at first, but you didn't believe anything I said. Later, I thought you knew. I guess, looking back, Kij and the others never did actually name me in front of you."

"You've done nothing but make us proud of you," Ren said quietly, clasping his hand. "You've been brave, clever, and selfless."

"Kij would have won the day without you." Odelia covered Ren's hand with her own.

"We love you." Halley cupped his hand and her sisters' hands between her two. "And we're not going to lose you again."

Chapter 16

Ren was jolted awake by someone leaping onto her bed. All annoyance vanished as Jerin squirmed into her arms.

"Get up! Get up!" He left her breathless with kisses between his demands. "Their ship is at the landing! They're here!"

"I'm awake!" She managed another kiss before he slipped away. He dashed across the room to peer out her window, kneeling on the window seat.

"I can't wait to see everyone, especially my new brother!" He looked adorable in his plum silk tunic and flowing trousers, his long black braid dangling between the bare soles of his feet.

"It will take them at least an hour to cross town and climb the hill. Come here, and give me a proper good-morning."

Nights, Jerin insisted on keeping order, Eldest to youngest, and last night had been Odelia's turn. Days, though, he was deliciously spontaneous.

There were wagons and wagons filled with Whistlers.

Wedding Keifer had been a solemn occasion, with all the pomp and joy of a state funeral. The day had been hot, the clothes uncomfortable, and the need for respectful silence reinforced with Eldest's riding crop. The Porters had stayed cool, quiet, and watchful as sharks. Much as Ren loved Jerin, she spent the first month of her betrothal dreading their actual marriage ceremony.

Cullen's wedding cured that dread. After that extended country frolic, it was a family decision to include the Annaboro Whistlers and make drastic changes to the royal traditions. So it was over a hundred of the Whistlers that tumbled out of the wagons into an extended, loud greeting: twenty-four mothers and aunts, sisters and female cousins numbering more than seventy (Jerin couldn't remember exactly how many cousins he had), and eight—*eight*—brothers and male cousins.

Ren's little sisters and both sets of the Whistler youngest thundered off like a pack of puppies, tumbling and yelping and squealing. It wasn't until they vanished, off to explore the palace, that Ren realized she hadn't seen Eldie Porter among them. All the little ones had been red- or black-haired.

"Where's Eldie?"

"She went with the others," Eldest reported, greeting Ren with a rough embrace. "We've dyed her hair. She felt out of place, being the only towhead. With her blue eyes, you'd nearly take her for one of us now. Oh, yes, we've had her pick a new name, Neddie Whistler."

"Gave her a tattoo, too." Corelle indicated her own Order of the Sword tattoo. "Since Kij told her that she'd been fathered out of a crib."

They had agreed that she wouldn't be told the truth about her parentage, nor what had happened between her mothers and aunts, until she was an adult. The Whistlers had whisked Eldie out of Avonar the very night her fate was decided, telling her nothing but that she was now one of them. Their letters reported that between Cullen's familiar presence and a child's acceptance of new situations, Eldie settled in quickly. Apparently she had been painfully lonely, and thrived on being one of twenty Whistler children.

Cullen folded Ren into a hug, and she laughed in surprise at how much taller he was since the last time she saw him.

"Look at you! What have they been feeding you?"

"Just all that exercise he gets, riding," Corelle said with a wink, obviously meaning more than horses, which earned her a cuff from Eldest.

"He's just hit his growth spurt." Eldest gave a slight, satisfied smile. Cullen echoed it, abandoning Ren to embrace his wife from behind, his large hands resting gently on her stomach.

Hoy! What's this? Ren eyed Eldest Whistler closer and found barely noticeable signs of a pregnancy. *Two months? Early in the third month?* Luckily it obviously wasn't into the second trimester—for then it would be proof that Ren and her sisters had been less than careful in chaperoning their cousin.

Ren glanced to Halley then, who was in the same state. Actually, comparing the two, Halley outstripped Eldest. Ren was going to be wearing her new title of Queen Mother Elder a week or two before Eldest became Mother Elder Whistler. Ren found the fact surprisingly pleasing.

Queen Mother Elder. Ren had been saying it often in attempt to get used to it.

The Whistler women brought fiddles, banjos, fifes, drums, and dulcimers, aged corn whiskey, fine cigars, and a determination to have a good time.

A royal circus, Ren had named their wedding, and Jerin marveled at how right a name it was. Admittedly, he had seen only one circus, when he was quite young, but certainly most of the elements he remembered appeared on his wedding day.

There was the brisk music—trumpets, drums, and bagpipes—playing thundering songs. The royal family had their own melody, and apparently all the noble houses had a song too. It had stumped them for a while what to play for the Whistlers, and finally the fighting song of his grandmothers' regiment was selected.

There were the bright coaches—the royal carriages—gilded instead of painted yellow, but just as colorful as circus wagons. Ten in all, and then ten more of the Moorland carriages close behind, carrying the overflow.

There were the matching horses—the princesses, his elder sisters, and his middle sisters all rode glossy black horses in two lines, one on either side of him. His mount was a fiery red stallion, its symbolism not lost to him.

There were the colorful costumes—his wives-to-be in the dress red of the royal marines, his sisters in a balancing dark blue with gold waistcoats, he in a walking robe of white silk and seed pearls that gleamed in the morning light, with a cloak so long it nearly brushed the ground.

And there were the crowds, an endless flood of women, their voices a constant roar of approval. Apparently everyone thought the crush too dangerous to bring out their own menfolk; the only men Jerin saw appeared in the upper windows of the buildings lining the parade route.

"I wish we could have been married at the palace temple," he told Ren.

"The point of the day is for you to be seen," Ren said. "When our daughter is born, we'll become the Queen Mothers, mothers of the country. On a basic level, these are our children. We protect them, we settle their disputes, and we guide them as they grow. They have a right to know their father."

If Ren said it to settle him, it did not help. He could not imagine being father to this press of humanity.

Eldest Whistler reached over from her horse and took his hand. "Chin up. Eyes front. Show no fear. You're a Whistler—and your family will always be there if you need us."

So his sisters brought him to the temple, escorted by his wives, while all the world seemed to watch. Wives and sisters flanked him up the tall steps to the altar, and there his sisters fell back, leaving him alone with his wives, before the gods.

It was not the marriage he thought he would have, so many months before, when the horse-faced Brindles seemed to loom huge on his horizon. They shrank away now, like a kite snatched by the wind, gone forever.

Jerin reached out and found Ren's hand with his right and Halley's with his left.

Surely, the gods were merciful and loving. Surely they smiled upon this union, and he and his wives—Ren, Halley, Odelia, Trini, Lylia, Zelie, Quin, Selina, Nora, and Mira—would live happily ever after.

Wen Spencer
The Legend of Ukiah Oregon

ALIEN TASTE
Living with wolves as a child gave tracker Ukiah
Oregon a heightened sense of smell and taste.
Or so he thought—until he crossed paths with a
criminal gang known as the Pack. Now, Ukiah is
about to discover just how much he has in
common with the Pack: a bond of blood,
brotherhood...and destiny.
0-451-45837-0

BITTER WATERS
Tracker Ukiah Oregon must put his skills to
the ultimate test—because kidnappers
have taken his son.
0-451-45922-9

DOG WARRIOR
On the run from a fanatical cult, Ukiah Oregon is
surprised to discover Atticus Steele, a brother
he didn't know he had—and who could end up
getting them both killed.
0-451-45990-3

David Eddings

Domes of Fire

Book one of
The Tamuli

PRINCE SPARHAWK AND
THE TROLL-GODS

Queen Ehlana and the Pandion Knight Sir Sparhawk are
married, their kingdom peaceful at last, their union
blessed with a very special daughter named Danae. But
soon trouble sweeps westward from the Tamul Empire to
disrupt not only the living of Eosia but the dead: horrific
armies are being raised from the dust of the long-past Age
of Heroes, threatening the peace won at such cost in
Zemoch.

Prince Sparhawk is called upon to help the Tamuli nations
defeat these ancient horrors. Perhaps the Troll-Gods are
once more loose in the world! With Ehlana and a retinue
of Pandion Knights, Sparhawk will make the hazardous
journey to the Tamul Empire . . . only to discover in fire-
domed Matherion, the incandescent Tamul capital, that
the enemy is already within its gates.

Full of marvels and humour, romance and shrewdness,
above all full of magic, the resources of the epic form are
mined deep by the greatest of modern fantasy writers.

ISBN 0 586 21313 9

THE LORD OF THE RINGS
J. R. R. Tolkien

Part 1: The Fellowship of the Ring
Part 2: The Two Towers
Part 3: The Return of the King

The Lord of the Rings cannot be described in a few words.
J. R. R. Tolkien's great work of imaginative fiction has been
labelled both a heroic romance and a classic of science fiction.
It is, however, impossible to convey to the new reader all of
the book's qualities, and the range of its creation. By turns
comic, homely, epic, monstrous and diabolic, the narrative
moves through countless changes of scenes and character in
an imaginary world which is totally convincing in its detail.
Tolkien created a new mythology in an invented world which
has proved timeless in its appeal.

'An extraordinary book. It deals with a stupendous theme. It
leads us through a succession of strange and astonishing
episodes, some of them magnificent, in a region where everything
is invented, forest, moor, river, wilderness, town, and the races
which inhabit them. As the story goes on the world of the
Ring grows more vast and mysterious and crowded with curious
figures, horrible, delightful or comic. The story itself is superb.'
                                                        – *The Observer*

'Among the greatest works of imaginative fiction of the twentieth
century.'   – *Sunday Telegraph*

'The English-speaking world is divided into those who have
read *The Hobbit* and *The Lord of the Rings* and those who
are going to read them.'   – *Sunday Times*

The Lord of the Rings is available as a three book paperback
edition and also in one volume.